A New Voyage Round the World by a Course Never Sailed Before by Daniel Defoe

BEING

A VOYAGE undertaken by some MERCHANTS, who afterwards proposed the Setting up an East-India Company in FLANDERS.

Daniel Defoe is most well-known for his classic novels *Robinson Crusoe* and *Moll Flanders*. Born around 1660, he was also a journalist, a pamphleteer, a businessman, a spy. His life was long and colourful, and the breadth of his work, still highly regarded, is infused with similar vigour.

It is said that only the bible has been printed in more languages than Robinson Crusoe. Defoe is also noted for being one of the earliest proponents of the novel. He was extremely prolific and a very versatile writer, producing several hundred books, pamphlets, and journals on various topics including politics, crime, religion, marriage, psychology and the supernatural. He was also a pioneer of economic journalism though was made bankrupt on more on one occasion and usually mired in debt.

In later life Defoe was often most seen on Sundays when bailiffs and the like could legally make no move on him. Allegedly it was whilst hiding from creditors that he died on April 24th, 1731. He was interred in Bunhill Fields, London.

Index of Contents

A NEW VOYAGE ROUND THE WORLD BY A COURSE NEVER SAILED BEFORE

It has for some ages been thought so wonderful a thing to sail the tour or circle of the globe, that when a man has done this mighty feat, he presently thinks it deserves to be recorded like Sir Francis Drake's. So soon as men have acted the sailor, they come ashore and write books of their voyage, not only to make a great noise of what they have done themselves, but pretending to show the way to others to come after them, they set up for teachers and chart makers to posterity. Though most of them have had this misfortune, that whatever success they have had in the voyage, they have had very little in the relation; except it be to tell us, that a seaman when he comes to the press, is pretty much out of his element, and a very good sailor may make but a very indifferent author.

I do not in this, lessen the merit of those gentlemen who have made such a long voyage as that round the globe; but I must be allowed to say, as the way is now a common road, the reason of it thoroughly known, and the occasion of it more frequent than in former times, so the world has done wondering at it; we no more look upon it as a mighty thing, a strange and never heard of undertaking; this cannot be now expected of us, the thing is made familiar, every ordinary sailor is able to do it, if his merchants are but qualified to furnish him for so long a voyage; and he that can carry a ship to Lisbon, may with the same ease carry it round the world.

Some tell us, it is enough to wonder at a thing nine days, one would reasonably then conclude, that it is enough that sailing round the world has been wondered at above a hundred years. I shall therefore let the reader know, that it is not the rarity of going round the world that has occasioned this publication, but if some incidents have happened in such a voyage, as either have not happened to others, or as no other people, though performing the same voyage have taken notice of, then this account may be worth publishing, though the thing, viz. The Voyage round the World, be in itself of no value.

It is to be observed, of the several navigators whose Voyages round the World have been published, that few, if any of them, have diverted us with that variety which a circle of that length must needs offer. We have a very little account of their landings, their diversions, the accidents which happened to them, or to others by their means; the stories of their engagements, when they have had any scuffle either with natives, or European enemies, are told superficially and by halves; the storms and difficulties at sea or on shore, have nowhere a full relation; and all the rest of their accounts are generally filled up with directions for sailors coming that way, the bearings of the land, the depth of the channels, entrances, and bars, at the several ports, anchorage in the bays, and creeks, and the like things, useful indeed for seamen going thither again, and how few are they? but not at all to the purpose when we come expecting to find the history of the voyage.

Another sort of these writers have just given us their long journals, tedious accounts of their log-work, how many leagues they sailed every day; where they had the winds, when it blew hard, and when softly; what latitude in every observation, what meridian distance, and what variation of the compass. Such is the account of Sir John Narborough's Voyage to the South Seas, adorned with I know not how many charts of the famous Strait of Magellan, a place only now famous for showing the ignorance of Sir John Narborough, and a great many wise gentlemen before him, and for being a passage they had no need to have troubled themselves with, and which nobody will ever go through anymore.

Such also are the Voyages of Captain John Wood, to Nova Zemla, at the charge of the public, in King Charles the Second's time, and Martin Frobisher to the North-West Passages, in Queen Elizabeth's time; all which, are indeed full of their own journals, and the incidents of sailing, but have little or nothing of story in them, for the use of such readers who never intend to go to sea, and yet such readers may desire to hear how it has fared with those that have, and how affairs stand in those remote parts of the world.

For these reasons, when first I set out upon a cruising and trading voyage to the East, and resolved to go anywhere, and everywhere that the advantage of trade or the hopes of purchase should guide us, I also resolved to take such exact notice of everything that past within my reach, that I would be able, if I lived to come home, to give an account of my voyage, differing from all that I had ever seen before, in the nature of the observations, as well as the manner of relating them. And as this is perfectly new in its form, so I cannot doubt but it will be agreeable in the particulars, seeing either no voyage ever made before, had such variety of incidents happening in it, so useful and so diverting, or no person that sailed on those voyages, has thought fit to publish them after this manner.

Having been fitted out in the river of Thames so lately as the year 1713, and on a design perhaps not very consistent with the measures taking at that time for the putting an end to the war, I must be allowed to own I was at first obliged to act not in my own name, but to put in a French commander into the ship, for the reasons which follow, and which those, who understand the manner of trade upon closing the late war, I mean the trade with Spain, will easily allow to be just and well grounded.

During the late war between Great Britain and her confederates on one side, and the united crowns of France and Spain on the other, we all know the French had a free trade into the South Seas; a trade carried on with the greatest advantage, and to the greatest degree, that any particular commerce has been carried on in the world for many ages past; insomuch, that we found the return of silver that came back to France by those ships, was not only the enriching of the merchants of St. Malo, Rochelle, and other ports in France, some of whom we saw get immense estates in a few years, even to a million sterling a man; but it was evident, the King of France himself was enabled, by the circulation of so much bullion through his mints, to carry on that war with very great advantage.

It was just at the close of this war, when some merchants of London, looking with envy on the success of that trade, and how the French, notwithstanding the peace, would apparently carry it on, for some years at least, to infinite advantage, began to consider whether it might not be possible to come in for a portion of it with France, as they were allied to Spain, and yet go abroad in the nature of a private cruiser.

To bring this to pass, it was thought proper, in the first place, to get a share if possible, in a new design of an East India trade in Flanders, just then intended to be set up by some British merchants, by the assistance of an imperial charter, or at least under colour of it: and so we might go to sea in a threefold capacity, to be made use of as occasion might present, viz., when on the coast of New Spain we sought to trade, we were Frenchmen, had a French captain, and a sufficient number of French seamen, and Flemish or Walloon seamen, who spoke French, so to appear on all proper occasions. When at sea we met with any Spanish ship worth our while, we were English cruisers, had letters of mart from England, had no account of the peace, and were fitted for the attack. And when in the East Indies we had occasion to trade, either at the English or Dutch settlements, we should have imperial colours, and two Flemish merchants, at least in appearance, to transact everything as we found occasion. However, this last part of our project failed us, that affair not being fully ripe.

As this mysterious equipment may be liable to some exceptions, and perhaps to some inquiries, I shall for the present conceal my name, and that of the ship also. By inquiries, I mean inquiries of private persons concerned; for, as to public inquiries, we have no uneasiness, having acted nothing in contradiction to the rules and laws of our country; but I say, as to private persons, it is thought fit to prevent their inquiries, to which end, the captain, in whose name I write this, gives me leave to make use of his name, and conceal my own.

The ship sailed from the river the 20th of December, 1713, and went directly over to the coast of Flanders, lying at an anchor in Newport Pitts, as they are called, where we took in our French Captain Jean Michael Merlotte, who, with thirty-two French seamen, came on board us in a large snow from Dunkirk, bringing with them one hundred and twenty-two small ankers or rundlets of brandy, and some hampers and casks of French wine in wickered bottles. While we were here, we lay under English colours, with pendants flying, our ship being upwards of five hundred ton, and had forty-six guns mounted, manned with three hundred and fifty-six men; we took the more men on board, because we resolved, as occasion should present, to fit ourselves with another ship, which we did not question we should meet with in the South Seas.

We had also a third design in our voyage, though it may be esteemed an accident to the rest, viz., we were resolved to make some attempts for new discoveries, as opportunity offered; and we had two persons on board who were exceeding well qualified for our direction in this part, all which was derived from the following occasion.

The person who was principally concerned in the adventure was a man not only of great wealth, but of great importance; he was particularly addicted to what we call new discoveries, and it was indeed upon his genius to such things, that the first thought of the voyage was founded. This gentleman told me, that he had already sent one ship fully equipped and furnished for a new attempt upon the North-West or North-East passages, which had been so often in vain tried by former navigators; and that he did not question the success, because he had directed them by new measures, and to steer a course that was never attempted yet; and his design in our voyage was to make like discoveries towards the South pole; where, as he said, and gave us very good reasons for it, he did not doubt but we might discover, even to the pole itself, and find out new worlds and new seas, which had never been heard of before.

With these designs, this gentleman came into the other part of our project, and contributed the more largely, and with the more freedom, to the whole, upon that account; in particular, all the needful preparations for such discoveries were made wholly at his expense, which I take notice of here, as being most proper in the beginning of our story, and that the reader may the less wonder at the particular way we took to perform a voyage which might with much more ease have been done by the usual and ordinary way.

We sailed from the coast of Flanders the 2nd of January, and, without any extraordinary incident, made the coast of Galway, in Ireland, the 10th, where we stayed, and took in a very extraordinary store of provisions, three times as much as usual, the beef being also well pickled or double packed, that we might have a sufficient reserve for the length of our voyage, resolving also to spare it as much as possible.

We had a very rich cargo on board, consisting of all sorts of British manufactures suitable for the Spanish trade in their West Indies; and, as we aimed at nothing of trade till we came to the Spanish coast, we sailed directly for the Canary Islands: having not fully resolved whether we would make our voyage to the South Seas first, and so round the globe by the East Indies, as has been the usual way, or whether we would go first by the East Indies, and upon the discoveries we were directed to, and then cross the great Pacific Ocean to the west coast of America, as was at last resolved.

We made the Canaries, the 11th of February; and, coming to an anchor there to take in some fresh water, we put out French colours, and sent our boat on shore, with a French boatswain and all French seamen, to buy what we wanted: they brought us on board five butts or pipes of wine, and some provisions, and having filled our water, we set sail again the 13th. In this time we called a council among ourselves, by which way we should go.

I confess I was for going by the Cape of Good Hope first, and so to the East Indies: then, keeping to the south of Java, go away to the Moluccas, where I made no doubt to make some purchase among the Dutch Spice Islands, and so away to the Philippines; but the whole ship's company, I mean of officers, were against me in this scheme, although I told them plainly, that the discoveries which would be made in such a voyage as that, were the principal reasons why our chief owner embarked in the adventure, and that we ought to regard the end and design of our voyage; that it would certainly in the conclusion amount to the same, as to trade, as if we went the usual way, seeing the places we were to go to were the same one way as the other, and it was only putting the question which we should go to first; that all the navigators, on such voyages as these, went by the South Seas first, which would be no honour to us at all: but, if we went by the East Indies first, we should be the first that ever went such a voyage, and that we might make many useful discoveries and experiments in trying that course; that it would be worth our while, not only to go that way, but to have all the world take notice of it, and of us for it.

I used a great many arguments of the like nature, but they answered me most effectually, with laying before me the difficulties of the voyage, and the contrary methods of trade, which, in a word, made the going that way impracticable: First, the difficulty of the voyage, over the vast ocean called the Pacific Sea, or South Sea, which, if we kept a southern latitude, and took the variable winds, as we should find them, as I proposed to do, might very well be a voyage of six or eight months, without any sight of land, or supply of provisions or water, which was intolerable; that, as to trade, it was preposterous, and just setting the voyage with the bottom upward; for as we were loaden with goods, and had no money, our first business, they said, was to go to the South Seas, where our goods were wanted, and would sell for money, and then to the East Indies, where our money would be wanting, to buy other goods to carry home, and not to go to the East Indies first, where our goods would not sell, and where we could buy no other for want of money.

This was seemingly so strong a way of reasoning, that they were all against me, as well French as English, and even the two agents for discoveries submitted to it; and so we resolved to stand away from the Canaries to the coast o Brazil, thence upon the eastern coast of South America to Cape Horn, and then into the South Seas; and, if we met with anything that was Spanish by the way, we resolved to make prize of it, as in a time of war.

Accordingly, we made the coast of Brazil in twenty-six days, from the Canary Islands, and went on shore at Cape St. Augustine, for fresh water; afterwards we put into the bay of All Saints, got some fresh provisions there, and about an hundred very good hogs, some of which we killed and pickled, and carried the rest on board alive, having taken on board a great quantity of roots and maize, or Indian corn, for their food, which they thrived on very well.

It was the last of March when we came to the bay, and having stayed there fourteen days, to furnish ourselves with all things we wanted, we got intelligence there, that there were three ships at Buenos Ayres, in the river Rio de la Plata, which were preparing to go for Europe, and that they expected two Spanish men of war to be their convoy, because of the Portuguese men of war which were in Brazil, to convoy the Brazil fleet.

Their having two Spanish men of war with them for their convoy, took away a great deal from the joy we had entertained at the news of their being there, and we began to think we should make little or nothing of it; however, we resolved to see the utmost of it, and, particularly, if our double appearance would not now stand us in some stead.

Accordingly, we went away for the river of Plata, and, as usual, spreading French colours, we went boldly up to Buenos Ayres, and sent in our boat, manned with Frenchmen, pretending to be homeward bound from the South Seas, and in want of provisions.

The Spaniards received us with civility, and granted us such provisions as we wanted; and here we found, to our great satisfaction, that there was no such thing as any Spanish man of war there; but they said they expected one, and the governor there for the King of Spain asked our French officer if we would take one of their ships under our convoy? Monsieur Merlotte answered him warily, that his ship was deep loaden, and foul, and he could not undertake anything; but, if they would keep him company, he would do them what service he could; but that also, as they were a rich ship, they did not design to go directly to France, but to Martinico, where they expected to meet with some French men of war to convoy them home.

This answer was so well managed; though there was not one word of truth in it, that one of the three ships, for the other two were not ready, resolved to come away with us, and, in an evil hour for them, they did so.

To be brief, we took the innocent Spaniard into our convoy, and sailed away to the northward with them, but were not far at sea before we let them know what circumstances they were in, by the following method. We were about half a league a head of them, when our captain bringing to, and hauling up our courses, made a signal to the Spaniards for the captain to come on board, which he very readily did; as soon as he was on board, our captain let him know that he was our prisoner, and all his men, and immediately manning their boat with thirty of our men, we sent them on board their ship, to take possession of her, but ordered them that they should behave civilly to the men on board, and plunder nothing. For we made a promise to the Spanish captain, that his ship should not be plundered, upon condition he would give us a just account of his loading, and deliver peaceably to us what riches he had on board; then we also agreed, that we would restore him his ship, which by the way, we found was chiefly loaden with hides, things of no value to us, and that the ship also was an old vessel, strong, but often doubled, and therefore a very heavy sailer, and consequently not at all fit for our purpose, though we greatly wanted a ship to take along with us, we having, as I have said, both too many men, and being too full of goods.

The Spanish captain, though surprised with the stratagem that had brought him thus into the hands of his enemies, and greatly enraged in his mind at being circumvented, and trepanned out of his ship, yet showed a great presence of mind under his misfortune; and, as I verily believe, he would have fought us very bravely, if we had let him know fairly what we were, so he did not at all appear dejected at his disaster, but capitulated with us as if he had been taken sword in hand. And one time, when Captain Merlotte and he could not agree, and the Spanish captain was a little threatened, he grew warm; told the captain that he might be ill used, being in his hands, but that he was not afraid to suffer whatever his ill fortune had prepared for him, and he would not, for fear of ill usage, yield to base conditions; that he was a man of honour, and if he was so too, he demanded to be put on board his own ship again, and he should see he knew how to behave himself. Captain Merlotte smiled at that, and told him, he was not afraid to put him on board his own ship, and fight for her again, and that, if he did so, he was sure he could not escape him; the Spanish captain smiled too, and told him he should see, if he did, that he knew the way to heaven from the bottom of the sea as well as any other road, and that men of courage were never at a loss to conquer their enemy one way or other; intimating, that he would sink by his side rather than be taken, and that he would take care to be but a very indifferent prize to him, if he was conquered.

However, we came to better terms with him afterwards. In short, having taken on board all the silver, which was about two hundred thousand pieces of eight, and whatever else we met with that was valuable, among the rest his ammunition, and six brass guns, we performed conditions, and sent him into the Rio de la Plata again with his ship, to let the other Spanish captains know what scouring they had escaped.

Though we got a good booty, we were disappointed of a ship; however, we were not so sensible of that disappointment now, as we were afterwards: for, as we depended upon going to the South Seas, we made no doubt of meeting with vessels enough for our purpose. Of what followed, the reader will soon be informed.

We had done our work here, and had neither any occasion or any desire to lie any longer on this coast, where the climate was bad, and the weather exceeding hot, and where our men began to be very uneasy, being crowded together so close all in one ship; so we made the best of our way south.

We met with some stormy weather in these seas, and particularly a north-west blast, which carried us for eleven days a great way off to sea; but, as we had sea-room enough, and a stout strong-built ship under us, perfectly well prepared, tight and firm, we made light of the storms we met with, and soon came into our right way again; so that, about the 4th of May, we made land in the latitude of 45° 12', south.

We put in here for fresh water; and, finding nothing of the land marked in our charts, we had no knowledge of the place, but, coming to an anchor at about a league from the shore, our boat went in quest of a good watering-place; in pursuit of this, they went up a creek about two leagues more, where they found good water, and filled some casks, and so came on board to make their report.

The next day we came into the creek's mouth, where we found six to eight fathom water within a cable's length of the shore, and found fresh water enough, but no people or cattle, though an excellent country for both.

Of this country I made many observations, suitable to the design and desire of our ingenious employer and owner; and those observations are one end of publishing this voyage. I shall mention only one observation here, because I shall have occasion to speak of them hereafter more largely. My observation here is as follows:—

An observation concerning the soil and climate of the continent of America, south of the river De la Plata; and how suitable to the genius, the constitution, and the manner of living of Englishmen, and consequently for an English colony.

The particular spot which I observe upon, is that part of the continent of America which lies on the shore of the North Seas, as they are called, though erroneously, for they are more properly the East Seas, being extended along the east shores of South America. The land lies on the same east side of America, extended north and south from Coasta Deserta, in 42°, to Port St. Julian, in 49½°, being almost five hundred miles in length, full of very good harbours, and some navigable rivers. The land is a plain for several scores of miles within the shore, with several little rising hills, but nowhere mountainous or stony; well adapted for enclosing, feeding, and grazing of cattle; also for corn, all sorts of which would certainly not only grow, but thrive very well here, especially wheat, rye, pease, and barley, things which would soon be improved by Englishmen, to the making the country rich and populous, the raising great quantities of grain of all sorts, and cattle in proportion. The trade which I propose for the consumption of all the produce, and the place whither to be carried, I refer to speak of by itself, in the farther progress of this work.

I return now to the pursuit of our voyage. We put to sea again the 10th of May, with fair weather and a fair wind; though a season of the year, it is true, when we might have reason to expect some storms, being what we might call the depth of their winter. However, the winds held northerly, which, there, are to be esteemed the warm winds, and bringing mild weather; and so they did, till we came into the latitude of 50°, when we had strong winds and squally weather, with much snow and cold, from the south-west and south-west by west, which, blowing very hard, we put back to Port St. Julian, where we were not able to stir for some time.

We weighed again the 29th, and stood south again past the mouth of the Straits of Magellan, a strait famous for many years, for being thought to be the only passage out of the North Seas into the South Seas, and therefore I say famous some ages; not only in the discovery of it by Magellan, a Spanish captain, but of such significance, that, for many years, it was counted a great exploit to pass this strait, and few have ever done it of our nation, but that they have thought fit to tell the world of it as an extraordinary business, fit to be made public as an honour to their names. Nay, King Charles the Second thought it worth while to send Sir John Narborough, on purpose to pass and take an exact survey of this strait; and the map or plan of it has been published by Sir John himself, at the public expense, as a useful thing.

Such a mighty and valuable thing also was the passing this strait, that Sir Francis Drake's going through it gave birth to that famous old wives' saying, viz., that Sir Francis Drake shot the gulf; a saying that was current in England for many years after Sir Francis Drake was gone his long journey of all; as if there had been but one gulf in the world, and that passing it had been a wonder next to that of Hercules cleansing the Augean stable.

Of this famous place I could not but observe, on this occasion, that, as ignorance gave it its first fame and made it for so many ages the most eminent part of the globe, as it was the only passage by which the whole world could be surrounded, and that it was to every man's honour that had passed it; so now it is come to the full end or period of its fame, and will in all probability never have the honour to have any ship, vessel, or boat, go through it more, while the world remains, unless, which is very improbable, that part of the world should come to be fully inhabited.

I know some are of opinion, that, before the full period of the earth's existence, all the remotest and most barren parts of it shall be peopled; but I see no ground for such a notion, but many reasons which would make it appear to be impracticable, and indeed impossible; unless it should please God to alter the situation of the globe as it respects the sun, and place it in a direct, as it now moves in an oblique position; or that a new species of mankind should be produced, who might be as well qualified to live in the frozen zone as we are in the temperate, and upon whom the extremity of cold could have no power. I say, as there are several parts of the globe where this would be impracticable, I shall say no more than this, that I think it is a groundless suggestion.

But to return to our voyage; we passed by the mouth of this famous Strait of Magellan, and those others which were passed through by Le Maire the Dutch sailor afterwards; and keeping an offing of six or seven leagues, went away south, till we came into the latitude of 58°, when we would, as we had tried three days before, have stretched away south-west, to have got into the South Seas, but a strong gale of wind took us at west-north-west, and though we could, lying near to it, stretch away to the southward, yet, as it over-blowed, we could make no westward way; and though we had under us an excellent strong-built vessel, that, we may say, valued not the waves, and made very good work of it, yet we went away to leeward in spite of all we could do, and lost ground apace. We held it out, however, the weather being clear, but excessive cold, till we found ourselves in the latitude of 64°.

We called our council several times, to consider what we should do, for we did but drive to leeward the longer we strove with it; the gale held still on, and, to our apprehensions, it was set in; blowing like a kind of monsoon, or trade-wind, though in those latitudes I know there is no such thing properly called, as a trade-wind.

We tried, the wind abating, to beat up again to the north, and we did so; but it was by running a great way to the east; and once, I believe, we were in the longitude of St. Helena, though so far south, but it cost us infinite labour, and near six weeks' time. At length we made the coast, and arrived again at the Port of St. Julian the 20th of June, which, by the way, is the depth of their winter.

Here we resolved to lay up for the winter, and not attempt to go so far south again at that time of the year, but our eager desire of pursuing our voyage prevailed, and we put out to sea again, having taken in fresh provisions, such as are to be had there; that is to say, seals, penguins, and such like, and with this recruit we put to sea, I say, a second time.

We had this time worse luck than we had before; for, the wind setting in at south-west, blew a storm, and drove us with such force away to sea eastward, that we were never able to make any way to the southward at all, but were carried away with a continued storm of wind, from the same corner, or near it. Our pilot, or master, as we called him, finding himself often obliged to go away before it, which kept us out long at sea, and drove us far to the north-east, eastward, that he advised us to stand away for the Cape of Good Hope; and accordingly we did so, and arrived there the last day of July.

We were now disheartened indeed, and I began to revive my proposal of going to the East Indies, as I at first proposed; and to answer the objection which they then made against it, as being against the nature of trade, and that we had nothing on board but European goods, which were not fitted for the East Indies, where money only was suitable to the market we were to make; I say, to answer this objection, I told them I would engage that I would sell our whole cargo at the Philippine Islands as well as on the coast of America; for that those islands being Spanish, our disguise of being French would serve us as well at the Philippines, as it would in New Spain; and with this particular advantage, that we should sell here for four times the value we should on the coast of Chili, or Peru; and that, when we had done, we could load our ship again there, or in other places in the Indies, with such goods as would come to a good market again in New Spain.

This I told them was indeed what had not been practised, nor at any other time would it be practicable: for as it was not usual for any ships to go from the East Indies to the Philippines, so neither was it usual for any European ships to trade with freedom in the South Seas, till, since the late war, when the French had the privilege; and I could not but be amazed that the French had never gone this way, where they might have made three or four voyages in one, and with much less hazard of meeting with the English or Dutch cruisers; and have made twice the profits which they made the other way, where they were frequently out three or four years upon one return; whereas here they might make no less than three returns, or perhaps four, in the same voyage and in much less time.

They were now a little surprised, for in all our first debates we had nothing of this matter brought in question; only they entertained a notion that I was going upon strange projects to make discoveries, search for the South pole, plant new colonies, and I know not how many whims of their own, which were neither in my design, or in my instructions. The person, therefore, who was our supercargo, and the other captain, whose name I have not mentioned, together with the French Captain, Merlotte, and the rest, who had all opposed me before, came cheerfully into my proposal; only the supercargo told me, in the name of the rest, that he began to be more sensible of the advantages of the voyage I had proposed, than he was before; but that, as he was equally intrusted with me in the government of the trading part, he begged I would not take it ill, that he desired I would let him farther into that particular, and explain myself, at least as far as I thought proper.

This was so just a request, and so easy for me to do, and, above all, was made with so much good manners and courtesy, that I told him, if I had been otherwise determined, the courteous and good-humoured way with which he required it, would constrain me to it; but that, however, I was very ready to do it, as he was intrusted with the cargo jointly with me, and that it was a piece of justice to the owners, that whom they thought fit to trust I should trust also; upon this I told him my scheme, which was as follows:

First, I said, that, as the Philippine Islands received all their European goods from Acapulco, in America, by the king of Spain's ships, they were obliged to give what price was imposed upon them by the merchants, who brought those goods by so many stages to Acapulco. For example, the European goods, or suppose English goods in particular, with which they were loaden, went first from England to Cadiz, from Cadiz by the galleons to Porto Bello, from Porto Bello, to Panama, from Panama to Acapulco; in all which places the merchants had their several commissions and other profits upon the sale; besides the extravagant charges of so many several ways of carriage, some by water, some by land, and besides the king's customs in all those places; and that, after all this, they were brought by sea from Acapulco to the Philippine Islands, which was a prodigious voyage, and were then generally sold in the Philippine Islands at three hundred per cent. advance.

That, in the room of all this, our cargo being well bought and well sorted, would come to the Philippine Islands at once, without any landing or re-landing, and without any of all the additions of charge to the first cost, as those by the way of New Spain had upon them; so that, if we were to sell them at the Philippine Islands a hundred per cent. cheaper than the Spaniards usually sold, yet we should get abundantly more than we could on the coast of Peru, though we had been allowed a free trade there.

That there were but two objections to this advantage, and these were, our liberty of trading, and whether the place would consume the quantity of goods we had; and to this I had much to answer. First, that it was well known at the Philippine Isles, that the kings of France and Spain were united firmly together; that the king of Spain had allowed the king of France's subjects a free trade in his American dominions, and consequently, that it would not be denied there; but, on the other hand, that, if it was denied by the governor, yet there would be room to find out a trade with the inhabitants, and especially with the Chinese and Japan merchants, who were always there, which trade the governor could not prevent; and thus we could not fear a market for all our cargo, if it was much greater than it was.

That as to the returns, we had the advantage either way: for, first, we should be sure to receive a great part of the price of our goods in Chinese or Japan gold and silver, or in pieces of eight; or, if we thought fit to trade another way, we might take on board such a quantity of China damasks, and other wrought silks, muslins and chintz, China ware, and Japan ware; all which, would be immediately sold in America; that we should carry a cargo of these goods to New Spain, infinitely to our advantage, being the same cargo which the four great Acapulco ships carry back with them every year: That when we had gone to the South Seas with this cargo, of which we knew we should make a good market, we had nothing to do but to come back, if we thought fit, to the East Indies again, where we might load for England or Flanders such goods as we thought proper; or, if we did not think fit to take so great a run, we might go away to the south, and round by Cape Horn into the Atlantic Ocean, and perfect those discoveries, which we made part of in the beginning of our voyage.

This was so clear a scheme of trade, that he seemed surprised with it, and fully satisfied in every part of it. But the captain then objected against the length of the voyage to the South Seas from the Philippines, and raised several scruples about the latitude which we should keep in such a voyage; that we should not be able to carry any provisions which we could take on board in those hot countries, that would keep for so long a run, and several other difficulties; to all which I made answer, that when we had sold our cargo at the Philippines, and found our advantages there to answer our desires, I would not oppose our returning from thence directly to England if they found it needful; or, if they thought a farther adventure would not answer the risks we were to expect in it, we would never have any dispute about that.

This satisfied them fully, and they went immediately with the news to the men, as what they thought would please them wonderfully, seeing they were mighty uneasy but two or three days before, about their being to go back again to the south of America, and the latitude of 64°, where we had not only been twice driven back, as if heaven had forbidden us to pass that way, but had been driven so far to the south, that we had met with a most severe cold, and which pinched our men exceedingly, who being come, as we might say, a hot-weather voyage, were but ill furnished for the state of the air usual in the latitudes of 64°.

But we had a harder task to go through than we expected, upon this occasion; and it may stand here upon record, as a buoy or beacon to warn officers and commanders of ships, supercargoes, and such as are trusted in the conduct of the voyage, never to have any disputes among themselves, (I say not among themselves), about the course they shall take, or whither they shall go; for it never fails to come among the men after them, and if the debate is but named on the outside of the great cabin door, it becomes immediately a dispute among the officers upon the quarter-deck, the lieutenants, mates, purser, &c.; from thence it gets afore the mast, and into the cook room, and the whole ship is immediately divided into factions and parties; every foremast man is a captain, or a director to the captain; every boatswain, gunner, carpenter, cockswain, nay, and even the cook, sets up for a leader of the men; and if two of them join parties, it is ten to one but it comes to a mutiny, and perhaps to one of the two last extremities of all mutinies, viz., running away from the ship, or, what is worse, running away with the ship.

Our case was exactly thus, and had issued accordingly, for aught I know, if we had not been in a port where, we got immediate assistance, and that by a more than ordinary vigour in the management too.

I have mentioned the first time when we called a council about our voyage at the Canaries, and how it was carried against my opinion not to go to the East Indies, but to go to the South Seas, about by Cape Horn. As the debate of this was not at all concealed, the officers of the ship, viz., the two lieutenants and two mates, the purser, and others, came in, and went out, and not only heard all we said, but talked of it at liberty on the quarter-deck, and where they pleased, till it went among the whole ship's crew. It is true, there came nothing of all this at that time, because almost all the votes being against my opinion, as I have said already, the ship's company seemed to join in naturally with it, and the men were so talked into the great prospects of gain to themselves, by a voyage to the South Seas, that they looked upon me, who ought to have had the chief direction in the business, to be nobody, and to have only made a ridiculous proposal, tending to hurt them; and I perceived clearly after this, that they looked upon me with an evil eye, as one that was against their interest; nay, and treated me with a sort of contempt too, as one that had no power to hurt them, but as one, that if things were left to me, would carry them on a wildgoosechase they knew not whither.

I took no notice of this at first, knowing that, in the process of things, I should have opportunity enough to let them know I had power to oblige them many ways; as also, that I had authority sufficient to command the whole ship, and that the direction of the voyage was principally in me, though I being willing to do everything in a friendly way, had too easily, and, I may say, too weakly, put that to the vote, which I had a right to have commanded their compliance with. The ill consequences of which appeared not for some time, but broke out upon the occasion of our new measures, as will presently appear.

As soon as we had determined our voyage among ourselves in the great cabin, the supercargo and Captain Merlotte went out upon the quarter-deck, and began to talk of it among the officers, midshipmen, &c.; and, to give them their due, they talked of it very honestly; not with any complaint of being over-ruled, or over-persuaded, but as a measure that was fully agreed to among us in the great cabin.

The boatswain, a blunt, surly, bold fellow, as soon as he heard of it, Very well, says he, so we are all come back into Captain Positive's blind proposal (for so he called me); why this is the same that everybody rejected at the Canaries; and now, because we are driven hither by contrary winds, those winds must be a reason why we must undertake a preposterous, ridiculous voyage, that never any sailor would have proposed, and that man never went before. What, does the captain think that we cannot find our way to the coast of America again, and because we have met with cross winds, we must never meet with fair ones? I warrant him, let us but go up the height of St. Helena, we will soon reach the Rio de la Plata and Port St. Julian again, and get into the South Seas too, as others have done before us.

The gunner took it from the boatswain, and he talks with one of the midshipmen in the same dialect. For my part, says he, I shipped myself for the South Seas when I first came aboard the ship, and in hopes of good booty; and if we go thither, I know nothing can hinder us, wind and weather permitting: but this is such a voyage as no man ever attempted before; and whatever the captain proposes, can have nothing in it for the men, but horrid fatigue, violent heats, sickness, and starving.

One of the mates takes it from him, and he says as openly, I wonder what a plague the rest of the gentlemen mean; they were all against the captain when he started this whimsical voyage before, and now they come all into it of a sudden, without any consideration; and so the project of one man must ruin the most promising voyage ever yet undertaken, and be the death of above two hundred as stout fellows as ever were together in one ship in this part of the world.

One of the midshipmen followed the mate, and said, We were all promised that another ship should be gotten, either purchased or taken, and that the first ship we took, should be manned and victualled out of this ship, where we were double manned, and crowded together enough to bring an infection among us, in such hot climates as we are going into; and if we were in the South Seas, we should easily buy a ship, or take a ship for our purpose, almost where we would; but in all this part of the world there is no such thing as a ship fit for an Englishman to set his foot in. We were promised, too, that when we got into such a ship, we that entered as midshipmen should be preferred to offices, as we were qualified, and as our merit should recommend us. What they are going to do with us now, I cannot imagine, unless it be to turn us afore the mast, when half the foremast men are dead, and thrown overboard.

The master, or pilot of the ship, heard all these things, and sent us word into the great cabin of all that passed, and, in short, assured us, that, if these things went a little farther, he was afraid they would come up to a mutiny; that there was great danger of it already, and that we ought to apply some immediate remedy to it, or else he thought it would be too late. He told me the particulars also, and how the whole weight of their resentment seemed to tend to quarrelling at my command, as believing that this project of going to the East Indies was wholly mine; and that the rest of the officers being a little influenced by the accident of our being driven so far out of our way, were only biassed in the rest by my opinion; and, as they were all against it before, would have been so still, if it had not been for me; and he feared, if they went on, they might enter into some fatal measures about me, and perhaps resolve to set me on shore in some barren uninhabited land or other, to give me my bellyful of new discoveries, as it seems some of them had hinted, and the second mate in particular.

I was far from being insensible of the danger I was in, and indeed of the danger the whole voyage, ship and all, was in; for I made no question, but that, if their brutish rage led them to one villanous action, they would soon go on to another; and the devil would take hold of that handle to represent the danger of their being punished for it when they came home; and so, as has been often the case, prompt them to mutiny against all command, and run away with the ship.

However, I had presence of mind enough to enter into prompt measures for our general safety, and to prevent the worse, in case of any attempt upon me. First, I represented the case to the rest of the gentlemen and asked if they would stand by me, and by the resolutions which we had taken for the voyage; then I called into our assistance the chief mate, who was a kinsman of one of our owners, a bold resolute gentleman, and a purser, who we knew was faithful to us; as also the surgeon and the carpenter. I engaged them all to give me first their opinions whether they were convinced of the reasonableness of my scheme for the voyage I had proposed; and that they might judge for themselves, laid it all before them again, arguing every part of it so clearly to them, that they were convinced entirely of its being the most rational prospect of the voyage for us, of any we could go about.

When I had done this, I recommended it to them to expostulate with the men, and if possible, to keep them in temper, and keep them to their duty; but at the same time, to stand all ready, and upon a signal which I gave them, to come all to the steerage, and defend the great cabin door with all the other hands, whom they could be sure of; and in the mean time to be very watchful over the motions of the men, and see what they drove at.

At the same time I fortified myself with the French captain, and the supercargo, and the other captain; and by the way, all the French captain's men were true to him, and he true to us, to a man. We then brought a sufficient store of ammunition and small arms into the great cabin, and secured the steerage, as also the roundhouse, so that we could not possibly be surprised.

There was nothing done that night, but the next morning I was informed, that the gunner and second mate were in a close cabal together, and one or two of the midshipmen, and that they had sworn to one another, not that they would not go the voyage as was proposed, for that might have ended in their running away, which I should not have been sorry for; but, in short, their oath was, that the ship should not go the voyage; by which I was presently to understand, that they had some measures to take to prevent my design of the voyage to the Philippines, and that, perhaps, this was to run away with the ship to Madagascar, which was not far off.

I had, however, this apparent encouragement, that as the contrivance was yet but two days' old, for it was but two days since they had any notice of our intentions to go, they would be some days caballing and forming an interest among the men, to make up a party strong enough to make any attempt; and that, as I had a trusty set of men, who would be as diligent the other way, they would be contriving every method to get the men over to their opinion, so that at least it would be some time before they could make their party up.

The affair was rightly conjectured, and the three men who had made themselves the head of the mutineers, went on apace, and my men increased too, as much as could be desired for the time; but the Friday after, which was about five days from the first discovery, one of the midshipmen came, and desired to speak with me, and begged it might not, if possible, be known that he was with me. I asked him if he desired to be alone; he said no, I might appoint whom I thought convenient that I could trust, but that what he had to say was of the last importance to all our lives, and that therefore, he hoped I would be very sure of those in whom I confided.

Upon this, I told him, I would name the chief mate, the French captain, and the supercargo, and in the mean time, I bade him not be too much surprised, for that I had already some warning of the scheme which I believed he had to tell me of, and that I was preparing all things to disappoint it: that, however, I should not value his fidelity the less, and that he might speak freely his mind before those men, for they were all in the secret already, and he might be sure both of protection and reward.

Accordingly, I bade him go out upon the quarter-deck, and walk there, and that, when the chief mate went off into the roundhouse, he should go down between decks as if he was going into his cabin to sleep, and that, when he heard the chief mate call the cabin boy, a black of mine, whose name was Spartivento, he should take that for a signal that the steerage was clear, and he might come up, and should be let into the great cabin; all which was so managed, and in so short a time, that he was with us in the great cabin in a quarter of an hour after the first conference, and none of the men perceived it.

Here he let me into the whole secret, and a wicked scheme it was; viz., that the second mate, the gunner, three midshipmen, the cockswain, and about six-and-thirty of the men, had resolved to mutiny, and seize upon all us who were in the new project, as they called it; and to confine us first, then to set us on shore, either there where we were, or somewhere else, and so carry the ship away to the South Seas, and then to do as they found convenient; that is to say, in a word, to seize upon me, the other captain, the French captain, the supercargo, the chief mate, doctor, and carpenter, with some others, and run away with the ship.

He told me, that they had not fully concluded on all their measures, nor gained so many of the men as they intended; that they were to sound some more of the men the next morning, and, as soon as they had made their number up fifty, they were resolved to make the attempt, which they did not question would be by Thursday, and this was Monday morning; and that, if they were then ready, they would make the onset at changing the watch the same evening. He added, that, as they were to go on shore the next morning for fresh water, I should know the truth of it by this; that the second mate would come to me, and tell me that they wanted more water, and to know if I pleased the boats should go on shore, and that, if I chose it, he would go with them, or any else whom I pleased to appoint; and that, upon supposition that I would leave it to him, to take those he thought fit to go with him, he would then take occasion to choose the principal conspirators, that they might, when they were on shore, conclude upon the measures they intended to pursue.

I had all that day (Monday) to order my preparations, and upon this plain intelligence, I determined to lose no time, nor was it long before I resolved what to do; for as their design was desperate, so I had nothing but desperate remedies to provide. Having therefore settled my measures, I called for the cockswain, and bade him man the pinnace, for that I was to go on shore, and I appointed only the supercargo, and the surgeon, and the French captain, to go with me.

There were no English ships in the road, but there were about five Dutch vessels homeward-bound, waiting for more, and three outward-bound. As I passed by one of the outward-bound East India ships, the French captain, as we had agreed before, pretended to know the ship, and that the commander was his old acquaintance, and asked me to give him leave to visit him, and told me he was sure he would make us all welcome. I seemed unwilling at first, telling him I intended to go on shore and pay my respects to the governor, and, as was usual, to ask him leave to buy some provisions, and that the governor would take it very ill if I did not go. However, upon his alleging that we would not stay, and that the Dutch captain, upon his going on board, would, he was sure, give us a letter of recommendation to the governor, by which we should have everything granted that we could desire, I consented to his importunity, and we went on board.

Captain Merlotte, who spoke Dutch very well, hailed the ship, asked the captain's name, and then asked if he was on board; they answered, Yes; then he bade them tell him the captain of the English ship was come to visit him; upon which, immediately their chief mate bade them man the side, and stood at the side to receive us, and, before we could get up, the Dutch captain came upon the quarter-deck, and with great civility invited us into his cabin; and, while we were there, the chief mate, by the captain's order, entertained the boat's crew with like civility.

When we were in the cabin, Captain Merlotte told the Dutch captain that we came indeed to him in the form of a visit, but that our business was of the greatest importance, and desired we might speak to him of it in the hearing of none but such as he could trust. The captain told us with the greatest open-heartedness imaginable, that though we were strangers to him, yet we looked like honest men, and he would grant our request; we should speak it in the hearing of none but those we could trust, for there should be nobody by but ourselves.

We made him fully sensible that we knew how obliging that compliment was, but begged he would admit any whom he thought worthy to be trusted with a secret of the last importance. He then carried it as far the other way, and told us, that then he must call in the whole ship's company, for that there was not a man in the ship but he could trust his life in his hands. However, upon the whole, he sent everybody out of the cabin but us three and himself, and then desired we would speak our minds freely.

Captain Merlotte, who spoke Dutch, began, but the Dutch captain interrupted him, and asked if the English captain, meaning me, spoke Dutch; he said no; upon which he asked Captain Merlotte if he spoke English, and he said yes, upon which he let me know that he understood English, and desired I would speak to him in English.

I was heartily glad of this, and began immediately with the story, for we had time little enough, I told him that he was particularly happy in having it in his power to say he could put his life in the hand of any man, the meanest in his ship; that my men were unhappily the reverse of his; and, then beginning at the first of the story, I gave him a full account of the whole, as related above.

He was extremely affected with it, and asked me what he could do to serve me, and assured me that he would not only do what in him lay, but would engage all the ships in the road to do the like, and the governor also on shore. I thanked him very sincerely, and told him what at present was the circumstance I thought lay before me, was this, viz., that the chief conspirators would be on shore on the morrow, with one, or perhaps two, of our boats, to fetch water and get some fresh provisions, and I should be very glad to have them seized upon by surprise, when they were on shore, and that then I thought I could master the rest on board well enough.

Leave that to me, says he, I will give the governor notice this evening, and as soon as they come on shore they shall be all seized; But, says he, if you think they may incline to make any resistance, I will write a line to the governor, and give it you now; then, when your men go on shore, order two of the principal rogues to go and wait on the governor with the letter from you, and when he receives it, he shall secure them there; so they will be divided, and taken with the more ease.

In the mean time, added he, while this is doing on shore, I will come on board your ship, with my long boat and pinnace, and as many men as you please, to repay you the compliment of this visit, and assist you in reducing the rest.

This was so kind, and so completely what I desired, that I could have asked nothing more; and I accepted his visit in his barge, which I thought would be enough, but was afraid that, if more came, our men might be alarmed, and take arms before I was ready; so we agreed upon that, and, if I desired more help, I should hang out a signal, viz., a red ancient, on the mizen top.

All things being thus consulted, I returned on board, pretending to our men that I had spent so much time on board the Dutch ship, that I could not go on shore; and indeed some of my men were so drunk, that they could scarce sit to their oars; and the coxswain was so very far gone, that I took occasion to ask publicly, to leave him on board till the next day, giving the Dutch captain also a hint that he was in the conspiracy, and I should be glad to leave him on that account.

The next day, about nine o'clock, the second mate came to me, and told me they wanted more water, and, if I pleased to order the boat on shore, he would go if I thought fit, and see if he could get any fresh provisions, the purser being indisposed.

I told him, yes, with all my heart; that the Dutch captain last night had given me a letter to the governor, to desire we might be furnished with whatever we had occasion for, and that I had thoughts of calling for him to go on shore and deliver it, and that, perhaps, the governor might make him some present in compliment to the English nation.

He seemed extremely pleased at this, and even elevated, and going out to give orders about the boat, ordered the long-boat and the shallop, and came in again, and asked me whom I pleased to have go along with him. I answered, smilingly to him. Pick and choose then yourself, only leave the pinnace's crew that went with me yesterday, because they must go on board again to carry the Dutch captain a little present of English beer that I am going to send him, and fetch aboard their drunken coxswain, who was so intoxicated that we were fain to leave him behind us.

This was just what he wanted; and we found he chose all the chief rogues of the conspiracy; such as the boatswain, the gunner, the midshipmen we spoke of, and such of the foremast men as he had secured in his design; and of the rest, we judged they were in the plot, because he took them with him; and thus having the long-boat and the shallop, with about six-and-thirty men with them, away they went to fill water.

When they came on shore, they had presently three Dutchmen, set by the Dutch captain, unperceived by them, to be spies upon them, and to mark exactly what they did; and at the same time found three boats of Dutchmen at the watering-place, (for the captain had procured two boats to go on shore from two other ships,) full of men also, having acquainted them with the design. As soon as our boats came on shore, the men appeared to be all very much engaged in something more than ordinary, and, instead of separating, as it was expected they should, they went all into one boat, and there they were mighty busily engaged in discourse one with another.

The Dutch captain had given the charge of these things to a brisk bold fellow, his mate, and he took the hints the captain gave him so well, that nothing could have been better; for, finding the men thus in a kind of a cabal, he takes four of his men with muskets on their shoulders, like the governor's men, and goes with them to the Englishmen's boat, and asks for their officer, the second mate, who, upon this, appears. He tells them he comes from the governor, to know if they were Englishmen, and what their business was on shore there: the mate answered, they came from on board the English ship, that they were driven there by stress of weather, and hoped they might have leave to fill water and buy necessaries for their money.

He told them he supposed the governor would not refuse them when he knew who they were, but that it was but good manners to ask leave: the Englishman told him, that he had not yet filled any water or bought any provisions, and that he had a letter to the governor from the captain, which he supposed was to pay the usual civilities to him, and to give him the civility of taking leave, as was expected.

The Dutchman answered, that was hael weel; that he might go and carry it, if he pleased, then, and, if the governor gave them leave, all was right and as it should be; but that the men could not be admitted to come on shore till his return.

Upon this, away goes the second mate of our ship and three of the men with him, whereof the gunner was one; for he had asked the Dutchman how many he might carry with him, and he told him three or four: and those he took you may be sure, were of the particular men whom he had a confidence in, because of their conversing together by the way.

When they came to the governor, the mate sent in a message first, viz., that he was come from on board the English ship in the road, and that he had a letter from the captain to his excellence.

The governor, who had notice given him of the business, sends out word, that the gentlemen should send in the letter, and the governor would give them an answer: in the mean time, there appeared a guard of soldiers at the governor's house, and the four Englishmen were let into the outer room, where the door was shut after them, and the soldiers stood without the door, and more soldiers in another room between them and the parlour which the governor sat in.

After some time, the mate was called in, and the governor told him that he had read the letter which he brought, and asked him if he knew the contents of it; he answered, No: the governor replied, he supposed not, for, if he had, he would scarce have brought it; at the same time told him, he was obliged to make him and all his men prisoners, at the request of their own captain, for a conspiracy to raise a mutiny and run away with the ship. Upon which, two great fat Dutchmen came up to him, and bid him deliver his sword, which he did with some reluctance; for he was a stout strong fellow; but he saw it all to no purpose to dispute or resist.

At the same time, the three men without were made prisoners also by the soldiers. When the governor had thus secured these men, he called them in, and inquired the particulars of the case, and expostulated with them very pathetically upon such a horrid, villanous design, and inquired of them what the occasion could be; and, hearing all they had to say in their defence, told them he could do nothing more in it till their captain came on shore, which would be in a day or two, and that, in the mean time, they must be content to remain in custody, which they did, separated from one another. They were very civilly treated, but strictly kept from speaking or sending any messages to one another, or to the boats.

When this was accomplished, the governor sent six files of musketeers down to the watering-place, with an order to secure all the Englishmen in the two boats, which was done. They seemed inclined to make some resistance at first, being all very well armed; but the seamen of the three Dutch long-boats, joining themselves to the soldiers, and notice being given the English seamen, that if they fired one gun, they should have no quarter; and especially their two principal men, the chief mate and the gunner, being absent, they submitted, and were all made prisoners also.

When this was done, of which the Dutch captain had notice by a signal from the shore, he came off in his shallop, with about sixteen seamen, and five or six gentlemen and officers, to pay his visit to me. I received him with all the appearance of ceremony imaginable, ordered an elegant dinner to be prepared for him, and caused his men to be all treated upon the deck, and made mighty preparations for the feast.

But in the middle of all this, Captain Merlotte, with all his Frenchmen, being thirty-two, appeared in arms on the quarter-deck; the Dutch captain's attendants stood to their arms on the main-deck, and I, with the supercargo, the doctor, and the other captain, leaving the Dutch captain and some men in the great cabin as a reserve, came to the steerage door, cleared the steerage behind me, and stood there with a cutlass in my hand, but said nothing; neither was there a word spoke anywhere all the while.

In this juncture, the chief mate, the faithful midshipmen, the carpenter, and the gunner's mate, with about twenty men whom they could trust, went fore and aft between decks, and secured all the particular men that we had the least suspicion of, being no less than thirty-five more. These they secured, bringing them up into the steerage, where their hands were tied behind them, and they were commanded not to speak a word to one another upon pain of present death.

When this was done, the chief mate came to me to the steerage door, and passing by, went forward with his men, entered the cook-room, and posted himself at the cook-room door. There might be still about eighty men upon the forecastle and midships upon the open decks; and there they stood staring, and surprised at what was doing, but not being able to guess in the least what was meant, what was the cause of it, or what was intended to be done farther.

When I found all things ready, I moved forward a step or two, and beckoning to the mate to command silence, I told the men that I was not disposed to hurt any man, nor had I done what I now did, but by necessity, and that I expected they should all submit; that, if any one of them made the least resistance, he was a dead man; but that, if they would be easy and quiet, I should give a very good account to them all, of every part of the voyage, or scheme of a voyage, which I had laid, and which had been so ill represented to them.

Then I caused my commissioner letter of mart to be read to them all, by which it appeared that I was really chief commander of the ship, and had a right to direct the voyage as I thought best; with a paper of written instructions, signed by the owners and adventurers, and directed to me, with another paper of instructions to all the officers, to be directed by me in all things; which, indeed, was all news to them, for they did not think I was the chief captain or commander of the ship and voyage.

When I had done this, I gave them a long and full account of the reasons why I thought it best, as our present circumstances were stated, not to go to the South Seas first, but to go away to the Philippine Islands, and what great prospect of advantage to the owners there was, as well as to the men; and that I wondered much that such measures were taken in the ship as I heard there were; and that I was not, they might see, unprovided of means to reduce every one of them to their duty by force, and to punish those that were guilty, as they deserved, but that I rather desired to win them with kindness; and that, therefore, I had resolved, that if any of them had any reason to dislike the voyage, they should be safely set on shore, and suffered to go to the second mate and his comrades: and farther, I told them what circumstances they were in and how effectually they were secured.

This astonished them, and surprised them exceedingly, and some of them inquired more particularly into the circumstances of the said second mate and his fellows: I told them they were safe enough, and should remain so; for, as I could prove they had all a villanous design to run away with the ship, and set me on shore, either here, or in a worse place, I thought that only upon account of my own safety, such men were not fit to go in the ship, being once capable to entertain such horrid mischievous thoughts, or that could be guilty of such a villany; and that, if any of them were of their minds, they were very welcome, if they thought fit, to go to them.

At this offer, some bold rogues upon the forecastle, which I did not discern, by reason of the number that stood there, cried out, One and all, which was a cry, at the same time, of mutiny and rebellion, that was certain, and in its kind very dangerous.

However, to let them see I was not to be daunted with it, I called out to one of the men among them, whom I saw upon the forecastle; You Jones, said I, tell me who they are, and come away from them, for I will make an example of them, whoever they are. Will Jones slunk in among the rest, and made me no answer, and immediately One and all was cried again, and a little huzza with it, and some of the men appeared to have fire-arms with them. There was a great many of them, and I presently foresaw, that, if I went to the extremity, I should spoil the voyage, though I conquered them; so I bridled my passion with all my power, and said calmly, Very well, gentlemen, let me know what you mean by one and all? I offered any of you that did not like to go the voyage to quit the ship; is that what you intend by one and all? If so, you are welcome, and pray take care to do it immediately; as for what chests or clothes you have in the ship, you shall have them all with you. Upon this I made the chief mate, who was now come to me again, advance a little with some more men, and get between the men upon the forecastle and those who were upon the main deck; and, as if he had wanted room, when he had gotten between them, he said to them, Stand aft a little, gentlemen, and so crowded them towards me.

As they came nearer and nearer to where I stood, I had an opportunity to speak to them singly, which I did calmly and smilingly.

Why, how now, Tom, says I, to one of them; what are you among the mutineers?

Lord, sir, says Tom, not I, they are mad, I think; I have nothing to say to them; I care not where I go, not I; I will go round the globe with you, it's all one to me.

Well, Tom, says I, but what do you do among them then? come away into the steerage, and show yourself an honest man.

So Tom comes in, and after him another, and then two more. Upon my saying to Tom, What do you do among them? one of the fellows says to one of the officers that stood at a little distance from me, What does the captain mean by saying, among them? What, does he reckon us to be in the plot? He is quite wrong, we are all ignorant, and surprised at it. He immediately tells me this, and I was glad, you may be sure, to hear it, and said aloud to the man that he spoke to, If they are honest men, and would not appear in this villany, let them go down between decks, and get out of the way, that they may have no share in the punishment, if they have none in the crime. With all my heart, says one; God bless you, captain, says another, and away they dropt one by one in at the steerage door, and down between decks, every one in his hammock or cabin, till there were not above five or six of them left.

By this time, our two boats appeared from the shore, being both manned with Dutchmen, viz. the Dutch captain's mate and about twenty of his men, all the water casks full, but not a man of mine with them, for they were left on shore in safe custody.

I waited till they came on board, and then turning to the men on the forecastle, I told them they should go on board the boats immediately, as soon as the butts of water were hoisted in. They still said, One and all, they were ready, desired they might go and fetch their clothes.

No, no, says I, not a man of you shall set your foot any more into the ship; but go get you into the boat, and what is your own shall be given you into the boat.

As I spoke this in an angry tone, and with a kind of passion, that bespoke resentment to a high degree, they began to see they had no opportunity to choose; and some of them slipt down the scuttle into the cook-room. I had ordered the officer who was there, who was one of the midshipmen, to wink at it, and let as many come down as offered it; and the honest man did more than that, for he went to the scuttle himself, and, as if he had whispered, so that I should not hear him, called them one by one by their names, and argued with them; Prithee, Jack, says he to one of them, do not you be distracted, and ruin yourself to gratify a rash drunken humour; if you go into the boat you are undone; you will be seized as soon as you come on shore, as the rest are, and will be sent to England in irons, and there you will be infallibly hanged; why you are certainly all mad.

Jack replies, he had no design to mutiny, but the second mate drew him in, and he did not know what to do, he wished he had not meddled; he knew he was undone; but now what could he do?

Do, says the midshipman, leave them for shame, and slip down here, and I will see and get you off if I can.

Accordingly he pulled him down, and after him so many got out of sight the same way, that there was not above seventeen or eighteen left upon the forecastle.

I seemed to take no notice of that, till at last one of the men that was left there, with his hat or cap in his hand, stepping just to the edge of the forecastle, which was next to me, said, in a very respectful manner, that I saw how many had slunk away and made their peace, or at least obtained pardon, and that I might, perhaps, know that they who were left were only such as had their duty there, being placed there of course before the mutiny began, and that they had no hand in it, but abhorred it with all their hearts, which he hoped I would consider, and not join them with those that had offended, merely because they came upon the forecastle, and mixed there with the men who had the watch.

I told him, if that was true, it would be in their favour, but I expected he would prove it to my satisfaction before I accepted that for an excuse. He told me, it might, perhaps, be hard to prove it, seeing the boatswain and his mate, and the second mate, were gone, but the rest of the ship's crew could all testify that they were a part of the men whose watch it was, and that they were upon the forecastle by the necessity of their duty, and no otherwise; and called several men who were upon duty with them to witness it, who did confirm it.

Upon this, I found myself under a necessity, in justice to the men, to approve it; but my own management was a bite upon myself in it; for, though I did allow the midshipman to wink at their slipping away, as before, yet I made no question but I should have some left to make examples of; but as I could not go back from the promise of mercy which I had allowed the midshipman to offer in my name, so I tricked myself by their mistake into a necessity of pardoning them all, which was very far from my design; but there was no remedy.

However, the men, when they were so happily escaped, desired the midshipman, who had been instrumental to their deliverance, to assure me, that as they were sensible that they had deserved very ill at my hands, and that yet I had treated them thus kindly, they would not only reveal to me all the particulars of the conspiracy, and the names of those principally concerned in it, but that they would assure me they would never more dispute any of my measures, but were very ready to do their duty as seamen, to what part of the world soever I might think fit to go, or which way I thought fit to carry them, whether outward or homeward; and that they gave me the tender of their duty in this manner with the utmost sincerity and with thankfulness, for my having forgiven them that conduct which was the worst that a seamen could be guilty of.

I took this very kindly, and sent them word I did so, and that they should see they had taken the wiser course; that I had an entire confidence in their fidelity; and that they should never find I would reproach them with, or use them the worse for, what had past.

I must confess, I was very glad of this submission of the men; for though, by the measures I had taken, I was satisfied I should conquer them, and that I was safe from their attempts; yet, carrying it on by resentment, and doing justice upon the offenders, whatever advantage it had one way, had this disadvantage in the consequence; viz., that it would ruin the voyage, for at least half the men were in the plot.

Having thus conquered them by good usage, I thought my next work was to inquire into the mistakes which had been the foundation of all this: so, before I parted with the men who had returned to their duty, I told them, that as I had freely forgiven what was past, so I would keep my word, that I would never reproach them with it; but that I thought it was necessary their judgments should be convinced how much they were imposed upon, as well as their tempers be reduced by my kindness to them. That I was of the opinion that they had been abused in the account given them of what I had designed to do, and of the reasons I had to give for doing it; and I would desire them to let me know afterwards, whether they had been faithfully informed or not; and whether in their own judgment, now when they were freed from the prepossessions they were under, they could object anything against it or no.

This I did with respect to the other men whom I had made prisoners in the steerage, whom I had the same design to be kind to as I had to these; but upon whom I resolved to work this way, because, after all, I might have this work to do over again, if I should meet with any disappointment or miscarriage in the voyage; or especially, if we should be put to any difficulties or distresses in the pursuing it.

In order to this I caused the voyage itself, and the reasons of it, the nature of the trade I was to carry on by it, the pursuit of it to the South Seas, and, in a word, everything just as we had argued and settled it in the great cabin, to be put into writing and read to them.

The fellows, every one of them, declared they were fully satisfied in the voyage itself, and that my reasons for it were perfectly good; and that they had received a quite different account of it; as that I would carry them into the island of the Moluccas, which was the most unhealthy part of the East Indies; that I would go away to the south for new discoveries; and that I would go away thence to the South Seas; which was a voyage of such a length, that no ship could victual for; that it was impossible to carry fresh water such a length; and, in a word, that it was a voyage that would destroy us all.

It was the chief mate and the midshipman who took them all down the scuttle, that brought me this account from them: so I made him take two of those penitent mutineers with him, and go to the men in the steerage, whom he had made prisoners at first, and see whether their delusions were of the same kind, and what kind of temper they were in; accordingly, he went to them directly, for this was not a business that admitted giving them time to club and cabal together, and form other societies or combinations which might have consequences fatal to us still.

When he came to them, he told them, the captain was willing to do all the justice possible to his men, and to use them, on all occasions, with equity and kindness; that I had ordered him to inquire calmly what it was had moved them to these disorders, and what it was which they had been made to believe was doing, that they could enter into measures so destructive to themselves, and to those who had intrusted them all with the ship and cargo; for that, in a voyage, every foremast-man, in his degree, is trusted with the safety of the whole ship.

They answered it was the second mate; that they had never shown themselves discontented, much less disorderly, in the ship; that they had, on all occasions, done their duty through the whole voyage till now; and that they had no ill design upon any one, much less had they any design to destroy the voyage, or injure the captain; but that they were all told by the second mate, that the captain had imposed upon them, by proposing a mad voyage to the south pole, that would be the death of them all, and that they were to lay aside the trading and cruising voyages which they came out upon, and were now to spend the whole voyage in new discoveries; by which the men could propose nothing to themselves but hardships, and perhaps perishing with hunger and cold; whereas, had they gone to the South Seas as was intended, they might all have been made; and that the hazards, with that prospect, had some consolation in them; whereas, in this project, there was nothing but certain destruction.

The mate delivered them a copy of the scheme I had proposed, the reasons of it, the trade I had designed, the return I was to make, and everything, as I have already mentioned, and bade them take it and consider of it.

As I was justly provoked to see how I had been abused and misrepresented to the men, so they were astonished when they read my scheme, and saw what mischiefs they had been led into, for they knew not what, and without any reason or just consideration: and, after they had debated things awhile among themselves, they desired the chief mate might come to them again, which he did; then they told him, that as they had been thus grossly abused, and drawn into mischiefs which they never designed, by such plausible pretences, and by being told such a long story full of lies, and to carry on an infernal project of the second mate's, they hoped their being so much imposed upon would a little extenuate their fault; that they were convinced the captain had proposed nothing but what was very rational, and a voyage that might be very profitable to the owners and to every individual; and they entirely threw themselves upon the captain's mercy, and humbly begged pardon; that, if I pleased to forgive them, they would endeavour to merit such forgiveness by their future behaviour; and that, in the mean time, they submitted to what punishment I pleased to lay upon them: and, particularly, that, as they had forfeited, by their conspiracy, all the claims they had upon the ship, and might justly have been turned on shore at the first land they came to, they were willing to sign a discharge for all their wages due to them, which was now near eight months a man, and to be considered for the rest of the voyage as they deserved: that they would all take a solemn oath of fidelity to me to do their duty, to go wherever I would carry them, and to behave with the greatest submission and diligence, in hopes to regain my favour by their future behaviour, and to show their gratitude for the pardon I should grant them.

This was, indeed, just as I would have it, for I wanted nothing more than to have something offered, which I might give them back again; for I ever thought, and have found it by experience, to be the best way; and men were always secured in their duty by a generous kindness, better than by absolute dominion and severity: indeed, my opinion was justified in all the measures I took with these men; for as I found they were sufficiently humbled, and that I had brought them low enough, I let them know that it was not their punishment but their amendment I desired; that I scorned to make a prey of them, and take that forfeiture they had offered, by putting the wages due to them for their labour in my pocket. I then sent them word I was very glad to hear that they were sensible how much they had been imposed upon; that, as it was not my design to offer anything to them which they or any honest men ought to refuse, so it was not my desire to make any advantages of their follies but what might tend to bring them back to their duty; that, as I had no prospect that was inconsistent with their safety and interest, so I scorned to make an advantage of their submission; that as to their wages, though they had forfeited them by their mutiny, yet God forbid I should convert them to my own profit; and since forgiving their offence was in my power, the crime being in one particular an offence against me, they should never be able to say I made a gain of their submission, and, like the Pope, should sell them my pardon; that, upon their solemnly engaging to me never to offer the least disturbance of any kind in the ship for the future, but to do their duty faithfully and cheerfully, I would forget all that was passed; only this I expected, that two of them, who were particularly guilty of threatening the life of Captain Merlotte, should be punished as they deserved.

They could not deny but this was most just; and they did not so much as offer to intercede for those two; but, when one of the two moved the rest to petition for them, they answered they could not do it, for they had received favour enough for themselves, and they could not desire anything of the captain for their sakes, for they had all deserved punishment as well as they.

In a word, the two men were brought upon deck, and soundly whipped and pickled; and they all proved very honest ever after: and these, as I said at first, were two-and-thirty in all.

All this while Captain Merlotte with his Frenchmen were in arms, and had possession on the quarter-deck to the number of twenty-three stout men; I had possession of the main-deck with eighteen men and the sixteen Dutchmen, and my chief mate with the midshipman, had possession of the cook-room and quarter-deck; the Dutch captain, our supercargo, the surgeon, and the other captain, kept the great cabins with a guard of twelve musketeers without the door, and about eight more within, besides servants. Captain Merlotte's man also had a guard of eight men in the roundhouse. I had now nothing to do but with my men who were on shore; and of these, six were no way culpable, being men not embarked in the design, but carried on shore by the chief mate, with a design to engage them with him; so that, indeed, they fell into a punishment before they fell into the crime, and what to do with these men was a nice point to manage.

The first thing I did, was to dismiss my visitor, the Dutch captain, whom I had a great deal of reason to think myself exceedingly obliged to: and, first, I handsomely rewarded his men, to whom I gave four pieces of eight a man; and having waited on the captain to the ship's side, and seen him into his boat, I fired him twenty-one guns at his going off; for which he fired twenty-five when he came on board his ship.

The same afternoon I sent my pinnace on board him for my drunken cockswain, and with the pinnace I sent the captain three dozen bottles of English beer, and a quarter cask of Canary, which was the best present I had to make him; and sent every one of his other seamen a piece of eight per man; and, indeed, the assistance I had from the ship deserved it; and to the mate, who acted so bravely with my men on shore, I sent fifty pieces of eight.

The next day I went on shore to pay my respects to the governor, when I had all the prisoners delivered up to me. Six men I caused to be immediately set at liberty, as having been innocent, and brought all the rest on board, tied hand and foot, as prisoners, and continued them so, a great while afterward, as the reader will find. As for the second mate, I tried him formally by a council of war, as I was empowered by my commission to do, and sentenced him to be hanged at the yard-arm: and though I suspended the execution from day to day, yet I kept him in expectation of the halter every hour; which, to some, would have been as grievous as the hanging itself.

Thus we conquered this desperate mutiny, all principally proceeding from suffering the private disputes among ourselves, which ought to have been the arcana of the whole voyage, and kept as secret as death itself could have kept it, I mean so as not to come among the seamen afore the mast.

We lay here twelve days, during which time we took in fresh water as much as we had casks for, and were able to stow. On the 13th day of August, we weighed and stood away to the east, designing to make no land any more till we came to Java Head, and the Straits of Sunda, for that way we intended to sail; but the wind sprung up at E. and E. S. E., and blew so fresh, that we were obliged, after two days' beating against it, to bear away afore it, and run back to the Cape of Good Hope.

While we were here, there came in two Dutch East Indiamen more, homeward-bound, to whom had happened a very odd accident.

They had been attacked by a large ship of forty-four guns, and a stout sloop of eight guns; the Dutch ships resolving to assist one another, stood up to the Frenchman, (for such it seems he was,) and fought him very warmly. The engagement lasted six or seven hours; in which the privateer had killed them some men; but in the heat of the fight, the sloop received a shot, which brought her mainmast by the board; and this caused the captain of the frigate to sheer off, fearing his sloop would be taken; but the sloop's men took care of themselves, for, hauling a little out of the fight, they got into their own boats, and a boat which the frigate sent to their help, and abandoned the sloop; which the Dutchmen perceiving, they manned out their boats, and sent and took the sloop with all that was in her, and brought her away with them.

The Dutchmen came into the road at the Cape with this prize while our ship was there the second time; and we saw them bringing the sloop in tow, having no mast standing, but a little pole-mast set up for the present, and her mizen, which was also disabled, and of little use to her.

I no sooner saw her, but it came into my thoughts, that, if she was anything of a sea-boat, she would do our business to a tittle; and, as we had always resolved to get another ship, but had been disappointed, this would answer our end exactly; accordingly I went with my chief mate, in our shallop, on board my old acquaintance the Dutch captain, and inquiring there, was informed that it was a prize taken, and that in all probability the captain that took her would be glad to part with her; and the captain promised me to go on board the ship that brought her in, and inquire about it, and let me know.

Accordingly, the next morning the captain sent me word I might have her; that she carried eight guns, had good store of provisions on board, with ammunition sufficient, and I might have her and all that was in her for twelve hundred pieces of eight. In a word, I sent my chief mate back with the same messenger and the money, giving him commission to pay for her, and take possession of her, if he liked her; and the Dutch captain, my friend, lent him twelve men to bring her off to us, which they did the same day.

I was a little put to it for a mast for her, having not anything on board we could spare that was fit for a main-mast; but resolving at last to mast her not as a sloop, but as a brigantine, we made shift with what pieces we had, and a spare foretop-mast, which one of the Dutch ships helped me to; so we fitted her up very handsomely, made her carry twelve guns, and put sixty men on board. One of the best things we found on board her, were casks, which we greatly wanted, especially for barrelling up beef and other provisions, which we found very difficult; but our cooper eked them out with making some new ones out of her old ones.

After staying here sixteen days more, we sailed again. Indeed, I thought once we should never have gone away at all; for it is certain above half the men in the ship had been made uneasy, and there remained still some misunderstanding of my design, and a supposition of all the frightful things the second mate had put in their heads; and, by his means, the boatswain and gunner.

As these three had the principal management of the conspiracy, and that I had pardoned all the rest, I had some thoughts of making an example of these; I took care to let them know it, too, in a manner that they had no room to think it was in jest, but I intended to have them all three hanged; and I kept them above three weeks in suspense about it: however, as I had no intention to put them to death, I thought it was a piece of cruelty, something worse than death, to keep them continually in expectation of it, and in a place too where they had but little more than room to breathe.

So, having been seventeen days gone from the Cape, I resolved to relieve them a little, and yet at the same time remove them out of the way of doing me any capital injury, if they should have any such design still in their heads. For this purpose, I caused them to be removed out of the ship into brigantine, and there I permitted them to have a little more liberty than they had on board the great ship; and where two of them entered into another conspiracy, as wild and foolish as ever I heard of, or as, perhaps, was ever heard of by any other; but of this I shall say more in its place.

We were now to sail in company, and we went away from the Cape, the 3rd of September, 1714. We found the brigantine was an excellent sea-boat, and could bear the weather to a miracle, and no bad sailer; she kept pace with us on all occasions, and in a storm we had at S. S. E., some days after, she shifted as well as we did in the great ship, which made us all well pleased with her.

This storm drove us away to the northward; and I once thought we should have been driven back to the Cape again; which, if it had happened, I believe we should never have gone on with the voyage; for the men began to murmur again, and say we were bewitched; that we were beaten off first from the south of America, that we could never get round there, and now driven back from the south of Africa; so that, in short, it looked as if fate had determined this voyage to be pursued no farther. The wind continued, and blew exceeding hard: and, in short, we were driven so far to the north, that we made the south point of the island of Madagascar.

My pilot knew it to be Madagascar as soon as he had a clear view of the land; and, having beaten so long against the sea to no purpose, and being in want of many things, we resolved to put in; and accordingly made for Port St. Augustine, on the west side of the island, where we came to an anchor in eleven fathom water, and a very good road.

I could not be without a great many anxious thoughts upon our coming into this island; for I knew very well that there was a gang of desperate rogues here, especially on the northern coast, who had been famous for their piracies; and I did not know but that they might be either strong enough as pirates to take us, or rogues enough to entice a great many of my men to run away; so I resolved neither to come near enough the shore to be surprised, nor to suffer any of my men to go on shore, such excepted as I could be very secure of.

But I was soon informed by a Dutchman, who came off to me with some of the natives in a kind of canvass boat, that there were no Europeans there but himself, and the pirates were on the north part of the island; that they had no ship with them of any force, and that they would be glad to be fetched off by any Christian ship; that they were not above two hundred in number, their chief leaders, with the only ships of force they had, being out a cruising on the coast of Arabia, and the Gulf of Persia.

After this, I went on shore myself with Captain Merlotte, and some of the men whom I could trust; and we found it true as the Dutchman had related. The Dutchman gave us a long history of his adventures, and how he came to be left there by a ship he came in from Europe, which, he running up into the country for sport with three more of his comrades, went away without them, and left them among the natives, who, however, used them extremely well; and that now he served them for an interpreter and a broker, to bargain for them with the European ships for provisions. Accordingly, he engaged to bring us what provisions we pleased, and proposed such trinkets in return as he knew the natives desired, and as were of value little enough to us; but he desired a consideration for himself in money, which, though it was of no use to him there, he said it might be hereafter; and, as his demand was but twenty pieces of eight, we thought he very well deserved them.

Here we bought a great quantity of beef, which, having no casks to spare, we salted, and then cured it in the sun, by the Dutchman's direction, and it proved of excellent use to us through the whole voyage; for we kept some of it till we came to England, but it was then so hard, that a good hatchet would hardly cut it.

While we lay here, it came into my thoughts, that now was a good time to execute justice upon my prisoners; so I called up the officers to a kind of council of war, and proposed it to them in general terms, not letting them know my mind as to the manner of it. They all agreed it was necessary, and the second mate, boatswain, and gunner, had so much intelligence of it from the men, that they prepared for death as much as if I had signed a dead-warrant for their execution, and that they were to be hanged at the yard-arm.

But, in the midst of those resolves, I told the council of officers, my design was to the north part of the island, where a gang of pirates were said to be settled, and that I was persuaded I might get a good ship among them, and as many men as we desired, for that I was satisfied the greatest part of them were so wearied of their present situation, that they would be glad of an opportunity to come away, and especially such as had, either by force, or rash, hasty resolutions, been, as it were, surprised into that sort of life; that I had been informed they were very far from being in such a formidable posture as they had been represented to us in Europe, or anything near so numerous; but that, on the contrary, we should find them poor, divided, in distress, and willing to get away upon any terms they could.

Some of the officers of the ship differed from me in my opinion. They had received such ideas of the figure those people made in Madagascar, from the common report in England, that they had no notion of them, but as of a little commonwealth of robbers; that they were immensely rich; that Captain Avery was king of the Island; that they were eight thousand men; that they had a good squadron of stout ships, and that they were able to resist a whole fleet of men of war; having a harbour so well fortified at the entrance into it, that there was no coming at them without a good army for land-service, to assist in the enterprise.

I convinced them how impossible this was to be true, and told them all the discourse I had with the Dutchman, at the place where I now was, who had received a full account of the particulars from several of them who had come down to St. Augustine's in little boats in order to make their escape from their comrades, and to get passage for Europe; that he had always assisted, and got them off, whenever any ship touched at that port; and that they all agreed in their relation of their state and condition, which was indeed miserable enough, saving that they wanted not for victuals.

In a word, I soon brought them to enter into the reason of it, and to be of my opinion; and, accordingly, I ordered to get ready, and in three days' time weighed anchor, and stood away for the north of the island, taking care not to communicate our debates and resolves to the men before the mast, as had been done before, we having had enough of that already.

While we were thus coasting the island to the north, and in the channel or sea between the island and the main of Africa, it came into my thoughts, that I might now make use of my traitors to my advantage and their own too, and that I might, if they were honest, gain my end, and get a full intelligence of the people I had my eye upon; and, if they were still traitors, they would desert and go over to the pirates, and I should be well rid of them, without the necessity of bringing them to the yard-arm; for I was very uneasy in my mind about hanging them, nor could I ever have been brought to do it, I believe, whatever risk I had run from their mutinous disposition.

I was now got in the latitude of fifteen degrees and a half south of the line, and began to think of standing in for the shore; when I ordered the second mate, who lay in irons in the brigantine, to be brought on board the great ship, and to be called up into the great cabin. He came in great concern, though he was of himself a very bold and resolute fellow, yet, as he made no doubt that he was sent for to execution, he appeared thoroughly softened, and quite another man than he was before.

When he was brought in, I caused him to be set down in a nook of the cabin where he could not stir to offer any violence to me, had he been so inclined, two large chests being just before him; and I ordered all my people to withdraw, except Captain Merlotte and the supercargo; and then, turning myself to the criminal, I told him, as he knew his circumstances, I need not repeat them, and the fact for which he was brought into that condition; that I had hitherto, from time to time, delayed his execution, contrary to the opinion of the rest of the chief officers, who in full council had unanimously condemned him; that a sudden thought had come into my mind, which, if he knew how to merit mercy, and to retrieve his circumstances by his future fidelity, might once again put it into his power, not only to save his life, but to be trusted in the ship again, if he inclined to be honest; that, however, if he had no inclination to merit by his service, I would put it to his choice, either to undertake with courage and fidelity what I had to propose to him, in which case he might expect to be very well treated, or, if not, I would pardon him as to the death he had reason to expect, and he with his two fellow-criminals should be set on shore to go whither they pleased.

He waited, without offering to speak a word, till I made a full stop, and then asked me if I gave him leave to answer.

I told him he might say whatever he thought proper.

Then he asked if I gave him leave to speak freely, and would not take offence at what he might say? I replied, he should speak as freely as if he had never offended; and that, as I had given him his life, I now would give him my word, nothing he could say should revoke the grant; and that he should not only go freely on shore, (for I expected by his words that he had made that choice) but I would give him the lives of his two fellow-prisoners; and would give them arms and ammunition, and anything else that was reasonable for them to ask, or necessary to their subsisting on shore in such a country.

He told me then, that had it been any other part of the world than at Madagascar, he would readily have chosen to have gone on shore; nay, though the place had been really desolate and uninhabited; that he did not object because my offer was not very generous and kind, and that it would be always with regret that he should look back upon the mercy he should have received, and how ill he had deserved it at my hands.

But that as it was at this place that I mentioned setting him at liberty, he told me, that though he had been mutinous and disorderly, for which he had acknowledged he had deserved to die, yet he hoped I could not think so ill of him as to believe he could turn pirate; and begged that, rather than entertain such hard thoughts of him, I would execute the worst part of the sentence, and send him out of the world a penitent and an honest man, which he should esteem far better than to give him his life in a condition in which he could preserve it upon no other terms than those of being the worst of villains. He added, that if there was anything he could do to deserve so much mercy as I intended him, he begged me that I would give him room to behave himself as became him, and he would leave it wholly to me to use him as he should deserve, even to the recalling the pardon that I had granted him.

I was extremely satisfied with what he said, and more particularly with the manner of his speaking it; I told him I was glad to see that he had a principle of so much honesty at the bottom of a part so unhappy as he had acted; and I would be very far from prompting him to turn pirate, and much more from forcing him to do so, and that I would, according to his desire, put an opportunity into his hands to show himself a new man, and, by his fidelity, to wipe out all that was past. And then, without any more ceremony, I told him my whole design, which was, to send him, and four or five more men with him, on shore among the pirates as spies, to see what condition they were in, and to see whether there were any apprehensions of violence from them, or whether they were in the mean circumstances that I had reason to believe they were in; and, lastly, whether they had any ship or vessel which might be bought of them, and whether men might be had to increase our company; that is to say, such men as, being penitent for their rogueries and tired with their miseries, would be glad of the opportunity of turning honest men before they were brought to it by distress and the gallows.

He embraced the offer with the greatest readiness, and gave me all the assurances that I could desire of his fidelity. I then asked him whether he thought his two fellow-prisoners might be trusted upon the same conditions.

In reply, he asked me if I would take it for a piece of sincerity, if, after a trial, he should tell me his mind, and would not be displeased if he declined speaking his thoughts till he had talked with them.

I told him he should be at liberty to give his farther answer after he had proposed it to them; but I insisted upon his opinion first, because it was only his opinion that I asked now; whereas, if he reported it to them, then he had no more to do but to report their answer.

He then asked me if I would please to grant him one thing, that, whatever his opinion should be, what he should say should be no prejudice to them in their present condition.

I told him it was a reasonable caution in him, and I would assure him that, whatever he said should not do them any prejudice; and, to convince him of it, I gave him my word that I would not put them to death on any account whatsoever, merely for his sake.

He bowed, and thanked me very heartily for that grant, which, he said, obliged him to be the plainer with me on that head; and as, he said, he would not deceive me in anything whatever, so he would not in this, especially; and therefore told me it was his opinion, they would not serve me faithfully; and he referred me to the experience I should find of it; and added, that he would be so just to me in the beginning, as that, while he begged to be merciful to them, yet for my own sake he would also beg me not to trust them.

I took the hint, and said no more at that time, but ordered his irons to be taken off, with direction for him to have leave to go to his former cabin, and to have his chests and things restored to him; so that he was at full liberty in the ship, though not in any office, or appointed to any particular business.

A day or two after this we made land, which appeared to be the north-west part of the island, in the latitude of 13° 30'; and now I thought it was time to put our design into execution; for I knew very well that it could not be a great way from this part of the island where the pirates were to be heard of: so I ordered the boat on shore, with about sixteen men, to make discoveries, and with them my new-restored man.

I gave him no instruction for anything extraordinary at this time, our work now being only to find out where they were. The boat came on board again at night, (for we had now stood in within two leagues of the shore) and brought us an account, that there were no English or Europeans on that part of the island, but that they were to be heard of a great way farther; so we stood away to the north all the night, and the next day, the wind being fair and the sea smooth, and by our reckoning we went in that time about forty leagues.

The next evening, the same company went on shore again, and were shown by some of the natives where the pirates inhabited; which, in short, was about five or six and twenty miles farther north still, in a river very commodious for shipping, where they had five or six European-built ships, and two or three sloops, but they were all laid up, except two sloops, with which they cruised sometimes a great distance off to the north, as far as the Arabian Gulf. The mate returned with this intelligence the same night; and by his direction we stood in as close under the shore as we could conveniently, about six leagues farther north; here we found a very good road under a little cape, which kept us perfectly undiscovered; and in the morning, before day, my man went on shore again with the boat, and keeping only four men with him, sent the boat on board again, agreeing on a signal for us to send the boat for him again when he should return.

There was a pretty high ledge of hills to the north of the place where he landed, and which, running west, made the little cape, under the lee of which our ship rode at anchor.

As soon as he came to the top of those hills, he plainly discovered the creek or harbour where the pirates' ships lay, and where they had formed their encampment on the shore. Our men took proper observations of the situation of the place they were in, upon the hill, that they might not fail to find their way back again, though it were in the night; and that, by agreeing in the account they should give of themselves, they might be all found in the same tale. They boldly went down the hill, and came to the edge of the creek, the pirates' camp being on the other shore.

Here they fired a gun, to raise a kind of alarm among them, and then, hanging out a white cloth on the top of a pole, a signal of peace, they hailed them in English, and asked them if they would send a boat and fetch them over.

The pirates were surprised at the noise of the piece, and came running to the shore with all speed; but they were much more surprised when they heard themselves hailed in English. Upon the whole, they immediately sent a boat to fetch them over, and received them with a great deal of kindness.

Our men pretended to be overjoyed at finding them there, told them a long story, that they came on shore on the west side of the island, where, not far off, there were two English ships; but that the natives quarrelling with their men, upon some rudeness offered to their women, and they being separated from their fellows, were obliged to fly; that the natives had surrounded the rest, and, they believed, had killed them all; that they wandered up to the top of the hill, intending to make signals to their ship, to send them some help, when, seeing some ships, and believing some Europeans were there, they came down to take some shelter, and begged of them a boat to carry them round the cape to their comrades, unless they would give them leave to stay with them, and do as they did, which they were very willing to do.

This was all a made story; but, however, the tale told so well, that they believed it thoroughly, and received our men very kindly, led them up to their camp, and gave them some victuals.

Our men observed they had provisions enough, and very good, as well beef as mutton, that is to say, of goats' flesh, which was excellent; also pork and veal; and they were tolerable good cooks too; for they found they had built several furnaces and boilers, which they had taken out of their ships, and dressed a great quantity of meat at a time: but, observing they had no liquor, the mate pulled a large bottle of good cordial water out of his pocket, and gave it about as far as it would go, and so did two others of the men, which their new landlords took very kindly.

They spent good part of the first day in looking about them, seeing the manner of the pirates' living there, and their strength, and soon perceived that they were indeed in but a sorry condition every way, except that they had live cattle and flesh meat sufficient. They had a good platform of guns indeed, and a covered pallisadoe round where they lodged their ammunition: but as for fortifications to the landward, they had none, except a double pallisadoe round their camp, and a sort of a bank thrown up within to fire from, and stand covered from the enemies' lances, which was all they had to fear from the natives. They had no bread but what they made of rice, and the store they had of that was very small: they told our men, indeed, that they had two ships abroad, which they expected back every day, with a quantity of rice, and what else they could get, especially some arrack, which they were to trade for with the Arabian merchants, or take it by force, which should first offer.

Our men pretended to like their way of living mighty well and talked of staying with them, if they would let them; and thus they passed their first day of meeting.

Our men had two tents or huts given them to lodge in, and hammocks hung in the huts very agreeably, being such, I suppose, as belonged to some of their company who were dead, or were out upon adventure; here they slept very securely, and in the morning walked about, as strangers might be suffered to do, to look about them. But my new manager's eye was chiefly here upon two things: first, to see if they had any shipping for our purpose; and, secondly, to see if he could pitch upon one man, more likely than the rest, to enter into some confidence with; and it was not long before he found an opportunity for both. The manner was thus:

He was walking by himself, having ordered his other men to straggle away, two and two, this way and that, as if they had not minded him, though always to keep him in sight; I say, he walked by himself towards that part of the creek where, as was said, three of their largest ships lay by the walls, and when he came to the shore right against them, he stood still, looking at them very earnestly.

While he was here, he observed a boat put off from one of them, with four oars and one sitter only, whom they set on shore just by him, and then put off again; the person whom they set on shore, was, it seems, one who had been with our men the evening before, but, having some particular office on board one of those ships, lay on board every night with about ten or twelve men, just to watch and guard the ship, and so came on shore in the morning, as is usual in men-of-war laid up.

As soon as he saw our man he knew him, and spoke very familiarly to him; and seeing he was looking so earnestly at the ship, he asked him if he would go on board; our man faintly declined it, as on purpose to be asked again, and upon just as much farther pressing as was sufficient to satisfy him that the gunner (for that was his office) was in earnest, he yielded; so the gunner called back the boat, and they went on board.

Our man viewed the ship very particularly, and pretended to like everything he saw; but, after some conversation, asked him this home question, namely, Why they did not go to sea, and seek purchase, having so many good ships at their command?

He shook his head, and told him very frankly, that they were in no condition to undertake anything, for that they were a crew of unresolved, divided rogues; that they were never two days of a mind; that they had nobody to command, and therefore nobody to obey; that several things had been offered, but nothing concluded; that, in short, they thought of nothing but of shifting every one for himself as well as he could.

My mate replied, he thought it had been quite otherwise, and that made him tell them the night before that he had an inclination to stay with them.

I heard you say so, said the gunner, and it made me smile; I thought in myself that you would be of another mind when ye knew us a little better; for, in a word, said he, if our people should agree to lend you a boat to go back to your ship, they would fall together by the ears about who should go with you, for not a man of them that went with you would ever come back again hither, if your captain would take them on board, though the terms were, to be hanged when they came to England.

My mate knew that this was my opinion before; but he was really of another mind himself, till he saw things and till he talked with the gunner, and this put new thoughts in his head; so he entertained the gunner with a scheme of his own, and told him, if it was so as he related it, and that he had really a mind to come off from the gang, he believed that he could put him in a way how to do it to his advantage, and to take a set of his people with him, if he could pick out some of them that might be depended upon.

The gunner replied, I can pick out a set of very brave fellows, good seamen, and most of them such as, having been forced into the pirates' ships, were dragged into that wicked life they had lived, not only against their consciences, but by a mere necessity to save their lives, and that they would be glad at any price to go off.

The mate then asked him, Pray, gunner, how many such men can you answer for?

Why, says he, after a short pause, I am sure I can answer for above a hundred.

Upon this my mate told him the circumstances we were in, the voyage we were upon; that we were a letter of mart ship of such a force, but that we were over-manned and double-stored, in hopes of getting a good ship upon our cruise to man out of the other; that we had been disappointed, and had only got the sloop or brigantine which we bought at the Cape; that, if he could persuade the men to sell us one of their ships, we would pay them for it in ready money, and perhaps entertain a hundred of their men into the bargain.

The gunner told him he would propose it to them; and added, in positive terms, that he knew it would be readily accepted, and that he should take which of the three ships I pleased.

The mate then desired that he would lend him his shallop to go on board our ship, to acquaint me with it, and bring back sufficient orders to treat.

He told him, he would not only do that, but, before I could be ready to go, he would propose it to the chief men that he had his eye upon, and would have their consent, and that then he would go along with him on board to make a bargain.

This was as well as our mate could expect; and the gunner had either so much authority among them, or the men were so forward to shift their station in the world, that the gunner came again to our mate in less than two hours, with an order, signed by about sixteen of their officers, empowering him to sell us the ship which the gunner was on board of, and to allot so many guns, and such a proportion of ammunition to her, as was sufficient, and to give the work of all their carpenters for so many days as were necessary to repair her, calk, and grave her, and put her in condition to go to sea.

She was a Spanish-built ship; where they had her the gunner said he did not know; but she was a very strong, tight ship, and a pretty good sailer.

We made her carry two-and-thirty guns, though she had not been used to carry above twenty-four.

The gunner being thus empowered to treat with my mate, came away in their shallop, and brought the said gunner and two more of their officers with him, and eight seamen. The gunner and I soon made a bargain for the ship, which I bought for five thousand pieces of eight, most of it in English goods such as they wanted; for they were many of them almost naked of clothes, and, as for other things, they had scarce a pair of stockings or shoes among them.

When our bargain was made, and the mate had related all the particulars of the conference he had had with the gunner, we came to talk of the people who were to go with us: the gunner told us that we might indeed have good reason to suspect a gang of men who had made themselves infamous all over the world by so many piracies and wicked actions; but, if I would put so much confidence in him, he would assure me, that, as he should have the power in his hands to pick and choose his men, so he would answer body for body for the fidelity of all the men he should choose; and that most, if not all of them, would be such as had been taken by force out of other ships, or wheedled away when they were drunk: and he added, there never was a ship load of such penitents went to sea together as he would bring us.

When he said this, he began to entreat me that I would please to give him the same post which he held in the ship, viz., of gunner, which I promised him; and then he desired I would permit him to speak with me in private; I was not at first very free to it, but he having consented to let the mate and Captain Merlotte be present, I yielded.

When all the rest were withdrawn, he told me, that having been five years in the pirates' service, as he might call it, and being obliged to do as they did, I might be sure he had some small share in the purchase; and however he had come into it against his will, yet, as he had been obliged to go with them, he had made some advantage; and that, being resolved to leave them, he had a good while ago packed up some of the best of what he had got, to make his escape, and begged I would let him deposit it with me as a security for his fidelity.

Upon this he ordered a chest to be taken out of the shallop, and brought into my great cabin; and, besides this, gave me out of his pocket, a bag, sealed up, the contents of which I shall speak of hereafter.

The shallop returned the next day, and I sent back the mate with my long-boat and twenty-four men, to go and take possession of the ship; and appointed my carpenter to go and see to the repairs that were necessary to be done to her: and some days after, I sent Captain Merlotte with the supercargo, in our sloop, to go and secure the possession, and to cover the retreat of any of the men who might have a mind to come away, and might be opposed by the rest; and this was done at the request of the gunner who foresaw there might be some debate about it.

They spent six weeks and some odd days in fitting out this ship, occasioned by the want of a convenient place to lay her on shore in, which they were obliged to make with a great deal of labour; however, she was at last completely fitted up.

When she was equipped, they laid in a good store of provisions, though not so well cured as to last a great while. One of the best things we got a recruit of here was casks, which, as said before, we greatly wanted, and which their coopers assisted us to trim, season, and fit up.

As to bread, we had no help from them; for they had none but what they made of rice, and they had not sufficient store of that.

But we had more to do yet: for, when the ship was fitted up, and our men had the possession of her, they were surprised one morning, on a sudden, with a most horrible tumult among the pirates: and had not our brigantine been at hand to secure the possession, I believe they had taken the ship from our men again, and perhaps have come down with her and their two sloops, and have attacked us. The case was this:

The gunner, who was a punctual fellow to his word, resolved that none of the men should go in the ship but such as he had singled out; and they were such as were generally taken out of merchant ships by force: but when he came to talk to the men of who should go, and who should stay, truly they would all go, to a man, there was not a man of them would stay behind; and, in a word, they fell out about it to that degree that they came to blows, and the gunner was forced to fly for it, with about twenty-two men that stood to him, and six or seven were wounded in the fray, whereof two died.

The gunner being thus driven to his shifts, made down to the shore to his boat, but the rogues were too nimble for him, and had got to his boat before him, and prepared to man her and two more, to go on board and secure the ship.

In this distress, the gunner, who had taken sanctuary in the woods at about a mile distance, but unhappily above the camp, so that the platform of guns was between him and the ship, had no remedy but to send one of his men, who swam very well, to take a compass round behind the pirates' camp and come to the water-side below the camp and platform, so to take the water and swim on board the ship, which lay near a league below their said camp, and give our men notice of what had happened; to warn them to suffer none of their men to come on board, unless the gunner was with them; and if possible, to send a boat on shore to fetch off the gunner and his men, who were following by the same way, and would be at the same place, and make a signal to them to come for him.

Our men had scarce received this notice, when they saw a boat full of men put off from the platform, and row down under shore towards them: but as they resolved not to suffer them to come on board, they called to them by a speaking-trumpet, and told them they might go back again, for they should not come on board, nor any other boat, unless the gunner was on board.

They rowed on for all that, when our men called to them again, and told them, if they offered to put off, in order to come on board, or, in short, to row down shore any farther than a little point which our men named, and which was just ahead of them, they would fire at them. They rowed on for all this, and even till they were past the point; which, our men seeing, they immediately let fly a shot, but fired a little ahead of them, so as not to hit the boat, and this brought them to a stop; so they lay upon their oars awhile, as if they were considering what to do, when our men perceived two boats more come off from the platform, likewise full of men, and rowing after the first.

Upon this, they called again to the first boat with their speaking-trumpet, and told them, if they did not all go immediately on shore, they would sink the boat. They had no remedy, seeing our men resolved, and that they lay open to the shot of the ship; so they went on shore accordingly, and then our men fired at the empty boat, till they split her in pieces, and made her useless to them.

Upon this firing, our brigantine, which lay about two leagues off in the mouth of a little creek, on the south of that river, weighed immediately, and stood away to the opening of the road where the ship lay; and the tide of flood being still running in, they drove up towards the ship, for her assistance, and came to an anchor about a cable's length ahead of her, but within pistol-shot of the shore; at the same time sending two-and-thirty of her men on board the great ship, to reinforce the men on board, who were but sixteen in number.

Just at this time, the gunner and his twenty-one men, who heard the firing, and had quickened their pace, though they had a great compass to fetch through woods and untrod paths, and some luggage to carry too, were come to the shore, and made the signal, which our men in the ship observing, gave notice to the officer of the brigantine to fetch them on board, which he did very safely. By the way, as the officer afterwards told us, most of their luggage consisted in money, with which, it seems, every man of them was very well furnished, having shared their wealth at their first coming on shore: as for clothes, they had very few, and those all in rags; and as for linen, they had scarce a shirt among them all, or linen enough to have made a white flag for a truce, if they had occasion for it: in short, a crew so rich and so ragged, were hardly ever seen before.

The ship was now pretty well manned: for the brigantine carried the gunner and his twenty-one men on board her; and the tide by this time being spent, she immediately unmoored, and loosed her topsails, which, as it happened, had been bent to the yards two days before; so with the first of the ebb she weighed, and fell down about a league farther, by which she was quite out of reach of the platform, and rid in the open sea; and the brigantine did the same.

But by this means, they missed the occasion of the rest of the gunner's men, who, having got together to the number of between seventy and eighty, had followed him, and come down to the shore, and made the signals, but were not understood by our ship, which put the poor men to great difficulties; for they had broken away from the rest by force, and had been pursued half a mile by the whole body, particularly at the entrance into a very thick woody place, and were so hard put to it, that they were obliged to make a desperate stand, and fire at their old friends, which had exasperated them to the last degree. But, as the case of these men was desperate, they took an effectual method for their own security, of which I shall give a farther account presently.

The general body of the pirates were now up in arms, and the new ship was, as it were, in open war with them, or at least they had declared war against her: but as they had been disappointed in their attempt to force her, and found they were not strong enough at sea to attack her, they sent a flag of truce on board. Our men admitted them to come to the ship's side; but as my mate, who now had the command, knew them to be a gang of desperate rogues, that would attempt anything, though ever so rash, he ordered that none of them should come on board the ship, except the officer and two more, who gave an account that they were sent to treat with us; so we called them the ambassadors.

When they came on board, they expostulated very warmly with my new agent, the second mate, that our men came in the posture of friends, and of friends too in distress, and had received favours from them, but had abused the kindness which had been shown them; that they had bought a ship of them, and had had leave and assistance to fit her up and furnish her; but had not paid for her, or paid for what assistance and what provisions had been given to them: and that now, to complete all, their men had been partially and unfairly treated; and when a certain number of men had been granted us, an inferior fellow, a gunner, was set to call such and such men out, just whom he pleased, to go with us; whereas the whole body ought to have had the appointing whom they would or would not give leave to, to go in the ship: that, when they came in a peaceable manner to have demanded justice, and to have treated amicably of these things, our men had denied them admittance, had committed hostilities against them, had fired at their men, and staved their boat, and had afterward received their deserters on board, all contrary to the rules of friendship. And in all these cases they demanded satisfaction.

Our new commander was a ready man enough, and he answered all their complaints with a great deal of gravity and calmness. He told them, that it was true we came to them as friends, and had received friendly usage from them, which we had not in the least dishonoured; but that as friends in distress, we had never pretended to be, and really were not; for that we were neither in danger of anything, or in want of anything; that as to provisions, we were strong enough if need were, to procure ourselves provisions in any part of the island, and had been several times supplied from the shore by the natives, for which we had always fully satisfied the people who furnished us; and that we scorned to be ungrateful for any favour we should have received, much less to abuse it, or them for it.

That we had paid the full price of all the provisions we had received, and for the work that had been done to the ship; that what we had bargained for, as the price of the ship, had been paid, as far as the agreement made it due, and that what remained, was ready to be paid as soon as the ship was finished, which was our contract.

That as to the people who were willing to take service with us, and enter themselves on board, it is true that the gunner and some other men offered themselves to us, and we had accepted of them, and we thought it was our part to accept or not to accept of such men as we thought fit. As for what was among themselves, that we had nothing to do with: that, if we had been publicly warned by them not to have entertained any of their men, but with consent of the whole body, then indeed we should have had reason to be cautious; otherwise, we were not in the least concerned about it. That it is true, we refused to let their boats come on board us, being assured that they came in a hostile manner, either to take away the men by force, which had been entered in our service, or perhaps even to seize the ship itself; and why else was the first boat followed by two more, full of men, armed and prepared to attack us? That we not only came in a friendly manner to them, but resolved to continue in friendship with them, if they thought fit to use us as friends; but that, considering what part of the world we were in, and what their circumstances were, they must allow us to be upon our guard, and not put ourselves in a condition to be used ill.

While he was talking thus with them in the cabin, he had ordered a can of flip to be made, and given their men in the boat, and every one a dram, but would not suffer them to come on board; however, one or two of them got leave to get in at one of the ports, and got between decks among our men; here they made terrible complaints of their condition, and begged hard to be entertained in our service; they were full of money, and gave twenty or thirty pieces of eight among our men, and by this present prevailed on two men to speak to my mate, who appeared as captain, to take the boat's crew on board.

The mate very gravely told the two ambassadors of it, and added, that, seeing they were come with a flag of truce, he would not stop their men without their consent, but the men being so earnest, he thought they would do better not to oppose them. The ambassadors, as I call them, opposed it, however, vehemently, and at last desired to go and talk with the men, which was granted them readily.

When they came into their boat, their men told them plainly, that, one and all, they would enter themselves with their countrymen; that they had been forced already to turn pirates, and they thought they might very justly turn honest men again by force, if they could not get leave to do it peaceably; and that, in short, they would go on shore no more; that, if the ambassadors desired it, they would set them on shore with the boat, but as for themselves, they would go along with the new captain.

When the ambassadors saw this, they had no more to do but to be satisfied, and so were set on shore where they desired, and their men stayed on board.

During this transaction, my mate had sent a full account to me of all that had passed, and had desired me to come on board and give farther directions in all that was to follow; so I took our supercargo and Captain Merlotte along with me, and some more of our officers, and went to them. It was my lot to come on board just when the aforesaid ambassadors were talking with my mate, so I heard most of what they had to say, and heard the answer my mate gave them, as above, which was extremely to my satisfaction; nor did I interrupt him, or take upon me any authority, though he would very submissively have had me shown myself as captain, but I bade him go on, and sat down, as not concerned in the affair at all.

After the ambassadors were gone, the first thing I did, was, in the presence of all the company, and, having before had the opinion of those I brought with me, to tell my second mate how well we were all satisfied with his conduct, and to declare him captain of the ship that he was in; only demanding his solemn oath, to be under orders of the great ship, as admiral, and to carry on no separate interests from us; which he thankfully accepted, and, to give him his due, as faithfully performed, all the rest of our very long voyage, and through all our adventures.

It was upon my seeming intercession, that he gave consent to the boat's crew, who brought the ambassadors, to remain in our service, and set their statesmen on shore; and in the end, I told him that as far as about one hundred and fifty, or two hundred men, he should entertain whom he thought fit. Thus having settled all things in the ship to our satisfaction, we went back to our great ship the next day.

I had not been many hours on board, till I was surprised with the firing of three muskets from the shore; we wondered what could be the meaning of it, knowing that it was an unusual thing in that place, where we knew the natives of the country had no fire-arms; so we could not tell what to make of it, and therefore took no notice, other than, as I say, to wonder at it. About half-an-hour after, we heard three muskets more, and still, not knowing anything of the matter, we made them no return to the signal.

Some time after three muskets were fired again, but still we took no notice, for we knew nothing of what return was to be made to it.

When night come on, we observed two great fires upon two several hills, on that part of the shore opposite to us, and after that, three rockets were fired, such as they were, for they were badly constructed; I suppose their gunner was ill provided for such things: but all signified nothing; we would have made any return to them that had been to be understood, but we knew nothing of any agreed signal; however, I resolved that I would send a boat on shore, well manned, to learn, if possible, what the meaning of all this was; and, accordingly, in the morning, I sent our long-boat and shallop on shore, with two-and-thirty men in them both, to get intelligence; ordering them, if possible, to speak with somebody, before they went on shore, and know how things stood; that then, if it was a party of the pirates, they should by no means come near them, but parley at a distance, till they knew the meaning of their behaviour.

As soon as my men came near the shore, they saw plainly that it was a body of above a hundred of the pirates; but seeing them so strong, they stood off, and would not come nearer, nor near enough to parley with them; upon this, the men on shore got one of the islanders' canvass boats, or rather boats made of skins, which are but sorry ones at best, and put off, with two men to manage the sail, and one sitter, and two paddles for oars and away they came towards us, carrying a flag of truce, that is to say, an old white rag; how they came to save so much linen among them all, was very hard to guess.

Our men could do no less than receive their ambassador, and a flag of truce gave no shadow of apprehension, especially considering the figure they made, and that the men on shore had no other boats to surprise or attack us with; so they lay by upon their oars till they came up, when they soon understood who they were, viz.—that they were the gunner's selected men; that they came too late to have their signal perceived from the other ship, which was gone out of sight of the place they were directed to; that they had with great difficulty, and five days and nights' marching, got through a woody and almost impassable country to come at us; that they had fetched a circuit of near a hundred miles to avoid being attacked by their comrades, and that they were pursued by them with their whole body, and therefore they begged to be taken on board; they added, if they should be overtaken by their comrades, they should be all cut in pieces, for that they had broke away from them by force, and moreover had been obliged, at the first of their pursuit, to face about and fire among them, by which they had killed six or seven of them, and wounded others, and that they had sworn they would give them no quarter, if they could come fairly up with them.

Our men told them they must be contented to remain on shore, where they were, for some time, for that they could do nothing till they had been on board, and acquainted their captain with all the particulars; so they came back immediately to me for orders.

As to me, I was a little uneasy at the thoughts of taking them on board; I knew they were a gang of pirates at best, and what they might do I knew not, but I sent them this message, that though all their tale might be very good for aught I knew, yet that I must take so much time as to send an express to the captain of the other ship, to be informed of the truth of it; and that if he brought a satisfactory answer, I would send for them all on board.

This was very uncomfortable news to them, for they expected to be surrounded every hour by their comrades, from whom they were to look for no mercy; however, seeing no remedy, they resolved to march about twenty miles farther south, and lie by in a place near the sea, where we agreed to send to them; concluding that their comrades not finding them near the place where we lay, would not imagine they could be gone farther that way. As they guessed, so it proved, for the pirates came to the shore, where they saw tokens enough of their having been there, but seeing they could not be found, concluded they were all gone on board our ship.

The wind proving contrary, it was no less than four days before our boat came back, so that the poor men were held in great suspense: but when they returned, they brought the gunner with them who had selected those men from all the rest for our new ship; and who, when he came, gave me a long account of them, and what care he had taken to pick them out for our service, delivering me also a letter from my new captain to the same purpose: upon all which concurring circumstances, we concluded to take them on board; so we sent our boats for them, which, at twice, brought them all on board, and very stout young fellows they were.

When they had been on board some days and refreshed themselves, I concluded to send all on board the new ship; but, upon advice, I resolved to send sixty of my own men joined to forty of these, and keep thirty-four of them on board my ship; for their number was just seventy-four, which with the gunner and his twenty-one men, and the sixteen men who came with the worthy ambassadors, and would not go on shore again, made one hundred and twelve men; and, as we all thought, were enough for us, though we took in between forty and fifty more afterwards.

We were now ready to go to sea, and I caused the new ship and the brigantine to come away from the place where they lay, and join us; which they did, and then we unloaded part of our provisions and ammunition; of which, as I observed at first, we had taken in double quantity; and, having furnished the new ship with a proportion of all things necessary, we prepared for our voyage.

I should here give a long account of a second infernal conspiracy, which my two remaining prisoners had formed among the men, which was to betray the new ship to the pirates; but it is too long a story to relate here; nor did I make it public among the ship's company: but as it was only, as it were, laid down in a scheme, and that they had no opportunity to put it in practice, I thought it was better to make as little noise about it as I could. So I ordered my new captain, for it was he who discovered it to me, to punish them in their own way, and, without taking notice of their new villanies, to set them on shore, and leave them to take their fate with a set of rogues whom they had intended to join with, and whose profession was likely, some time or other, to bring them to the gallows. And thus I was rid of two incorrigible mutineers; what became of them afterwards I never heard.

We were now a little fleet, viz., two large ships and a brigantine, well manned, and furnished with all sorts of necessaries for any voyage or any enterprise that was fit for men in our situation to undertake; and, particularly, here I made a full design of the whole voyage, to be again openly declared to the men, and had them asked, one by one, if they were willing and resolved to undertake it, which they all very cheerfully answered in the affirmative.

Here we had an opportunity to furnish ourselves with a plentiful stock of excellent beef, which, as I said before, we cured with little or no salt, by drying it in the sun; and, I believe, we laid in such a store, that, in all our three vessels, we had near a hundred and fifty tons of it; and it was of excellent use to us, and served us through the whole voyage. There was little else to be had in this place that was fit to be carried to sea; except that, as there was plenty of milk, some of our men, who were more dexterous than others, made several large cheeses; nor were they very far short of English cheese, only that we were but indifferent dairy folks. Our men made some butter also, and salted it to keep, but it grew rank and oily, and was of little use to us.

It was on the 15th of December that we left this place, a country fruitful, populous, full of cattle, large and excellent good beef, and very fat; and the land able to produce all manner of good things; but the people wild, naked, black, barbarous, perfectly untractable, and insensible of any state of life being better than their own.

We stood away towards the shore of Arabia, till we passed the line, and came into the latitude of 18° north, and then stood away east, and east-by-north, for the English factories of Surat, and the coast of Malabar; not that we had any business there, or designed any, only that we had a mind to take on board a quantity of rice, if we could come at it; which at last, we effected by a Portuguese vessel, which we met with at sea, bound to Goa, from the Gulf of Persia. We chased her, and brought her too, indeed, as if we resolved to attack and take the ship; but, finding a quantity of rice on board, which was what we wanted, with a parcel of coffee, we took all the rice, but paid the supercargo, who was a Persian or Armenian merchant, very honestly for the whole parcel, his full price, and to his satisfaction; as for the coffee, we had no occasion for it. We put in at several ports on the Indian coast for fresh water and fresh provisions, but came near none of the factories, because we had no mind to discover ourselves; for though we were to sail through the very centre of the India trade, yet it was perfectly without any business among them. We met indeed on this coast with some pearl fishers, who had been in the mouth of the Arabian Gulf, and had a large quantity of pearl on board. I would have traded with them for goods, but they understood nothing but money, and I refused to part with it; upon which the fellows gave our supercargo some scornful language, which though he did not well understand what they said, yet he pretended to take it as a great affront, and threatened to make prize of their barks, and slaves of the men; upon which they grew very humble; and one of them, a Malabar Indian, who spoke a little English, spoke for them, that they would willingly trade with us for such goods as we had; whereupon I produced three bales of English cloth, which I showed them, and said they would be of good merchandise at Gombaroon in the Gulf, for that the Persians made their long vests of such cloths.

In short, for this cloth, and some money, we bought a box of choice pearls, which the chief of them had picked out from the rest for the Portuguese merchants at Goa; and which, when I came to London, was valued at two thousand two hundred pounds sterling.

We were near two months on our voyage from Madagascar to the coast of India, and from thence to Ceylon, where we put in on the south-west part of the island, to see what provisions we could get, and to take in a large supply of water.

The people here we found willing to supply us with provisions; but withal so sharp, imposing upon us their own rates for everything, and withal, so false, that we were often provoked to treat them very rudely. However, I gave strict orders that they should not be hurt upon any occasion, at least till we had filled all our water-casks and taken in what fresh provisions we could get, and especially rice, which we valued very much. But they provoked us at last beyond all patience; for they were such thieves when they were on board, and such treacherous rogues when we were on shore, that there was no bearing with them; and two accidents fell out upon this occasion which fully broke the peace between us; one was on board, and the other on shore, and both happened the same day.

The case on board was this. There came on board us a small boat, in which were eleven men and three boys, to sell us roots, yams, mangoes, and such other articles as was frequent for them to do every day;

but this boat having more goods of that kind than usual, they were longer than ordinary in making their market. While they were thus chaffering on board, one of them having wandered about the ship, and pretending to admire everything he saw, and being gotten between decks, was taken stealing a pair of shoes which belonged to one of the seamen. The fellow being stopped for his theft, appeared angry, raised a hideous screaming noise to alarm his fellows; and, at the same time, having stolen a long pair of scissors, pulled them out, and stabbed the man who had laid hold of him into the shoulder, and was going to repeat his blow, when the poor fellow who had been wounded, having struck up his heels and fallen upon him, had killed him if I had not called to take him off, and bring the thief up to me.

Upon this order, they laid hold of the barbarian, and brought him up with the shoes and the scissors that he had stolen, and as the fact was plain, and needed no witnesses, I caused all the rest of them to be brought up also; and, as well as we could, made them understand what he had done.

They made pitiful signs of fear, lest they should all be punished for his crime, and particularly when they saw the man whom he had wounded brought in; then they expected nothing but death, and they made a sad lamentation and howling, as if they were all to die immediately.

It was not without a great deal of difficulty that I found ways to satisfy them, that nobody was to be punished but the man that had committed the fact; and then I caused him to be brought to the gears, with a halter about his neck, and be soundly whipped; and indeed, our people did scourge him severely from head to foot; and, I believe, if I had not run myself to put an end to it, they would have whipped him to death.

When this punishment was over, they put him into their boat, and let them all go on shore. But no sooner were they on shore, but they raised a terrible outcry in all the villages and towns near them, and they were not a few, the country being very populous; and great numbers came down to the shore, staring at us, and making confused ugly noises, and abundance of arrows they shot at the ship, but we rode too far from the shore for them to do us any hurt.

While this was doing, another fray happened on shore, where two of our men, bargaining with an islander and his wife for some fowls, they took their money and gave them part of the fowls, and pretended the woman should go and fetch the rest. While the woman was gone, three or four fellows came to the man who was left; when talking a while together, and seeing our men were but two, they began to take hold of the fowls which had been sold, and would take them away again; when one of our men stepped up to the fellow who had taken them, and went to lay hold of him, but he was too nimble for him, and ran away, and carried off the fowls and the money too. The seamen were so enraged to be so served, that they took up their pieces, for they had both fire-arms with them, and fired immediately after him, and aimed their shot so well, that though the fellow flew like the wind, he shot him through the head, and he dropped down dead upon the spot.

The rest of them, though terribly frightened, yet, seeing our men were but two, and the noise bringing twenty or thirty more immediately to them, attacked our men with their lances, and bows and arrows; and in a moment there was a pitched battle of two men only against twenty or thirty, and their number increasing too.

In short, our men spent their shot freely among them as long as it lasted, and killed six or seven, besides wounding ten or eleven more, and this cooled their courage, and they seemed to give over the battle;

and our men, whose ammunition was almost spent, began to think of retreating to their boat, which was near a mile off, for they were very unhappily gotten from their boat so far up the country.

They made their retreat pretty well for about half the way, when, on a sudden, they saw they were not pursued only, but surrounded, and that some of their enemies were before them. This made them double their pace, and, seeing no remedy, they resolved to break through those that were before them, who were about eleven or twelve. Accordingly, as soon as they came within pistol shot of them, one of our men having, for want of shot, put almost a handful of gravel and small stones into his piece, fired among them, and the gravel and stones scattering, wounded almost all of them; for they being naked from the waist upwards, the least grain of sand scratched and hurt them, and made them bleed if it only entered the skin.

Being thus completely scared, and indeed more afraid than hurt, they all ran away, except two, who were really wounded with the shot or stones, and lay upon the ground. Our men let them lie, and made the best of their way to their boat; where, at last, they got safe, but with a great number of the people at their heels. Our men did not stay to fire from the boat, but put off with all the speed they could, for fear of poisoned arrows, and the country people poured so many of their arrows into the boat after them, and aimed them also so truly, that two of our men were hurt with them; but, whether they were poisoned or not, our surgeons cured them both.

We had enough of Ceylon; and having no business to make such a kind of war as this must have been, in which we might have lost but could get nothing, we weighed, and stood away to the East. What became of the fellow that was lashed we knew not; but, as he had but little flesh left on his back, which was not mangled and torn with our whipping him, and we supposed they were but indifferent surgeons, our people said the fellow could not live; and the reason they gave for it was, because they did not pickle him after it. Truly, they said, that they would not be so kind to him as to pickle him: for though pickling, that is to say, throwing salt and vinegar on the back after the whipping, is cruel enough as to the pain it is to the patient, yet it is certainly the way to prevent mortification, and causes it to heal again with more ease.

We stood over from Ceylon east-south-east cross the great Bay of Bengal, leaving all the coast of Coromandel, and standing directly for Achen, on the north point of the great island of Sumatra, and in the latitude of 6° 81' north.

Here we spread our French colours, and, coming to an anchor, suffered none of our men to go on shore but Captain Merlotte and his Frenchmen; and, having nothing to do there, or anywhere else in the Indian seas, but to take in provisions and fresh water, we stayed but five days; in which time we supplied ourselves with what the place would afford; and, pretending to be bound for China, we went on to the south through the straits of Malacca, between the island of Sumatra and the main or isthmus of Malacca.

We had here a very difficult passage, though we took two pilots on board at Achen, who pretended to know the straits perfectly well; twice we were in very great danger of being lost, and once our Madagascar ship was so entangled among rocks and currents, that we gave her up for lost, and twice she struck upon the rocks, but she did but touch, and went clear.

We went several times on shore among the Malayans, as well on the shore of Malacca itself, as on the side of Sumatra. They are as fierce, cruel, treacherous, and merciless a crew of human devils as any I have met with on the face of the whole earth; and we had some skirmishes with them, but not of any consequence. We made no stay anywhere in this strait but just for fresh water, and what other fresh provisions we could get, such as roots, greens, hogs, and fowls, of which they have plenty and a great variety: but nothing to be had but for ready money; which our men took so unkindly, and especially their offering two or three times to cheat them, and once to murder them, that afterwards they made no scruple to go on shore a hundred or more at a time, and plunder and burn what they could not carry off; till at last we began to be such a terror to them, that they fled from us wherever we came.

On the 5th of March we made the southernmost part of the Isthmus of Malacca, and the island and straits of Sincapora, famous for its being the great outlet into the Chinese sea, and lying in the latitude of 1° 15' north latitude.

We had good weather through these straits, which was very much to our comfort; the different currents and number of little islands making it otherwise very dangerous, especially to strangers. We got, by very good luck, a Dutch pilot to carry us through this strait, who was a very useful, skilful fellow, but withal so impertinent and inquisitive, that we knew not what to say to him nor what to do with him; at last he grew saucy and insolent, and told our chief mate that he did not know but we might be pirates, or at least enemies to his countrymen the Dutch; and if we would not tell him who we were and whither we were bound, he would not pilot us any farther.

This I thought very insolent, to a degree beyond what was sufferable; and bade the boatswain put a halter about the fellow's neck, and tell him that, the moment he omitted to direct the steerage as a pilot, or the moment the ship come to any misfortune, or struck upon any rock, he should be hung up.

The boatswain, a rugged fellow, provided himself with a halter, and coming up to the pilot, asked him what it was he wanted to be satisfied in?

The pilot said he desired to have a true account whither we were going.

Why, says the boatswain, we are agoing to the devil, and I shall send you before to tell him we are coming; and with that he pulled the halter out of his pocket and put it over his head, and taking the other end in his hand, Come, says the boatswain, come along with me; do you think we can't go through the strait of Sincapora without your help? I warrant you, says he, we will do without you.

By this time it may be supposed the Dutchman was in a mortal fright, and half choked too with being dragged by the throat with the halter, and, full heartily he begged for his life: at length the boatswain, who had pulled him along a good way, stopped and the Dutchman fell down on his knees; but the boatswain said, he had the captain's orders to hang him, and hang him he would, unless the captain recalled his orders; but that he would stay so long, if anybody would go up to the captain and tell him what the Dutchman said, and bring back an answer.

I had no design to hang the poor fellow, it is true, and the boatswain knew that well enough. However, I was resolved to humble him effectually, so I sent back two men to the boatswain, the first was to tell the boatswain aloud that the captain was resolved to have the fellow hanged, for having been so impudent to threaten to run the ship aground; but then the second, who was to stay a little behind, was to call out, as if he came since the first from me, and that I had been prevailed with to pardon him, on his promises of better behaviour. This was all acted to admiration; for the first messenger called aloud to the boatswain, that the captain said he would have the Dutchman hanged for a warning to all pilots, and to teach them not to insult men when they are in difficulties, as the midwives do whores in labour, and will not deliver them till they confess who is the father.

The boatswain had the end of the halter in his hand all the while; I told you so, says he, before. Come, come along Mynheer, I shall quickly do your work, and put you out of your pain; and then he dragged the poor fellow along to the main-mast. By this time the second messenger came in, and delivered his part of the errand, and so the poor Dutchman was put out of his fright, and they gave him a dram to restore him a little, and he did his business very honestly afterwards.

And now we were at liberty again, being in the open sea, which was what we were very impatient for before. We made a long run over that part which we call the sea of Borneo, and the upper part of the Indian Arches, called so from its being full of islands, like the Archipelago of the Levant. It was a long run, but, as we were to the north of the islands, we had the more sea-room; so we steered east half a point, one way or other, for the Manillas, or Philippine Islands, which was the true design of our voyage; and, perhaps, we were the first ship that ever came to those islands, freighted from Europe, since the Portuguese lost their footing there.

We put in on the north coast of Borneo for fresh water, and were civilly used by the inhabitants of the place, who brought us roots and fruits of several kinds, and some goats, which we were glad of: we paid them in trifles, such as knives, scissors, toys, and several sorts of wrought iron, hatchets, hammers, glass-work, looking-glasses, and drinking-glasses; and from hence we went away, as I said, for the Philippine Islands.

We saw several islands in our way, but made no stop, except once for water, and arrived at Manilla the 22nd of May, all our vessels in very good condition, our men healthy, and our ships sound; having met with very few contrary winds, and not one storm in the whole voyage from Madagascar. We had now been seventeen months and two days on our voyage from England.

When we arrived, we saluted the Spanish flag, and came to an anchor, carrying French colours. Captain Merlotte, who now acted as commander, sent his boat on shore the next day to the governor, with a respectful letter in French; telling him that, having the King of France's commission, and being come into those seas, he hoped that, for the friendship which was between their most Christian and catholic majesties, he should be allowed the freedom of commerce and the use of the port; the like having been granted to his most Christian majesty's subjects in all the ports of new Spain, as well in the southern as in the northern seas.

The Spanish governor returned a very civil and obliging answer, and immediately permitted us to buy what provisions we pleased for our supply, or anything else for our use; but added, that, as for allowing any exchange of merchandises, or giving leave for European goods to be brought on shore there, he was not empowered to grant.

We made it appear as if this answer was satisfactory; and the next morning Captain Merlotte sent his boat on shore with all French sailors and a French midshipman, with a handsome present to the governor, consisting of some bottles of French wines, some brandy, two pieces of fine Holland, two pieces of English black baize, one piece of fine French drugget, and five yards of scarlet woollen-cloth.

This was too considerable a present for a Spaniard to refuse; and yet these were all European goods, which he seemed not to allow to come on shore. The governor let the captain know that he accepted his present; and the men who brought it were very handsomely entertained by the governor's order, and had every one a small piece of gold; and the officer who went at their head had five pieces of gold given him: what coin it was I could not tell, but I think it was a Japan coin, and the value something less than a pistole.

The next day the governor sent a gentleman with a large boat, and in it a present to our captain, consisting of two cows, ten sheep, or goats, for they were between both; a number of fowls of several sorts, and twelve great boxes of sweetmeats and conserves; all of which were indeed very acceptable; and invited the captain and any of his attendants on shore, offering to send hostages on board for our safe return; and concluding with his word of honour for our safety, and free going back to our ships.

The captain received the present with very great respect, and indeed it was a very noble present; for at the same time a boat was sent to both the other ships with provisions and sweetmeats, in proportion to the size of the vessels. Our captain caused the gentleman who came with this present, to have a fine piece of crimson English cloth given him, sufficient to make a waistcoat and breeches of their fashion, with a very good hat, two pair of silk stockings, and two pair of gloves: and all his people had a piece of drugget given them sufficient to make the like suit of clothes; the persons who went to the other ship, and to the brigantine, had presents in proportion.

This, in short, was neither more nor less than trading and bartering, though, from supercilious punctilio, we had in a manner been denied it.

The next day the captain went on shore to visit the governor, and with him several of our officers; and the captain of the Madagascar ship, formerly my second mate, and the captain of the brigantine. I did not go myself for that time, nor the supercargo, because, whatever might happen, I would be reserved on board; besides, I did not care to appear in this part of the business.

The captain went on shore like a captain, attended with his two trumpeters, and the ship firing eleven guns at his going off. The governor received him like himself, with prodigious state and formality; sending five gentlemen and a guard of soldiers to receive him and his men at their landing, and to conduct them to his palace.

When they came there they were entertained with the utmost profusion and magnificence, after the Spanish manner; and they all had the honour to dine with his excellence; that is to say, all the officers. At the same time the men were entertained very handsomely in another house, and had very good cheer; but it was observed that they had but very little wine, except such as we had sent them, which the governor apologised for, by saying his store, which he had yearly from New Spain, was nearly spent. This deficiency we supplied the next day by sending him a quarter cask of very good Canary, and half a hogshead of Madeira; which was a present so acceptable, that, in short, after this, we might do just as we pleased with him and all his men.

While they were thus conversing together after dinner, Captain Merlotte was made to understand, that though the governor could not admit an open avowed trade, yet that the merchants would not be forbid coming on board our ship, and trading with us in such manner as we should be very well satisfied with; after which, we should be at no hazard of getting the goods we should sell put on shore; and we had an experiment of this made in a few days, as follows:

When Captain Merlotte took his leave of the governor, he invited his excellence to come on board our ship, with such of his attendants as he pleased to bring with him, and in like manner offered hostages for his return. The governor accepted the invitation, and with the same generosity, said he would take his parole of honour given, as he was the King of France's captain, and would come on board.

The governor did not come to the shore side with our people; but stood in the window of the palace, and gave them the compliment of his hat and leg at their going into their boats, and made a signal to the platform, to fire eleven guns at their boats putting off.

These were unusual and unexpected honours to us, who, but for this stratagem of the French commission, had been declared enemies. It was suggested to me here, that I might with great ease surprise the whole island, nay, all the islands, the governor putting such confidence in us, that we might go on shore in the very fort unsuspected. But though this was true, and that we did play them a trick at the Rio de la Plata, I could not bear the thoughts of it here; besides, I had quite another game to play, which would turn out more advantageous to us and to our voyage, than an enterprise of so much treachery could be to England, which also we might not be able to support from thence, before the Spaniards might beat us out again from Acapulco, and then we might pass our time ill enough.

Upon the whole, I resolved to keep every punctilio with the governor very justly, and we found our account in it presently.

About three days afterwards we had notice that the governor would pay us a visit, and we prepared to entertain his excellence with as much state as possible. By the way, we had private notice that the governor would bring with him some merchants, who, perhaps, might lay out some money, and buy some of our cargo; nor was it without a secret intimation that even the governor himself was concerned in the market that should be made.

Upon this intelligence, our supercargo caused several bales of English and French goods to be brought up and opened, and laid so in the steerage and upon the quarter-deck of the ship, that the governor and his attendants should see them of course as they passed by.

When the boats came off from the shore, which we knew by their fort firing eleven guns, our ship appeared as fine as we could make her, having the French flag at the main-top, as admiral, and streamers and pendants at the yard-arms, waste cloths out, and a very fine awning over the quarter-deck. When his excellency entered the ship, we fired one-and-twenty guns, the Madagascar ship fired the like number, and the brigantine fifteen, having loaded her guns nimbly enough to fire twice.

As the governor's entertainment to us was more meat than liquor, so we gave him more liquor than meat; for, as we had several sorts of very good wines on board, we spared nothing to let him see he was very welcome. After dinner we brought a large bowl of punch upon the table, a liquor he was a stranger to: however, to do him justice, he drank very moderately, and so did most of those that were with him. As to the men that belonged to his retinue, I mean servants and attendants, and the crews of the boats, we made some of them drunk enough.

While this was doing, two gentlemen of the governor's company took occasion to leave the rest and walk about the ship; and, in so doing, they seemed, as it were by chance, to cast their eyes upon our bales of cloth and stuffs, baize, linen, silks, &c, and our supercargo and they began to make bargains apace, for he found they had not only money enough, but had abundance of other things which we were as willing to take as money, and of which they had brought specimens with them; as particularly spices, such as cloves and nutmegs; also China ware, tea, japanned ware, wrought silks, raw silk, and the like.

However, our supercargo dealt with them at present for nothing but ready money, and they paid all in gold: the price he made here, was to us indeed extravagant, though to them moderate, seeing they had been used to buy these goods from the Acapulco ships, which came in yearly, from whom to be sure they bought them dear enough. They bought as many goods at this time as they paid the value of fifteen thousand pieces of eight for, but all in gold by weight.

As for carrying our goods on shore, the governor, being present, no officer had anything to say to them; so they were carried on shore as presents, made by us to the governor and his retinue.

The next day three Spanish merchants came on board us, early in the morning, before it was light, and desired to see the supercargo. They brought with them a box of diamonds and some pearl, and a great quantity of gold, and to work they went with our cargo, and I thought once they would have bought the whole ship's loading; but they contented themselves to buy about the value of two-and-twenty thousand pieces of eight, which did not cost, in England, one-sixth part of the money.

We had some difficulty about the diamonds, because we did not understand the worth of them, but our supercargo ventured upon them at ten thousand pieces of eight, and took the rest in gold. They desired to stay on board till the next night, when, soon after it was dark, a small sloop came on board and took in all their goods, and, as we were told, carried them away to some other island.

The same day, and before these merchants were gone, came a large shallop on board with a square sail, towing after her a great heavy boat, which had a deck, but seemed to have been a large ship's long-boat, built into a kind of yacht, but ill masted, and sailed heavily. In these two boats they brought seven tons of cloves in mats, some chests of China ware, some pieces of China silks, of several sorts, and a great sum of money also.

In short, the merchants sold so cheap and bought so dear, that our supercargo declared he would sell the whole cargo for goods, if they would bring them, for, by his calculation, he had disposed of as many goods as he received the value of one hundred thousand pieces of eight for, all which, by his accounts, did not amount to, first cost, above three thousand pounds sterling in England.

Our ship was now an open fair; for, two or three days after, came the vessel back which went away in the night, and with them a Chinese junk, and seven or eight Chinese or Japanners; strange, ugly, ill-looking fellows they were, but brought a Spaniard to be their interpreter, and they came to trade also, bringing with them seventy great chests of China ware exceeding fine, twelve chests of China silks of several sorts, and some lackered cabinets, very fine. We dealt with them for all those, for our supercargo left nothing, he took everything they brought. Our traders were more difficult to please than we: for as for baize and druggets, and such goods, they would not meddle with them; but our fine cloths and some bales of linen they bought very freely. So we unloaded their vessel and put our goods on board. We took a good sum of money of them besides; but whither they went we knew not, for they both came and went in the night too, as the other did.

This trade held a good while, and we found that our customers came more from other islands than from the island where the governor resided; the reason of which, as we understood afterwards, was, because, as the governor had not openly granted a freedom of commerce, but privately winked at it, so they were not willing to carry it on openly before his face, or, as we say, under his nose; whereas, in other islands, they could convey their goods on shore with very little hazard, agreeing with the custom-house officer for a small matter.

These boats came and went thus several times, till, in short, we had disposed almost of the whole cargo; and now our men began to be convinced that we had laid out our voyage very right, for never was cargo better sold; and, as we resolved to pursue our voyage for New Spain, we had taken in a cargo very proper to sell there, and so, perhaps, to double the advantage we had already made.

In the mean time, all our hands were at work to store ourselves anew, with such provisions as could be had here for so long a run as we knew we were to have next; namely, over the vast Pacific Ocean, or South Sea, a voyage where we might expect to see no land for four months, except we touched at the Ladrones, as it might happen; and our greatest anxiety was for want of water, which our whole ship could scarce be able to stow sufficient for our use; and our want of casks was still as bad as the want of water, for we really knew not what to put water in when we had it.

The Spaniards had helped us to some casks, but not many; those that they could spare were but small, and at last we were obliged to make use of about two hundred large earthen jars, which were of singular use to us. We got a large quantity of good rice here, which we bought of a Chinese merchant, who came in here with a large China vessel to trade, who bought of us also several of our European goods.

Just as we were ready to sail, a boat came from the town of Manilla, and brought a new merchant, who wanted more English goods, but we had but few left; he brought with him thirty chests of calicoes, muslins, wrought silks, some of them admirably fine indeed, with fifteen bales of romals, and twelve tons of nutmegs. We sold him what goods we had left, and gave him money for the rest, but had them at a price so cheap, as was sufficient to let us know that it was always well worth while for ships to trade from Europe to the East Indies; from whence they are sure to make five or six of one. Had more of these merchants come on board, we were resolved to have laid out all the gold and silver we had, which was a very considerable quantity.

The last merchant who came on board us was a Spaniard; but I found that he spoke very good French, and some English; that he had been in England some years before, and understood English woollen manufactures very well. He told me he had all his present goods from Acapulco, but that they were then excessively dear. He had considerable dealings with the Chinese, and some with the coast of Coromandel and Bengal, and kept a vessel or two of his own to go to Bengal, which generally went twice in a year.

I found be had great business with New Spain, and that he generally had one of the Acapulco ships chiefly consigned to him; so that he was full of all such goods as those ships generally carried away from the Manillas, and, had we traded with him sooner, we should have had more calicoes and muslins than we now had; however, we were exceedingly well stored with goods of all sorts, suitable for a market in Peru, whither I resolved to go.

We continued chaffering after this manner about nine weeks, during which time we careened our ships, cleaned their bottoms, rummaged our gold, and repacked some of our provisions; endeavouring, as much as possible, to keep all our men as fully employed as we could, to preserve them in health, and yet not to overwork them, considering the heat of the climate.

Some time before we were ready to sail, I called all the warrant officers together, and told them, that as we were come to a country where abundance of small things were to be bought, and going to a country where we might possibly have an opportunity to sell them again to advantage, I would advance to every officer a hundred dollars, upon account of their pay, that they might lay it out here, and dispose of it again on the coast of New Spain to advantage. This was very acceptable to them, and they acknowledged it; and here, besides this, by the consent of all our superior officers, I gave a largess or bounty of five dollars a man, to all our foremast men; most of which I believe they laid out in arrack and sugar, to cheer them up in the rest of the voyage, which they all knew would be long enough.

We went away from Manilla, in the island of Luconia, the 15th of August, 1714; and, sailing awhile to the southward, passed the Straits between that island and Mindora, another of the Philippines, where we met with little extraordinary, except extraordinary lightning and thunders, such as we never heard or saw before, though, it seems, it is very familiar in that climate; till, after sixteen days' sailing, we saw the isle of Guam, one of the Ladrones, or Islands of Thieves, for so much the word imports; here we came to an anchor, Sept. 3, under the lee of a steep shore, on the north side of the isle of Guam; but, as we wanted no trade here, we did not at first inquire after the chief port, or Spanish governor, or anything of that kind; but we changed our situation the next day, and went through the passage to the east side of the island, and came to an anchor near the town.

The people came off, and brought us hogs and fowls, and several sorts of roots and greens, articles which we were very glad of, and which we bought the more of because we always found that such things were good to keep the men from the scurvy, and even to cure them of it if they had it. We took in fresh water here also, though it was with some difficulty, the water lying half a mile from the shore.

When I parted from Manilla, and was getting through the Strait between the island of Luconia and that of Mindora, I had some thoughts of steering away north, to try what land we might meet with to the north-east of the Philippines; and with intent to have endeavoured to make up into the latitude of 50 or 60°, and have come about again to the south, between the island of California and the mainland of America; in which course, I did not question meeting with extraordinary new discoveries, and, perhaps, such as the age might not expect to hear of, relating to the northern world, and the possibility of a passage out of those seas, either east or west, both which, I doubt not, would be found, if they were searched after this way; and which, for aught I know, remain undiscovered for want only of an attempt being made by those seas, where it would be easy to find whether the Tartarian seas are navigable or not; and whether Nova Zembla be an island or joined to the main; whether the inlets of Hudson's Bay have any opening into the West Sea; and whether the vast lakes, from whence the great river of Canada is said to flow, have any communication this way or not.

But though these were valuable discoveries, yet, when I began to cast up the account in a more serious manner, they appeared to have no relation to, or coherence with, our intended voyage, or with the design of our employers, which we were to consider in the first place, for though it is true that we were encouraged to make all such kinds of useful discoveries as might tend to the advantage of trade, and the improvement of geographical knowledge and experience, yet it was all to be so directed as to be subservient to the profits and advantages of a trading and cruising voyage.

It is true that these northern discoveries might be infinitely great, and most glorious to the British nation, by opening new sources of wealth and commerce in general: yet, as I have said, it was evident that they tended directly to destroy the voyage, either as to trading or to cruising, and might perhaps end in our own destruction also. For example, first of all, if adventuring into those northern seas, we should, by our industry, make out the discovery, and find a passage, either east or west, we must follow the discovery so as to venture quite through, or else we could not be sure that it was really a discovery; for these passages would not be like doubling Cape de Bon Esperance, on the point of Africa, or going round Cape Horn, the southernmost point of America, either of which were compassed in a few days, and then immediately gave an opening into the Indian or Southern Oceans, where good weather and certain refreshment were to be had.

Whereas, for the discovery in the north, after having passed the northernmost land of Grand Tartary, in the latitude of 74 even to 80°, and perhaps to the very north pole, there must be a run west, beyond the most northerly point of Nova Zembla, and on again west-south-west, about the North Kyn and North Cape, about six hundred leagues, before we could come to have any relief of the climate; after that, one hundred and sixty leagues more, and even to Shetland and the north of Scotland, before we could meet with any relief of provisions, which, after the length we must have run, from the latitude of 3½°, where we now were at the Philippine Islands, to 74° north, being near five thousand miles, would be impossible to be done, unless we were sure to victual, and furnish ourselves again with provisions and water by the way, and that in several places.

As to the other passage east, towards the continent of America, we had this uncertainty also; namely, that it was not yet discovered whether the land of California was an island or a continent, and if it should prove the latter, so as that we should be obliged to come back to the west, and not be able to find an opening between California and the land of north America, so as to come away to the coast of Mexico, to Acapulco, and so into the South Sea, and at the same time should not find a passage through Hudson's Bay, &c., into the North Sea, and so to Europe, we should not only spoil the voyage that way also, but should infallibly perish by the severity of the season and want of provisions.

All these things argued against any attempt that way; whereas, on the other hand, for southern discoveries, we had this particular encouragement; that whatever disappointment we might meet with, in the search after unknown countries, yet we were sure of an open sea behind us; and that whenever we thought fit to run south beyond the tropic, we should find innumerable islands where we might get water, and some sort of provisions, or come back into a favourable climate, and have the benefit of the trade winds, to carry us either backward or forward, as the season should happen to guide us.

Last of all, we had this assurance, that, the dangers of the seas excepted, we were sure of an outlet before us, if we went forward, or behind us, if we were forced back; and, having a rich cargo, if we were to do nothing but go home, we should be able to give our employers such an account of ourselves, as that they would be very far from being losers by the voyage; but that, if we reached safe the coast of New Spain, and met with an open commerce there, as we expected, we should perhaps make the most prosperous voyage that was ever made round the globe before.

These considerations put an end to all my thoughts of going northward; some of our secret council, (for, by the way, we consulted our foremast men no more, but had a secret council among ourselves, the resolutions of which we solemnly engaged not to disclose); some of these, I say, were for steering the usual course, from the Philippines to New Spain, viz., keeping in the latitudes of 11 or 13° north the line, and so making directly for California; in which latitude they proposed that we might, perhaps, by cruising thereabout, meet with the Manilla ships, going from New Spain to Manilla, which we might take as prizes, and then stand directly for the coast of Peru. But I opposed this, principally because it would effectually overthrow all my meditated discoveries to the southward; and, secondly, because I had observed, that, on the north of the line, there are no islands to be met with, in all the long run of near two thousand leagues, from Guam, one of the Ladrones, to the land of California; and that we did not find we were able to subsist during so long a run, especially for want of water; whereas, on the south of the line, as well within the tropic as without, we were sure to meet with islands innumerable, and that even all the way; so that we were sure of frequent relief of fresh water, of plants, fowl, and fish, if not of bread and flesh, almost all the way.

This was a main consideration to our men, and so we soon resolved to take the southern course; yet, as I said, we stood away for the Ladrones first. These are a cluster of islands, which lie in about 11 to 13° north latitude, north-east from the Moluccas, or Spice Islands, and east and by north from that part of the Philippines where we were, and at the distance of about four hundred leagues, and all the ships which go or come between the Philippines and New Spain touch at them, for the convenience of provisions, water, &c.; those that go to Spain put in there, in order to recruit and furnish for, and those that come from Spain, to relieve themselves after so long a run as that of six thousand miles, for so much it is at least from Guam to Acapulco; on these accounts, and with these reasonings, we came to the isles of the Ladrones.

During our run between the Philippine and Ladrone islands, we lived wholly upon our fresh provisions, of which we laid in a great stock at Manilla, such as hogs, fowls, calves, and six or seven cows, all alive, so that our English beef and pork, which lay well stored, was not touched for a long time.

At the Ladrones we recruited, and particularly took on board, as well alive as pickled up, near two hundred hogs, with a vast store of roots, and such things as are their usual food in that country. We took in also above three thousand cocoa-nuts and cabbages; yams, potatoes, and other roots, for our own use; and, in particular, we got a large quantity of maize, or Indian wheat, for bread, and some rice.

We stored ourselves likewise with oranges and lemons; and, buying a great quantity of very good limes, we made three or four hogsheads of lime-juice, which was a great relief to our men in the hot season, to mix with their water; as for making punch, we had some arrack and some sugar, but neither of them in such quantity as to have much punch made afore the mast.

We were eighteen days on our passage from the Strait of Mindora to Guam, and stayed six days at the latter, furnishing ourselves with provisions, appearing all this while with French colours, and Captain Merlotte as commander. However we made no great ceremony here with the Spanish governor, as I have said already, only that Captain Merlotte, after we had been here two days, sent a letter to him by a French officer, who, showing his commission from the king of France, the governor presently gave us product, as we call it, and leave to buy what provisions we wanted.

In compliment for this civility, we sent the governor a small present of fine scarlet camlet and two pieces of baize; and he made a very handsome return, in such refreshments as he thought we most wanted.

There was another reason for our keeping in this latitude till we came to the Ladrones; namely, that all the southern side of that part of the way, between the Philippines and the Ladrones, is so full of islands, that, unless we had been provided with very good pilots, it would have been extremely hazardous; and, add to this, that, beyond these islands south, is no passage; the land, which they call Nova Guinea, lying away east and east-south-east, farther than has yet been discovered; so that it is not yet known whether that country be an island or the continent.

Having for all these reasons gone to the Ladrones, and being sufficiently satisfied in our reasons for going away from thence to the southward, and having stored ourselves, as above, with whatever those islands produced, we left the Ladrones the 10th day of September in the evening, and stood away east-south-east, with the wind north-north-west, a fresh gale; after this, I think it was about five days, when, having stretched, by our account, about a hundred and fifty leagues, we steered away more to the southward, our course south-east-by-south.

And now, if ever, I expected to do something by way of discovery. I knew very well there were few, if any, had ever steered that course; or that, if they had, they had given very little account of their travels. The only persons who leave anything worth notice being Cornelius Vanschouten and Francis Le Mare, who, though they sailed very much to the south, yet say little to the purpose, as I shall presently show.

The sixteenth day after we parted from the Ladrones, being, by observation, in the latitude of 17° south of the line, one of our men cried, A sail! a sail! which put us into some fit of wonder, knowing nothing of a ship of any bulk could be met with in those seas; but our fit of wonder was soon turned to a fit of laughter, when one of our men from the foretop, cried out, Land! which, indeed, was the case; and the first sailor was sufficiently laughed at for his mistake, though, giving him his due, it looked at first as like a sail as ever any land at a distance could look.

Towards evening we made the land very plain, distance about seven leagues south-by-east, and found that it was not an island, but a vast tract of land, extended, as we had reason to believe, from the side of Gilolo, and the Spice Islands, or that which we call Nova Guinea, and never yet fully discovered. The land lying away from the west-north-west to the south-east-by-south, still southerly.

I, that was for making all possible discovery, was willing, besides the convenience of water, and perhaps fresh provisions, to put in here, and see what kind of country it was; so I ordered the brigantine to stand in for the shore. They sounded, but found no ground within half a league of the shore; so they hoisted out their boat, and went close in with the shore, where they found good anchor-hold in about thirty-six fathom, and a large creek, or mouth of a river; here they found eleven to thirteen fathom soft oozy sand, and the water half fresh at the mouth of the creek.

Upon notice of this, we stood in, and came all to an anchor in the very creek; and, sending our boats up the creek, found the water perfectly fresh and very good upon the ebb, about a league up the river.

Among all the islands in this part of the world, that is to say, from the Philippines eastward, of which there are an infinite number, we never came near any but we found ourselves surrounded with canoes and a variety of boats, bringing off to us cocoa-nuts, plantains, roots, and greens, to traffic for such things as they could get; and that in such numbers, we were tired with them, and sometimes alarmed, and obliged to fire at them. But here, though we saw great numbers of people at a distance from the shore, yet we saw not one boat or bark, nor anything else upon the water.

We stayed two or three days taking in fresh water, but it was impossible to restrain our men from going on shore, to see what sort of a country it was; and I was very willing they should do so. Accordingly, two of our boats, with about thirty men in both of them, went on shore on the east side of the creek or harbour where our ship lay.

They found the country looked wild and savage; but, though they could find no houses, or speak with the inhabitants, they saw their footsteps and their seats where they had sat down under some trees; and after wandering about a little, they saw people, both men and women, at a distance; but they ran away from our men, at first sight, like frightened deer; nor could they make any signal to them to be understood; for when our men hallooed and called after them, they ran again as if they had been bewitched.

Our men gathered a great variety of green stuff, though they knew not of what kind, and brought it all on board, and we eat a great deal of it; some we boiled and made broth of, and some of our men, who had the scurvy, found it did them a great deal of good; for the herbs were of a spicy kind, and had a most pleasant agreeable taste: but none of us could tell what to call them, though we had several men on board who had been among the Spice Islands before in Dutch ships.

We were very uneasy that we could get nothing here but a little grass and potherbs, as our men called it, and the men importuned me to let them have two boats, and go up the river as high as the tide would carry them; this I consented to, being as willing to make the discovery as they; so I ordered the captain of the Madagascar ship, who had, as I have said, been formerly my second mate, to go along with them.

But in the morning, a little before the flood was made, I was called out of my cabin to see an army, as they told me, coming to attack us. I turned out hastily enough, as may be easily conjectured, and such an army appeared as no ship was ever attacked with; for we spied three or four hundred black creatures, come playing and tumbling down the stream towards us, like so many porpoises in the water. I was not satisfied at first that they were human creatures, but would have persuaded our men, that they were sea-monsters, or fishes of some strange kind.

But they quickly undeceived us, for they came swimming about our ships, staring and wondering and calling to one another, but said not one word to us, at least, if they did, we could not understand them.

Some of them came very near our ships, and we made signs to them to come on board, but they would not venture. We tossed one of them a rope, and he took hold of it boldly; but as soon as we offered to pull, he let go, and laughed at us; another of them did the like, and when he let go, turned up his black buttocks, as in sport at us; the language of which, in our country, we all knew, but whether it had the same meaning here, we were at a loss to know.

However, this dumb manner of conversing with them we did not like, neither was it to any purpose to us; and I was resolved, if possible, to know something more of them than we could get thus; so I ordered out our pinnace with six oars, and as many other men well armed, to row among them; and, if possible, to take some of them and bring them on board. They went off, but the six-oar pinnace, though a very nimble boat, could not row so fast as they could swim; for, if pulling with all their might, they came near one of them, immediately, like dog and duck, they would dive, and come up again thirty or forty yards off; so that our men did not know which way to row after them; however, at last getting among the thickest of them, they got hold of two, and with some difficulty dragged them in; but think of our surprise, to find they were not men, but both young women. However, they were brought on board naked as they were.

When they came on board, I ordered they should have two pieces of linen wrapped round their waists to cover them, which they seemed well pleased with. We gave them also several strings of beads, and our men tied them about their necks, and about their arms like bracelets, and they were wonderfully delighted with their ornaments. Others of our men gave each of them a pair of scissors, with needles and some thread, and threading the needles, showed them how to sew with them; we also gave them food, and each of them a dram of arrack, and made signs to know of them where they lived; they pointed up to the river, but we could by no means understand them.

When we had dressed them up thus with necklaces, and bracelets, and linen, we brought them up upon the deck, and made them call to their country folk, and let them see how well they were used, and the girls beckoned them to come on board, but they would not venture.

However, as I thought the discovery we were to make, would be something the easier on account of the usage of these two young women; for they were not, as we guessed, above twenty or two-and-twenty years of age; we resolved that the boat should go on, as we intended, up the river; and that, as the two women pointed that way, we should carry them along with us.

Accordingly we sent two shallops, or large boats, which carried together sixty men, all well armed. We gave them store of beads and knives and scissors, and such baubles with them, with hatchets and nails, and hooks, looking-glasses, and the like; and we built up the sides and sterns of the boats, and covered them with boards, to keep off arrows and darts, if they should find occasion, so that they looked like London barges. In this posture, as soon as the tide or flood was made up, our men went away, carrying a drum and a trumpet in each boat; and each boat had also two patereroes, or small cannon, fixed on the gunnel near the bow.

Thus furnished, they went off about eleven o'clock in the forenoon, and to my very great uneasiness, I heard no more of them for four days. The whole ship's company were indeed surprised at their stay, and the captain of the sloop would fain have had me let him have sailed up the river with the sloop, as far as the channel would serve; which really we found was deep enough. Indeed, as I was unwilling to run any more risks, I could not persuade myself, but that the force I had already sent was sufficient to fight five thousand naked creatures, such as the natives seemed to be, and therefore, I was very unwilling to send. However, I consented at last to have our long-boat and two smaller boats manned with fifty-four men more, very well armed, and covered from arrows and darts as the other had been, to go up the river, upon their solemn promise, and with express order, to return the next day, at farthest; ordering them to fire guns as they went up the river, to give notice to their fellows, if they could be heard, that they were coming; and that, in the mean time, if I fired three guns they should immediately return.

They went away with the tide of flood, a little before noon, and went up the river about five leagues, the tide running but slowly, and a strong fresh of land-water that checked the current coming down; so that when the tide was spent they came to an anchor. They found the river, contrary to their expectation, continued both deep enough, and was wider in breadth than where the ships were at anchor; and that it had another mouth or outlet into the sea some leagues farther east, so that the land to the east of us, where our men went on shore, was but an island, and had not many inhabitants, if any; the people they had seen there having possibly swam over the other arm or branch of the river, to observe our ships the nearer. As our men found they could go no farther for want of the tide, they resolved to come to an anchor; but, just as they were sounding, to see what ground they had, and what depth, a small breeze at north-east sprang up, by which they stemmed the current and reached up about two leagues farther, when they hove over their grappling in five fathom water, soft ground; so that all this way, and much farther, every one of our ships might have gone up the channel, being as broad as the Thames is about Vauxhall.

It must be observed, that all along this river they found the land, after they came past the place where the other branch of the river broke off, eastward, was full of inhabitants on both sides, who frequently came down to the water-side in haste to look at our boats; but always when our men called to them, as if they thought our men inquired after their fellows, they pointed up the river, which was as much as to say, they were gone farther that way.

However, our men not being able to go any farther against the tide, took no notice of that; but, after a little while some of them, in one of the smaller boats, rowed towards the shore, holding up a white flag to the people in token of friendship; but it was all one, and would have been all one for aught we knew, if they had held up a red flag, for they all ran away, men, women, and children; nor could our men by any persuasions, by gestures and signs of any kind, prevail on them to stay, or hardly so much as to look at them.

The night coming on, our men knew not well what course to take; they saw several of the Indians' dwellings and habitations, but they were all at a distance from the river, occasioned, as our men supposed, by the river's overflowing the flat grounds near its banks, so as to render those lands not habitable.

Our men had a great inclination to have gone up to one of the towns they saw, but he that commanded would not permit it; but told them, if they could find a good landing-place, that they might all go on shore, except a few to keep the boats, if they chose to venture; upon which the smallest boat rowed up about a mile, and found a small river running into the greater, and here they all resolved to land; but first they fired two muskets, to give notice, if possible, to their comrades, that they were at hand; however, they heard nothing of them.

What impression the noise of the two muskets made among the Indians they could not tell, for they were all run away before.

They were no sooner on shore, but, considering they had not above two hours day, and that the Indian villages were at least two miles off, they called a council, and resolved not to march so far into a country they knew so little of, and be left to come back in the dark; so they went on board again, and waited till morning. However, they viewed the country, found it was a fertile soil, and a great herbage on the ground; there were few trees near the river; but farther up where the Indian dwellings were, the little hills seemed to be covered with woods, but of what kind they knew not.

In the morning, before break of day, some of our men fancied they heard a gun fired up the river; upon which the officer ordered two muskets to be fired again, as had been done the evening before; and in about a quarter of an hour they were answered by the like firing, by which our men knew that their comrades heard them; so, without pursuing their intended landing, the tide being then running upwards, they weighed, and set to their oars, having little or no wind, and that which they had blowing down the stream.

After they had gone about a league, they heard a confused noise at a great distance, which surprised them a little at first; but, as they perceived it drew nearer and nearer, they waited awhile, when they discovered first here and there some people, then more, and then about two or three hundred men and women together, running, and every one carrying something.

Where it was they were going to, or what it was they carried, our men could not tell till they came nearer, when they found that they were all loaded with provisions, cocoa-nuts, roots, cabbages, and a great variety of things which the men knew little of; and all these were carrying down to our ships, as we understood afterwards, in gratitude for our kind usage of the two young women.

When these people saw our men and their three boats, they were at a full stop, and once or twice they were ready to lay down all their loads, and run for it; but ours made signs of peace, and held up a white flag to them.

Some of them, it seems, having, as we found, conversed with our men, had a little more courage than the rest, and came to the shore side, and looked at the boats. One of our men thought of a stratagem to make known our desire of peace with them. Taking a string of beads and some toys, he held them up at the end of the boat-hook staff, and showed them to the Indians, pointing to them with his hand, and then pointing with the other hand to what the Indians carried, and to his mouth, intimating that we wanted such things to eat, and would give him the beads for them.

One of the Indians presently understood him, and threw himself into the water, holding a bundle of plants, such as he had trussed up together, upon his head, and swimming with the other hand, came so near the boat, where our men held out the staff, as to reach the end of the staff, take off the string of beads and toys, and hang his bunch of trash, for it was not better, upon the hook, and then went back again, for he would come no nearer.

When he was gotten on shore again, all his comrades came about him to see what he had got; he hung the string of beads round his neck, and ran dancing about with the other things in his hand, as if he had been mad.

What our men got was a trifle of less worth than a good bunch of carrots in England, but yet it was useful, as it brought the people to converse with us; for after this they brought us roots and fruits innumerable, and began to be very well acquainted with us.

By that time our men had chaffered thus four or five times they first heard, and in a little while after saw, their two great boats, with their fellows, coming down the river, at about two miles' distance, with their drums and trumpets, and making noise enough.

They had been, it seems, about three leagues higher up, where they had been on shore among the Indians, and had set at liberty the two maidens, for such they understood they were; who, letting their friends see how fine they were dressed, and how well they were used, the Indians were so exceedingly obliged, and showed themselves so grateful, that they thought nothing too much for them, but brought out all the sorts of provisions which their country produced, which, it seem, amounted to nothing but fruits, such as plantains, cocoa-nuts, oranges and lemons, and such things, and roots, which we could give no name to; but that which was most for our use, was a very good sort of maize, or Indian corn, which made us excellent bread.

They had, it seems, some hogs and some goats; but our men got only six of the latter, which were at hand, and were very good. But that which was most remarkable was, that whereas in all the islands within the tropics the people are thievish, treacherous, fierce, and mischievous, and are armed with lances, or darts, or bows and arrows; these appeared to be a peaceable, quiet, inoffensive people; nor did our men see any weapon among them except a long staff, which most of the men carried in their hands, being made of a cane, about eight foot long, and an inch and a half in diameter, much like a quarter-staff, with which they would leap over small brooks of water with admirable dexterity.

The people were black, or rather of a tawny dark brown; their hair long, but curling in very handsome ringlets: they went generally quite naked, both men and women; except that in two places, our men said, they found some of the women covered from the middle downward. They seemed to have been strangers to the sea; nor did we find so much as any one boat among them: nor did any of the inhabitants dwell near the sea; but cultivated their lands very well, in their way; having abundance of greens and fruits growing about their houses; and upon which we found they chiefly lived. The climate seemed to be very hot, and yet the country very fruitful.

These people, by all we could perceive, had never had any converse with the rest of the world by sea; what they might have by land we know not; but, as they lie quite out of the way of all commerce, so it might be probable they never had seen a ship or boat, whether any European ship, or so much as a periagua of the islands. We have mentioned their nearest distance to the Ladrones, being at least four hundred leagues; and from the Spice Islands, and the country of New Guinea, much more; but as to the European shipping, I never heard of any that ever went that way, nor do I believe any ever did.

I take the more notice of these people's not having conversed, as I say, with the world, because of the innocence of their behaviour, their peaceable disposition, and their way of living upon the fruits and produce of the earth; also their cultivation, and the manner of their habitations; no signs of rapine or violence appearing among them. Our stay here was so little, that we could make no inquiry into their religion, manner of government, and other customs; nor have I room to crowd many of these things into this account. They went, indeed, as I have said, naked, some of them stark naked, both men and women, but I thought they differed in their countenances from all the wild people I ever saw; that they had something singularly honest and sincere in their faces, nor did we find anything of falsehood or treachery among them.

The gratitude they expressed for our kindly using the two young women I have mentioned, was a token of generous principles; and our men told us, that they would have given them whatever they could have asked, that was in their power to bestow.

In a word, it was on their account they sent that little army of people to us loaden with provisions, which our men met before the two shallops came down. But all the provisions they had consisted chiefly in fruits of the earth, cocoa-nuts, plantains, oranges, lemons, &c., and maize, or Indian corn. We were not a sufficient time with them to inquire after what traffick they had, or whether anything fit for us. They had several fragrant plants, and some spices, particularly cinnamon, which we found, but what else the country produced we knew not.

We came away from hence after seven days' stay, having observed little of the country, more than that it seemed to be very pleasant, but very hot; the woods were all flourishing and green and the soil rich, but containing little that could be the subject of trade; but an excellent place to be a baitland, or port of refreshment, in any voyage that might afterwards be undertaken that way.

We set sail, I say, from hence in seven days, and, finding the coast lie fairly on our starboard side, kept the land on board all the way, distance about three leagues; and it held us thus, about a hundred and twenty leagues due east, when on a sudden we lost sight of the land; whether it broke off, or whether it only drew off farther south, we could not tell.

We went on two or three days more, our course south-east, when we made land again; but found it only to be two small islands, lying south and by east, distance nine leagues. We stood on to them, and two of our boats went on shore, but found nothing for our purpose; no inhabitants, nor any living creatures, except sea fowls, and some large snakes; neither was there any fresh water. So we called that land Cape Dismal.

The same evening we stood away full south, to see if we could find out the continuance of the former land; but as we found no land, so a great sea coming from the south we concluded we should find no land that way. And, varying our course easterly, we ran with a fair fresh gale at north-west and by west, for seven days more; in all which time, we saw nothing but the open sea every way; and making an observation found we had passed the southern tropic; and that we were in the latitude of 26° 13', after which we continued our course still southerly for several days more, until we found, by another observation, that we were in 32° 20'.

This evening we made land over our starboard bow, distance six leagues, and stood away south and by east: but the wind slackening we lay by in the night; and in the morning found the land bearing east and by south, distance one league and a half; a good shore, and on sounding, about five-and-thirty fathom, stony ground. We now hoisted our boat out, and sent it on shore for discoveries, to sound the depth of the water, and see for a good harbour to put in at.

Our people went quite in with the shore, where they found several men and women crowded together to look at us. When our men came close to the land they hung out a white flag, but the wild people understood nothing of the meaning of it, but stood looking and amazed, and we have great reason to believe that they never had seen any ship or bark of any nation before. We found on our landing, no boats or sails, or anything they had to make use of on the water; but some days after we saw several small canoes, with three or four men in each.

Our men not being able to speak a word for them to understand, or to know what was said to them, the first thing they did, was to make signs to them for something to eat; upon which three of them seemed to go away, and coming again in a few minutes, brought with them several bundles or bunches of roots, some plantains, and some green lemons, or limes, and laid down all upon the coast. Our men took courage then to go on shore, and, taking up what they brought, set up a stick, and upon the end of it hung five bunches or strings of blue and white beads, and went on board again.

Never was such joy among a wild people discovered, as these natives showed, when they took the beads off the stick; they danced and capered, and made a thousand antic gestures, and, inviting our men on shore, laid their hands upon their breasts across, and then looked up, intimating a solemn oath not to hurt us.

Our men made signs, by which they made them understand, that they would come again next morning, and also that they should bring us more eatables; accordingly, we sent three boats the next morning, and our men carried knives, scissors, beads, looking-glasses, combs, and any toys they had, not forgetting glass beads and glass ear-rings in abundance.

The Indians were very ready to meet us, and brought us fruits and herbs as before; but three of them, who stood at a distance, held each of them a creature exactly like a goat, but without horns or beard; and these were brought to traffick with us.

We brought out our goods, and offered every one something; but the variety was surprising to them who had never seen such things before. But that which was most valuable of all our things, was a hatchet, which one of their principal men took up and looked at it, felt the edge, and laid it down; then took it up again, and wanted to know the use of it: upon which one of our men took it, and stepping to a tree that stood near, cut off a small bough of it at one blow. The man was surprised, and ran to the tree with it, to see if he could do the same, and finding he could, he laid it down, ran with all his might into the country, and by-and-by returning, came with two men more with him, to show them this wonderful thing, a hatchet.

But if they were surprised with the novelty of a hatchet, our men were as much surprised to see hanging round the ears of both the men that he brought with him, large flat pieces of pure gold. The thread which they hung by was made of the hair of the goats, twisted very prettily together and very strong.

Our men offering to handle them, to see if they were gold, one of the men took off his two gold bobs, and offered them to our men for the hatchet. Our men seemed to make much difficulty of it, as if the hatchet was of much greater value than those trifles; upon which he, being as we found, superior, made the other, who came with him, pull off his two ear-jewels also; and so our unreasonable people took them all four, being of pure gold, and weighing together some grains above two ounces, in exchange for an old rusty hatchet. However unreasonable the price was, the purchaser did not think it so; and so over-fond was he of the hatchet, that as soon as he had it for his own, he ran to the tree, and in a few minutes had so laid about him with the hatchet, that there was not a twig left on it that was within his reach.

This exchange was a particular hint to me; and I presently directly my chief mate, and Captain Merlotte, to go on shore the next day, and acquaint themselves as much as they could with the natives, and, if possible, to find out where they had this gold, and if any quantity was to be found.

Captain Merlotte and my chief mate bestowed their time so well, and obliged the natives so much, by the toys and trifles they gave them, that they presently told them that the gold, which they called Aarah, was picked up in the rivers that came down from a mountain which they pointed to, a great way off. Our men prevailed with three of them, to go with them to one of these rivers, and gave them beads and such things to encourage them, but no hatchet; that was kept up at a high rate, and as a rarity fit only for a king, or some great man who wore Aarah on his ears.

In a word, they came to the river where they said they found this Aarah; and the first thing our men observed there, was an Indian sitting on the ground, and beating something upon a great stone, with another stone in his hand for his hammer: they went to see what he was doing, and found he had got a lump of gold from the sand, as big as a swan-shot, of no regular shape, but full of corners, neither round nor square; and the man was beating it flat as well as he could.

One of our men, who had a hatchet in his hand, made signs to him to let him flatten it for him; and so turning the back part of the hatchet, which served the purpose of a hammer, he beat the piece of gold flat in an instant; and then turning it upon the edge, beat it that way until he brought it to be round also.

This was so surprising to the man who had been beating, that he stood looking on with all the tokens of joy and amazement; and, desiring to see the hatchet, looked this way and that way, upon those of his countrymen who came with us, as if asking them if ever they saw the like.

When our man had done, he made signs to know if he had any more Aarah; the man said nothing, but went down to the brink of the river, and, putting his hand into a hole, he brought out three little lumps of gold, and a great many smaller, some of them about as big as a large pin's head; all which he had laid up there, in the hollow of a stone. Our man thought it was too much, to take all that for the hatchet; and therefore pulled out some beads, and pieces of glass, and such toys; and, in short, bought all this cargo of gold, which in the whole weighed near five ounces, for about the value of two shillings.

Though these bargains were very agreeable to us, yet the discovery of such a place, and of such a fund of treasure, in a part of the world, which it is very very probable, was never before seen by any European eyes, nor so much as inquired after, was the greatest satisfaction imaginable to me; knowing the adventurous temper of the gentleman who was our principal employer. Upon this account, while my men busied themselves in their daily search after gold, and in finding out the rivers from whence it came, or rather where it was found, I employed myself to be fully informed where this place was; whether it was an island or a continent; and having found a tolerable good road for our ships to ride in, I caused my two shallops, well manned, to run along the coast, both east and west, to find which way it lay, and whether they could find any end of it; as also to see what rivers, what people, and what provisions they could meet with.

By my observation, I found that we were in the latitude of 27° 13' south meridian; distance from the Ladrones about 16° east. While my shallops were gone, I went on shore, and some of my men set up tents, as well for the convenience of their traffick, as for their resting on shore all night; keeping, however, a good guard, and having two of our ship's dogs with them, who never failed giving them notice, whenever any of the natives came near them; for what ailed the dogs I know not, but neither of them could bear the sight of the Indians, and we had much to do to keep them from flying at them.

While we rode here, we had the most violent storm of wind with rain, and with great claps of thunder, that we had yet sustained since we came out of England. It was our comfort that the wind came off shore, for it blew at south, and shifting between the south, south-east, and south-west, with such excessive gusts, and so furious, and withal, not only by squalls and sudden flaws, but a settled terrible tempest, that had it been from off sea, as it was off shore, we must have perished, there had been no remedy, and even as it was, we rode in great danger. My boatswain called out twice to me to cut my masts by the board, protesting we should either bring our anchors home, or founder as we rode; and indeed the sea broke over us many times in a terrible manner. As I said before, we had an indifferent good road, and so we had, but not a very good one, for the land was low; and on the east we lay a little open. However, our ground-tackle was good, and our ship very tight, and I told the boatswain I would rather slip the cable and go off to sea than cut the masts. However, in about four hours' time more we found the wind abate, though it blew very hard for three days after.

I was in great pain for my two shallops in this tempest, but they had both the good luck to lie close under the shore; and one indeed had hauled quite upon the land, where the men lay on shore under their sail, so that they got no damage; and about three days after, one of them returned, and brought me word they had been to the west, where they had made very little discovery, as to the situation of the country, or whether it was an island or a continent, but they had conversed with the natives very often, and found several who had pieces of gold hanging, some in their hair, some about their necks; and they made a shift to bring as many with them as weighed, all put together, seventeen or eighteen ounces, for which they had bartered toys and trifles, as we did; but they found no rivers, where they could discover any gold in the sands, as We had done, so that they believed it all came from the side where we were.

But our other shallop had much better luck; she went away to the east, and by the time she had gone about sixteen leagues she found the shore break off a little, and soon after a little more, until at length they came as it were to the land's end; when, the shore running due south, they followed, according to their account, near thirteen leagues more.

In this interval they went several times on shore, entered three rivers, indifferently large, and one of them very large at the mouth, but grew narrow again in three or four leagues; but a deep channel, with two-and-twenty to eight-and-twenty fathom water in it all the way, as far as they went.

Here they went on shore and trafficked with the natives, whom they found rude and unpolished, but a very mild inoffensive people; nor did they find them anything thievish, much less treacherous, as in some countries is the case. They had the good luck to find out the place where, as they supposed, the king of the country resided; which was a kind of a city, encompassed all round, the river making a kind of double horse-shoe. The manner of their living is too long to describe; neither could our men give any account of their government, or of the customs of the place; but what they sought for was gold and provisions, and of those they got pretty considerable quantities.

They found the Indians terribly surprised at the first sight of them; but after some time they found means to let them know they desired a truce, and to make them understand what they meant by it.

At length a truce being established, the king came, and with him near three hundred men; and soon after the queen, with half as many women. They were not stark naked, neither men nor women, but wearing a loose piece of cloth about their middles; what it was made of we could not imagine, for it was neither linen or woollen, cotton or silk; nor was it woven, but twisted and braided by hand, as our women make bone lace with bobbins. It seems it was the stalk of an herb, which this was made with; and was so strong that I doubt not it would have made cables for our ships, if we had wanted to make such an experiment.

When the king first came to our men they were a little shy of his company, he had so many with him, and they began to retire; which the king perceiving, he caused all his men to stop, and keep at a distance; and advanced himself with about ten or twelve of his men, and no more.

When he was come quite up, our men, to show their breeding, pulled off their hats, but that he did not understand, for his men had no hats on. But the officer making a bow to him, he understood that presently, and bowed again; at which all his men fell down flat upon their faces, as flat to the ground as if they had been shot to death with a volley of our shot; and they did not fall so quick but they were up again as nimbly, and then down flat on the ground again; and this they did three times, their king bowing himself to our men at the same time.

This ceremony being over, our men made signs to them that they wanted victuals to eat, and something to drink: and pulled out several things, to let the people see they would give something for what they might bring them.

The king understood them presently, and turning to some of his men he talked awhile to them; and our men observed, that while he spoke they seemed to be terrified, as if he had been threatening them with death. However, as soon as he had done, three of them went away, and our men supposed they went to fetch something that the king would give them; upon which, that they might be beforehand with them, our men presented his majesty with two pair of bracelets of fine glass beads of several colours, and put them upon his arms, which he took most kindly; and then they gave him a knife, with a good plain ivory handle, and some other odd things. Upon receiving these noble presents, he sends away another of his men, and a little after two more.

Our men observed that two of the men went a great way off toward the hill, but the other man that he sent away first went to his queen, who, with her retinue of tawny ladies, stood but a little way off, and soon after her majesty came with four women only attending her.

The officer who commanded our men, finding he should have another kind of compliment to pay the ladies, retired a little; and, being an ingenious handy sort of a man, in less than half-an-hour, he and another of his men made a nice garland, or rather a coronet, of sundry strings of beads, and with glass bobs and pendants, all hanging about it, most wonderful gay; and when the queen was come, he went up to the king, and showing it to him, made signs that he would give it to the queen.

The king took it, and was so pleased with the present, that truly he desired our officer to put it upon his own head, which he did; but, when he had got it so placed, he let our men see he was king over his wife, as well as over the rest of the country, and that he would wear it himself.

Our men then pulled out a little pocket looking-glass, and, holding it up, let his majesty see his own face, which we might reasonably suppose he had never seen before, especially with a crown on his head too. Before he saw his own face in the glass he was grave and majestic, and carried it something like a king; but he was so delighted with the novelty that he was quite beside himself, and jumped and capered and danced about like a madman.

All this while our men saw nothing coming, but that all was given on their side; whereupon they made signs again, that they wanted provisions.

The king then made signs, pointing to a hill a good way off, as if it would come from thence very quickly; and then looked to see if his people were coming, as if he was impatient till they came, as well as our men.

During this time, one of our men observed that the queen had several pieces of gold, as they thought them to be, hanging about her, particularly in her hair, and large flat plates of gold upon the hinder part of her head, something in the place of a roll, such as our women wear; that her hair was wound about it in rolls, braided together very curiously; and having informed our officer, he made signs to the king for leave to give the queen something, which he consented to. So he went to her majesty, making a bow as before; but this complaisance surprised her, for, upon his bowing, on a sudden falls the queen and all her four ladies flat on the ground, but were up again in a moment; and our people wondered how they could throw themselves so flat on their faces, and not hurt themselves; nor was it less to be wondered at, how they could so suddenly jump up again, for they did not rise up gradually as we must do, with the help of our hands and knees, if we were extended so flat on our faces, but they, with a spring, whether with their hands or their whole bodies, we knew not, sprang up at once, and were upon their feet immediately.

This compliment over, our officer stepped up to the queen, and tied about her neck a most delicate necklace of pearl; that is to say, of large handsome white glass beads, which might in England cost about fourpence halfpenny, and to every one of her ladies he gave another of smaller beads, differing in colour from those which he gave the queen. Then he presented her majesty with a long string of glass beads, which, being put over her head, reached down to her waist before, and joined in a kind of tassel, with a little knot of blue riband, which she was also extremely pleased with; and very fine she was.

The queen made, it seems, the first return; for, stepping to one of her women, our men observed that her attendant took something out of her hair, and then the queen let her tie her hair up again; after which her majesty brought it and gave it to our officer, making signs to know if it was acceptable. It was a piece of gold that weighed about two ounces and a half; it had been beaten as flat as they knew how to beat it. But the metal was of much more beauty to our men than the shape.

Our officer soon let the queen and people see that he accepted the present, by laying it to his mouth and to his breast, which he found was the way when they liked anything. In short, our officer went to work again, and in a little while he made a little coronet for the queen, as he had done before for the king, though less; and, without asking leave of his majesty, went up to her and put it upon her head; and then gave her a little looking-glass, as he had done to the king, that she might view her face in it.

She was so surprised at the sight, that she knew not how to contain herself; but, to show her gratitude, she pulled out another plate of gold out of her own hair, and gave it to our officer; and, not content with that, she sent one of her women to the crowd of females who first attended her, and whether she stripped them of all the gold they had, or only a part, she brought so many pieces, that, when together, they weighed almost two pounds.

When she was thus dressed she stepped forward very nimbly and gracefully towards the king, to show him what she had got; and, finding he was dressed as fine as herself, they had work enough for near two hours to look at one another, and admire their new ornaments.

Our men reported, that the king was a tall, well-shaped man, of a very majestic deportment, only that when he laughed he showed his teeth too much, which, however, were as white as ivory: as for the queen, saving that her skin was of a tawny colour, she was a very pretty woman; very tall, a sweet countenance, admirable features, and, in a word, a complete handsome lady.

She was very oddly dressed; she was quite naked from her head to below her breasts; her breasts were plump and round, not flaggy and hanging down, as it generally is with the Indian women, some of whose breasts hang as low as their bellies, but projecting as beautifully as if they had been laced up with stays round her body; and below her breast she had a broad piece of a skin of some curious creature, spotted like a leopard, probably of some fine spotted deer. This was wrapped round her very tight, like a body-girt to a horse; and under this she had a kind of petticoat, as before described, hanging down to her ankles. As for shoes or stockings, they were only such as nature had furnished. Her hair was black, and, as supposed, very long, being wreathed up and twisted in long locks about the plate of gold she wore; for when she pulled off the plate above mentioned, it hung down her back and upon her shoulders very gracefully; but it seems she did not think so, for, as soon as she found it so fallen down, she caused one of her women to roll it up, and tie it in a great knot which hung down in her neck, and did not look so well as when it was loose.

While the king and the queen were conversing together about their fine things, as above, our men went back to the boat, where they left the purchase they had got, and furnished themselves with other things fit to traffick with as they saw occasion; and they were not quite come up to the king again, when they perceived that the men the king had sent up into the country were returned, and that they brought with them a great quantity of such provisions as they had, which chiefly consisted of roots and maize, or Indian corn, and several fruits which we had never seen before. Some of them resembled the large European figs, but were not really figs; with some great jars of water, having herbs steeped in it, and roots, that made it look as white as milk, and drank like milk sweetened with sugar, but more delicious, and exceeding cool and refreshing. They brought also a great quantity of oranges, but they were neither sweet nor sour, and our men believed they were not ripe; but when they were dressed after the manner of the country, which they showed our men, and which was to roast them before the fire, they had an admirable flavour, and our men brought a great many away to us, and when we roasted them they exceeded anything of the kind I had ever tasted.

After our men had received what was brought, and shown that the whole was very acceptable, the king made signs that he would be gone, but would come again to them the next morning; and, pointing to the queen's head, where the plate of gold had been that she had given to our men, intimated that he would bring some of the same with him the next day. But while he was making these signs, one of his other messengers came back, and gave the king something into his hand wrapped up, which our men could not see. As soon as the king had it, as if he had been proud to show our men that he could make himself and his queen as fine as they could make him, he undid the parcel, and decked out his queen with a short thing like a robe, which reached from her neck down to the spotted skin which she wore before, and so it covered her shoulders and breast. It was made of an infinite number and variety of feathers, oddly, and yet very curiously put together; and was spangled all over with little drops or lumps of gold; some no bigger than a pin's head, which had holes made through them, and were strung six or seven together, and so tied on to the feathers; some as big as a large pea, hanging single, some as big as a horse-bean, and beaten flat, and all hanging promiscuously among the feathers, without any order or shape, which, notwithstanding, were very beautiful in the whole, and made the thing look rich and handsome enough.

As soon as he had thus equipped his queen, he put another upon himself, which was larger, and had this particular in its shape, that it covered his arms almost to his elbows, and was so made that it came round under the arm, and being fastened there with a string, made a kind of sleeve.

As the king's robe, or whatever it may be called, was longer, for it came down to his waist, so it had a great deal more gold about it, and larger pieces than that the queen wore. When their majesties had thus put on their robes, it may be guessed how glorious they looked, but especially the queen, who being a most charming beautiful creature, as said before, was much more so when glistening thus with gold. Our men looked very narrowly to observe whether there were any diamonds or pearls among their finery, but they could not perceive any.

The king and queen now withdrew for that evening, but their people did not leave our men so, for they thronged about them; and some brought them jars of the white liquor, some brought them roots, others fruits, some one thing, some another; and our men gave every one of them some small matter or other in proportion to what they brought. At last, there came four particular tall lusty men, with bows and arrows; but before they came close up to our men, they laid down their bows and arrows on the ground, and came forward with all the tokens of friendship they were able to make.

They had two youths with them, each of whom led a tame fawn of pretty large growth, and when the men came up, they gave the two fawns to our men; who, in return, gave each of them a knife, and some strings of beads, and such toys as they had.

Our men observed, that all these men had little bits of gold, some of one shape, and some of another, hanging at their ears; and when our men came to be familiar, they asked them as well as they could, where they found that stuff? and they made signs to the sand in the river, and then pointed towards that part of the country where our ships lay, which signified to our men that the gold was, most of it, where we lay, not there where the king and queen resided. Nay, when our men pointed again to the river where they were, and went and took up some of the sand, as if they would look for gold in it, they made signs of laughing at it, and that there was nothing to be found there, but that it lay all the other way.

And yet two or three of the men, who, when the tide was out, went up the bank of the river, two or three miles upon the sands, peeping and trying the sands as they went, they found three or four little bits of pure gold, though not bigger than pins heads; but no doubt farther up the country they might have found more.

These four men seeing how fond our people were of the gold, made signs they could fetch gold to them if they would give them such things as they liked; and ours again told them they should have anything they pleased; and, as earnest, gave them some pieces of iron and bits of glass of small value, both which they were much delighted with.

Early in the morning their four customers came again, and brought several men, who seemed to be servants, along with them, loaden with refreshments, such as the white water, mentioned above, which they brought in earthen pots, very hard, made so by the heat of the sun. They brought also three small deer with them, and a kind of coney or rabbit, but larger, which our men were very glad of. But that which was above all the rest, they brought a good quantity of gold-dust, that is to say, some in small lumps, some in bigger; and one of them had near a pound weight wrapped up in a piece of coney-skin, which was all so very small that it was like dust; which, as our men understood afterwards, was reckoned little worth, because all the lumps had been picked out of it.

Our men, to be sure, were very willing to trade for this commodity, and therefore they brought out great variety of things to truck with them, making signs to them to pick out what they liked; but still keeping a reserve for the king and queen, whom they expected. Above all they had made a reserve for the king of some extraordinary hatchets, which they had not yet suffered to be seen, with a hammer or two, and some drinking-glasses, and the like, with some particular toys for the queen.

But they had variety enough left besides for the four men: who, in short, bought so many trinkets and trifles, that our men not only got all the gold they brought, but the very pieces of gold out of their ears; in return for which our men gave them every one a pair of ear-rings, to hang about their ears, with a fine drop; some of green glass, some red, some blue; and they were wonderfully pleased with the exchange, and went back, we may venture to say, much richer in opinion than they came.

As soon as these people had done their market, and indeed a little before, they perceived at a distance the king and queen coming with a great retinue; so they made signs to our men that they must be gone, and that they would not have the king know that they had been there.

I must confess, the relation of all this made me very much repent that I had not happened to have put in there with the ships; though indeed, as the road lay open to the east and south winds, it might have been worse another way; I mean, when the storm blew. However, as it is, I must report this part, from the account given us by my men.

When the king and queen came the second time, they were together, and dressed up, as our men supposed, with the utmost magnificence, having the fine feathered spangled things about their shoulders; and the king had over all his habit, a fine spotted robe of deer skins, neatly joined together; and which, as he managed it, covered him from head to foot; and, in short, it was so very beautiful that he really looked like a king with it.

When he came to our men, and the ceremony of their meeting was over, the king, turning round, showed them, that he had brought them stores of provisions; and indeed, so he had; for he had at least fifty men attending him, loaden with roots, and oranges, and maize, and such things; in short, he brought them above twenty thousand oranges; a great parcel of that fruit like a fig, which I mentioned above, and other fruits. After which another party followed, and brought twenty live deer, and as many of their rabbits, dead; the latter are as big as our hares.

As they came up, the king made signs to our men to take them; and our officer making signs to thank his majesty, he ordered one of the queen's attendants to give him one of the feathered robes, such an one as the king himself had on; and made mighty fine with lumps and tassels of gold, as the other. And a tawny lass advancing to him offered to put it over his head, but he took it in his hand and put it on himself, and looked as like a jack pudding in it, as any one could desire; for it made no figure at all upon him, compared to what it did upon the Indians.

When they had received all this, they could not but make a suitable return; and therefore our officer caused his reserve to be brought out; and first he gave his majesty a dozen of very handsome drinking-glasses of several sizes; with half a dozen of glass beakers, or cups, to the queen, for the same use. Then he gave the king a little hanger, and a belt to wear it by his side; and showed him how to buckle it on and take it off, and how to draw it out, and put it in again.

This was such a present, and the king was so delighted with it, that our officer said he believed the king did nothing but draw it and put it up again, put it on and pull it off, for near two hours together.

Besides this he gave the king three hatchets, and showed him the uses of them; also two large hammers, and a pair of very strong large shears, particularly showing him, that with those hammers they might beat out the gold lumps which they found in the rivers, and with the shears might cut the edges round, or into what shape they pleased, when they were beaten thin.

To the queen he gave six little knives, and a dozen small looking-glasses for her ladies; six pairs of scissors, and a small box full of large needles; then he gave her some coarse brown thread, and showed her how to thread the needle, and sew anything together with the thread; all which she admired exceedingly, and called her tawny maids of honour about her, that they might learn also. And whilst they were standing all together, our officer, to divert the king, sewed two of her women one to another by the lap of their waistcoats, or what else it might be called; and when they were a little surprised at it, and began, as he thought, to be a little uneasy, he took the scissors, and at one snap set them at liberty again, which passed for such an extraordinary piece of dexterity, that the king would needs have two of them sewed together again, on purpose to see it cut again. And then the king desired he might have a needle and thread himself, and a pair of scissors; then he would sew some things together, and cut them asunder again several times, and laugh most heartily at the ingenuity of it.

Besides the above things, they gave her majesty a pair of ear-rings to hang on her ears, the glass in them looking green like an emerald; a ring of silver, with false stones in it, like a rose diamond ring, the middle stone red like a ruby, which she went presently and gave to the king; but our officer made signs that he had one that was bigger for the king, and accordingly gave the king one much larger; and now they had done giving presents, as they thought, when the king made a sign to the queen, which she understood, and, calling one of her women, she brought a small parcel, which the queen gave our officer into his hand, wherein was about eleven pounds weight of gold-dust, but, as before, no lumps in it.

Our men having thus finished their traffick, and being about to come away, they made signs to the king, that they would come again and bring him more fine things; at which the king smiled, and pointing to the gold, as if telling them he would have more of that for them when they came again.

Our men had now their expectations fully answered; and, as I said, had ended their traffick; and, taking leave of the king and all his retinue, retired to their shallop, the king and queen going away to their city as above. The wind blowing northerly, they were seven days before they got down to us in the ship; during which time they had almost famished the deer they had left, five of which they had kept to bring us alive, and yet they went two or three times on shore to get food for them by the way.

We were all glad to see them again, and I had a great deal of reason to be very well satisfied with the account of their traffick, though not much with their discovery, for they were not able to give us the least account whether the land was a continent or an island.

But let that be how it will, it is certainly a country yet unfrequented by any of the Christian part of mankind, and perhaps, may ever be so, and yet may be as rich as any other part of the world yet discovered. The mountains in most of the islands, as well as of the mainland in those parts, abounding in gold or silver, and, no question, as well worth searching after as the coast of Guinea; where, though the quantity they find is considerable, yet it is at this time sought after by so many, and the negroes taught so well how to value it, that but a little is brought away at a time, and so much given for it, that, computing the charge of the voyage, is oftentimes more than it is worth.

But though it is true that what gold is found here is a great way off, yet, I am persuaded such quantities are to be had, and the price given for it so very trifling, that it would be well worth searching for.

I reckon, that, including the gold our shallop brought, and what we got on shore where we lay, we brought away about twenty-four pounds weight of gold; the expense of which we could not value at above ten or eleven pounds in England, put it all together; and reckoning for all the provisions we got there, which supplied us for twenty days after we came away.

For while our shallop was making her visit thus to the royal family, &c., as is related, our men were not idle on shore, but, partly by trade with the natives, and by washing the sands in the small rivers, we got such a quantity of gold as well satisfied us for the stay we made.

We had been about eighteen days here when our shallop returned, and we stayed a week more trafficking with the people; and I am persuaded, if we had been in the mind to have settled there and stayed till now, we should have been very welcome to the people. We saw neither horse or cow, mule, ass, dog, or cat, or any of our European animals, excepting that our men shot some wild ducks and widgeons, exactly the same which we see in England, and very fat and good, but much easier to shoot than in England, having never been acquainted with the flash and noise of guns as ours have been; we also found a sort of partridges in the country not much unlike our own, and a great many of the whistling plover, the same with ours.

Though this month's stay was unexpected, yet we had no reason to think our time ill spent. However, we did not think we ought to lie here too long whatever we got; so we weighed and stood off to sea, steering still south-east, keeping the shore of this golden country in sight, till our men told us they found the land fall off to the south. Then we steered away more southerly for six or eight days, not losing sight of, land all the time, till by an observation we found we were in the latitude of 34° 30' south of the line, our meridian distance from the Ladrones 22° 30' east, when a fresh gale of wind springing up at south and by east, obliged us to haul close for that evening. At night it blew such a storm that we were obliged to yield to the force of it, and go away afore it to the north, or north-by-west, till we came to the point of that land we passed before. Here, the land tending to the west, we ran in under the lee of a steep shore, and came to an anchor in twenty-five fathoms water, being the same country we were in before. Here we rode very safe for five days, the wind continuing to blow very hard all the time from the south-east.

My men would fain have had me gone ashore again and trafficked with the people for more gold; but I, who was still in quest of further discoveries, thought I knew enough of this place to tempt my friend the merchant, whose favourite design was that of making new discoveries, to another voyage there, and that was enough for me. So I declined going on shore again, except that we sent our boats for a recruit of fresh water; and our men, while they were filling it, shot a brace of deer, as they were feeding by the side of a swamp or moist ground, and also some wild ducks. Here we set up a great wooden cross, and wrote on it the names of our ships and commanders, and the time that we came to an anchor there.

But we were obliged to a farther discovery of this country than we intended, by the following accident. We had unmoored early in the morning, and by eight o'clock were under sail; by ten we had doubled the point I mentioned above, and stood away south keeping the shore on board, at the distance of about two leagues west.

The next day, the officer who had been with the shallop, showed us the opening or mouth where he had put in, and where he had made his traffick with the king of the country, as said before.

We went on still for two days, and still we found the land extending itself south, till the third day in the morning, when we were a little surprised to find ourselves, as it were, embayed, being in the bottom of a deep gulf, and the land appearing right ahead, distance about three leagues; the coast having turned away to the east and by south, very high land and mountainous, and the tops of some of the hills covered with snow.

Our second mate and the boatswain, upon this discovery, were for coming about, and sent to me for orders to make signals to the other ship and our brigantine, who were both ahead, to do the like; but I, who was willing to acquaint myself as fully as I could with the coast of the country, which I made no question I should have occasion to come to again, said, No, no, I will see a little farther first. So I ran on, having an easy gale at north-east and good weather, till I came within about a league and a half of the shore, when I found, that in the very bite or nook of the bay, there was a great inlet of water, which either must be a passage or strait between the land we had been on shore upon; which, in that case, must be a great island, or that it must be the mouth of some extraordinary great river.

This was a discovery too great to be omitted, so I ordered the brigantine to stand in with an easy sail, and see what account could be had of the place; accordingly they stood in, and we followed about a league, and then lay by, waiting their signals. I had particularly ordered them to keep two boats ahead to sound the depth all the way, and they did so; and how it happened we knew not, but on a sudden we heard the sloop fire two guns first, and then one gun; the first was a signal to us to bring to, and come no farther: the next was a signal of distress. We immediately tacked to stand off, but found a strong current setting directly into the bite, and there not being wind enough for us to stem the current, we let go our anchors in twenty fathoms water.

Immediately we manned out all the boats we had, great and small, to go and assist our brigantine, not knowing what distress she might be in; and they found that she had driven up, as we were like to have done, too far into the channel of a large river, the mouth of which, being very broad, had several shoals in it: and though she had dropped her anchor just upon notice, which the boats who were sounding gave her, yet she tailed aground upon a sand-bank, and stuck fast; our men made no doubt but she would be lost, and began to think of saving the provisions and ammunition out of her. The two long boats accordingly began to lighten her; and first they took in her guns, and let out all her casks of water: then they began to take in her great shot and the heavy goods. But by this time they found their mistake, for the current, which I mentioned, was nothing but a strong tide of flood, which, the indraught of the river being considerable, ran up with a very great force, and in something less than an hour the brigantine floated again.

However, she had stuck so long upon the sand, and the force of the current or tide had been so great, that she received considerable damage; and had a great deal of water in her hold. I immediately ordered out boats to row to the land, on both sides, to see if they could find a good place to lay her on shore in; they obeyed the order, and found a very convenient harbour in the mouth of a small river, which emptied itself into the great river about two leagues within the foreland of it, on the north side, as the river Medway runs into the Thames, within the mouth of it, on the south, side, only this was not so far up.

Here they ran in the sloop immediately, and the next day we came thither also; our boats having sounded the whole breadth, of the main river, and found a very good channel, half a league broad, having from seventeen to four-and-twenty fathoms water all the way, and very good riding.

Here we found it absolutely necessary to take everything out of the brigantine to search her bottom, for her lying on shore had strained her seams, and broke one of her floor timbers; and having hands enough, our men unloaded her in a very little time, and making a little dock for her, mended all the damage in about ten days' time. But seeing her in so good a condition, and the place so convenient, I resolved to have her whole bottom new calked and cleaned, that we made her as tight as she was when she first came off the stocks.

This I took for a good opportunity to careen and clean our other ships too; for we had done little to them since we came from Madagascar. We found our Madagascar ship much worm-eaten in her sheathing, which we helped as well as we could by new nailing and by taking out some pieces of her sheathing, and putting new ones in. But as to our great ship, she was sheathed with lead, and had received no damage at all; only that she was very foul, which we remedied by scraping and cleaning, and new graving her quite over.

We were not all employed in this work, and therefore we had leisure to make the best of our time for the main work of new discoveries. And now I resolved to leave it no more to under officers, as I had done before, viz., when I gave the command of the shallop that traded with the king and queen, as above, to a midshipman, which I was very sorry for, though the fellow did his business very well too; but, I say, I resolved not to trust any one now but myself.

In the first place, I took the two shallops and went across the mouth of the great river to the south shore, to see what kind of a country was to be found there. For, as to the north side, where we were, we found it to be much the same with that part where we had been before; with this difference only, whereas, in the other place gold was to be had in plenty, but here was none we could find; nor did we perceive that the people had any.

I found the mouth of this river, or inlet, to be about four leagues over where I crossed it, which was about three leagues and a half within the inlet itself. But the weather being very calm, and the flood-tide running sharp, we let our boat drive up, in our crossing, about two leagues more; and we found the channel grew narrow so fast, that, where we came to land, it was not full a league over; that about three leagues farther we found it a mere river, not above as broad as the Thames at Blackwall.

We found it a steep shore, and, observing a little creek very convenient for our purpose, we ran in our boats among some flags or rushes, and laid them as soft and as safe as if they had been in a dock; we went all on shore immediately, except two men in each boat left to guard our provisions.

We had for arms, every man a musket, a pistol, and a cutlass; and in each boat we had six half pikes, to use as we might have occasion. We had also every man a hatchet, hung in a little frog at his belt; and in each boat a broad axe and a saw.

We were furnished with strings of beads, bits of glass, glass rings, ear-rings, pearl necklaces, and suchlike jewellery ware innumerable; besides knives, scissors, needles, pins, looking-glasses, drinking-glasses, and toys in great plenty.

We were no sooner on shore but we found people in abundance; for there were two or three, small towns within a little way of the shore; and I suppose we might have the more people about us, because, as we understood afterwards, they had seen us before, though we had not seen them.

We made signs to them, by putting our fingers to our mouths, and moving our chaps as if we were eating, that we wanted provisions; and we hung up a white flag for a truce. They presently understood the first signal, but knew nothing of the last; and as to provisions, just as had been the case before, they brought us out roots and fruits, such as they ate themselves, but such as we had never seen before. Some of them, however, were very sweet and good, and when we boiled them they tasted much like an English parsnip; and we gave them strings of beads, pieces of glass, and such things as we remarked they were fond of.

We found the people, as I observed of the other, very inoffensive and sincere; not quarrelsome, nor treacherous, nor mischievous in the least. And we took care not so much as to let them know the use or manner of our fire-arms for a great while; neither was there one piece fired all the time we were among the other people, where we had so much gold. If there had, it had been very probable that they would have fled the country, in spite of all the good usage we could have been able to have shown them.

The people where we were now were not so rich in gold as those where we were before, but we found them much better stored with provisions; for besides deer, of which they had great plenty and variety, for they had some of a sort which I had never seen before, and besides an infinite number of those rabbits I have mentioned, which were as big as our hares, and which do not burrow in the ground as our rabbits do, they had also a kind of sheep, large, (like those of Peru, where they are used to carry burdens), and very good. They have no wool nor horns, but are rather hairy like a goat; nor should I call them sheep, but that their flesh eats like mutton, and I knew not what else to call them. The natives called them huttash; but what breed, or from what part of the world, or whether peculiar to this division alone, I know not.

However, their flesh was very agreeable, and they were fat and good; and as the Indians were mightily pleased with the price we paid them, and the goods we paid them in, they brought us more of these huttashes than we knew what to do with; and as I can calculate the rate, I suppose we might have them for about eight-pence, or sometimes not above sixpence cost each; for they would give us one very thankfully for a string or two of small beads, and think themselves mighty well paid.

I found them so plentiful, and so easy to come at, that in short I sent fifty of them alive, tied neck and heels, in one of the shallops back to our ships, and ordered them to send their long-boats over for more; for though it was so little a way over, we did not find they had any of them on that side the river.

We did the Indians another piece of service, for, if they gave us meat, we taught them to be cooks, for we showed them how to roast it upon a stick or spit before the fire; whereas they ate all their meat before, either stewed in earthen pots over the fire, with herbs, such as we did not understand, or thrown on burning fuel of green wood, which always made it taste and stink of the smoke most intolerably.

We had a great deal of opportunity now to converse with the people on both sides the river; and we found them to be not only different nations, but of different speech and different customs. These on the south side, where I now was, seemed to be the best furnished with provisions, and to live in the greatest plenty. But those on the north side appeared better clothed, and a more civilized sort of people; and of the two, seemed to have in their countenances something more agreeable.

However, as they were near neighbours, for the river only parted them, they were not very much unlike each other. That which seemed most strange to me was, that we found they had little knowledge or communication one with another. They had indeed some boats in the river, but they were very small, and rather served to just waft them over, or to fish in them, than for any other use; for we found none that could carry above four men, and those very oddly made, partly as a canoe, by hollowing a tree, and partly by skins of beasts, dried and stuck on in such a manner that they would paddle along at a great rate with them.

For want of understanding their language I could come at no knowledge of their religion or worship; nor did I see any idols among them, or any adoration paid to the sun or moon. But yet, as a confirmation that all nations, however barbarous, have some notion of a God, and some awe of a superior power, I observed here, that, in making a bargain with one of the principal men, (such I perceived him to be by the respect the rest showed him), I say, being making a bargain with him, as well as could be done between two people who understood not one word of what either said, he had made signs to bring me twelve sheep the next morning, for some things that I was to deliver him of mine. I am sure the goods were not all of them of value sufficient to give me the least distrust; but when I gave him the goods without the sheep, being, as I said, to trust him till the next day, he called two men to him, and pointing to the goods that I had put into his hands, he tells upon his fingers twelve, letting them know, as I supposed, that he was to give me twelve sheep the next day in return, and so far it appeared they were to be witnesses of the agreement. He then placed his two hands, one upon each breast, with the fingers turned up towards his face, and holding them thus he looked towards heaven, with his face turned upward also, and with the utmost gravity, seriousness, and solemnity in his countenance that ever I saw in any man's face in my life, he moved his lips in the action of speaking. When he had continued in this posture about a quarter of a minute, he took the two men, and put them in the same attitude, and then pointed to me, and next to himself; by which I understood, first, that he solemnly swore to me that he would bring the sheep punctually and faithfully to me, and then brought the two men to be bail or security for the performance; that is to say, to oblige themselves to perform it if he did not.

Doubtless those people who have any notion of a God must represent him to themselves as something superior, and something that sees, and hears, and knows what they say or do. Whether these people meant the sun, or the moon, or the stars, or other visible object, or whatever else, I do not pretend to determine, but it is certain they understood it to be something to swear by; something that could bear witness of their engagement, and that being called to witness it would resent their breach of promise if they made it. As to those whose gods are monsters, and hideous shapes, frightful images, and terrible figures, the motive of their adoration being that of mere terror, they have certainly gross ideas; but these people seem to act upon a more solid foundation, paying their reverence in a manner much more rational, and to something which it was much more reasonable to worship, as appeared in the solemnity of their countenances, and their behaviour in making a solemn promise.

We found those people clothed, generally speaking, over their whole bodies, their heads, arms, legs and feet excepted, but not so agreeably as those we mentioned above; and we found that the clothing of these were generally made of the skins of beasts, but very artfully put together, so that though they had neither needle nor thread, yet they had the same plant as I mentioned before, the stalk of which would so strongly tie like a thread, that they peeled it off thicker or finer as they had occasion, and made use of it abundance of ways to tie and twist, and make their clothes with it, as well for their occasion as if it had been woven in a loom.

We found several of these people had little bits of gold about them; but when we made signs to them to know where they got it, and where it might be had, they made signs to us, pointing to the country on the north side of the river; so that we had, it seems, fallen upon the right gold coast in our first coming. They pointed indeed likewise to some very high mountains, which we saw at a great distance south-west, so that it seems as if there was gold found that way also; but it appeared the people here had not much of it for their share.

The men here had bows and arrows, and they used them so dexterously, that a wild goose flying over our heads, one of the Indians shot it quite through with an arrow. One of our men was so provoked to see them, as it were, to outdo him, that, some time after, seeing a couple of ducks flying fair for a mark, he presented his piece, and shot them both flying.

I was very angry when I heard the gun; had I been there he had never got leave to fire; however, when it was done, I was pleased well enough to see the effect it had upon these poor innocent well-meaning people. At first it frightened them to the last degree, and I may truly say it frightened them out of their senses, for they that were near it started so violently, that they fell down and lay speechless for some time; those that were farther off ran away, as if it had been some new kind of lightning and thunder, and came out of the earth instead of out of the clouds; but when they saw the two creatures fall down dead from above, and could see nothing that flew upward to kill them, they were perfectly astonished, and laid their two hands on their breasts and looked up to heaven, as if they were saying their prayers, in the most solemn manner imaginable.

However, this accident gave them terrible ideas of us, and I was afraid at first they would run all away from us through fear. I therefore used them after it with all the kindness and tenderness imaginable, gave them every day some trifle or other, which, though of no value to me, they were exceedingly fond of; and we asked nothing of them in return but provisions, of which they had great plenty, and gave us enough every day to satisfy us. As for drink, they had none of the milky liquor which we had in the other part of the country, but they had a root which they steeped in water, and made it taste hot, as if pepper had been in it, which made it so strong, that though it would not make our men drunk, it was worse, for it made them nearly mad.

I was so pleased with these people that I came over to them every other day, and some of our men lay on shore, under a sail pitched for a tent; and they were so safe, that at last they kept no watch, for the poor people neither thought any harm, nor did any; and we never gave them the least occasion to apprehend anything from us, at least not till our man fired the gun, and that only let them know we were able to hurt them, without giving them the least suspicion that we intended it; on the contrary, one of our men played an odd prank with a child, and fully satisfied them that we would do them no harm. This man having seen one of their children, a little laughing speechless creature, of about two years old, the mother having gone from it a little way, on some particular occasion, the fellow took it and led it home to the tent, and kept it there all night.

The next morning, he dressed it up with beads and jewels wondrous fine, a necklace about its neck, and bracelets of beads about its wrists, and several strings of beads wrapped up and tied in its hair, having fed it and laid it to sleep, and made much of it.

In this figure he carried it up in his arms to the Indian's hut where he had found it, and where there had been a lamentable outcry for the child all the night, the mother crying and raising her neighbours, and in a most strange concern.

But when some of the women, her neighbours, saw the child brought back, there was a contrary extreme of joy; and the mother of it being fetched, she fell a-jumping and dancing to see her child, but also making so many odd gestures, as that our men could not well know for awhile whether she was pleased or not: the reason it seems was, she did not know whether to hope or fear, for she did not know whether the man would give back her child or take it away again.

But when the man who had the child in his arms had been told by signs that this was the mother, he beckoned to have her come to him, and she came, but trembling for fear. Then he took the child, and kissing it two or three times, gave it into her arms. But it is impossible to express by words the agony the poor woman was in; she took the child, and holding it in her arms fixed her eyes upon it without motion, or, as it were, without life, for a good while; then she took it and embraced it in the most passionate manner imaginable; when this was over, she fell a-crying so vehemently till she sobbed; and all this while spoke not one word. When the crying had given sufficient vent to her passion, then she fell a-dancing and making a strange odd noise, that cannot be described, and at last she left the child, and came back to the place where our men were, and to the man that brought her child, and, as soon as she came up to him, she fell flat on the ground, as I have described above the queen and her women did, and up again immediately; and thus she did three times, which it seems was her acknowledgment to him for bringing it back.

The next day, for her gratitude did not end here, she came down to our tent, and brought with her two sheep, with a great back-burden of roots of the kind which I said the natives steep in the water, and several fruits of the country, as much as two men who came with her could carry, and these she gave all to the man who had brought back her child. Our men were so moved at the affectionate carriage of this poor woman to her infant, that they told me it brought tears from their eyes.

The man who received the present took the woman and dressed her up almost as fine as he had done the child, and she went home like a kind of a queen among them.

We observed while we stayed here that this was a most incomparable soil; that the earth was a fat loamy mould; that the herbage was strong; that the grass in some places was very flourishing and good, being as high as our mid-thigh; and that the air was neither very hot, nor, as we believed, very cold. We made an experiment of the fruitfulness of the soil, for we took some white peas, and digging the ground up with a spade, we sowed some, and before we went away we saw them come out of the ground again, which was in about nine days.

We made signs to the people that they should let them grow, and that if they gathered them they were good to eat; we also sowed some English wheat, and let them know, as well as we could, what the use of them both was. But I make no doubt but they have been better acquainted with, both by this time, by an occasion which followed.

Our men were so fond of this place, and so pleased with the temper of the people, the fruitfulness of the soil, and agreeableness of the climate, that about twenty of them offered me, if I would give them my word to come again, or send to them to relieve and supply them with necessaries, they would go on shore and begin a colony, and live all their days there. Nay, after this, their number came up to three-and-thirty; or they offered that, if I would give them the sloop, and leave them a quantity of goods, especially of such toys as they knew would oblige the people to use them well, they would stay at all hazards, not doubting, as they told me, but they should come to England again at last, with the sloop full of gold.

I was not very willing to encourage either of these proposals, because, as I told them, I might perhaps find a place as fit to settle a colony in before we came home, which was not at such an excessive distance from England, so that it was scarce possible ever to relieve them. This satisfied them pretty well, and they were content to give over the project; and yet, at last, which was more preposterous than all the rest, five of our men and a boy ran away from us and went on shore, and what sort of life they led, or how they managed, we could not tell, for they were too far off us to inquire after them again. They took a small yawl with them, and it seems had furnished themselves privately with some necessary things, especially, tools, a grindstone, a barrel of powder, some peas, some wheat, and some barley; so that it seems they are resolved to plant there. I confess I pitied them, and when I had searched for them, and could not find them, I caused a letter to be written to them, and fixed it upon a post at the place where our ship careened; and another letter on the south side, to tell them that in such a certain place I had left other necessaries for them, which I did, made up in a large case of boards or planks, and covered with boards like a shed.

Here I left them hammocks for lodging, all sorts of tools for building them a house, spades, shovels, pickaxes, an axe, and two saws, with clothes, shoes, stockings, hats, shirts, and, in a word, every thing that I could think of for their use; and a large box of toys, beads, &c., to invite the natives to trade with them.

One of our men, whom they had made privy to their design, but made him promise not to reveal it until they were gone, had told them that he would persuade me, if he could, to leave them a farther supply; and bade them come to the place after the ships were gone, and that they should find directions left for them on a piece of a board, or a letter from him set up upon a post. Thus they were well furnished with all things for immediate living.

I make no doubt but they came to find these things; and, since they had a mind to make trial of a wild retired life, they might shift very well; nor would they want anything but English women to raise a new nation of English people, in a part of the world that belongs neither to Europe, Asia, Africa, or America. I also left them every man another gun, a cutlass, and a horn for powder; and I left two barrels of fine powder, and two pigs of lead for shot, in another chest by itself.

I doubt not but the natives will bestow wives upon them, but what sort of a posterity they will make, I cannot foresee, for I do not find by inquiry that the fellows had any great store of knowledge or religion in them, being all Madagascar men, as we called them, that is to say, pirates and rogues; so that, for aught I know, there may be a generation of English heathens in an age or two more; though I left them five Bibles, and six or seven Prayer-books, and good books of several sorts, that they might not want instruction, if they thought fit to make use of it for themselves or their progeny.

It is true, that this is a country that is remote from us of any in the yet discovered world, and consequently it would be suggested as unprofitable to our commerce; but I have something to allege in its defence, which will prove it to be infinitely more advantageous to England than any of our East India trade can be, or that can be pretended for it. The reason is plain in a few words; our East India trade is all carried on, or most part of it, by an exportation of bullion in specie, and a return of foreign manufactures or produce; and most of these manufactures also, either trifling and unnecessary in themselves, or such as are injurious to our own manufactures. The solid goods brought from India, which may be said to be necessary to us, and worth sending our money for, are but few; for example,

1. The returns which I reckon trifling and unnecessary, are such as China ware, coffee, tea, Japan work, pictures, fans, screens, &c.

2. The returns that are injurious to our manufactures, or growth of our own country, are printed calicoes, chintz, wrought silks, stuffs, of herbs and barks, block-tin, sugar, cotton, arrack, copper, and indigo.

3. The necessary or useful things are, pepper, saltpetre, dying-woods and dying-earths, drugs, lacs, such as shell-lac, stick-lac, &c., diamonds, some pearl, and raw-silk.

For all these we carry nothing or very little but money, the innumerable nations of the Indies, China, &c., despising our manufactures, and filling us with their own.

On the contrary, the people in the southern unknown countries, being first of all very numerous, and living in a temperate climate, which requires clothing, and having no manufactures, or materials for manufactures, of their own, would consequently take off a very great quantity of English woollen manufactures, especially when civilized by our dwelling among them, and taught the manner of clothing themselves for their ease and convenience; and, in return for these manufactures, it is evident we should have gold in specie, and perhaps spices, the best merchandise and return in the world.

I need say no more to excite adventurous heads to search out a country by which such an improvement might be made, and which would be such an increase of, or addition to, the wealth and commerce of our country.

Nor can it be objected here, that this nook of the country may not easily be found by any one but by us, who have been there before, and perhaps not by us again exactly; for, not to enter into our journal of observations for their direction, I lay it down as a foundation, that whoever sailing over the South Seas keeps a stated distance from the tropic, to the latitude of 56 to 60°, and steers eastward towards the Straits of Magellan, shall never fail to discover new worlds, new nations, and new inexhaustible funds of wealth and commerce, such as never were yet known to the merchants of Europe.

This is the true ocean called the South Sea; that part which we corruptly call so can be so in no geographical account, or by any rule, but by the mere imposition of custom, it being only originally called so, because they that sailed to it were obliged to go round the southernmost part of America to come into it; whereas it ought indeed to be called the West Sea, as it lies on the west side of America, and washes the western shore of that great continent for near eight thousand miles in length; to wit, from 56° south of the line to 70° north, and how much farther we know not; on this account I think it ought to be called the American Ocean, rather than with such impropriety the South Sea.

But this part of the world where we were may rightly be called the South Sea, by way of distinction, as it extends from India round the globe, to India again, and lies all south of the line even, for aught we know, to the very South Pole, and which, except some interposition of land, whether islands or continent, really surrounds the South Pole.

We were now in the very centre or middle of this South Sea, being, as I have said, in the latitude of 34° 20'; but having had such good success in our inquiry or search after new continents, I resolved to steer to the south and south-east, as far as till we should be interrupted by land or ice, determining to search this unknown part of the globe as far as nature would permit, that I might be able to give some account to my employers, and some light to other people that might come that way, whether by accident or by design.

We had spent six-and-twenty days in this place, as well in repairing our brigantine and careening, as trimming our ship; we had not been so long, but, that we did not resolve to careen our ships till we had spent ten days about the brigantine, and then we found more work to do to the sheathing of the Madagascar ship than we expected.

We stored ourselves here with fresh provisions and water, but got nothing that we could properly call a store, except the flesh of about thirty deer, which we dried in the sun, and which proved indifferently good afterwards, but not extraordinary.

We sailed again the six-and-twentieth day after we came in, having a fair wind at north and north-north-west, and a fresh gale which held us five days without intermission; in which time, running away south and south-south-east, we reached the former latitude, where we had been, and meeting with nothing remarkable, we steered a little farther to the eastward; but keeping a southerly course still, till we came into the latitude of 41°, and then going due east, with the wind at north and by west, we reckoned our meridian distance from the Ladrones, to be 50° 30'.

In all this run we saw no land, so we hauled two points more southerly, and went on for six or seven days more; when one of our men on the round top, cried Land! It was a clear fine morning, and the land he espied being very high, it was found to be sixteen leagues distance; and the wind slackening, we could not get in that night, so we lay by till morning, when being fair with the land, we hoisted our boat to go and sound the shore, as usual. The men rowed in close with the shore and found a little cove, where there was good riding, but very deep water, being no less than sixty fathoms within cable's length of the shore.

We went in, however, and after we were moored sent our boat on shore to look for water, and what else the country afforded. Our men found water, and a good sort of country, but saw no inhabitants; and, upon coasting a little both ways on the shore, they found it to be an island, and without people; but said that about three leagues off to the southward, there seemed to be a Terra Firma, or continent of land, where it was more likely we should make some discovery.

The next day we filled water again, and shot some ducks, and the day after weighed and stood over for the main, as we thought it to be. Here, using the same caution as we always had done, viz., of sounding the coast, we found a bold shore and very good anchor hold, in six-and-twenty to thirty fathoms.

When we came on shore, we found people, but of a quite different condition from those we had met with before, being wild, furious, and untractable; surprised at the sight of us, but not intimidated; preparing for battle, not for trade; and no sooner were we on shore but they saluted us with their bows and arrows. We made signals of truce to them, but they did not understand us, and we knew not what to offer them more but the muzzles of our muskets; for we were resolved to see what sort of folks they were, either by fair means or foul.

The first time, therefore, that they shot at our men with their bows and arrows, we returned the salute with our musket-ball, and kill two of their foremost archers. We could easily perceive that the noise of our pieces terrified them, and the two men being killed, they knew not how, or with what, perfectly astonished them; so that they ran, as it were, clean out of the country, that is to say, clean out of our reach, for we could never set our eyes upon them after it. We coasted this place also, according to our usual custom; and, to our great surprise, found it was an island too, though a large one; and that the mainland lay still more to the southward, about six leagues distance, so we resolved to look out farther, and accordingly set sail the next day, and anchored under the shore of this last land, which we were persuaded was really the main.

We went on shore here peaceably, for we neither saw any people, or the appearance of any, but a charming pleasant valley, of about ten or eleven miles long, and five or six miles broad; and then it was surrounded with mountains, which reached the full length, running parallel with the valley, and closing it in to the sea at both ends; so that it was a natural park, having the sea on the north side, and the mountains in a semicircle round all the rest of it. These hills were so high, and the ways so untrod and so steep, that our men, who were curious enough to have climbed up to the top of them, could find no way that was practicable to get up, and after two or three attempts gave it over.

In this vale we found abundance of deer, and abundance of the same kind of sheep which I mentioned lately. We killed as many of both as we had occasion for; and, finding nothing here worth our staying any longer for, except that we saw something like wild rice growing here, we weighed after three days, and stood away still to the south.

We had not sailed above two days with little wind and an easy sail, when we perceived this also was an island, though it must be a large one; for, by our account, we sailed near a hundred and fifty miles along the shore of it, and we found the south part a flat pleasant country enough; and our men said they saw people upon it on the south side, but we went not on shore there any more.

Steering due south from hence in quest of the mainland, we went on eleven days more, and saw nothing significant, and, upon a fair observation, I found we were in the latitude of 47° 8' south; then I altered my course a little to the eastward, finding no land, and the weather very cold, and going on with a fresh gale at south-south-west for four days, we made land again; but it was now to the east-north-east, so that we were gotten, as we may say, beyond it.

We fell in with this land in the evening, so that it was not perceived till we were within half a league of it, which very much alarmed us, the land being low; and having found our error, we brought to and stood off and on till morning, when we saw the shore lie, as it were, under our larboard bow, within a mile and a quarter distance, the land low, but the sea deep and soft ground. We came to anchor immediately, and sent our shallops to sound the shore, and the men found very good riding in a little bay, under the shelter of two points of land, one of which made a kind of hook, under which we lay secure from all winds that could blow, in seventeen fathoms good ground. Here we had a good observation, and found ourselves in the latitude of 50° 21'. Our next work was to find water, and our boats going on shore, found plenty of good water and some cattle, but told us they could give no account what the cattle were, or what they were like. In searching the coast, we soon found this was an island also, about eleven leagues in length, from north-west to south-east, what breadth we could not tell. Our men also saw some signs of inhabitants. The next day six men appeared at a distance, but would take notice of no signals, and fled as soon as our men advanced. Our people went up to the place were they lay, and found they had made a fire of some dry wood; that they had laid there, as they suppose, all night, though without covering. They found two pieces of old ragged skins of deer, which looked as if worn out by some that had used them for clothing, and one piece of a skin of some other creature, which had been rolled up into a cap for the head; also a couple of arrows of about four feet long, very thick, and made of a hard and heavy wood; so they must have very large and strong bows to shoot such arrows, and consequently must be men of an uncommon strength.

Our men wandered about the country three or four days, with less caution than the nature of their situation required; for they were not among a people of an innocent, inoffensive temper here, as before, but among a wild, untractable nation, that perhaps had never seen creatures in their own likeness before, and had no thought of themselves but of being killed and destroyed, and consequently had no thought of those they had seen but as of enemies, whom they must either destroy, if they were able, or escape from them if they were not. However, we got no harm, neither would the natives ever appear to accept any kindnesses from us.

We had no business here, after we found what sort of people they were who inhabited this place; so, as soon as we had taken in fresh water, and caught some fish, of which we found good store in the bay or harbour where we rode, we prepared to be gone. Here we found the first oysters that we saw anywhere in the South Seas; and, as our men found them but the day before we were to sail, they made great entreaty to me to let them stay one day to get a quantity on board, they being very refreshing, as well as nourishing, to our men.

But I was more easily prevailed with to stay, when Captain Merlotte brought me, out of one oyster that he happened to open, a true oriental pearl, so large and so fine, that I sold it, since my return, for three-and-fifty pounds.

After taking this oyster, I ordered all our boats out a dredging, and in two days' time so great a quantity there was, that our men had taken above fifty bushels, most of them very large. But we were surprised and disappointed, when, at the opening all those oysters, we found not one pearl, small or great, of any kind whatever, so we concluded that the other was a lucky hit only, and that perhaps there might not be any more of that kind in these seas.

While we were musing on the oddness of this accident, the boatswain of the Madagascar ship, whose boat's crew had brought in the great oyster in which the pearl was found, and who had been examining the matter, came and told me that it was true that their boat had brought in the oyster, and that it was before they went out a dredging in the offing, but that their boat took these oysters on the west side of the island, where they had been shoring, as they called it, that is to say, coasting along the shore, to see if they could find anything worth their labour, but that afterwards the boats went a dredging in the mouth of the bay where we rode, and where, finding good store of oysters, they had gone no farther.

Upon this intelligence we ordered all hands to dredging again, on the west side of the island. This was in a narrow channel, between this island and a little cluster of islands which we found together extended west, the channel where our men fished might be about a league over, or something better, and the water about five or seven fathoms deep.

They came home well tired and ill pleased, having taken nothing near so many oysters, as before; but I was much better pleased, when, in opening them, we found a hundred and fifty-eight pearls, of the most perfect colour, and of extraordinary shape and size, besides double the number of a less size, and irregular shape.

This quickened our diligence, and encouraged our men, for I promised the men two pieces of eight to each man above his pay, if I got any considerable quantity of pearl. Upon this they spread themselves among the islands, and fished for a whole week, and I got such a quantity of pearl as made it very well worth our while; and, besides that, I had reason to believe the men, at least the officers who went with them, concealed a considerable quantity among themselves; which, however, I did not think fit to inquire very strictly after at that time.

Had we been nearer home, and not at so very great an expense, as three ships, and so many men at victuals and wages, or had we been where we might have left one of our vessels to fish, and have come to them again, we would not have given it over while there had been an oyster left in the sea, or, at least, that we could come at: but as things stood, I resolved to give it over, and put to sea.

But when I was just giving orders, Captain Merlotte came to me, and told me that all the officers in the three ships had joined together to make an humble petition to me, which was, that I would give them one day to fish for themselves; that the men had promised that, if I would consent, they would work for them gratis; and likewise, if they gained anything considerable, they would account for as much out of their wages as should defray the ships' expense, victuals, and wages, for the day.

This was so small a request, that I readily consented to it, and told them I would give them three days, provided they were willing to give the men a largess, as I had done, in proportion to their gain. This they agreed to, and to work they went; but whether it was that the fellows worked with a better will, or that the officers gave them more liquor, or that they found a new bank of oysters, which had not been found out before, but so it was, that the officers got as many pearls, and some of extraordinary size and beauty, as they afterwards sold, when they came to Peru, for three thousand two hundred and seventeen pieces of eight.

When they had done this, I told them it was but right that, as they had made so good a purchase for themselves by the labour of the men, the men should have the consideration which I had proposed to them. But now I would make another condition with them, that we would stay three days more, and whatever was caught in these three days should be shared among the men at the first port we came at, where they could be sold, that the men who had now been out so long might have something to buy clothes and liquors, without anticipating their wages; but then I made a condition with the men too, viz., that whatever was taken they should deposit it in my hands, and with the joint trust of three men of their own choosing, one out of each ship, and that we would sell the pearl, and I should divide the money among them equally, that so there might be no quarrelling or discontent, and that none of them should play any part of it away. These engagements they all came willingly into, and away they went a dredging, relieving one another punctually, so that in the three whole days every man worked an equal share of hours with the rest.

But the poor men had not so good luck for themselves as they had for their officers. However, they got a considerable quantity, and some very fine ones; among the rest they had two in the exact shape of a pear, and very exactly matched; and these they would needs make me a present of, because I had been so kind to them to make the proposal for them. I would have paid for them two hundred pieces of eight, but one and all, they would not be paid, and would certainly have been very much troubled if I had not accepted of them. And yet the success of the men was not so small but, joined with the two pieces of eight a man which I allowed them on the ships' account, and the like allowance the officers made them, and the produce of their own purchase, they divided afterwards about fifteen pieces of eight a man, which was a great encouragement to them.

Thus we spent in the whole, near three weeks here, and called these the Pearl Islands, though we had given no names to any of the places before. We were the more surprised with this unexpected booty, because we all thought it very unusual to find pearl of so excellent a kind in such a latitude as that of 49 to 50°; but it seems there are riches yet unknown in those parts of the world, where they have never been yet expected, and I have been told, by those who pretend to give a reason for it, that if there was any land directly under the poles, either south or north, there would be found gold of a fineness more than double to any that was ever yet found in the world: and this is the reason, they say, why the magnetic influence directs to the poles, that being the centre of the most pure metals, and why the needle touched with the loadstone or magnet always points to the north or south pole. But I do not recommend this, as a certainty, because it is evident no demonstration could ever be arrived at, nor could any creature reach to that particular spot of land under the pole, if such there should be, those lands being surrounded with mountains of snow and frozen seas, which never thaw, and are utterly impassable either for ships or men.

But to return to our voyage; having thus spent as I have said, three weeks on this unexpected expedition, we set sail, and as I was almost satisfied with the discoveries we had made, I was for bending my course due east and so directly for the south part of America; but the winds now blowing fresh from the north-west, and good weather, I took the occasion as a favourable summons, to keep still on southing as well as east till we came into the latitude of 56°, when our men, who had been all along a warm weather voyage, began to be pinched very much with the cold, and particularly complained that they had no clothes sufficient for it.

But they were brought to be content by force; for the wind continuing at north and north-north-west, and blowing very hard, we were obliged to keep on our course farther south, indeed, than I ever intended, and one of the men swore we should be driven to the south pole. Indeed, we rather ran afore it than kept our course, and in this run we suffered the extremest cold, though a northerly wind in those latitudes is the warm wind, as a southerly is here; but it was attended with rain and snow, and both freezing violently. At length one of our men cried out, Land, and our men began to rejoice; but I was quite of a different opinion, and my fears were but too just, for as soon as ever he cried Land, and that I asked him in what quarter, and he answered due south, which was almost right ahead, I gave orders to wear the ship, and put her about immediately, not doubting but instead of land I should find it a mountain of ice, and so it was; and it was happy for us that we had a stout ship under us, for it blew a fret of wind. However, the ship came very well about, though when she filled again, we found the ice not half a league distance under our stern.

As I happened to be the headmost ship, I fired two guns to give notice to our other vessels, for that was our signal to come about, but that which was very uneasy to me, the weather was hazy, and they were both out of sight; which was the first time that we lost one another in those seas; however, being both to windward, and within hearing of my guns, they took the warning, and came about with more leisure and less hazard than I had done.

I stood away now to the eastward, firing guns continually, that they might know which way to follow; and they answered me duly, to let me know that they heard me.

It was our good fortune also, that it was day when we were so near running into this danger. In the afternoon the wind abated, and the weather cleared up; we then called a council, and resolved to go no farther south, being then in the latitude of 67° south, which I suppose is the farthest southern latitude that any European ship ever saw in those seas.

That night it froze extremely hard, and the wind veering to the south-west, it was the severest cold that ever I felt in my life; a barrel or cask of water, which stood on the deck, froze entirely in one night into one lump, and our cooper, knocking off the hoops from the cask, took it to pieces, and the barrel of ice stood by itself, in the true shape of the vessel it had been in. This wind was, however, favourable to our deliverance, for we stood away now north-east and north-east-by-north, making fresh way with a fair wind.

We made no more land till we came into the latitude of 62°, when we saw some islands at a great distance, on both sides of us; we believed them to be islands, because we saw many of them with large openings between. But we were all so willing to get into a warmer climate, that we did not incline to put in anywhere, till, having run thus fifteen days and the wind still holding southerly, with small alteration and clear weather, we could easily perceive the climate to change, and the weather grow milder. And here taking an observation, I found we were in the latitude of 50° 30', and that our meridian distance from the Ladrones west was 87°, being almost one semi-diameter of the globe, so that we could not be far from the coast of America, which was my next design, and indeed the chief design of the whole voyage.

On this expectation I changed my course a little, and went away north-by-east, till by an observation I found myself in 47° 7', and then standing away east for about eleven days more, we made the tops of the Andes, the great mountains of Chili, in South America, to our great joy and satisfaction, though at a very great distance.

We found our distance from the shore not less than twenty leagues, the mountains being so very high; and our next business was to consider what part of the Andes it must be, and to what port we should direct ourselves first. Upon the whole, we found we were too much to the south still, and resolved to make directly for the river or port of Valdivia, or Baldivia, as it is sometimes called, in the latitude of 40°; so we stood away to the north. The next day the pacific, quiet sea, as it is termed, showed us a very frowning rough countenance, and proved the very extreme of a contrary disposition; for it blew a storm of wind at east-by-south, and drove us off the coast again, but it abated again for a day or two; and then for six days together it blew excessive hard, almost all at east, so that I found no possibility of getting into the shore; and besides, I found that the winds came off that mountainous country in squalls, and that the nearer we came to the hills the gusts were the more violent. So I resolved to run for the island of Juan Fernandez, to refresh ourselves there until the weather was settled; and besides, we wanted fresh water very much.

The little that the wind stood southerly helped me in this run, and we came in five days more, fair with the island, to our great joy, and brought all our ships to an anchor as near the watering-place as is usual, where we rode easy, though, the wind continued to blow very hard; and being, I say, now about the middle of our voyage, I shall break off my account here, as of the first part of my work, and begin again at our departure from hence.

It is true, we had got over much the greater run, as to length of way; but the most important part of our voyage was yet to come, and we had no inconsiderable length to run neither, for as we purposed to sail north, the height of Panama, in the latitude of 9° north, and back again by Cape Horn, in the latitude of, perhaps, 60° south, and that we were now in 40° south; those three added to the run, from Cape Horn home to England made a prodigious length, as will be seen by this following account, in which also the meridian distances are not all reckoned, though those also are very great.

From Juan Fernandez to the Line	30
From the Line to Panama	9
From Panama to Cape Horn, including the distance we take in going round	60
From Cape Horn to the Line again in the North Seas	60
From the Line to England	51
	—
	210 Deg.
	—

N.B. There must be deducted from this account the distance from Lima to Panama, because we did not go up to Panama, as we intended to do.

By this account we had almost 30° to run more than a diameter of the globe, besides our distance west, where we then were, from the meridian of England, whither we were to go; which, if exactly calculated, is above 70°, take it from the island of Juan Fernandez.

But to return a little to our stay in this place, for that belongs to this part of my account, and of which I must make a few short observations.

It was scarce possible to restrain Englishmen, after so long beating the sea, from going on shore when they came to such a place of refreshment as this; nor indeed was it reasonable to restrain them, considering how we all might be supposed to stand in need of refreshment, and considering that here was no length of ground for the men to wander in, no liquors to come at to distract them with their excess, and, which was still more, no women to disorder or debauch them. We all knew their chief exercise would be hunting goats for their subsistence, and we knew also, that, however they wanted the benefit of fresh provision, they must work hard to catch it before they could taste the sweet of it. Upon these considerations, I say, our ships being well moored, and riding safe, we restrained none of them, except a proper number to take care of each ship; and those were taken out by lot, and then had their turn also to go on shore some days afterwards, and in the mean time had both fresh water and fresh meat sent them immediately, and that in sufficient quantity to their satisfaction. As soon as we were on shore, and had looked about us, we began first with getting some fresh water, for we greatly wanted it. Then carrying a small cask of arrack on shore, I made a quantity of it be put into a whole butt of water before I let our men drink a drop; so correcting a little the chilness of the water, because I knew they would drink an immoderate quantity, and endanger their healths, and the effect answered my care; for, those who drank at the spring where they took in the water, before I got this butt filled, and before the arrack was put into it, fell into swoonings and faint sweats, having gorged themselves too much with the cool water; and two or three I thought would have died, but our surgeons took such care of them, that they recovered.

While this was doing, others cut down branches of trees and built us two large booths, and five or six smaller, and we made two tents with some old sails; and thus we encamped, as if we had been to take up our dwelling, and intended to people the island.

At the same time, others of our men began to look out for goats, for it may be believed we all longed for a meal of fresh meat. They were a little too hasty at their work at first, for firing among the first goats they came at, when there were but a few men together, they frighted all the creatures, and they ran all away into holes, and among the rocks and places where we could not find them; so that for that day they made little of it. However, sending for more firemen, they made a shift to bring in seventeen goats the same day, whereof we sent five on board the ships, and feasted with the rest on shore. But the next day the men went to work in another manner, and with better conduct; for as we had hands enough, and fire-arms enough, they spread themselves so far, that they, as it were, surrounded the creatures; and so driving them out of their fastnesses and retreats, they had no occasion to shoot, for the goats could not get from them, and they took them everywhere with their hands, except some of the old he-goats, which were so surly, that they would stand at bay and rise at them, and would not be taken; and these, as being old also, and as they thought, good for nothing, they let go.

In short, so many of our men went on shore, and these divided themselves into so many little parties, and plyed their work so hard, and had such good luck, that I told them it looked as if they had made a general massacre of the goats, rather than a hunting.

Our men also might be said not to refresh themselves, but to feast themselves here with fresh provisions; for though we stayed but thirteen days, yet we killed three hundred and seventy goats, and our men who were on board were very merrily employed, most assuredly, for they might be said to do very little but roast and stew, and broil and fry, from morning to night. It was indeed an exceeding good supply to them, for they had been extremely fatigued with the last part of their voyage, and had tasted of no fresh provisions for six weeks before.

This made them hunt the goats with the more eagerness, and indeed, they surrounded them so dexterously, and followed them so nimbly, that notwithstanding the difficulties of the rocks, yet the goats could hardly ever escape them. Here our men found also very good fish, and some few tortoises, or turtles, as the seamen call them, but they valued them not, when they had such plenty of venison; also they found some very good herbs in the island, which they boiled with the goats' flesh, and which made their broth very savoury and comfortable, and withal very healing, and good against the scurvy, which in those climates Englishmen are very subject to.

We were now come to the month of April, 1715, having spent almost eight months in this trafficking wandering voyage from Manilla hither. And whoever shall follow the same, or a like track, if ever such a thing shall happen, will do well to make a year of it, and may find it very well worth while.

I doubt not but there are many undiscovered parts of land to the west, and to the south also, of the first shore, of which I mentioned, that we stayed trafficking for little bits of gold. And though it is true that such traffick, as I have given an account of, is very advantageous in itself, and worth while to look for, especially after having had a good market for an out-ward-bound European cargo, according to the pattern of ours, at the Philippines, and which, by the way, they need not miss, I say, as this trade for gold would be well worth while, so had we gone the best way, and taken a course more to the south from Manilla, not going away east to the Ladrones, we should certainly have fallen in with a country, from the coast of New Guinea, where we might have found plenty of spices, as well as of gold.

For why may we not be allowed to suppose that the country on the same continent, and in the same latitude, should produce the same growth? Especially considering them situated, as it may be called, in the neighbourhood of one another.

Had we then proceeded this way, no question but we might have fixed on some place for a settlement, either English or French, whence a correspondence being established with Europe, either by Cape Horn east, or the Cape De Bona Esperance west, as we had thought fit, they might have found as great a production of the nutmegs and the cloves as at Banda and Ternate, or have made those productions have been planted there for the future, where no doubt they would grow and thrive as well as they do now in the Moluccas.

But we spun out too much time for the business we did; and though we might, as above, discover new places, and get very well too, yet we did nothing in comparison of what we might be supposed to have done, had we made the discovery more our business.

I cannot doubt, also, but that when we stood away south it was too late; for had we stood into the latitude of 67° at first, as we did afterwards, I have good reason to believe that those islands which we call the Moluccas, and which lie so thick and for so great an extent, go on yet farther, and it is scarce to be imagined that they break off just with Gilloto.

This I call a mistake in me, namely, that I stood away east from the Philippines to the Ladrones, before I had gone any length to the south.

But to come to the course set down in this work, namely, south-east and by east from the Ladrones, the places I have taken notice of, as these do not, in my opinion, appear to be inconsiderable and of no value, so had we searched farther into them, I doubt not but there are greater things to be discovered, and perhaps a much greater extent of land also. For as I have but just, as it were, described the shell, having made no search for the kernel, it is more than probable, that within the country there might be greater discoveries made, of immense value too. For even, as I observed several times, whenever we found any people who had gold, and asked them, as well as by signs we could make them understand, they always pointed to the rivers and the mountains which lay farther up the country, and which we never made any discovery of, having little in our view but the getting what little share of gold the poor people had about them. Whereas had we taken possession of the place, and left a number of men sufficient to support themselves, in making a farther search, I cannot doubt but there must be a great deal of that of which the inactive Indians had gotten but a little.

Nor had we one skilful man among us to view the face of the earth, and see what treasure of choice vegetables might be there. We had indeed six very good surgeons, and one of them, whom we took in among the Madagascar men, was a man of great reading and judgment; but he acknowledged he had no skill in botanics, having never made it his study.

But to say the truth, our doctors themselves (so we call the surgeons at sea) were so taken up in their traffick for gold, that they had no leisure to think of anything else. They did indeed pick up some shells, and some strange figured skeletons of fishes and small beasts, and other things, which they esteemed as rarities; but they never went a simpling, as we call it, or to inquire what the earth brought forth that was rare, and not to be found anywhere else.

I think, likewise, it is worth observing, how the people we met with, where it is probable no ships, much less European ships, had ever been, and where they had never conversed with enemies, or with nations accustomed to steal and plunder; I say, the people who lived thus, had no fire, no rage in their looks, no jealous fears of strangers doing them harm, and consequently no desire to do harm to others. They had bows and arrows indeed, but it was rather to kill the deer and fowls, and to provide themselves with food, than to offend their enemies, for they had none.

When, therefore, removing from thence, we came to other and different nations, who were ravenous and mischievous, treacherous and fierce, we concluded they had conversed with other nations, either by going to them, or their vessels coming there. And to confirm me in this opinion, I found these fierce false Indians had canoes and boats, some of one kind, and some of another, by which perhaps, they conversed with the islands or other nations near them, and that they also received ships and vessels from other nations, by which they had several occasions to be upon their guard, and learned the treacherous and cruel parts from others which nature gave them no ideas of before.

As the natives of these places were tractable and courteous, so they would be made easily subservient and assistant to any European nation that would come to make settlements among them, especially if those European nations treated them with humanity and courtesy; for I have made it a general observation, concerning the natural disposition of all the savage nations that ever I met with, that if they are once but really obliged they will always be very faithful.

But it is our people, I mean the Europeans, who, by breaking faith with them, teach them ingratitude, and inure them to treat their new comers with breach of faith, and with cruelty and barbarity. If you once win them by kindness, and doing them good, I mean at first, before they are taught to be rogues by example, they will generally be honest, and be kind also, to the uttermost of their power.

It is to be observed, that it has been the opinion of all the sailors who have navigated those parts of the world, that farther south there are great tracts of undiscovered land; and some have told us they have seen them, and have called them by such and such name, as, particularly, the Isles of Solomon, of which yet we can read of nobody that ever went on shore on them, or that could give any account of them, except such as are romantic, and not to be depended upon.

But what has been the reason why we have hitherto had nothing but guesses made at those things, and that all that has been said of such lands has been imperfect? The reason, if I may speak my opinion, has been, because it is such a prodigious run from the coast of America to the islands of the Ladrones, that the few people who have performed it never durst venture to go out of the way of the trade-winds, lest they should not be able to subsist for want of water and provisions; and this is particularly the case in the voyage from the coast of America only.

Whereas, to go the way which I have marked out, had we seen a necessity, and that there was no land to be found to the south of the tropic for a supply of provisions and fresh water, it is evident we could have gone back again, from one place to another, and have been constantly supplied; and this makes it certain also, that it cannot be reasonably undertaken by a ship going from the east, I mean the coast of America, to the west; but, from the west, viz., the Spice Islands to America west, it may be adventured with ease, as I have shown.

It is true, that William Cornelius Van Schouten and Francis le Maire, who first found the passage into the South Sea by Cape Horn, and not to pass the Straits of Magellan, I say, they did keep to the southward of the tropic, and pass in part the same way I have here given an account of, as by their journals, which I have by me at this time, is apparent.

And it is as true also, that they did meet with many islands and unknown shores in those seas, where they got refreshment, especially fresh water: perhaps some of the places were the same I have described in this voyage, but why they never pursued that discovery, or marked those islands and places they got refreshments at, so that others in quest of business might have touched at them and have received the like benefit, that I can give no account of.

I cannot help being of opinion, let our map makers place them where they will, that those islands where we so successfully fished for oysters, or rather for pearl, are the same which the ancient geographers have called Solomon's Islands; and though they are so far south, the riches of them may not be the less, nor are they more out of the way. On the contrary, they lie directly in the track which our navigators would take, if they thought fit, either to go or come between Europe and the East Indies, seeing they that come about Cape Horn seldom go less south than the latitude of 63 or 64°; and these islands, as I have said, lie in the latitude of 40 to 48° south, and extend themselves near one hundred and sixty leagues in breadth from north to south.

Without doubt those islands would make a very noble settlement, in order to victual and relieve the European merchants in so long a run as they have to make; and when this trade came to be more frequented, the calling of those ships there would enrich the islands, as the English at St. Helena are enriched by the refreshing which the East India ships find that meet there.

But to return to our present situation at Juan Fernandez. The refreshment which our men found here greatly encouraged and revived them; and the broths and stewings which we made of the goats' flesh which we killed there, than which nothing could be wholesomer, restored all our sick men, so that we lost but two men in our whole passage from the East Indies, and had lost but eight men in our whole voyage from England, except I should reckon those five men and a boy to be lost which run away from us in the country among the Indians, as I have already related.

I should have added, that we careened and cleaned our ships here, and put ourselves into a posture for whatever adventures might happen; for as I resolved upon a trading voyage upon the coast of Chili and Peru, and a cruising voyage also, as it might happen, so I resolved also to put our ships into a condition for both, as occasion should present.

Our men were nimble at this work, especially having been so well refreshed and heartened up by their extraordinary supply of fresh meats, and the additions of good broths and soups which they fed on every day in the island, and with which they were supplied without any manner of limitation all the time they were at work.

This I say being their case, they got the Madagascar ship hauled down, and her bottom washed and tallowed, and she was as clean as when she first came off the stocks in five days' time: and she was rigged, and all set to rights, and fit for sailing in two more.

The great ship was not so soon fitted, nor was I in so much haste, for I had a design in my head which I had not yet communicated to anybody, and that was to send the Madagascar ship a-cruising as soon as she was fitted up; accordingly, I say, the fifth day she was ready, and I managed it so that the captain of the Madagascar ship openly, before all the men, made the motion, as if it had been his own project, and desired I would let him go and try his fortune, as he called it.

I seemed unwilling at first, but he added to his importunity, that he and all his crew were desirous, if they made any purchase, it should be divided among all the crews in shares, according as they were shipped; that if it was provisions, the captain should buy it at half price, for the use of the whole, and the money to be shared.

Upon hearing his proposals, which were esteemed very just, and the men all agreeing, I gave consent, and so he had my orders and instructions, and leave to be out twelve days on his cruise, and away he went. His ship was an excellent sailer, as has been said, and being now a very clean vessel, I thought he might speak with any other, or get away from her if he pleased; by the way, I ordered him to put out none but French colours.

He cruised a week without seeing a sail, and stood in quite to the Spanish shore in one place, but in that he was wrong. The eighth day, giving over all expectations, he stood off again to sea, and the next morning he spied a sail, which proved to be a large Spanish ship, and that seemed to stand down directly upon him, which a little checked his forwardness; however, he kept on his course, when the Spaniard seeing him plainer than probably he had done at first, tacked, and crowding all the sail he could carry, stood in for the shore.

The Spaniard was a good sailer, but our ship plainly gained upon her, and in the evening came almost up with her; when he saw the land, though at a great distance, he was loath to be seen chasing her from the shore; however, he followed, and night coming on, the Spaniard changed his course, thinking to get away, but as the moon was just rising, our men, who resolved to keep her in sight, if possible, perceived her, and stretched after her with all the canvass they could lay on.

This chase held till about midnight, when our ship coming up with her, took her after a little dispute. They pretended, at first, to have nothing on board but timber, which they were carrying, as they said, to some port for the building of ships; but our men had the secret to make the Spaniards confess their treasure, if they had any, so that after some hard words with the Spanish commander, he confessed he had some money on board, which, on our men's promise of good usage, he afterwards very honestly delivered, and which might amount to about sixteen thousand pieces of eight.

But he had what we were very glad of besides, viz., about two hundred great jars of very good wheat flour, a large quantity of oil, and some casks of sweetmeats, all which was to us very good prize.

But now our difficulty was, what we should do with the ship, and with the Spaniards; and this was so real a difficulty that I began to wish he had not taken her, lest her being suffered to go, she should alarm the country, or if detained, discover us all.

It was not above one day beyond his orders that we had the pleasure of seeing the captain of the Madagascar come into the road, with his prize in tow, and the flour and oil was a very good booty to us; but upon second and better thoughts, we brought the Spaniards to a fair treaty, and, which was more difficult, brought all our men to consent to it. The case was this. Knowing what I proposed to myself to do, namely, to trade all the way up the Spanish coast, and to pass for French ships, I knew the taking this Spanish ship would betray us all, unless I resolved to sink the ship and murder all the men; so I came to a resolution of talking with the Spanish captain, and making terms with him, which I soon made him very glad to accept of.

First, I pretended to be angry with the captain of the Madagascar ship, and ordered him to be put under confinement, for having made a prize of his catholic majesty's subjects, we being subjects to the king of France, who was in perfect peace with the king of Spain.

Then I told him that I would restore him his ship and all his money, and as to his flour and oil, which the men had fallen greedily upon, having a want of it, I would pay him the full value in money for it all, and for any other loss he had sustained, only that I would oblige him to lie in the road at the island where we were, till we returned from our voyage to Lima, whither we were going to trade, for which lying I also agreed to pay him demurrage for his ship, after the rate of eight hundred pieces of eight per month, and if I returned not in four months, he was to be at his liberty to go.

The captain, who thought himself a prisoner and undone, readily embraced this offer; and so we secured his ship till our return, and there we found him very honestly at an anchor, of which I shall give a farther account in its place.

We were now, as I have said, much about the middle of our voyage, at least as I had intended it; and having stored ourselves with every thing the place afforded, we got ready to proceed, for we had, as it were, dwelt here near a fortnight.

By this time the weather was good again, and we stood away to the south-east for the port of Baldivia, as above, and reached to the mouth, of the harbour in twelve days' sail.

I was now to change faces again, and Captain Merlotte appeared as captain, all things being transacted in his name, and French captains were put into the brigantine, and into the Madagascar ship also. The first thing the captain did was to send a civil message to the Spanish governor, to acquaint him, that being come into those seas as friends, under his most Christian majesty's commission, and with the king of Spain's permission, we desired to be treated as allies, and to be allowed to take water and wood, and to buy such refreshments as we wanted, for which we would pay ready money; also we carried French colours, but took not the least notice of our intention to trade with them.

We received a very civil answer from the governor, viz., That being the king of France's subjects, and that they were in alliance with us, we were very welcome to wood and water, and any provision the place would afford, and that our persons should be safe, and in perfect liberty to go on shore; but that he could not allow any of our men to lie on shore, it being express in his orders that he should not permit any nation not actually in commission from the king of Spain to come on shore and stay there, not even one night; and that this was done to prevent disorders.

We answered, that we were content with that order, seeing we did not desire our men should go on shore to stay there, we not being able to answer for any misbehaviour, which was frequent among seamen.

While we continued here, several Spaniards came on board and visited us, and we often went on shore on the same pretence; but our supercargo, who understood his business too well not to make use of the occasion, presently let the Spaniards see that he had a great cargo of goods to dispose of; they as freely took the hint, and let him know that they had money enough to pay for whatever they bought; so they fell to work, and they bought East India and China silks, Japan ware, China ware, spice, and something of everything we had. We knew we should not sell all our cargo here; nor any extraordinary quantity; but we knew, on the other hand, that, what we did sell here, we should sell for £100 per cent. extraordinary, I mean more than we should sell for at Lima, or any other ports on that side, and so we did; for here we sold a bottle of arrack for four pieces of eight, a pound of cloves for five pieces of eight, and a pound of nutmegs for six pieces of eight; and the like of other things.

They would gladly have purchased some European goods, and especially English cloth and baize; but as we had indeed very few such things left, so we were not willing they should see them, that they might not have any suspicion of our being Englishmen, and English ships, which would soon have put an end to all our commerce.

While we lay here trafficking with the Spaniards, I set some of my men to work to converse among the native Chilians, or Indians, as we call them, of the country, and several things they learned of them, according to the instructions which I gave them; for example, first, I understood by them that the country people, who do not live among the Spaniards, have a mortal aversion to them; that it is rivetted in their minds by tradition from father to son, ever since the wars which had formerly been among them, and that though they did not now carry on those wars, yet the animosity remained; and the pride and cruel haughty temper of the Spaniards were such still to those of the country people who came under their government, as make that aversion continually increase. They let us know, that if any nation in the world would but come in and assist them against the Spaniards, and support them in their rising against them, they would soon rid their hands of the whole nation. This was to the purpose exactly, as to what I wanted to know.

I then ordered particular inquiry to be made, whether the mountains of Andes, which are indeed prodigious to look at, and so frightful for their height, that it is not to be thought of without some horror, were in any places passable? what country there was beyond them? and whether any of their people had gone, over and knew the passages?

The Indians concurred with the Spaniards in this (for our men inquired of both), that though the Andes were to be supposed, indeed, to be the highest mountains in the world, and that, generally speaking, they were impassable, yet that there had been passages found by the vales among the mountains; where, with fetching several compasses and windings partly on the hills, and partly in the valleys, men went with a great deal of ease and safety quite through or over, call it as we will, to the other, named the east side, and as often returned again.

Some of the more knowing Indians or Chilians went farther than this, and when our men inquired after the manners, situation, and produce of the country on the other side, they told them, that when they passed the mountains from that part of the country, they went chiefly to fetch cattle and kill deer, of which there were great numbers in that part of the land; but that when they went from St. Jago they turned away north some leagues, when they came to a town called St. Anthonio de los Vejos, or, the town of St. Anthony and the Old Men; that there was a great river at that city, from whence they found means to go down to the Rio de la Plata, and so to the Buenos Ayres, and that they frequently carried thither great sums of money in Chilian gold, and brought back European goods from thence.

I had all I wanted now, and bade my men say no more to them on that subject, and only to tell them, that they would come back and travel a little that way to see the country. The people appeared very well pleased with this intelligence, and answered, that if they would do so, they should find some, as well Spaniards as Chilians, who would be guides to them through the hills; also assuring them, that they would find the hills very practicable, and the people as they went along very ready to assist and furnish them with whatever they found they wanted, especially if they come to know that they were not Spaniards, or that they would protect them from the Spaniards, which would be the most agreeable thing to them in the world; for it seems many of the nations of the Chilians had been driven to live among the hills, and some even beyond them, to avoid the cruelty and tyranny of the Spaniards, especially in the beginning of their planting in that country.

The next inquiry I ordered them to make was, whether it was possible to pass those hills with horses or mules, or any kind of carriages? and they assured them, they might travel with mules, and even with horses also, but rather with mules; but as to carriages, such as carts or waggons, they allowed that was not practicable. They assured us, that some of those ways through the hills were much frequented, and that there were towns, or villages rather, of people to be found in the valleys between the said hills; some of which villages were very large, and the soil very rich and fruitful, bearing sufficient provisions for the inhabitants, who were very numerous. They added, that the people were not much inclined to live in towns as the Spaniards do, but that they lived scattered up and down the country, as they were guided by the goodness of the land; that they lived very secure and unguarded, never offering any injury to one another, nor fearing injury from any but the Spaniards.

I caused these inquiries to be made with the utmost prudence and caution, so that the Spaniards had not the least suspicion of our design; and thus, having finished our traffick, and taken in water and provisions, we sailed from Baldivia, having settled a little correspondence there with two Spaniards, who were very faithful to us, and with two Chilian Indians, whom we had in a particular manner engaged, and whom, to make sure of, we took along with us; and having spent about thirteen days here, and taken the value of about six thousand pieces of eight in silver and gold, but most of it in gold, we set sail.

Our next port was the Bay of the Conception; here, having two or three men on board who were well acquainted with the coast, we ran boldly into the bay, and came to an anchor in that which they call the Bite, or little bay, under the island Quinquina; and from thence we sent our boat, with French mariners to row, and a French cockswain, with a letter to the Spanish governor, from Captain Merlotte. Our pretence was always the same as before, that we had his most Christian majesty's commission, &c., and that we desired liberty to wood and water, and to buy provisions, having been a very long voyage, and the like.

Under these pretences, we lay here about ten days, and drove a very considerable trade for such goods as we were sure they wanted; and having taken about the value of eight thousand pieces of eight, we set sail for the port or river that goes up to St. Jago, where we expected a very good market, being distant from the Conception about sixty-five leagues.

St. Jago is the capital city of Chili, and stands twelve leagues within the land; there are two ports, which are made use of to carry on the traffic of this place, viz., R. de Ropocalmo, and port de Valparaiso. We were bound to the last, as being the only port for ships of burden, and where there is security from bad weather.

We found means here, without going up to the city of St. Jago, to have merchants enough to come down to us; for this being a very rich city, and full of money, we found all our valuable silks of China, our atlases, China damasks, satins, &c., were very much valued, and very much wanted, and no price was too high for us to ask for them. For, in a word, the Spanish ladies, who, for pride, do not come behind any in the world, whatever they do for beauty, were so eager for those fine things, that almost any reasonable quantity might have been sold there; but the truth is, we had an unreasonable quantity, and therefore, as we had other markets to go to, we did not let them know what a great stock of goods we had, but took care they had something of everything they wanted. We likewise found our spices were an excellent commodity in those parts, and sold for a great profit too, as indeed everything else did, as is said above.

We found it very easy to sell here to the value of one hundred and thirty thousand pieces of eight, in all sorts of China and East-India goods; for still, though we had some of the English cargo loose, we let none of it be seen. We took most of the money in gold uncoined, which is got out of the mountains in great quantities, and of which we shall have occasion to speak more hereafter.

Our next trading port was Coquimbo, a small town but a good port. Here we went in without ceremony, and upon the same foot, of being French, we were well received, traded underhand with the Spanish merchants, and got letters to some other merchants at Guasco, a port in a little bay about fifteen leagues north from Coquimbo.

From hence to the port of Copiapo, is twenty-five leagues. Here we found a very good port, though no trading town or city; but the country being well inhabited, we found means to acquaint some of the principal Spaniards in the country of what we were, and (with which they were pleased well enough) that they might trade with us for such things, which it was easy to see they gave double price for to the merchants who came from Lima, and other places. This brought them to us with so much eagerness, that though they bought for their own use, not for sale, yet they came furnished with orders, perhaps for two or three families together, and being generally rich, would frequently lay out six hundred or eight hundred pieces of eight a man; so that we had a most excellent market here, and took above thirty thousand pieces of eight; that is to say, the value of it, for they still paid all in gold.

Here we had opportunity to get a quantity of good flour, or wheat meal, of very good European wheat, that is to say, of that sort of wheat; and withal, had good biscuit baked on shore, so that now we got a large recruit of bread, and our men began to make puddings, and lived very comfortably. We likewise got good sugar at the ingenioes, or sugar-mills, of which there were several here, and the farther north we went their number increased, for we were now in the latitude of 28° 2' south.

We had but one port now of any consequence that we intended to touch at, until we came to the main place we aimed at, which was Lima, and this was about two-thirds of the way thither; I mean Porto Rica, or Arica, which is in the latitude of 18° of thereabouts. The people were very shy of us here, as having been much upon their guard for some years past, for fear of buccaneers and English privateers: but when they understood we were French, and our French captain sent two recommendations to them from a merchant at St. Jago, they were then very well satisfied, and we had full freedom of commerce here also.

From hence we came the height of Lima, the capital port, if not the capital city, of Peru, lying in the latitude of 12° 30'. Had we made the least pretence of trading here, we should, at least, have had soldiers put on board our ships to have prevented it, and the people would have been forbidden to trade with us upon pain of death. But Captain Merlotte having brought letters to a principal merchant of Lima, he instructed him how to manage himself at his first coming into that port; which was to ride without the town of Callao, out of the command of the puntals or castles there, and not to come any nearer, upon what occasion soever, and then to leave the rest to him.

Upon this, the merchant applied himself to the governor for leave to go on board the French ship at Callao; but the governor understood him, and would not grant it by any means. The reason was, because there had been such a general complaint by the merchants from Carthagena, Porto Bello, and other places, of the great trade carried on here with French ships from Europe, to the destruction of the merchants, and to the ruin of the trade of the galleons, that the governor, or viceroy of Peru, had forbid the French ships landing any goods.

Now, though this made our traffick impracticable at Lima itself, yet it did by no means hinder the merchants trading with us under cover, &c., but especially when they came to understand that we were not loaden from Europe with baize, long ells, druggets, broadcloth, serges, stuffs, stockings, hats, and such like woollen manufactures of France, England, &c.; but that our cargo was the same with that of the Manilla ships at Acapulca, and that we were loaden with calicoes, muslins, fine-wrought China silks, damasks, Japan wares, China wares, spices, &c., there was then no withholding them: but they came on board us in the night with canoes, and, staying all day, went on shore again in the night, carrying their goods to different places, where they knew they could convey them on shore without difficulty.

In this manner we traded publicly enough, not much unlike the manner of our trade at the Manillas; and here we effectually cleared ourselves of our whole cargo, as well English goods as Indian, to an immense sum. Here our men, officers as well as seamen, sold their fine pearl, particularly one large parcel, containing one hundred and seventy-three very fine pearls, but of different sizes, which a priest bought, as we are told, to dress up the image of the blessed Virgin Mary in one of their churches.

In a word, we came to a balance here, for we sold everything that we had the least intention to part with; the chief things we kept in reserve, were some bales of English goods, also all the remainder of our beads and bugles, toys, ironwork, knives, scissors, hatchets, needles, pins, glass-ware, and such things as we knew the Spaniards did not regard, and which might be useful in our farther designs, of which my head was yet very full. Those, I say, we kept still.

Here, likewise, we sold our brigantine, which, though an excellent sea-boat, as may well be supposed, considering the long voyage we had made in her, was yet so worm-eaten in her bottom, that, unless we would have new sheathed her, and perhaps shifted most of her planks too, which would have taken up a great deal of time, she was by no means fit to have gone any farther, at least not so long a run as we had now to make, viz., round the whole southern part of America, and where we should find no port to put in at, (I mean, where we should have been able to have got anything done for the repair of a ship), until we had come home to England.

It was proposed here to have gone to the governor or viceroy of Peru, and have obtained his license or pass to have traversed the Isthmus of America, from port St. Maria to the river of Darien. This we could easily have obtained under the character that we then bore, viz., of having the King of France's commission; and had we been really all French, I believe I should have done it, but as we were so many Englishmen, and as such were then at open war with Spain, I did not think it a safe adventure, I mean not a rational adventure, especially considering what a considerable treasure we had with us.

On the other hand, as we were now a strong body of able seamen, and had two stout ships under us, we had no reason to apprehend either the toil or the danger of a voyage round Cape Horn, after which we should be in a very good condition to make the rest of our voyage to England. Whereas, if we travelled over the Isthmus of America, we should be all like a company of freebooters and buccaneers, loose and unshipped, and should perhaps run some one way and some another, among the logwood cutters at the bay of Campeachy, and other places, to get passage, some to Jamaica and some to New England; and, which was worse than all, should be exposed to a thousand dangers on account of the treasure we had with us, perhaps even to that of murdering and robbing one another. And, as Captain Merlotte said, who was really a Frenchman, it were much more eligible for us, as French, or, if we had been such, to have gone up to Acapulca, and there to sell our ships and get license to travel to Mexico, and then to have got the viceroy's assiento to have come to Europe in the galleons; but, as we were so many Englishmen, it was impracticable; our seamen also being Protestants, such as seamen generally are, and bold mad fellows, they would never have carried on a disguise, both of their nation and of their religion, for so long a time as it would have been necessary to do for such a journey and voyage.

But, besides all these difficulties, I had other projects in my head, which made me against all the proposals of passing by land to the North Sea; otherwise, had I resolved it, I should not have much concerned myself about obtaining a license from the Spaniards, for, as we were a sufficient number of men to have forced our way, we should not much have stood upon their giving us leave, or not giving us leave, to go.

But, as I have said, my views lay another way, and my head had been long working upon the discourse my men had had with the Spaniards at Baldavia. I frequently talked with the two Chilian Indians whom I had on board, and who spoke Spanish pretty well, and whom we had taught to speak a little English.

I had taken care that they should have all the good usage imaginable on board. I had given them each a very good suit of clothes made by our tailor, but after their own manner, with each of them a baize cloak; and had given them hats, shoes, stockings, and everything they desired, and they were mighty well pleased, and I talked very freely with them about the passage of the mountains, for that was now my grand design.

While I was coming up the Chilian shore, as you have heard, that is to say, at St. Jago, at the Conception, at Arica, and even at Lima itself, we inquired on all occasions into the situation of the country, the manner of travelling, and what kind of country it was beyond the mountains, and we found them all agreeing in the same story; and that passing the mountains of Les Cordelieras, for so they call them in Peru, though it was the same ridge of hills as we call the Andes, was no strange thing. That there were not one or two, but a great many places found out, where they passed as well with horses and mules as on foot, and even some with carriages; and, in particular, they told us at Lima, that from Potosi, and the towns thereabouts, there was a long valley, which ran for one hundred and sixty leagues in length southward, and south-east, and that it continued until the hills parting, it opened into the main level country on the other side; and that there were several rivers which began in that great valley, and which all of them ran away to the south and south-east, and afterwards went away east, and east-north-east, and so fell into the great Rio de la Plata, and emptied themselves into the North Seas; and that merchants travelled to those rivers, and then went down in boats as far as the town or the city of the Ascension, and the Buenos Ayres.

This was very satisfying you may be sure, especially to hear them agree in it, that the Andes were to be passed; though passing them hereabouts, (where I knew the mainland from the west shore, where we now were, must be at least one thousand five hundred miles broad), was no part of my project; but I laid up all these things in my mind, and resolved to go away to the south again, and act as I should see cause.

We were now got into a very hot climate, and, whatever was the cause, my men began to grow very sickly, and that to such a degree that I was once afraid we had got the plague among us; but our surgeons, who we all call doctors at sea, assured me there was nothing of that among them, and yet we buried seventeen men here, and had between twenty and thirty more sick, and, as I thought, dangerously too.

In this extremity, for I was really very much concerned about it, one of my doctors came to me, and told me he had been at the city (that is, at Lima) to buy some drugs and medicines, to recruit his chest, and he had fallen into company with an Irish Jesuit, who, he found, was an extraordinary good physician, and that he had had some discourse with him about our sick men, and he believed for a good word or two, he could persuade him to come and visit them.

I was very loath to consent to it, and said to the surgeon, If he is an Irishman, he speaks English, and he will presently perceive that we are all Englishmen, and so we shall be betrayed; all our designs will be blown up at once, and our farther measures be all broken; and therefore I would not consent. This I did not speak from the fear of any hurt they could have done me by force, for I had no reason to value that, being able to have fought my way clear out of their seas, if I had been put to it; but, as I had traded all the way by stratagem, and had many considerable views still behind, I was unwilling to be disappointed by the discovery of my schemes, or that the Spaniards should know upon what a double foundation I acted, and how I was a French ally and merchant, or an English enemy and privateer, just as I pleased, and as opportunity should offer; in which case they would have been sure to have trepanned me if possible, under pretence of the former, and have used me, if they ever should get an advantage over me, as one of the latter.

This made me very cautious, and I had good reason for it too; and yet the sickness and danger of my men pressed me very hard to have the advice of a good physician, if it was possible, and especially to be satisfied whether it was really the plague or no, for I was very uneasy about that.

But my surgeon told me, that, as to my apprehension of discovery, he would undertake to prevent it by this method. First, he said, he found that the Irishman did not understand French at all, and so I had nothing to do but to order, that, when he came on board, as little English should be spoke in his hearing as possible; and this was not difficult, for almost all our men had a little French at their tongue's end, by having so many Frenchmen on board of them; others had the Levant jargon, which they call Lingua Frank; so that, if they had but due caution, it could not be suddenly perceived what countrymen they were.

Besides this, the surgeon ordered, that as soon as the Padre came on board, he should be surrounded with French seamen only, some of whom should be ordered to follow him from place to place, and chop in with their nimble tongues, upon some occasion or other, so that he should hear French spoken wherever he turned himself.

Upon this, which indeed appeared very easy to be done, I agreed to let the doctor come on board, and accordingly the surgeon brought him the next day, where Captain Merlotte received him in the cabin, and treated him very handsomely, but nothing was spoken but French or Spanish; and the surgeon, who had pretended himself to be an Irishman, acted as interpreter between the doctor and us.

Here we told him the case of our men that were sick; some of them, indeed, were French, and others that could speak French, were instructed to speak to him as if they could speak no other tongue, and those the surgeon interpreted; others, who were English, were called Irishmen, and two or three were allowed to be English seamen picked up in the East Indies, as we had seamen, we told him, of all nations.

The matter, in short, was so carried that the good man, for such I really think he was, had no manner of suspicion; and, to do him justice, he was an admirable physician, and did our men a great deal of good; for all of them, excepting three, recovered under his hands, and those three had recovered if they had not, like madmen, drank large quantities of punch when they were almost well; and, by their intemperance, inflamed their blood, and thereby thrown themselves back again into their fever, and put themselves, as the Padre said of them, out of the reach of medicine.

We treated this man of art with a great deal of respect, made him some very handsome presents, and particularly such as he could not come at in the country where he was; besides which, I ordered he should have the value of one hundred dollars in gold given him; but he, on the other hand, thanking Captain Merlotte for his bounty, would have no money, but he accepted a present of some linen, a few handkerchiefs, some nutmegs, and a piece of black baize: most of which, however, he afterwards said, he made presents of again in the city, among some of his acquaintance.

But he had a farther design in his head, which, on a future day, he communicated in confidence to the surgeon I have mentioned, who conversed with him, and by him to me, and which was to him, indeed, of the highest importance. The case was this.

He took our surgeon on shore with him one day from the Madagascar ship, where he had been with him to visit some of our sick men, and, drinking a glass of wine with him, he told him he had a favour to ask of him, and a thing to reveal to him in confidence, which was of the utmost consequence to himself though of no great value to him, (the surgeon), and, if he would promise the utmost secrecy to him, on his faith and honour, he would put his life into his hands. For, seignior, said he, it will be no other, nor would anything less than my life pay for it, if you should discover it to any of the people here, or anywhere else on this coast.

The surgeon was a very honest man, and carried indeed the index of it in his face; and the Padre said afterwards, he inclined to put this confidence in him because he thought he saw something of an honest man in his very countenance. After so frank a beginning, the surgeon made no scruple to tell him, that, seeing he inclined to treat him with such confidence, and to put a trust of so great importance in him, he would give him all the assurance in his power that he would be as faithful to him as it was possible to be to himself, and that the secret should never go out of his mouth to any one in the world, but to such and at such time as he should consent to and direct. In short, he used so many solemn protestations, that the Padre made no scruple to trust him with the secret, which, indeed, was no less than putting his life into his hands. The case was this.

He told him he had heard them talk of going to Ireland in their return, and, as he had been thirty years out of his own country, in such a remote part of the world, where it was never likely that he should ever see it again, the notion he had entertained that this ship was going thither, and might set him on shore there, that he might once more see his native country, and his family and friends, had filled his mind with such a surprising joy, that he could no longer contain himself; and that, therefore, if he would procure leave of the captain that he might come privately on board and take his passage home, he would willingly pay whatever the captain should desire of him, but that it must be done with the greatest secrecy imaginable, or else he was ruined; for that, if he should be discovered and stopped, he should be confined in the Jesuit's house there as long as he lived, without hope of redemption.

The surgeon told him the thing was easy to be done if he would give him leave to acquaint one man in the ship with it, which was not Captain Merlotte, but a certain Englishman, who was a considerable person in the ship, without whom the captain did nothing, and who would be more secure to trust, by far, than Captain Merlotte. The Padre told him, that, without asking him for any reasons, since he had put his life and liberty in his hands, he would trust him with the management of the whole, in whatever way he chose to conduct it.

The surgeon accordingly brought him on board to me, and making a confidence of the whole matter to me, I turned to the Padre, and told him in English, giving him my hand, that I would be under all the engagements and promises of secrecy that our surgeon had been in, for his security and satisfaction; that he had merited too well of us to wish him any ill, and, in short, that the whole ship should be engaged for his security. That, as to his coming on board and bringing anything off that belonged to him, he must take his own measures, and answer to himself for the success; but that, after he was on board, we would sink the ship under him, or blow her aloft in the air, before we would deliver him up on any account whatever.

He was so pleased with my frank way of talking to him, that he told me he would put his life into my hands with the same freedom as he had done before with my surgeon; so we began to concert measures for his coming on board with secrecy.

He told us there was no need of any proposals, for he would acquaint the head of the house that he intended to go on board the French ship in the road, and to go to St. Jago, where he had several times been in the same manner; and that, as they had not the least suspicion of him, he was very well satisfied that they would make no scruple of it.

But his mistake in this might have been his ruin; for though, had it been a Spanish ship, they would not have mistrusted him, yet, when he named the French ship in the road of Callao, they began to question him very smartly about it. Upon which, he was obliged to tell them, that, since they were doubtful of him, he would not go at all, telling them withal, that it was hard to suspect him, who had been so faithful to his vows, as to reside for near thirty years among them, when he might frequently have made an escape from them, if he had been so disposed. So, for three or four days, he made no appearance of going at all; but having had private notice from me the evening before we sailed, he found means to get out of their hands, came down to Callao on a mule in the night, and our surgeon, lying ready with our boat about half a league from the town, as by appointment, took him on board, with a negro, his servant, and brought him safe to the ship; nor had we received him on board half an hour, but, being unmoored and ready to sail, we put out to sea, and carried him clear off.

He made his excuses to me that he was come away naked, according to his profession; that he had purposed to have furnished himself with some provisions for the voyage, but that the unexpected suspicions of the head of their college, or house, had obliged him to come away in a manner that would not admit of it; for that he might rather be said to have made his escape than to have come fairly off.

I told him he was very welcome (and indeed so he was, for he had been already more worth to us than ten times his passage came to), and that he should be entered into immediate pay, as physician to both the ships, which I was sure none of our surgeons would repine at, but rather be glad of; and accordingly I immediately ordered him a cabin, with a very good apartment adjoining to it, and appointed him to eat in my own mess whenever he pleased, or by himself, on his particular days, when he thought proper.

And now it was impossible to conceal from him that we were indeed an English ship, and that I was the captain in chief, except, as has been said, upon occasion of coming to any particular town of Spain. I let him know I had a commission to make prize of the Spaniards, and appear their open enemy, but that I had chosen to treat them as friends, in a way of commerce, as he had seen. He admired much the moderation I had used, and how I had avoided enriching myself with the spoil, as I might have done; and he made me many compliments upon that head, which I excused hearing, and begged him to forbear. I told him we were Christians, and as we had made a very prosperous voyage, I was resolved not to do any honest man the least injustice, if I could avoid it.

But I must observe here, that I did not enter immediately into all this confidence with him neither, nor all at once; neither did I let him into any part of it, but under the same solemn engagements of secrecy that he had laid upon us, nor till I was come above eighty leagues south from Lima.

The first thing I took the freedom to speak to him upon was this. Finding his habit a little offensive to our rude seamen, I took him into the cabin the very next day after we came to sea, and told him that I was obliged to mention to him what I knew he would soon perceive; namely, that we were all Protestants, except three or four of the Frenchmen, and I did not know how agreeable that might be to him. He answered, he was not at all offended with that part; that it was none of his business to inquire into any one's opinion any farther than they gave him leave; that if it was his business to cure the souls of men on shore, his business on board was to cure their bodies; and as for the rest, he would exercise no other function than that of a physician on board the ship without my leave.

I told him that was very obliging; but that for his own sake I had a proposal to make him, which was, whether it would be disagreeable to him to lay aside the habit of a religious, and put on that of a gentleman, so to accommodate himself the more easily to the men on board, who perhaps might be rude to him in his habit, seamen being not always men of the most refined manners.

He thanked me very sincerely; told me that he had been in England as well as in Ireland, and that he went dressed there as a gentleman, and was ready to do so now, if I thought fit, to avoid giving any offence; and added that he chose to do so. But then, smiling, said he was at a great loss, for he had no clothes. I bade him take no care about that, for I would furnish him; and immediately we dressed him up like an Englishman, in a suit of very good clothes, which belonged to one of our midshipmen who died. I gave him also a good wig and a sword, and he presently appeared upon the quarter-deck like a grave physician, and was called doctor.

From that minute, by whose contrivance we knew not, it went current among the seamen that the Spanish doctor was an Englishman and a protestant, and only had put on the other habit to disguise himself and make his escape to us; and this was so universally believed that it held to the last day of the whole voyage, for as soon as I knew it, I took care that nobody should ever contradict it: and as for the doctor himself, when he first heard of it, he said nothing could be more to his satisfaction, and that he would take care to confirm the opinion of it among all the men, as far as lay in his power.

However, the doctor earnestly desired we would be mindful, that as he should never offer to go on shore, whatever port we came to afterwards, none of the Spaniards might, by inquiry, hear upon any occasion of his being on board our ship; but above all, that none of our men, the officers especially, would ever come so much in reach of the Spaniards on shore as to put it in their power to seize upon them by reprisal, and so oblige us to deliver him up by way of exchange.

I went so far with him, and so did Captain Merlotte also, as to assure him, that if the Spaniards should by any stratagem, or by force, get any of our men, nay, though it were ourselves, into their hands, yet he should, upon no conditions whatever be delivered up. And indeed for this very reason we were very shy of going on shore at all; and as we had really no business any where but just for water and fresh provisions, which we had also taken in a very good store of at Lima, so we put in nowhere at all on the coast of Peru, because there we might have been more particularly liable to the impertinencies of the Spaniard's inquiry; as to force, we were furnished not to be in the least apprehensive of that.

Being thus, I say, resolved to have no more to do with the coast of Peru, we stood off to sea, and the first land we made was a little unfrequented island in the latitude of 17° 13', where our men went on shore in the boats three or four times, to catch tortoises or turtles, being the first we had met with since we came from the East Indies. And here they took so many, and had such a prodigious quantity of eggs out of them, that the whole company of both ships lived on them till within four or five days of our coming to the island of Juan Fernandez, which was our next port. Some of these tortoises were so large and so heavy that no single man could turn them, and sometimes as much as four men could carry to the boats.

We met with some bad weather after this, which blew us off to sea, the wind blowing very hard at the south-east; but it was not so great a wind as to endanger us, though we lost sight of one another more in this storm than we had done in all our voyage. However, we were none of us in any great concern for it now, because we had agreed before, that if we should lose one another, we should make the best of our way to the island of Juan Fernandez; and this we observed now so directly, that both of us shaping our course for the island, as soon as the storm abated, came in sight of one another long before we came thither, which proved very agreeable to us all.

We were, including the time of the storm, two hundred and eighteen days from Lima to the Island of Juan Fernandez, having most of the time cross contrary winds, and more bad weather than is usual in those seas; however, we were all in good condition, both ships and men.

Here we fell to the old trade of hunting of goats. And here our new doctor set some of our men to simpling, that is to say, to gather some physical herbs, which he let them see afterwards were very well worth their while. Our surgeons assisted, and saw the plants, but had never observed the same kind in England. They gave me the names of them, and it is the only discovery in all my travels which I have not reserved so carefully as to publish for the advantage of others, and which I regret the omission of very much.

While we were here, an odd accident gave me some uneasiness, which, however, did not come to much. Early in the grey of the morning, little wind, and a smooth sea, a small frigate-built vessel, under Spanish colours, pennant flying, appeared off at sea, at the opening of the north-east point of the island. As soon as she came fair with the road, she lay by, as if she came to look into the port only; and when she perceived that we began to loose our sails to speak with her, she stretched away to the northward, and then altering her course, stood away north-east, using oars to assist her, and so she got away.

Nothing could be more evident to us than that she came to look at us, nor could we imagine anything less; from whence we immediately concluded that we were discovered, and that our taking away the doctor had given a great alarm among the Spaniards, as we afterwards came to understand it had done. But we came a little while afterwards to a better understanding about the frigate.

I was so uneasy about it, that I resolved to speak with her if possible, so I ordered the Madagascar ship, which of the two, was rather a better sailer than our own, to stand in directly to the coast of Chili, and then to ply to the northward, just in sight of the shore, till he came into the latitude of 22°; and, if he saw nothing in all that run, then to come down again directly into the latitude of the island of Juan Fernandez, but keeping the distance of ten leagues off farther than before, and to ply off and on in that latitude for five days; and then, if he did not meet with me, to stand in for the island.

While he did this, I did the same at the distance of near fifty leagues from the shore, being the distance which I thought the frigate kept in as she stood away from me. We made our cruise both of us very punctually; I found him in the station we agreed on, and we both stood into the road again from whence we came.

We no sooner made the road, but we saw the frigate, as I called her, with another ship at an anchor in the same road where she had seen us; and it was easy to see that they were both of them in a great surprise and hurry at our appearing, and that they were under sail in so very little time as that we easily saw they had slipped their cables, or cut away their anchors. They fired guns twice, which we found was a signal for their boats, which were on shore, to come on board; and soon after we saw three boats go off to them, though, as we understood afterwards, they were obliged to leave sixteen or seventeen of their men behind them, who, being among the rocks catching of goats, either did not hear the signals, or could not come to their boats time enough.

When we saw them in this hurry, we thought it must be something extraordinary, and bore down upon them, having the weather-gage.

They were ships of pretty good force, and full of men, and when they saw we were resolved to speak with them, and that there was no getting away from us, they made ready to engage; and putting themselves upon a-wind, first stretching ahead to get the weather-gage of us, when they thought they were pretty well, boldly tacked, and lay by for us, hoisting the English ancient and union jack.

We had our French colours out till now; but being just, as we thought, going to engage, I told Captain Merlotte I scorned to hide what nation I was of when I came to fight for the honour of our country; and, besides, as these people had spread English colours, I ought to let them know what I was; that, if they were really English and friends, we might not fight by mistake, and shed the innocent blood of our own countrymen; and that, if they were rogues, and counterfeited their being English, we should soon perceive it.

However, when they saw us put out English colours, they knew not what to think of it, but lay by awhile to see what we would do. I was as much puzzled as they, for, as I came nearer, I thought they seemed to be English ships, as well by their bulk as by their way of working; and as I came still nearer, I thought I could perceive so plainly by my glasses that they were English seamen, that I made a signal to our other ship, who had the van, and was just bearing down upon them, to bring to; and I sent my boat to him to know his opinion. He sent me word, he did believe them to be English; and the more, said he, because they could be no other nation but English or French, and the latter he was sure they were not; but, since we were the largest ships, and that they might as plainly see us to be English as we could see them, he said he was for fighting them, because they ought to have let us known who they were first. However, as I had fired a gun to bring him too, he lay by a little time till we spoke thus together.

While this was doing we could see one of their boats come off with six oars and two men, a lieutenant and trumpeter it seems they were, sitting in the stern, and one of them holding up a flag of truce; we let them come forward, and when they came nearer, so that we could hail them with a speaking trumpet, we asked them what countrymen they were? and they answered Englishmen. Then we asked them whence their ship? Their answer was, from London. At which we bade them come on board, which they did; and we soon found that we were all countrymen and friends, and their boat went immediately back to let them know it. We found afterwards that they were mere privateers, fitted out from London also, but coming last from Jamaica; and we let them know no other of ourselves, but declined keeping company, telling them we were bound now upon traffick, and not for purchase; that we had been at the East Indies, had made some prizes, and were going back thither again. They told us they were come into the South Seas for purchase, but that they had made little of it, having heard there were three large French men-of-war in those seas, in the Spanish service, which made them wish they had not come about; and that they were still very doubtful what to do.

We assured them we had been the height of Lima, and that we had not heard of any men-of-war, but that we had passed for such ourselves, and perhaps were the ships they had heard of; for that we were three sail at first, and had sometimes carried French colours.

This made them very glad, for it was certainly so that we had passed for three French men-of-war, and they were so assured of it, that they went afterwards boldly up the coast, and made several very good prizes. We then found also that it was one of these ships that looked into the road, as above, when we were here before, and seeing us then with French colours, took us for the men-of-war they had heard of; and, they added, that, when we came in upon them again, they gave themselves up for lost men, but were resolved to have fought it out to the last, or rather to have sunk by our side, or blown themselves up, than be taken.

I was not at all sorry that we had made this discovery before we engaged; for the captains were two brave resolute fellows, and had two very good ships under them, one of thirty-six guns, but able to have carried forty-four; the other, which we called the frigate-built ship, carried twenty-eight guns, and they were both full of men. Now, though we should not have feared their force, yet my case differed from what it did at first, for we had that on board that makes all men cowards, I mean money, of which we had such a cargo as few British ships ever brought out of those seas, and I was one of those that had now no occasion to run needless hazards. So that, in short, I was as well pleased without fighting as they could be; besides, I had other projects now in my head, and those of no less consequence than of planting a new world, and settling new kingdoms, to the honour and advantage of my country; and many a time I wished heartily that all my rich cargo was safe at London; that my merchants were sharing the silver and gold, and the pearl among themselves; and, that I was but safe on shore, with a thousand good families, upon the south of Chili, and about fifteen hundred good soldiers, and arms for ten thousand more, of which by and by, and, with the two ships I had now with me, I would not fear all the power of the Spaniards; I mean, that they could bring against me in the South Seas.

I had all these things, I say, in my head already, though nothing like to what I had afterwards, when I saw farther into the matter myself; however, these things made me very glad that I had no occasion to engage those ships.

When we came thus to understand one another, we went all into the road together, and I invited the captains of the two privateers on board me, where I treated them with the best I had, though I had no great dainties now, having been so long out of England. They invited me and Captain Merlotte, and the captain of the Madagascar ship in return, and, indeed, treated us very nobly.

After this, we exchanged some presents of refreshments, and, particularly, they sent me a hogshead of rum, which, was very acceptable; and I sent them in return a runlet of arrack, excusing myself that I had no great store. I sent them also the quantity of one hundred weight of nutmegs and cloves; but the most agreeable present I sent them was twenty pieces of Madagascar dried beef, cured in the sun, the like of which they had never seen or tasted before; and without question, it is such an excellent way of curing beef, that if I were to be at Madagascar again, I would take in a sufficient quantity of beef so preserved to victual the whole ship for the voyage; and I leave it as a direction to all English seamen that have occasion to use East-India voyages.

I bought afterwards six hogsheads of rum of these privateers, for I found they were very well stored with liquors, whatever else they wanted.

We stayed here twelve or fourteen days, but took care, by agreement, that our men should never go on shore the same days that their men went on shore, or theirs when ours went, as well to avoid their caballing together, as to avoid quarrelling, though the latter was the pretence. We agreed, also, not to receive on board any of our ships respectively, any of the crews belonging to the other; and this was their advantage, for, if we would have given way to that, half their men would, for aught I know, have come over to us.

While we lay here, one of them went a-cruising, finding the wind fair to run in for the shore; and, in about five days, she came back with a Spanish prize, laden with meal, cocoa, and a large quantity of biscuit, ready baked; she was bound to Lima, from Baldivia, or some port nearer, I do not remember exactly which. They had some gold on board, but not much, and had bought their lading at St. Jago. As soon as we saw them coming in with a prize in tow, we put out our French colours, and gave notice to the privateers that it was for their advantage that we did so; and so indeed it was, for it would presently have alarmed all the country, if such a fleet of privateers had appeared on the coast. We prevailed with them to give us their Spanish prisoners, and to allow us to set them on shore, I having assured them I would not land them till I came to Baldivia, nor suffer them to have the least correspondence with anybody till they came thither; the said Spaniards also giving their parole of honour not to give any account of their being taken till fourteen days after they were on shore.

This being the farthest port south which the Spaniards are masters of in Chili, or, indeed, on the whole continent of America, they could not desire me to carry them any farther. They allowed us a quantity of meal and cocoa out of their booty for the subsistence of the prisoners, and I bought a larger quantity besides, there being more than they knew how to stow, and they did not resolve to keep the Spanish ship which they took; by this means I was doubly stocked with flour and bread, but, as the first was very good, and well packed in casks and very good jars, it received no injury.

We bought also some of their cocoa, and made chocolate, till our men gorged themselves with it, and would have no more.

Having furnished ourselves here with goats' flesh, as usual, and taking in water sufficient, we left Juan Fernandez, and saw the cruisers go out the same tide, they steering north-north-east, and we south-south-east. They saluted us at parting, and we bade them good-bye in the same language.

While we were now sailing for the coast of Chili, with fair wind and pleasant weather, my Spanish doctor came to me and told me he had a piece of news to acquaint me with, which, he said, he believed would please me very well; and this was, that one of the Spanish prisoners was a planter, as it is called in the West Indies, or a farmer, as we should call it in England, of Villa Rica, a town built by the Spaniards, near the foot of the Andes, above the town of Baldivia; and that he had entered into discourse with him upon the situation of those hills, the nature of the surface, the rivers, hollows, passages into them, &c. Whether there were any valleys within the hills, of what extent, how watered, what cattle, what people, how disposed, and the like; and, in short, if there was any way of passing over the Andes, or hills above mentioned; and he told me, in few words, that he found him to be a very honest, frank, open sort of a person, who seemed to speak without reserve, without the least jealousy or apprehension; and that he believed I might have an ample discovery from him of all that I desired to know.

I was very glad of this news; and, at my request, it was not many hours before he brought the Spaniard into the great cabin to me, where I treated him very civilly, and gave him opportunity several times to see himself very well used; and, indeed, all the Spaniards in the ship were very thankful for my bringing them out of the hands of the privateers, and took all occasions to let us see it.

I said little the first time, but discoursed in general of America, of the greatness and opulency of the Spaniards there, the infinite wealth of the country, &c.; and I remember well, discoursing once of the great riches of the Spaniards in America, the silver mines of Potosi, and other places, he turned short upon me, smiling, and said, We Spaniards are the worst nation in the world that such a treasure as this could have belonged to; for if it had fallen into any other hands than ours, they would have searched farther into it before now. I asked him what he meant by that? and added, I thought they had searched it thoroughly enough; for that I believed no other nation in the world could ever have spread such vast dominions, and planted a country of such a prodigious extent, they having not only kept possession of it, but maintained the government also, and even inhabited it with only a few people.

Perhaps, seignior, says he, you think, notwithstanding that opinion of yours, that we have many more people of our nation in New Spain than we have. I do not know, said I, how many you may have; but, if I should believe you have as many here as in Old Spain, it would be but a few in comparison of the infinite extent of the King of Spain's dominions in America. And then, replied he, I assure you, seignior, there is not one Spaniard to a thousand acres of land, take one place with another, throughout New Spain.

Very well, said I, then I think the riches and wealth of America is very well searched, in comparison to the number of people you have to search after it. No, says he, it is not, neither; for the greatest number of our people live in that part where the wealth is not the greatest, and where even the governor and viceroy, enjoying a plentiful and luxurious life, they take no thought for the increase either of the king's revenues, or the national wealth. This he spoke of the city of Mexico, whose greatness, and the number of its inhabitants, he said, was a disease to the rest of the body. And what, think you, seignior, said he, that in that one city, where there is neither silver nor gold but what is brought from the mountains of St. Clara, the mines at St. Augustine's and Our Lady, some of which are a hundred leagues from it, and yet there are more Spaniards in Mexico than in both those two prodigious empires of Chili and Peru?

I seemed not to believe him; and, indeed, I did not believe him at first, till he returned to me with a question. Pray, seignior capitain, says he, how many Spaniards do you think there may be in this vast country of Chili? I told him I could make no guess of the numbers; but, without doubt, there were many thousands, intimating that I might suppose, near a hundred thousand. At which he laughed heartily, and assured me, that there were not above two thousand five hundred in the whole kingdom, besides women and children, and some few soldiers, which they looked upon as nothing to inhabitants, because they were not settled anywhere.

I was indeed surprised, and began to name several large places, which, I thought, had singly more Spaniards in them than what he talked of. He presently ran over some of them, and, naming Baldivia first, as the most southward, he asked me how many I thought were there? And I told him about three hundred families. He smiled, and assured me there were not above three or four-and-fifty families in the whole place, and about twenty-five soldiers, although it was a fortification, and a frontier. At Villa Rica, or the Rich Town, where he lived, he said there might be about sixty families, and a lieutenant, with twenty soldiers. In a word, we passed over the many places between and came to the capital, St. Jago, where after I had supposed there were five thousand Spaniards, he protested to me there were not above eight hundred, including the viceroy's court, and including the families at Valparaiso, which is the seaport, and excluding only the soldiers, which as he said, being the capital of the whole kingdom, might be about two hundred, and excluding the religious, who he added, laughing, signified nothing to the planting a country, for they neither cultivated the land nor increased the people.

Our doctor, who was our interpreter, smiled at this, but merrily said, that was very true, or ought to be so, intimating, that though the priests do not cultivate the land, yet they might chance to increase the people a little; but that was by the way. As to the number of inhabitants at St. Jago, the doctor agreed with him, and said, he believed he had said more than there were, rather than less.

As to the kingdom or empire of Peru, in which there are many considerable cities and places of note, such as Lima, Quito, Cusco, la Plata, and others, there are besides a great number of towns on the seacoasts, such as Porto Arica, St. Miguel, Prayta, Guyaquil, Truxillo, and many others.

He answered, that it was true that the city of Lima, with the town of Callao, was much increased within a few years, and particularly of late, by the settling of between three and four hundred French there, who came by the King of Spain's license; but that, before the coming of those gentlemen, at which he shook his head, the country was richer, though the inhabitants were not so many; and that, take it as it was now, there could not be reckoned above fifteen hundred families of Spaniards, excluding the soldiers and the clergy, which, as above, he reckoned nothing as to the planting of the country.

We came then to discourse of the silver mines at Potosi, and here he supposed, as I did also, a very great number of people. But seignior, says he, what people is it you are speaking of? There are many thousands of servants, but few masters; there is a garrison of four hundred soldiers always kept in arms and in good order, to secure the place, and keep the negroes, and criminals who work in the mines, in subjection; but that there were not besides five hundred Spaniards, that is to say, men, in the whole place and its adjacents. So that, in short, he would not allow above seven thousand Spaniards in the whole empire of Peru, and two thousand five hundred in Chili; at the same time, allowing twice as many as both these in the city of Mexico only.

After this discourse was over, I asked him what he inferred from it, as to the wealth of the country not being discovered? He answered, It was evident that it was for want of people that the wealth of the country lay hid; that there was infinitely more lay uninquired after than had yet been known; that there were several mountains in Peru equally rich in silver with that of Potosi; and, as for Chili, says he, and the country where we live, there is more gold at this time in the mountains of the Andes, and more easy to come at, than in all the world besides. Nay, says he, with some passion, there is more gold every year washed down out of the Andes of Chili into the sea, and lost there, than all the riches that go from New Spain to Europe in twenty years amount to.

This discourse fired my imagination you may be sure, and I renewed it upon all occasions, taking more or less time every day to talk with this Spaniard upon the subject of cultivation of the lands, improvement of the country, and the like; always making such inquiries into the state of the mountains of the Andes as best suited my purpose, but yet so as not to give him the least intimation of my design.

One day, conversing with him again about the great riches of the country, and of the mountains and rivers, as above, I asked him, that, seeing the place was so rich, why were they not all princes, or as rich as princes, who dwelt there? He shook his head, and said, it was a great reproach upon them many ways; and, when I pressed him to explain himself, he answered, it was occasioned by two things, namely, pride and sloth. Seignior, says he, we have so much pride that we have no avarice, and we do not covet enough to make us work for it. We walk about sometimes, says he, on the banks of the streams that come down from the mountains, and, if we see a bit of gold lie on the shore, it may be we will vouchsafe to lay off our cloak, and step forward to take it up; but, if we were sure to carry home as much as we could stand under, we would not strip and go to work in the water to wash it out of the sand, or take the pains to get it together; nor perhaps dishonour ourselves so much as to be seen carrying a load, no, not for all the value of the gold itself.

I laughed then, indeed, and told him he was disposed to jest with his countrymen, or to speak ironically; meaning, that they did not take so much pains as was required, to make them effectually rich, but that I supposed he would not have me understand him as he spoke. He said I might understand as favourably as I pleased, but I should find the fact to be true if I would go up with him to Villa Rica, when I came to Baldivia; and, with that, he made his compliment to me, and invited me to his house.

I asked him with a con licentia, seignior, that is, with pardon for so much freedom, that, if he lived in so rich a country, and where there was so inexhaustible a treasure of gold, how came he to fall into this state of captivity? and what made him venture himself upon the sea, to fall into the hands of pirates?

He answered, that it was on the very foot of what he had been complaining of; and that, having seen so much of the wealth of the country he lived in, and having reproached himself with that very indolence which he now blamed all his countrymen for, he had resolved in conjunction with two of his neighbours, the Spaniards, and men of good substance, to set to work in a place in the mountains where they had found some gold, and had seen much washed down by the water, and to find what might be done in a thorough search after the fund or mine of it, which they were sure was not far off; and that he was going to Lima, and from thence, if he could not be supplied, to Panama, to buy negroes for the work, that they might carry it on with the better success.

This was a feeling discourse to me, and made such an impression on me, that I secretly resolved that when I came to Baldivia, I would go up with this sincere Spaniard, for so I thought him to be, and so I found him, and would be an eyewitness to the discovery which I thought was made to my hand, and which I found now I could make more effectual than by all the attempts I was like to make by secondhand.

From this time I treated the Spaniard with more than ordinary courtesy, and told him, if I was not captain of a great ship, and had a cargo upon me of other gentleman's estates, he had said so much of those things, that I should be tempted to give him a visit as he desired, and see those wonderful mountains of the Andes.

He told me that if I would do him so much honour, I should not be obliged to any long stay; that he would procure mules for me at Baldivia, and that I should go not to his house only, but to the mountain itself, and see all that I desired, and be back again in fourteen days at the farthest. I shook my head, as if it could not be, but he never left importuning me; and once or twice, as if I had been afraid to venture myself with him, he told me he would send for his two sons, and leave them in the ship, as hostages for my safety.

I was fully satisfied as to that point, but did not let him know my mind yet; but every day we dwelt upon the same subject, and I travelled through the mountains and valleys so duly in every day's discourse with him, that when I afterwards came to the places we had talked of, it was as if I had looked over them in a map before.

I asked him if the Andes were a mere wall of mountains, contiguous and without intervals and spaces, like a fortification, or boundary to a country? or whether they lay promiscuous, and distant from one another? and whether there lay any way over them into the country beyond?

He smiled when I talked of going over them. He told me they were so infinitely high, that no human creature could live upon the top; and withal so steep and so frightful, that if there was even a pair of stairs up on one side, and down on the other, no man would dare to mount up, or venture down.

But that as for the notion of the hills being contiguous, like a wall that had no gates, that was all fabulous; that there were several fair entrances in among the mountains, and large pleasant and fruitful valleys among the hills, with pleasant rivers, and numbers of inhabitants, and cattle and provisions of all sorts; and that some of the most delightful places to live in that were in the whole world were among the valleys, in the very centre of the highest and most dreadful mountains.

Well, said I, seignior, but how do they go out of one valley into another? and whither do they go at last? He answered me, those valleys are always full of pleasant rivers and brooks, which fall from the hills, and are formed generally into one principal stream to every vale: and that as these must have their outlets on one side of the hills or on the other, so, following the course of those streams, one is always sure to find the way out of one valley into another, and at last out of the whole into the open country; so that it was very frequent to pass from one side to the other of the whole body of the mountains, and not go much higher up hill or down hill, compared to the hills in other places. It was true, he said, there was no abrupt visible parting in the mountains, that should seem like a way cut through from the bottom to the top, which would be indeed frightful; but that as they pass from some of the valleys to others, there are ascents and descents, windings and turnings, sloping up and sloping down, where we may stand on those little ridges, and see the waters on one side run to the west, and on the other side to the east.

I asked him what kind of a country was on the other side? and how long time it would take up to go through from one side to the other? He told me there were ways indeed that were more mountainous and uneasy, in which men kept upon the sides or declivity of the hills; in which the natives would go, and guide others to go, and so might pass the whole ridge of the Andes in eight or nine days, but that those ways were esteemed very dismal, lonely, and dangerous, because of wild beasts; but that through the valleys, the way was easy and pleasant, and perfectly safe, only farther about; and that those ways a man might be sixteen or seventeen days going through.

I laid up all this in my heart, to make use of as I should have occasion, but I acknowledged that it was surprising to me, as it was so perfectly agreeing with the notion that I always entertained of those mountains, of the riches of them, the facility of access to and from them, and the easy passage from one side to another.

The next discourse I had with him upon this subject I began thus: Well, seignior, said I, we are now come quite through the valleys and passages of the Andes, and, methinks I see a vast open country before me on the other side; pray tell me, have you ever been so far as to look into that part of the world, and what kind of a country it is?

He answered gravely, that he had been far enough several times to look at a distance into the vast country I spoke of; And such, indeed, it is, said he; and, as we come upon the rising part of the hills we see a great way, and a country without end; but, as to any descriptions of it, I can say but little, added he, only this, that it is a very fruitful country on that side next the hills; what it is farther, I know not.

I asked him if there were any considerable rivers in it, and which way they generally run? He said it could not be but that from such a ridge of mountains as the Andes there must be a great many rivers on that side, as there were apparently on this; and that, as the country was infinitely larger, and their course, in proportion, longer, it would necessarily follow that those small rivers would run one into another, and so form great navigable rivers, as was the case in the Rio de la Plata, which originally sprung from the same hills, about the city La Plata, in Peru, and swallowing up all the streams of less note, became, by the mere length of its course, one of the greatest rivers in the world. That, as he observed, most of those rivers ran rather south-eastward than northward, he believed they ran away to the sea, a great way farther to the south than the Rio de la Plata; but, as to what part of the coast they might come to the sea in, that he knew nothing of it.

This account was so rational that nothing could be more, and was, indeed, extremely satisfactory. It was also very remarkable that this agreed exactly with the accounts before given me by the two Chilian Indians, or natives, which I had on board, and with whom I still continued to discourse, as occasion presented; but whom, at this time, I removed into the Madagascar ship, to make-room for these Spanish prisoners.

I observed the Spaniard was made very sensible, by my doctor, of the obligation both he and his fellow-prisoners were under to me, in my persuading the privateers to set them at liberty, and in undertaking to carry them home to that part of Spain from whence they came; for, as they had lost their cargo, their voyage seemed to be at an end. The sense of the favour, I say, which I had done him, and was still doing him, in the civil treatment which I gave him, made this gentleman, for such he was in himself and in his disposition, whatever he was by family, for that I knew nothing of, I say, it made him exceedingly importunate with me, and with my doctor, who spoke Spanish perfectly well, to go with him to Villa Rica.

I made him no promise, but talked at a distance. I told him, if he had lived by the sea, and I could have sailed to his door in my ship, I would have made him a visit. He returned, that he wished he could make the river of Baldivia navigable for me, that I might bring my ship up to his door; and, he would venture to say, that neither I, nor any of my ship's company, should starve while we were with him. In the interval of these discourses, I asked my doctor his opinion, whether he thought I might trust this Spaniard, if I had a mind to go up and see the country for a few days?

Seignior, says he, the Spaniards are, in some respects, the worst nation under the sun; they are cruel, inexorable, uncharitable, voracious, and, in several cases, treacherous; but, in two things, they are to be depended upon beyond all the nations in the world; that is to say, when they give their honour, to perform anything, and when they have a return to make for any favour received. And here he entertained me with a long story of a merchant of Carthagena, who, in a sloop, was shipwrecked at sea, and was taken up by an English merchant on board a ship bound to London from Barbadoes, or some other of our islands; that the English merchant, meeting another English ship bound to Jamaica, put the Spanish merchant on board him, paid him for his passage, and desired him to set him on shore on the Spanish coast, as near to Carthagena as he could. This Spanish merchant could never rest till he found means to ship himself from Carthagena to the Havannah, in the galleons; from thence to Cadiz in Old Spain; and from thence to London, to find out the English merchant, and make him a present to the value of a thousand pistoles for saving his life, and for his civility in returning him to Jamaica, &c.

Whether the story was true or not, his inference from it was just, namely, that a Spaniard never forgot a kindness. But take it withal, says the doctor, that I believe it is as much the effect of their pride as of their virtue; for at the same time, said he, they never forget an ill turn any more than they do a good one; and they frequently entail their enmities on their families, and prosecute the revenge from one generation to another, so that the heir has, with the estate of his ancestors, all the family broils upon his hands as he comes to his estate.

From all this he inferred that, as this Spaniard found himself so very much obliged to me, I might depend upon it that he had so much pride in him, that if he could pull down the Andes for me to go through, and I wanted it, he would do it for me; and that nothing would be a greater satisfaction to him, than to find some way or other how to requite me.

All these discourses shortened our voyage, and we arrived fair and softly (for it was very good weather, and little wind) at Tucapel, or the river Imperial, within ten leagues of Baldivia, that is to say, of Cape Bonifacio, which is the north point of the entrance into the river of Baldivia. And here I took one of the most unaccountable, and I must needs acknowledge, unjustifiably resolutions, that ever any commander, intrusted with a ship of such force, and a cargo of such consequence, adventured upon before, and which I by no means recommend to any commander of any ship to imitate; and this was, to venture up into the country above a hundred and fifty miles from my ship, leaving the success of the whole voyage, the estates of my employers, and the richest ship and cargo that ever came out of those seas, to the care and fidelity of two or three men. Such was the unsatisfied thirst of new discoveries which I brought out of England with me, and which I nourished, at all hazards, to the end of the voyage.

However, though I condemn myself in the main for the rashness of the undertaking, yet let me do myself so much justice as to leave it on record too, that I did not run this risk without all needful precautions for the safety of the ship and cargo.

And first, I found out a safe place for the ships to ride, and this neither in the river of Tucapel, nor in the river of Baldivia, but in an opening or inlet of water, without a name, about a league to the south of Tucapel, embayed and secured from almost all the winds that could blow. Here the ships lay easy, with water enough, having about eleven fathoms good holding ground, and about half a league from shore.

I left the supercargo and my mate, also a kinsman of my own, a true sailor, who had been a midshipman, but was now a lieutenant; I say, to those I left the command of both my ships, but with express orders not to stir nor unmoor, upon any account whatever, unavoidable accidents excepted, until my return, or until, if I should die, they should hear of that event; no, though they were to stay there six months, for they had provisions enough, and an excellent place for watering lay just by them. And I made all the men swear to me that they would make no mutiny or disorder, but obey my said kinsman in one ship, and the supercargo in the other, in all things, except removing from that place; and that, if they should command them to stir from thence, they would not so much as touch a sail or a rope for the purpose.

When I made all these conditions, and told my men that the design I went upon was for the good of their voyage, for the service of the owners, and should, if it succeeded, be for all their advantages, I asked them if they were all willing I should go? To which they all answered, that they were very willing, and would take the same care of the ships, and of all things belonging to them, as if I were on board. This encouraged me greatly, and I now resolved nothing should hinder me.

Having thus concluded everything, then, and not till then, I told my Spaniard that I had almost resolved to go along with him, at which he appeared exceedingly pleased, and, indeed, in a surprise of joy. I should have said, that, before I told him this, I had set all the rest of the prisoners on shore, at their own request, just between the port of Tucapel and the bay of the Conception, excepting two men, who, as he told me, lived in the open country beyond Baldivia, and, as he observed, were very glad to be set on shore with him, so to travel home, having lost what little they had in the ship, and to whom he communicated nothing of the discourse we had so frequently held, concerning the affair of the mountains.

I also dismissed now the two Chilian Indians, but not without a very good reward, not proportioned to their trouble and time only, but proportioned to what I seemed to expect of them, and filled them still with expectations that I would come again, and take a journey with them into the mountains.

And now it became necessary that I should, use the utmost freedom with my new friend, the Spaniard, being, as I told him, to put my life in his hands, and the prosperity of my whole adventure, both ship and ship's company.

He told me he was sensible that I did put my life into his hands, and that it was a very great token of my confidence in him, even such a one that he, being a stranger to me, had no reason to expect; but he desired me to consider that he was a Christian, not a savage; that he was one I had laid the highest obligation upon, in voluntarily taking him out of the hands of the freebooters, where he might have lost his life. And, in the next place, he said, it was some recommendation that he was a gentleman, and that I should find him to be a man of honour; and, lastly, that it did not appear that he could make any advantage of me, or that he could get anything by using me ill; and, if even that was no argument, yet I should find, when I came to his house, that he was not in a condition to want anything that might be gained, so much as to procure it by such a piece of villany and treachery as to betray and destroy the man who had saved his life, and brought him out of the hands of the devil safe to his country and family, when he might have been carried away God knows whither. But to conclude all, he desired me to accept the offer he had made me at sea, viz., that he would send for his two sons, and leave them on board the ship as hostages for my safety, and desired they might be used on board no otherwise than I was used with him in the country.

I was ashamed to accept such an offer as this, but he pressed it earnestly, and importuned the doctor to move me to accept it, telling him that he should not be easy if I did not; so that, in short, the doctor advised me to agree to it, and, accordingly, he hired a messenger and a mule, and sent away for his two sons to come to him; and such expedition the messenger made, that in six days he returned with the two sons and three servants, all on horseback. His two sons were very pretty, well-behaved youths, who appeared to be gentlemen in their very countenances; the eldest was about thirteen years old, and the other about eleven. I treated them on board, as I had done their father, with all possible respect; and, having entertained them two days, left orders that they should be treated in the same manner when I was gone; and to this I added aloud, that their father might hear it, that whenever they had a mind to go away, they should let them go. But their father laid a great many solemn charges upon them that they should not stir out of the ship till I came back safe, and that I gave them leave, and he made them promise they would not; and the young gentlemen kept their word so punctually, that, when our supercargo, whom I left in command, offered to let them go on shore several times, to divert them with shooting and hunting, they would not stir out of the ship, and did not till I came back again.

Having gone this length, and made everything ready for my adventure, we set out, viz., Captain Merlotte, the Spanish doctor, the old mutineer who had been my second mate, but who was now captain of the Madagascar ship, and myself, with two midshipmen, whom he took as servants, but whom I resolved to make the directors of the main enterprise. As to the number, I found my Spaniard made no scruple of that, if it had been half my ship's company.

We set out, some on horses and some on mules, as we could get them, but the Spaniard and myself rode on two very good horses, being the same that his two sons came on. We arrived at a noble country-seat, about a league short of the town, where, at first, I thought we had been only to put in for refreshment, but I soon found that it was really his dwelling-house, and where his family and servants resided.

Here we were received like princes, and with as much ceremony as if he had been a prince that entertained us. The major-domo, or steward of his house, received us, took in our baggage, and ordered our servants to be taken care of.

It is sufficient to say, that the Spaniard did all that pride and ostentation was capable of inspiring him with, to entertain us; and the truth is, he could not have lived in a country in the world more capable of gratifying his pride; for here, without anything uncommon, he was able to show more gold plate than many good families in our country have of silver; and as for silver, it quite eclipsed the appearance, or rather took away the very use of pewter, of which we did not see one vessel, no not in the meanest part of his house. It is true, I believe, the Spaniard had not a piece of plate, or of any household furniture, which we did not see, except what belonged to the apartment of his wife; and, it is to be observed, that the women never appeared, except at a distance, and in the gardens, and then, being under veils, we could not know the lady from her women, or the maids from the mistress.

We were lodged every one in separate apartments, very well furnished, but two of them very nobly indeed, though all the materials for furniture there must be at an excessive price. The way of lodging upon quilts, and in beds made pavilion-wise, after the Spanish custom, I need not describe; but it surprised me to see the rooms hung with very rich tapestries, in a part of the world where they must cost so dear.

We had Chilian wine served us up in round gold cups, and water in large silver decanters, that held, at least, five quarts apiece; these stood in our chamber. Our chocolate was brought up in the same manner, in deep cups, all of gold, and it was made in vessels all of silver.

It would be tiresome to the reader to particularise my account with the relation of all the fine things our host had in his house, and I could not be persuaded but that he had borrowed all the plate in the town to furnish out his sideboard and table. But my doctor told me it was nothing but what was very usual among them that were men of any substance, as it was apparent he was; and that the silversmiths at St. Jago supplied them generally with their plate ready wrought, in exchange (with allowance for the quality) for the gold which they found in the mountains, or in the brooks and streams which came from the mountains, into which the hasty showers of winter rain frequently washed down pretty large lumps, and others, which were smaller, they washed out of the sands by the ordinary methods of washing of ore.

I was better satisfied in this particular when, the next day, talking to our new landlord about the mountains, and the wealth of them, I asked him if he could show me any of the gold which was usually washed out of the hills by the rain, in the natural figure in which it was found? He smiled, and told me he could show me a little, and immediately conducted us into a kind of a closet, where he had a great variety of odd things gathered up about the mountains and rivers, such as fine shells, stones in the form of stars, heavy pieces of ore, and the like, and, after this, he pulled out a great leather bag, which had, I believe, near fifty pounds weight in it. Here, seignior, says he, here is some of the dirt of the earth; and turning it out upon the table, it was easy to see that it was all mixed with gold, though the pieces were of different forms, and some scarce looking like gold at all, being so mixed with the spar or with earth, that it did not appear so plain; but, in every bit there was something of the clear gold to be seen, and, the smaller the lumps, the purer the gold appeared.

I was surprised at the quantity, more than at the quality of the metal, having, as I have said, seen the gold which the Indians found in the countries I have described, which seemed to have little or no mixture. But then I was to have considered, that what those Indians gathered was farther from the hills which it came from, and that those rough, irregular pieces would not drive so far in the water, but would lodge themselves in the earth and sand of the rivers nearer home; and also, that the Indians, not knowing how to separate the gold by fire from the dross and mixture above, did not think those rough pieces worth their taking up, whereas, the Spaniards here understood much better what they were about.

But, to return to the closet. When he had shown us this leather pouch of gold, he swept the ore to one side of the table, which had ledges round it to keep it from running off, and took up another bag full of large pieces of stone, great lumps of earth, and pieces of various shapes, all of which had some gold in them, but not to be gotten out but by fire. These, he told us, their servants bring home as they find them in the mountains, lying loose here and there, when they go after their cattle.

But still, I asked him if they found no pieces of pure gold; upon this he turned to a great old cabinet, full of pretty large drawers, and, pulling out one drawer, he showed us a surprising number of pieces of pure clean gold, some round, some long, some flat, some thick, all of irregular shapes, and worked roundish at the ends with rolling along on the sands; some of these weighed a quarter of an ounce, some more, and some less; and, as I lifted the drawer, I thought there could be no less than between twenty and thirty pounds weight of it.

Then he pulled out another drawer, which was almost full of the same kind of metal, but as small as sand, the biggest not so big as pins heads, and which might very properly be called gold dust.

After this sight, we were not to be surprised at anything he could show us of the kind. I asked him how long such a treasure might be amassing together in that country? He told me that was according to the pains they might take in the search; that he had been twelve years here, and had done little or nothing; but, had he had twenty negroes to have set on work, as he might have had, he might have procured more than this in one year. I asked him how much gold in weight he thought there might be in all he had shown me? He told me, he could not tell; that they never troubled themselves to weigh, but when the silversmith at St. Jago came to bring home any vessel, or when the merchants from Lima came to Baldivia with European goods, then they bought what they wanted of them. That they were sensible they gave excessive prices for everything, even ten or twenty for one; but as gold, he said, was the growth of that country, and the other things, such as cloth, linen, fine silks, &c, were the gold of Europe, they did not think much to give what was asked for those things. In short, I found that the people in this country, though they kept large plantations in their hands, had great numbers of cattle, ingenios, as they call them, for making sugar, and land, under management, for the maintenance of themselves and families, yet did not wholly neglect the getting gold out of the mountains, where it was in such plenty; and, therefore, it seems the town adjacent is called Villa Rica, or the Rich Town, being seated, as it were, at the foot of the mountains, and in the richest part of them.

After I had sufficiently admired the vast quantity of gold he had, he made signs to the doctor that I should take any piece or any quantity that I pleased; but thought I might take it as an affront to have him offer me any particular small parcel. The doctor hinted to me, and I bade him return him thanks; but to let him know that I would by no means have any of that, but that I would be glad to take up a piece or two, such as chance should present to me, in the mountains, that I might show in my own country, and tell them that I took it up with my own hands. He answered, he would go with me himself; and doubted not but to carry me where I should fully satisfy my curiosity, if I would be content to climb a little among the rocks.

I now began to see plainly that I had no manner of need to have taken his sons for hostages for my safety, and would fain have sent for them back again, but he would by no means give me leave; so I was obliged to give that over. A day or two after, I desired he would give me leave to send for one person more from the ships, who I had a great mind should see the country with me, and to send for some few things that I should want, and, withal, to satisfy my men that I was safe and well.

This he consented to; so I sent away one of the two midshipmen, whom I called my servants, and with him two servants of the Spaniard, my landlord, as I styled him, with four mules and two horses. I gave my midshipman my orders and directions, under my hand, to my supercargo, what to do, for I was resolved to be even with my Spaniard for all his good usage of me. The midshipman and his two companions did not return in less than ten days, for they came back pretty well laden, and were obliged to come all the way on foot.

The whole of this time my landlord and I spent in surveying the country, and viewing his plantation. As for the city of Villa Rica, it was not the most proper to go there in public, and the doctor knew that as well as the Spaniard, and, therefore, though we went several times incognito, yet it was of no consequence to me, neither did I desire it.

One night I had a very strange fright here, and behaved myself very much like a simpleton about it. The case was this. I waked in the middle of the night, and, chancing to open my eyes, I saw a great light of fire, which, to me, seemed as if the house, or some part of it, had been on fire, I, as if I had been at Wapping or Rotherhithe, where people are always terrified with such things, jumped out of bed, and called my friend, Captain Merlotte, and cried out, Fire! fire! The first thing I should have thought of on this occasion should have been, that the Spaniards did not understand what the words fire! fire! meant; and that, if I expected they should understand me, I should have cried Fuego, Fuego!

However, Captain Merlotte got up, and my Madagascar captain, for we all lay near one another, and, with the noise, they waked the whole house; and my landlord, as he afterwards confessed, began to suspect some mischief, his steward having come to his chamber door, and told him that the strangers were up in arms; in which mistake we might have all had our throats cut, and the poor Spaniard not to blame neither.

But our doctor coming hastily in to me, unriddled the whole matter, which was this: that a volcano, or burning vent among the hills, being pretty near the Spanish side of the country, as there are many of them in the Andes, had flamed out that night, and gave such a terrible light in the air as made us think the fire had at least been in the outhouses, or in part of the house, and, accordingly, had put me in such a fright.

Upon this, having told me what it was, he ran away to the Spanish servants, and told them what the meaning of it all was, and bade them go and satisfy their master, which they did, and all was well again; but, as for myself, I sat up almost all the night staring out from the window at the eruption of fire upon the hills, for the like wonderful appearance I had never seen before.

I sincerely begged my landlord's pardon for disturbing his house, and asked him if those eruptions were frequent? He said no, they were not frequent, for they were constant, either in one part of the hills or another; and that in my passing the mountains I should see several of them. I asked him if they were not alarmed with them? and if they were not attended with earthquakes? He said, he believed that among the hills themselves they might have some shakings of the earth, because sometimes were found pieces of the rocks that had been broken off and fallen down; and that it was among those that sometimes parts of stone were found which had gold interspersed in them, as if they had been melted and run together, of which he had shown me some; but that, as for earthquakes in the country, he had never heard of any since he came thither, which had been upwards of fifteen years, including three years that he dwelt at St. Jago.

One day, being out on horseback with my landlord, we rode up close to the mountains, and he showed me at a distance, an entrance as he called it, into them, frightful enough, indeed, as shall be described in its place. He then told me, that was the way he intended to carry me when he should go to show me the highest hills in the world; but he turned short, and, smiling, said it should not be yet; for, though he had promised me a safe return, and left hostages for it, yet he had not capitulated for time.

I told him he need not capitulate with me for time; for if I had not two ships to stay my coming, and between three and four hundred men eating me up all the while, I did not know whether I should ever go away again or not, if he would give me house room. He told me as to that, he had sent my men some provisions, so that they would not starve if I did not go back for some days. This surprised me not a little, and I discovered it in my countenance. Nay, seignior, says he, I have only sent them some victuals to maintain my two hostages, for you know they must not want. It was not good manners in me to ask what he had sent; but I understood, as soon as my midshipman returned, that he had sent down sixteen cows or runts, I know not what else to call them, but they were black cattle, thirty hogs, thirteen large Peruvian sheep, as big as great calves, and three casks of Chilian wine, with an assurance that they should have more provisions when that was spent.

I was amazed at all this munificence of the Spaniard, and very glad I was that I had sent my midshipman for the things I intended to present him with, for I was as well able to requite him for a large present as he was to make it, and had resolved it before I knew he had sent anything to the ships; so that this exchanging of presents was but a kind of generous barter or commerce; for as to gold, we had either of us so much, that it was not at all equal in value to what we had to give on both sides, as we were at present situated.

In short, my midshipman returned with the horses and servants, and when he had brought what I had sent for into a place which I desired the Spaniard to allow me to open my things in, I sent my doctor to desire the Spaniard to let me speak with him.

I told him first, that he must give me his parole of honour not to take amiss what I had to say to him; that it was the custom in our country, at any time, to make presents to the ladies, with the knowledge and consent of their husbands or parents, without any evil design, or without giving any offence, but that I knew it was not so among the Spaniards. That I had not had the honour yet either to see his lady or his daughter, but that I had heard he had both; however, that if he pleased to be the messenger of a trifle I had caused my man to bring, and would present it for me, and not take it as an offence, he should see beforehand what it was, and I would content myself with his accepting it in their behalf.

He told me, smiling, he did not bring me thither to take any presents of me. I had already done enough, in that I had given him his liberty, which was the most valuable gift in the world: and, as to his wife, I had already made her the best present I was able, having given her back her husband. That it is true, it was not the custom of the Spaniards to let their wives appear in any public entertainment of friends, but that he had resolved to break through that custom; and that he had told his wife what a friend I had been to her family, and that she should thank me for it in person; and that then, what present I had designed for her, since I would be a maker of presents, she should do herself the honour to take it with her own hands, and he would be very far from mistaking them, or taking it ill from his wife.

As this was the highest compliment he was able to make me, the more he was obliging in the manner, for he returned in about two hours, leading his wife into the room by the hand, and his daughter following.

I must confess I was surprised, for I did not expect to have seen such a sight in America. The lady's dress, indeed, I cannot easily describe; but she was really a charming woman, of about forty years of age, and covered over with emeralds and diamonds; I mean as to her head. She was veiled till she came into the room, but gave her veil to her woman when her husband took her by the hand. Her daughter I took to be about twelve years old, which the Spaniards count marriageable; she was pretty, but not so handsome as her mother.

After the compliments on both sides, my landlord, as I now call him, told her very handsomely what a benefactor I had been to her family, by redeeming him from the hands of villains; and she, turning to me, thanked me in the most obliging manner, and with a modest graceful way of speech, such as I cannot describe, and which indeed I did not think the Spaniards, who are said to be so haughty, had been acquainted with.

I then desired the doctor to tell the Spaniard, her husband, that I requested his lady to accept a small present which my midshipman had brought for her from the ship, and which I took in my hand, and the Spaniard led his wife forward to take it; and I must needs say it was not a mean present, besides its being of ten times the value in that place as it would have been at London; and I was now very glad that, as I mentioned above, I always reserved a small quantity of all goods unsold, that I might have them to dispose of as occasion should offer.

First, I presented her with a very fine piece of Dutch Holland, worth in London about seven shillings an ell, and thirty-six ells in length, and worth in Chili, to be sure, fifteen pieces of eight per ell, at least; or it was rather likely that all the kingdom of Chili had not such another.

Then I gave her two pieces of China damask, and two pieces of China silks, called atlasses, flowered with gold; two pieces of fine muslin, one flowered the other plain, and a piece of very fine chintz, or printed calico; also a large parcel of spices, made up in elegant papers, being about six pounds of nutmegs, and about twice as many cloves.

And lastly, to the young lady I gave one piece of damask, two pieces of China taffity, and a piece of fine striped muslin.

After all this was delivered, and the ladies had received them, and given them their women to hold, I pulled out a little box in which I had two couple of large pearls, of that pearl which I mentioned we found at the Pearl Islands, very well matched for ear-rings, and gave the lady one pair, and the daughter the other; and now, I think, I had made a present fit for an ambassador to carry to a prince.

The ladies made all possible acknowledgment, and we had the honour that day to dine with them in public. My landlord, the Spaniard, told me I had given them such a present as the viceroy of Mexico's lady would have gone fifty leagues to have received.

But I had not done with my host; for after dinner, I took him into the same room, and told him I hoped he did not think I had made all my presents to the ladies, and had nothing left to show my respect to him; and therefore, first, I presented him with three negro men, which I had bought at Callao for my own use, but knew I could supply myself again, at or in my way home, at a moderate price; in the next place, I gave him three pieces of black Colchester baize, which, though they are coarse ordinary things in England, that a footman would scarce wear, are a habit for a prince in that country. I then gave him a piece of very fine English serge, which was really very valuable in England, but much more there, and another piece of crimson broadcloth, and six pieces of fine silk druggets for his two sons; and thus I finished my presents. The Spaniard stood still and looked on all the while I was laying out my presents to him, as one in a transport, and said not one word till all was over; but then he told me very gravely, that it was now time for him to turn me out of his house: For seignior, says he, no man ought to suffer himself to be obliged beyond his power of return, and I have no possible way of making any return to you equal to such things as these.

It is true the present I had made him, if it was to be rated by the value of things in the country where it then was, would have been valued at six or seven hundred pounds sterling; but, to reckon them as they cost me, did not altogether amount to above one hundred pounds, except the three negroes, which, indeed, cost me at Lima one thousand two hundred pieces of eight.

He was as sensible of the price of those negroes as I was of the occasion he had of them, and of the work he had to do for them; and he came to me about an hour after, and told me he had looked over all the particulars of the noble presents which I had made them; and though the value was too great for him to accept, or for any man to offer him, yet since I had been at so much trouble to send for the things, and that I thought him worthy such a bounty, he was come back to tell me that he accepted thankfully all my presents, both to himself and to his wife and daughter, except only the three negroes; and as they were bought in the country, and were the particular traffick of the place, he could not take them as a present, but would be equally obliged, and take it for as much a favour if I would allow him to pay for them.

I smiled, and told him he and I would agree upon that; for he did not yet know what favours I had to ask of him, and what expense I should put him to; that I had a great design in my view, which I was to crave his assistance in, and which I had not yet communicated to him, in which he might perhaps find that he would pay dear enough for all the little presents I had made him; and, in the meantime, to make himself easy as to the three negro men, I gave him my word that he should pay for them, only not yet.

He could have nothing to object against an offer of this kind, because he could not guess what I meant, but gave me all the assurance of service and assistance that lay in his power in anything that I might have to do in that country.

But here, by the way, it ought to be understood, that all this was carried on with a supposition that we acted under a commission from the King of France; and though he knew many of us were English, and that I was an Englishman in particular, yet as we had such a commission, and produced it, we were Frenchmen in that sense to him, nor did he entertain us under any other idea.

The sequel of this story will also make it sufficiently appear that I did not make such presents as these in mere ostentation, or only upon the compliment of a visit to a Spanish gentleman, any more than I would leave my ship and a cargo of such value, in the manner I had done, to make a tour into the country, if I had not had views sufficient to justify such measures; and the consequence of those measures will be the best apology for my conduct, with all who will impartially consider them.

We had now spent a fortnight, and something more, in ceremony and civilities, and in now and then taking a little tour about the fields and towards the mountains. However, even in this way of living I was not so idle as I seemed to be, for I not only made due observations of all the country which I saw, but informed myself sufficiently of the parts which I did not see. I found the country not only fruitful in the soil, but wonderfully temperate and agreeable in its climate. The air, though hot, according to its proper latitude, yet that heat so moderated by the cool breezes from the mountains, that it was rather equal to the plain countries in other parts of the world in the latitude of 50° than to a climate in 38 to 40°.

This gave the inhabitants the advantages, not only of pleasant and agreeable living, but also of a particular fertility which hot climates are not blessed with, especially as to corn, the most necessary of all productions, such as wheat, I mean European wheat, or English wheat, which grew here as well and as kindly as in England, which in Peru and in the Isthmus of America will by no means thrive for want of moisture and cold.

Here were also an excellent middling breed of black cattle, which the natives fed under the shade of the mountains and on the banks of the rivers till they came to be very fat. In a word, here were, or might be produced, all the plants, fruits, and grain, of a temperate climate. At the same time, the orange, lemon, citron, pomegranate, and figs, with a moderate care would come to a very tolerable perfection in their gardens, and even sugar canes in some places, though these last but rarely, and not without great art in the cultivation, and chiefly in gardens.

I was assured, that farther southward, beyond Baldivia, and to the latitude of 47 to 49°, the lands were esteemed richer than where we now were, the grass more strengthening and nourishing for the cattle, and that, consequently, the black cattle, horses, and hogs, were all of a larger breed. But that, as the Spaniards had no settlement beyond Baldivia to the south, so they did not find the natives so tractable as where we then were; where, though the Spaniards were but few, and the strength they had was but small, yet, as upon any occasion they had always been assisted with forces sufficient from St. Jago, and, if need were, even from Peru, so the natives had always been subdued, and had found themselves obliged to submit; and that now they were entirely reduced, and were, and had been for several years, very easy and quiet. Besides, the plentiful harvest which they made of gold from the mountains (which appeared to be the great allurement of the Spaniards), had drawn them rather to settle here than farther southward, being naturally addicted, as my new landlord confessed to me, to reap the harvest which had the least labour and hazard attending it, and the most profit.

Not but that, at the same time, he confessed that he believed and had heard that there was as much gold to be found farther to the south, as far as the mountains continued; but that, as I have said, the natives were more troublesome there, and more dangerous, and that the king of Spain did not allow troops sufficient to civilize and reduce them.

I asked him concerning the natives in the country where we were? He told me they were the most quiet and inoffensive people, since the Spaniards had reduced them by force, that could be desired; that they were not, indeed, numerous or warlike, the warlike and obstinate part of them having fled farther off to the south, as they were overpowered by the Spaniards; that, for those who were left, they lived secure under the protection of the Spanish governor; that they fed cattle and planted the country, and sold the product of their lands chiefly to the Spaniards; but that they did not covet to be rich, only to obtain clothes, arms, powder and shot, which, however, they were suffered to have but sparingly, and with good assurance of their fidelity. I asked him if they were not treacherous and perfidious, and if it was not dangerous trusting themselves among them in the mountains, and in the retired places where they dwelt? He told me that it was quite the contrary; that they were so honest, and so harmless, that he would at any time venture to send his two sons into the mountains a-hunting, with each of them a Chilian for his guide; and let them stay with the said natives two or three nights and days at a time, and be in no uneasiness about them; and that none of them were ever known to do any foul or treacherous thing by the Spaniards, since he had been in that country.

Having thus finally informed myself of things, I began now to think it was high time to have a sight of the particulars which I came to inquire after, viz., the passages of the mountains, and the wonders that were to be discovered on the other side; and, accordingly, I took my patron, the Spaniard, by himself, and told him that as I was a traveller, and was now in such a remote part of the world, he could not but think I should be glad to see everything extraordinary that was to be seen, that I might be able to give some account of the world when I came into Europe, better and differing from what others had done who had been there before me; and that I had a great mind, if he would give me his assistance, to enter into the passages and valleys which he had told me so much of in the mountains; and, if it was possible, which, indeed, I had always thought it was not, to take a prospect of the world on the other side.

He told me it was not a light piece of work, and perhaps the discoveries might not answer my trouble, there being little to be seen but steep precipices, inhospitable rocks, and impassable mountains, immuring us on every side, innumerable rills and brooks of water falling from the cliffs, making a barbarous and unpleasant sound, and that sound echoed and reverberated from innumerable cavities among the rocks, and these all pouring down into one middle stream, which we should always find on one side or other of us as we went; and that sometimes we should be obliged to pass those middle streams, as well as the rills and brooks on the sides, without a bridge, and at the trouble of pulling off our clothes.

He told us that we should meet, indeed, with provisions enough, and with an innocent, harmless people, who, according to their ability, would entertain us very willingly; but that I, who was a stranger, would be sorely put to it for lodging, especially for so many of us.

However, he said, as he had perhaps at first raised this curiosity in me, by giving me a favourable account of the place, he would be very far from discouraging me now; and that, if I resolved to go, he would not only endeavour to make everything as pleasant to me as he could, but that he and his major-domo would go along with me, and see us safe through and safe home again; but desired me not to be in too much haste, for that he must make some little preparation for the journey, which, as he told us, might perhaps take us up fourteen or sixteen days forward, and as much back again; not, he said, that it was necessary that we should be so long going and coming, as that he supposed I would take time to see everything which I might think worth seeing, and not be in so much haste as if I was sent express. I told him he was very much in the right; that I did not desire to make a thing which I had expected so much pleasure in, be a toil to me more than needs must; and, above all, that as I supposed I should not return into these parts very soon, I would not take a cursory view of a place which I expected would be so well worth seeing, and let it be known to all I should speak of it to, that I wanted to see it again before I could give a full account of it.

Well, seignior, says he, we will not be in haste, or view it by halves; for, if wild and uncouth places be a diversion to you, I promise myself your curiosity shall be fully gratified; but as to extraordinary things, rarities in nature, and surprising incidents, which foreigners expect, I cannot say much to those. However, what think you, seignior, says he, if we should take a tour a little way into the entrance of the hills which I showed you the other day, and look upon the gate of this gulf? Perhaps your curiosity may be satisfied with the first day's prospect, which I assure you will be none of the most pleasant, and you may find yourself sick of the enterprise.

I told him, no; I was so resolved upon the attempt, since he, who I was satisfied would not deceive me, had represented it as so feasible, and especially since he had offered to conduct me through it, that I would not, for all the gold that was in the mountains, lay it aside. He shook his head at that expression, and, smiling at the doctor, says he, This gentleman little thinks that there is more gold in these mountains, nay, even in this part where we are, than there is above ground in the whole world. Partly understanding what he said, I answered, my meaning was to let him see that nothing could divert me from the purpose of viewing the place, unless he himself forbade me, which I hoped he would not; and that, as for looking a little way into the passage, to try if the horror of the place would put a check to my curiosity, I would not give him that trouble, seeing, the more terrible and frightful, the more difficult and impracticable it was, provided it could be mastered at last, the more it would please me to attempt and overcome it.

Nay, nay, seignior, said he, pleasantly, there is nothing difficult or impracticable in it, nor is it anything but what the country people, and even some of our nation, perform every day; and that not only by themselves, either for sport in pursuit of game, but even with droves of cattle, which they go with from place to place, as to a market or a fair; and, therefore, if the horror of the cliffs and precipices, the noises of the volcanos, the fire, and such things as you may hear and see above you, will not put a stop to your curiosity, I assure you, you shall not meet with anything impassable or impracticable below, nor anything but, with the assistance of God and the Blessed Virgin (and then he crossed himself, and so we did all), we shall go cheerfully over.

Finding, therefore, that I was thus resolutely bent upon the enterprise, but not in the least guessing at my design, he gave order to have servants and mules provided, for mules are much fitter to travel among the hills than horses; and, in four days he promised to be ready for a march.

I had nothing to do in all these four days but to walk abroad, and, as we say, look about me; but I took this opportunity to give instructions to my two midshipmen, who were called my servants, in what they were to do.

First, I charged them to make landmarks, bearings, and beacons, as we might call them, upon the rocks above them, and at every turning in the way below them, also at the reaches and windings of the rivers and brooks, falls of water, and everything remarkable, and to keep each of them separate and distinct journals of those things, not only to find the way back again by the same steps, but that they might be able to find that way afterwards by themselves, and without guides, which was the foundation and true intent of all the rest of my undertaking; and, as I knew these were both capable to do it, and had courage and fidelity to undertake it, I had singled them out for the attempt, and had made them fully acquainted with my whole scheme, and, consequently, they knew the meaning and reason of my present discourse with them. They promised not to fail to show me a plan of the hills, with the bearings of every point, one with another, where every step was to be taken, and every turning to the right hand or to the left, and such a journal, I believe, was never seen before or since, but it is too long for this place. I shall, however, take out the heads of it as I proceed, which may serve as a general description of the place.

The evening of the fourth day, as he had appointed, my friend, the Spaniard, let me know, that he was ready to set out, and accordingly we began our cavalcade. My retinue consisted of six, as before, and we had mules provided for us; my two midshipmen, as servants, had two mules given them also for their baggage, the Spaniard had six also, viz., his gentleman, or, as I called him before, his major-domo, on horseback, that is to say, on muleback, with mules for his baggage, and four servants on foot. Just before we set out, his gentleman brought each of us a fuzee, and our two servants each a harquebuss, or short musket, with cartouches, powder, and ball, together with a pouch and small shot, such as we call swan-shot, for fowls or deer, as we saw occasion.

I was as well pleased with this circumstance as with any my landlord had done, because I had not so entire a confidence in the native Chilians as he had; but I saw plainly, some time after, that I was wrong, for nothing could be more honest, quiet, and free from design, than those people, except the poor honest people where we dressed up the king and queen, as already mentioned.

We were late in the morning before we got out, having all this equipage to furnish, and, travelling very gently, it was about two hours before sunset when we came to the entrance of the mountains, where, to my surprise, I found we were to go in upon a level, without any ascent, at least that was considerable. We had, indeed, gone up upon a sharp ascent, for near two miles, before we came to the place.

The entrance was agreeable enough, the passage being near half a mile broad. On the left hand was a small river, whose channel was deep, but the water shallow, there having been but little rain for some time; the water ran very rapid, and, as my Spaniard told me, was sometimes exceeding fierce. The entrance lay inclining a little south, and was so straight, that we could see near a mile before us; but the prodigious height of the hills on both sides, and before us, appearing one over another, gave such a prospect of horror, that I confess it was frightful at first to look on the stupendous altitude of the rocks; everything above us looking one higher than another was amazing; and to see how in some places they hung over the river, and over the passage, it created a dread of being overwhelmed with them.

The rocks and precipices of the Andes, on our right hand, had here and there vast cliffs and entrances, which looked as if they had been different thoroughfares; but, when we came to look full into them, we could see no passage at the farther end, and that they went off in slopes, and with gulleys made by the water, which, in hasty rains, came pouring down from the hills, and which, at a distance, made such noises as it is impossible to conceive, unless by having seen and heard the like before; for the water, falling from a height twenty times as high as our own Monument, and, perhaps, much higher, and meeting in the passage with many dashes and interruptions, it is impossible to describe how the sound, crossing and interfering, mingled itself, and the several noises sunk one into another, increasing the whole, as the many waters joining increased the main stream.

We entered this passage about two miles the first night; after the first length, which as I said, held about three quarters of a mile, we turned away to the south, short on the right hand; the river leaving us, seemed to come through a very narrow but deep hollow of the mountains, where there was little more breadth at the bottom than the channel took up, though the rocks inclined backward as they ascended, as placed in several stages, though all horrid and irregular; and we could see nothing but blackness and terror all the way. I was glad our passage did not turn on that side, but wondered that we should leave the river, and the more when I found, that in the way we went, having first mounted gently a green pleasant slope, it declined again, and we saw a new rivulet begin in the middle, and the water running south-east or thereabouts. This discovery made me ask if the water went away into the new world beyond the hills? My patron smiled, and said, No seignior, not yet; we shall meet with the other river again very quickly; and so we found it again the next morning.

When we came a little farther, we found the passage open, and we came to a very pleasant plain, which declined a little gradually, widening to the left, or east side; on the right side of this we saw another vast opening like the first, which went in about half a mile, and then closed up as the first had done, sloping up to the top of the hills, a most astonishing inconceivable height.

My patron stopping here, and getting down, or alighting from his mule, gave him to his man, and asking me to alight, told me this was the first night's entertainment I was to meet with in the Andes, and hoped I was prepared for it. I told him, that I might very well consent to accept of such entertainment, in a journey of my own contriving, as he was content to take up with, in compliment to me.

I looked round to see if there were any huts or cots of the mountaineers thereabouts, but I perceived none; only I observed something like a house, and it was really a house of some of the said mountaineers, upon the top of a precipice as high from where we stood, as the summit of the cupola of St. Paul's, and I saw some living creatures, whether men or women I could not tell, looking from thence down upon us. However, I understood afterwards that they had ways to come at their dwelling, which were very easy and agreeable, and had lanes and plains where they fed their cattle, and had everything growing that they desired.

My patron, making a kind of an invitation to me to walk, took me up that dark chasm, or opening, on the right hand, which I have just mentioned. Here, sir, said he, if you will venture to walk a few steps, it is likely we may show you some of the product of this country; but, recollecting that night was approaching, he added, I see it is too dark; perhaps it will be better to defer it till the morning. Accordingly, we walked back towards the place where we had left our mules and servants, and, when we came thither, there was a complete camp fixed, three very handsome tents raised, and a bar set up at a distance, where the mules were tied one to another to graze, and the servants and the baggage lay together, with an open tent over them.

My patron led me into the first tent, and told me he was obliged to let me know that I must make a shift with that lodging, the place not affording any better.

Here we had quilts laid very commodiously for me and my three comrades, and we lodged very comfortably; but, before we went to rest, we had the third tent to go to, in which there was a very handsome table, covered with a cold treat of roasted mutton and beef, very well dressed, some potted or baked venison, with pickles, conserves, and fine sweetmeats of various sorts.

Here we ate very freely, but he bade us depend upon it that we should not fare so well the next night, and so it would be worse every night, till we came to lie entirely at a mountaineer's; but he was better to us than he pretended.

In the morning, we had our chocolate as regularly as we used to have it in his own house, and we were soon ready to pursue our journey. We went winding now from the south-east to the left, till our course looked east by north, when we came again to have the river in view. But I should have observed here, that my two midshipmen, and two of my patron's servants, had, by his direction, been very early in the morning climbing up the rocks in the opening on the right hand, and had come back again about a quarter of an hour after we set out; when, missing my two men, I inquired for them, and my patron said they were coming; for, it seems he saw them at a distance, and so we halted for them.

When they were come almost up to us, he called to his men in Spanish, to ask if they had had Una bon vejo? They answered, Poco, poco; and when they came quite up, one of my midshipmen showed me three or four small bits of clean perfect gold, which they had picked up in the hill or gullet where the water trickled down from the rocks; and the Spaniard told them that, had they had time, they should have found much more, the water being quite down, and nobody having been there since the last hard rain. One of the Spaniards had three small bits in his hand also. I said nothing for the present, but charged my midshipmen to mark the place, and so we went on.

We followed up the stream of this water for three days more, encamping every night as before, in which time we passed by several such openings into the rocks on either side. On the fourth day we had the prospect of a very pleasant valley and river below us, on the north side, keeping its course almost in the middle; the valley reaching near four miles in length, and in some places near two miles broad.

This sight was perfectly surprising, because here we found the vale fruitful, level, and inhabited, there being several small villages or clusters of houses, such as the Chilians live in, which are low houses, covered with a kind of sedge, and sheltered with little rows of thick grown trees, but of what kind we knew not.

We saw no way through the valley, nor which way we were to go out, but perceived it everywhere bounded with prodigious mountains, look to which side of it we would. We kept still on the right, which was now the south-east side of the river, and as we followed it up the stream, it was still less than at first, and lessened every step we went, because of the number of rills we left behind us; and here we encamped the fifth time, and all this time the Spanish gentleman victualled us; then we turned again to the right, where we had a new and beautiful prospect of another valley, as broad as the other, but not above a mile in length.

After we had passed through this valley, my patron rode up to a poor cottage of a Chilian Indian without any ceremony, and calling us all about him, told us that there we would go to dinner. We saw a smoke indeed in the house, rather than coming out of it; and the little that did, smothered through a hole in the roof instead of a chimney. However, to this house, as an inn, my patron had sent away his major-domo and another servant; and there they were, as busy as two professed cooks, boiling and stewing goats' flesh and fowls, making up soups, broths, and other messes, which it seems they were used to provide, and which, however homely the cottage was, we found very savoury and good.

Immediately a loose tent was pitched, and we had our table set up, and dinner served in; and afterwards, having reposed ourselves (as the custom there is), we were ready to travel again.

I had leisure all this while to observe and wonder at the admirable structure of this part of the country, which may serve, in my opinion, for the eighth wonder of the world; that is to say, supposing there were but seven before. We had in the middle of the day, indeed, a very hot sun, and the reflection from the mountains made it still hotter; but the height of the rocks on every side began to cast long shadows before three o'clock, except where the openings looked towards the west; and as soon as those shadows reached us, the cool breezes of the air came naturally on, and made our way exceeding pleasant and refreshing.

The place we were in was green and flourishing, and the soil well cultivated by the poor industrious Chilians, who lived here in perfect solitude, and pleased with their liberty from the tyranny of the Spaniards, who very seldom visited them, and never molested them, being pretty much out of their way, except when they came for hunting and diversion, and then they used the Chilians always civilly, because they were obliged to them for their assistance in their diversions, the Chilians of those valleys being very active, strong, and nimble fellows.

By this means most of them were furnished with fire-arms, powder, and shot, and were very good marksmen; but, as to violence against any one, they entertained no thought of that kind, as I could perceive, but were content with their way of living, which was easy and free.

The tops of the mountains here, the valleys being so large, were much plainer to be seen than where the passages were narrow, for there the height was so great that we could see but little. Here, at several distances (the rocks towering one over another), we might see smoke come out of some, snow lying upon others, trees and bushes growing all around; and goats, wild asses, and other creatures, which we could hardly distinguish, running about in various parts of the country.

When we had passed through this second valley, I perceived we came to a narrower passage, and something like the first; the entrance into it indeed was smooth, and above a quarter of a mile broad, and it went winding away to the north, and then again turned round to the north-east, afterwards almost due-east, and then to the south-east, and so to south-south-east; and this frightful narrow strait, with the hanging rocks almost closing together on the top, whose height we could neither see nor guess at, continued about three days' journey more, most of the way ascending gently before us. As to the river, it was by this time quite lost; but we might see, that on any occasion of rain, or of the melting of the snow on the mountains, there was a hollow in the middle of the valley through which the water made its way, and on either hand, the sides of the hills were full of the like gulleys, made by the violence of the rain, where, not the earth only, but the rocks themselves, even the very stone, seemed to be worn and penetrated by the continual fall of the water.

Here my patron showed me, that in the hollow which I mentioned in the middle of this way, and at the bottom of those gulleys, or places worn as above in the rocks, there were often found pieces of gold, and sometimes, after a rain, very great quantities; and that there were few of the little Chilian cottages which I had seen where they had not sometimes a pound or two of gold dust and lumps of gold by them, and he was mistaken, if I was willing to stay and make the experiment, if we did not find some even then, in a very little search.

The Chilian mountaineer at whose house we stopped to dine had gone with us, and he hearing my patron say thus, ran presently to the hollow channel in the middle, where there was a kind of fail or break in it, which the water, by falling perhaps two or three feet, had made a hollow deeper than the rest, and which, though there was no water then running, yet had water in it, perhaps the quantity of a barrel or two. Here, with the help of two of the servants and a kind of scoop, he presently threw out the water, with the sand, and whatever was at bottom among it, into the ordinary watercourse; the water falling thus hard, every scoopful upon the sand or earth that came out of the scoop before it, washed a great deal of it away; and among that which remained, we might plainly see little lumps of gold shining as big as grains of sand, and sometimes one or two a little bigger.

This was demonstration enough to us. I took up some small grains of it, about the quantity of half a quarter of an ounce, and left my midshipmen to take up more, and they stayed indeed so long, that they could scarce see their way to overtake us, and brought away about two ounces in all, the Chilian and the servants freely giving them all they found.

When we had travelled about nine miles more in this winding frightful narrow way, it began to grow towards night, and my patron talked of taking up our quarters as we had before; but his gentleman put him in a mind of a Chilian, one of their old servants, who lived in a turning among the mountains, about half a mile out of our way, and where we might be accommodated with a house, or place at least, for our cookery. Very true, says our patron, we will go thither; and there, seignior, says he, turning to me, you shall see an emblem of complete felicity, even in the middle of this seat of horror; and you shall see a prince greater, and more truly so, than King Philip, who is the greatest man in the world.

Accordingly we went softly on, his gentleman having advanced before, and in about half a mile we found a turning or opening on our left, where we beheld a deep large valley, almost circular, and of about a mile diameter, and abundance of houses or cottages interspersed all over it, so that the whole valley looked like an inhabited village, and the ground like a planted garden.

We who, as I said, had been for some miles ascending, were so high above the valley, that it looked as the lowlands in England do below Box Hill in Surrey; and I was going to ask how we should get down? but, as we were come into a wider space than before, so we had more daylight; for though the hollow way had rendered it near dusk before, now it was almost clear day again.

Here we parted with the first Chilian that I mentioned, and I ordered one of my midshipmen to give him a hat, and a piece of black baize, enough to make him a cloak, which so obliged the man that he knew not what way to testify his joy; but I knew what I was doing in this, and I ordered my midshipman to do it that he might make his acquaintance with him against another time, and it was not a gift ill bestowed, as will appear in its place.

We were now obliged to quit our mules, who all took up their quarters at the top of the hill, while we, by footings made in the rocks, descended, as we might say, down a pair of stairs of half a mile long, but with many plain places between, like foot-paces, for the ease of going and coming.

Thus, winding and turning to avoid the declivity of the hill, we came very safe to the bottom, where my patron's gentleman brought our new landlord, that was to be, who came to pay his compliments to us.

He was dressed in a jerkin made of otter-skin, like a doublet, a pair of long Spanish breeches, of leather dressed after the Spanish fashion, green, and very soft, and which looked very well, but what the skin was, I could not guess; he had over it a mantle of a kind of cotton, dyed in two or three grave brown colours, and thrown about him like a Scotsman's plaid; he had shoes of a particular make, tied on like sandals, flat-heeled, no stockings, his breeches hanging down below the calf of his leg, and his shoes lacing up above his ancles. He had on a cap of the skin of some small beast like a racoon, with a bit of the tail hanging out from the crown of his head backward, a long pole in his hand, and a servant, as oddly dressed as himself, carried his gun; he had neither spado nor dagger.

When our patron came up, the Chilian stepped forward and made him three very low bows, and then they talked together, not in Spanish, but in a kind of mountain jargon, some Spanish, and some Chilian, of which I scarce understood one word. After a few words, I understood he said something of a stranger come to see, and then, I supposed, added, the passages of the mountains; then the Chilian came towards me, made me three bows, and bade me welcome in Spanish. As soon as he had said that, he turns to his barbarian, I mean his servant, for he was as ugly a looked fellow as ever I saw, and taking his gun from him presented it to me. My patron bade me take it, for he saw me at a loss what to do, telling me that it was the greatest compliment that a Chilian could pay to me; he would be very ill pleased and out of humour if it was not accepted, and would think we did not want to be friendly with him.

As we had not given this Chilian any notice of our coming, more than a quarter of an hour, we could not expect great matters of entertainment, and, as we carried our provision with us, we did not stand in much need of it; but we had no reason to complain.

This man's habitation was the same as the rest, low, and covered with a sedge, or a kind of reed which we found grew very plentifully in the valley where he lived; he had several pieces of ground round his dwelling, enclosed with walls made very artificially with small stones and no mortar; these enclosed grounds were planted with several kinds of garden-stuff for his household, such as plantains, Spanish cabbages, green cocoa, and other things of the growth of their own country, and two of them with European wheat.

He had five or six apartments in his house, every one of them had a door into the open air, and into one another, and two of them were very large and decent, had long tables on one side, made after their own way, and benches to sit to them, like our country people's long tables in England, and mattresses like couches all along the other side, with skins of several sorts of wild creatures laid on them to repose on in the heat of the day, as is the usage among the Spaniards.

Our people set up their tents and beds abroad as before; but my patron told me the Chilian would take it very ill if he and I did not take up our lodging in his house, and we had two rooms provided, very magnificent in their way.

The mattress we lay on had a large canopy over it, spread like the crown of a tent, and covered with a large piece of cotton, white as milk, and which came round every way like a curtain, so that if it had been in the open field it would have been a complete covering. The bed, such as it was, might be nearly as hard as a quilt, and the covering was of the same cotton as the curtain-work, which, it seems, is the manufacture of the Chilian women, and is made very dexterously; it looked wild, but agreeably enough, and proper to the place, so I slept very comfortably in it.

But, I must confess, I was surprised at the aspect of things in the night here. It was, as I told you above, near night when we came to this man's cottage (palace I should have called it), and, while we were taking our repast, which was very good, it grew quite night.

We had wax candles brought in to accommodate us with light, which, it seems, my patron's man had provided; and the place had so little communication with the air by windows, that we saw nothing of what was without doors.

After supper my patron turned to me and said, Come, seignior, prepare yourself to take a walk. What! in the dark, said I, in such a country as this? No, no, says he, it is never dark here, you are now come to the country of everlasting day; what think you? is not this Elysium? I do not understand you, answered I. But you will presently, says he, when I shall show you that it is now lighter abroad than when we came in. Soon after this some of the servants opened the door that went into the next room, and the door of that room, which opened in the air, stood open, from whence a light of fire shone into the outer room, and so farther into ours. What are they burning there? said I to my patron. You will see presently, says he, adding, I hope you will not be surprised, and then he led me to the outer door.

But who can express the thoughts of a man's heart, coming on a sudden into a place where the whole world seemed to be on fire! The valley was, on one side, so exceeding bright the eye could scarce bear to look at it; the sides of the mountains were shining like the fire itself; the flame from the top of the mountain on the other side casting its light directly upon them. From thence the reflection into other parts looked red, and more terrible; for the first was white and clear, like the light of the sun; but the other, being, as it were, a reflection of light mixed with some darker cavities, represented the fire of a furnace; and, in short, it might well be said here was no darkness; but certainly, at the first view, it gives a traveller no other idea than that of being at the very entrance into eternal horror.

All this while there was no fire, that is to say, no real flame to be seen, only, that where the flame was it shone clearly into the valley; but the vulcano, or vulcanoes, from whence the fire issued out (for it seems there was no less than three of them, though at the distance of some miles from one another), were on the south and east sides of the valley, which was so much on that side where we were, that we could see nothing but the light; neither on the other side could they see any more, it seems, than just the top of the flame, not knowing anything of the places from whence it issued out, which no mortal creature, no, not of the Chilians themselves, were ever hardy enough to go near. Nor would it be possible, if any should attempt it, the tops of the hills, for many leagues about them, being covered with new mountains of ashes and stones, which are daily cast out of the mouths of those volcanoes, by which they grew every day higher than they were before, and which would overwhelm, not only men, but whole armies of men, if they should venture to come near them.

When first we came into the long narrow way I mentioned last, I observed, as I thought, the wind blew very hard aloft among the hills, and that it made a noise like thunder, which I thought nothing of, but as a thing usual. But now, when I came to this terrible sight, and that I heard the same thunder, and yet found the air calm and quiet, I soon understood that it was a continued thunder, occasioned by the roaring of the fire in the bowels of the mountains.

It must be some time, as may be supposed, before a traveller, unacquainted with such things, could make them familiar to him; and though the horror and surprise might abate, after proper reflections on the nature and reason of them, yet I had a kind of astonishment upon me for a great while; every different place to which I turned my eye presented me with a new scene of horror. I was for some time frighted at the fire being, as it were, over my head, for I could see nothing of it; but that the air looked as if it were all on fire; and I could not persuade myself but it would cast down the rocks and mountains on my head; but I was laughed out of that notion by the company.

After a while, I asked them if these volcanoes did not cast out a kind of liquid fire, as I had seen an account of on the eruptions at Mount-Ætna, which cast out, as we are told, a prodigious stream of fire, and run several leagues into the sea?

Upon my putting this question to my patron, he asked the Chilian how long ago it was since such a stream, calling it by a name of their own, ran fire? He answered, it ran now, and if we were disposed to walk but three furlongs we should see it.

He said little to me, but asked me if I cared to walk a little way by this kind of light? I told him it was a surprising place we were in, but I supposed he would lead me into no danger.

He said he would assure me he would lead me into no danger; that these things were very familiar to them, but that I might depend there was no hazard, and that the flames which gave all this light were six or seven miles off, and some of them more.

We walked along the plain of the valley about half a mile, when another great valley opened to the right, and gave us a more dreadful prospect than any we had seen before; for at the farther end of this second valley, but at the distance of three miles from where we stood, we saw a livid stream of fire come running down the sides of the mountain for near three quarters of a mile in length, running like melted metal into a mould, until, I supposed, as it came nearer the bottom, it cooled and separated, and so went out of itself.

Beyond this, over the summit of a prodigious mountain, we could see the tops of the clear flame of a volcano, a dreadful one, no doubt, could we have seen it all; and from the mouth of which it was supposed this stream of fire came, though the Chilian assured us that the fire itself was eight leagues off, and that the liquid fire which we saw came out of the side of the mountain, and was two leagues from the great volcano itself, running like liquid metal out of a furnace.

They told me there was a great deal of melted gold ran down with the other inflamed earth in that stream, and that much of the metal was afterwards found there; but this I was to take upon trust.

The sight, as will easily be supposed, was best at a distance, and, indeed, I had enough of it. As for my two midshipmen, they were almost frightened out of all their resolutions of going any farther in this horrible place; and when we stopped they came mighty seriously to me, and begged, for God's sake, not to venture any farther upon the faith of these Spaniards, for that they would certainly carry us all into some mischief or other, and betray us.

I bade them be easy, for I saw nothing in it all that looked like treachery; that it was true, indeed, it was a terrible place to look on, but it seemed to be no more than what was natural and familiar there, and we should be soon out of it.

They told me very seriously that they believed it was the mouth of hell, and that, in short, they were not able to bear it, and entreated me to go back. I told them I could not think of that, but if they could not endure it, I would give consent that they should go back in the morning. However, we went for the present to the Chilian's house again, where we got a plentiful draught of Chilian wine, for my patron had taken care to have a good quantity of it with us; and in the morning my two midshipmen, who got very drunk over night, had courage enough to venture forward again; for the light of the sun put quite another face upon things, and nothing of the fire was then to be seen, only the smoke.

All our company lodged in the tents here, but myself and my patron, the Spaniard, who lodged within the Chilian's house, as I have said.

This Chilian was a great man among the natives, and all the valley I spoke of, which lay round his dwelling, was called his own. He lived in a perfect state of tranquility, neither enjoying or coveting anything but what was necessary, and wanting nothing that was so. He had gold merely for the trouble of picking it up, for it was found in all the little gulleys and rills of water which, as I have said, came down from the mountains on every side; yet I did not find that he troubled himself to lay up any great quantity, more than served to go to Villa Rica and buy what he wanted for himself and family.

He had, it seems, a wife and some daughters, but no sons; these lived in a separate house, about a furlong from that where he lived, and were kept there as a family by themselves, and if he had any sons they would have lived with him.

He did not offer to go with us any part of our way, as the other had done, but, having entertained us with great civility, took his leave. I caused one of my midshipmen to make him a present, when we came away, of a piece of black baize, enough to make him a cloak, as I did the other, and a piece of blue English serge, enough to make him a jerkin and breeches, which he accepted as a great bounty.

We set out again, though not very early in the morning, having, as I said, sat up late, and drank freely over night, and we found, that after we had been gone to sleep it had rained very hard, and though the rain was over before we went out, yet the falling of the water from the hills made such a confused noise, and was echoed so backward and forward from all sides, that it was like a strange mixture of distant thunder, and though we knew the causes, yet it could not but be surprising to us for awhile.

However, we set forward, the way under foot being pretty good; and first he went up the steps again by which we had come down, our last host waiting on us thither, and there I gave him back his gun, for he would not take it before.

In this valley, which was the pleasantest by day and the most dismal by night that ever I saw, I observed abundance of goats, as well tame in the enclosures, as wild upon the rocks; and we found afterwards, that the last were perfectly wild, and to be had, like those at Juan Fernandez, by any one who could catch them. My patron sent off two of his men, just as a huntsman casts off his hounds, to go and catch goats, and they brought us in three, which they shot in less than half an hour, and these we carried with us for our evening supply; for we made no dinner this day, having fed heartily in the morning about nine, and had chocolate two hours before that.

We travelled now along the narrow winding passage, which I mentioned before, for about four hours, until I found, that though we had ascended but gently, yet that, as we had done so for almost twenty miles together, we were got up to a frightful height, and I began to expect some very difficult descent on the other side; but we were made easy about two o'clock, when the way not only declined again to the east, but grew wider, though with frequent turnings and windings about, so that we could seldom see above half a mile before us.

We went on thus pretty much on a level, now rising, now falling; but still I found that we were a very great height from our first entrance, and, as to the running of the water, I found that it flowed neither east nor west, but ran all down the little turnings that we frequently met with on the north side of our way, which my patron told me fell all into the great valley where we saw the fire, and so passed off by a general channel north-west, until it found its way out into the open country of Chili, and so to the South Seas.

We were now come to another night's lodging, which we were obliged to take up with on the green grass, as we did the first night; but, by the help of our proveditor-general, my patron, we fared very well, our goat's flesh being reduced into so many sorts of venison, that none of us could distinguish it from the best venison we ever tasted.

Here we slept without any of the frightful things we saw the night before, except that we might see the light of the fire in the air at a great distance, like a great city in flames, but that gave us no disturbance at all.

In the morning our two hunters shot a deer, or rather a young fawn, before we were awake, and this was the first we met with in this part of our travel, and thus we were provided for dinner even before breakfast-time; as for our breakfast, it was always a Spanish one, that is to say, about a pint of chocolate.

We set out very merrily in the morning, and we that were Englishmen could not refrain smiling at one another, to think how we passed through a country where the gold lay in every ditch, as we might call it, and never troubled ourselves so much as to stoop to take it up; so certain is it, that it is easy to be placed in a station of life where that very gold, the heaping up of which is elsewhere made the main business of man's living in the world, would be of no value, and not worth taking off from the ground; nay, not of signification enough to make a present of, for that was the case here.

Two or three yards of Colchester baize, a coarse rug-like manufacture, worth in London about 15½d. per yard, was here a present for a man of quality, when, for a handful of gold dust, the same person would scarce say, Thank you; or, perhaps, would think himself not kindly treated to have it offered him.

We travelled this day pretty smartly, having rested at noon about two hours, as before, and, by my calculation, went about twenty-two English miles in all. About five o'clock in the afternoon, we came into a broad, plain open place, where, though it was not properly a valley, yet we found it lay very level for a good way together, our way lying almost east-south-east. After we had marched so about two miles, I found the way go evidently down hill, and, in half a mile more, to our singular satisfaction we found the water from the mountains ran plainly eastward, and, consequently, to the North Sea.

We saw at a distance several huts or houses of the mountaineer inhabitants, but went near none of them, but kept on our way, going down two or three pretty steep places, not at all dangerous, though something difficult.

We encamped again the next night as before, and still our good caterer had plenty of food for us; but I observed that the next morning, when we set forward, our tents were left standing, the baggage mules tied together to graze, and our company lessened by all my patron's servants, which, when I inquired about, he told me he hoped we should have good quarters quickly without them.

I did not understand him for the present, but it unriddled itself soon after; for, though we travelled four days more in that narrow way, yet he always found us lodging at the cottages of the mountaineers.

The sixth day we went all day up hill; at last, on a sudden, the way turned short east, and opened into a vast wide country, boundless to the eye every way, and delivered us entirely from the mountains of the Andes, in which we had wandered so long.

Any one may guess what an agreeable surprise this was to us, to whom it was the main end of our travels. We made no question that this was the open country extending to the North, or Atlantic Ocean; but how far it was thither, or what inhabitants it was possessed by, what travelling, what provisions to be found by the way, what rivers to pass, and whether any navigable or not, this our patron himself could not tell us one word of, owning frankly to us, that he had never been one step farther than the place where we then stood, and that he had been there only once, to satisfy his curiosity, as I did now.

I told him, that if I had lived where he did, and had servants and provisions at command as he had, it would have been impossible for me to have restrained my curiosity so far as not to have searched through that whole country to the sea-side long ago. I also told him it seemed to be a pleasant and fruitful soil, and, no doubt, was capable of cultivations and improvements; and, if it had been only to have possessed such a country in his Catholic majesty's name, it must have been worth while to undertake the discovery for the honour of Spain; and that there could be no room to question but his Catholic majesty would have honoured the man who should have undertaken such a thing with some particular mark of his favour, which might be of consequence to him and his family.

He answered me, as to that, the Spaniards seemed already to have more dominions in America than they could keep, and much more than they were able to reap the benefit of, and still more infinitely than they could improve, and especially in those parts called South America.

And he, moreover, told me, that it was next to a miracle they could keep possession of the place we were in; and, were not the natives so utterly destitute of support from any other part of the world, as not to be able to have either arms or ammunition put into their hands, it would be impossible, since I might easily see they were men that wanted not strength of body or courage; and it was evident they did not want numbers, seeing they were already ten thousand natives to one Spaniard, taking the whole country from one end to the other.

Thus you see, seignior, added he, how far we are from improvement in that part of the country which we possess, and many more, which you may be sure are among these vast mountains, and which we never discovered, seeing all these valleys and passages among the mountains, where gold is to be had in such quantities, and with so much ease, that every poor Chilian gathers it up with his hands, and may have as much as he pleases, are all left open, naked, and unregarded, in the possession of the wild mountaineers, who are heathens and savages; and the Spaniards, you see, are so few, and those few so indolent, so slothful, and so satisfied with the gold they get of the Chilians for things of small value in trade, that all this vast treasure lies unregarded by them. Nay, continued he, is it not very strange to observe, that, when for our diversion we come into the hills, and among these places where you see the gold is so easily found, we come, as we call it, a-hunting, and divert ourselves more with shooting wild parrots, or a fawn or two, for which also we ride and run, and make our servants weary themselves more than they would in searching for the gold among the gulleys and holes that the water makes in the rocks, and more than would suffice to find fifty, nay, one hundred times the value in gold! To what purpose, then, should we seek the possession of more countries, who are already possessed of more land than we can improve, and of more wealth than we know what to do with? Perceiving me very attentive, he went on thus:

Were these mountains valued in Europe according to the riches to be found in them, the viceroy would obtain orders from the king to have strong forts erected at the entrance in, and at the coming out of them, as well on the side of Chili, as here, and strong garrisons maintained in them, to prevent foreign nations landing, either on our side in Chili, or on this side in the North Seas, and taking the possession from us. He would then order thirty thousand slaves, negroes or Chilians, to be constantly employed, not only in picking up what gold might be found in the channels of the water, which might easily be formed into proper receivers, so as that if any gold washed from the rocks it should soon be found, and be so secured, as that none of it would escape; also others, with miners and engineers, might search into the very rocks themselves, and would no doubt find out such mines of gold, or other secret stores of it in those mountains, as would be sufficient to enrich the world.

While we omit such things as these, seignior, says he, what signifies Spain making new acquisitions, or the people of Spain seeking new countries? This vast tract of land you see here, and some hundreds of miles every way which your eye cannot reach to, is a fruitful, pleasant, and agreeable part of the creation, but perfectly uncultivated, and most of it uninhabited; and any nation in Europe that thinks fit to settle in it are free to do so, for anything we are able to do to prevent them.

But, seignior, says I, does not his Catholic majesty claim a title to the possession of it? and have the Spaniards no governor over it? nor any ports or towns, settlements, or colonies in it, as is the case here in Chili? Seignior, replied he, the king of Spain is lord of all America, as well that which he possesses as that which he possesses not, that right being given him by the Pope, in the right of his being a Christian prince, making new discoveries for propagating the Christian faith among infidels; how far that may pass for a title among the European powers I know not. I have heard that it has always passed for a maxim in Europe, that no country which is not planted by any prince or people can be said to belong to them; and, indeed, I cannot say but it seems to be rational, that no prince should pretend to any title to a country where he does not think fit to plant and to keep possession. For, if he leaves the country unpossessed, he leaves it free for any other nation to come and possess; and this is the reason why the former kings of Spain did not dispute that right of the French to the colonies of the Mississipi and Canada, or the right of the English to the Caribee islands, or to their colonies of Virginia and New England.

In like manner, from the Buenos Ayres, in the Rio de la Plata, which lies that way (pointing north-east), to the Fretum Magellanicum, which lies that way (pointing south-east), which comprehends a vast number of leagues, is called by us Coasta Deserta, being unpossessed by Spain, and disregarded of all our nation; neither is there one Spaniard in it. Nevertheless, you see how fruitful, how pleasant, and how agreeable a climate it is; how apt for planting and peopling it seems to be, and, above all, what a place of wealth here would be behind them, sufficient, and more than enough, both for them and us; for we should have no reason to offer them any disturbance, neither should we be in any condition to do it, the passages of the mountains being but few and difficult, as you have seen, and our numbers not sufficient to do anything more than to block them up, to keep such people from breaking in upon our settlements on the coast of the South Seas.

I asked him if these notions of his were common among those of his country who were settled in Chili and Peru? or whether they were his own private opinions only? I told him I believed the latter, because I found he acted in all his affairs upon generous principles, and was for propagating the good of mankind; but, that I questioned whether their governor of Old Spain, or the sub-governor and viceroy of New Spain, acted upon those notions; and, since he had mentioned the Buenos Ayres and the Rio de la Plata, I should take that as an example, seeing the Spaniards would never suffer any nation to set foot in that great river, where so many countries might have been discovered, and colonies planted; though, at the same time, they had not possessed, or fully discovered those places themselves.

He answered me, smiling; Seignior, says he, you have given the reason for this yourself, in that very part which you think is a reason against it. We have a colony at Buenos Ayres, and at the city of Ascension, higher up in the Rio de la Plata, and we are not willing to let any other nation settle there, because we would not let them see how weak we are, and what a vast extent of land we possess there with a few men; and this for two reasons:

First, We are possessed of the country, and daily increasing there, and may in time extend ourselves farther. The great rivers Parana and Paraguay being yet left for us to plant in, and we are not willing to put ourselves out of a capacity of planting farther, and therefore we keep the possession.

Secondly, We have a communication from thence with Peru. The great river la Plata rises at the city of that name, and out of the mountain Potosi, in Peru, and a great trade is carried on by that river, and it would be dangerous to let foreigners into the secret of that trade, which they might entirely cut off, especially when they should find how small a number of Spaniards are planted there to preserve it, seeing there are not six hundred Spaniards in all that vast country, which, by the course of that river, is more than one thousand six hundred miles in length.

I confess, said I, these are just grounds for your keeping the possession of that river. They are so, said he, and the more because of so powerful a colony as the Portuguese have in the Brazils, which bound immediately upon it, and who are always encroaching upon it from the land side, and would gladly have a passage up the Rio Parana to the back of their colony.

But here, seignior, says he, the case differs; for we neither take nor keep possession here, neither have we one Spaniard, as I said, in the whole country now before you, and therefore we call this country Coasta Deserta. Not that it is a desert, as that name is generally taken to signify, a barren, sandy, dry country; on the contrary, the infinite prodigious increase of the European black cattle which were brought by the Spaniards to the Buenos Ayres, and suffered to run loose, is a sufficient testimony of the fruitfulness and richness of the soil, their numbers being such, that they kill above twenty thousand in a year for nothing but the hides, which they carry away to Spain, leaving the flesh, though fat and wholesome, to perish on the ground, or be devoured by birds of prey.

And the number is so great, notwithstanding all they destroy, that they are found to wander sometimes in droves of many thousands together over all the vast country between the Rio de la Plata, the city of Ascension, and the frontier of Peru, and even down into this country which you see before us, and up to the very foot of these mountains.

Well, said I, and is it not a great pity that all this part of the country, and in such a climate as this is, should lie uncultivated, or uninhabited rather? for I understand there are not any great numbers of people to be found among them.

It is true, added he, there are some notions prevailing of people being spread about in this country, but, as the terror of our people, the Spaniards, drove them at first from the seacoast towards these mountains, so the greatest part of them continue on this side still, for towards the coast it is very rare that they find any people.

I would have inquired of him about rivers and navigable streams which might be in this country, but he told me frankly that he could give me no account of those; only thus, that if any of the rivers went away towards the north, they certainly run all into the great Rio de la Plata; but that if they went east, or southerly, they must go directly to the coast, which was ordinarily called, as he said, La Costa Deserta, or, as by some, the coast of Patagonia. That, as to the magnitude of those rivers he could say little, but it was reasonable to suppose there must be some very considerable rivers, and whose streams must needs be capable of navigation, seeing abundance of water must continually flow from the mountains where we then were, and its being at least four hundred miles from the sea-side, those small streams must necessarily join together, and form large rivers in the plain country.

I had enough in this discourse fully to satisfy all my curiosity, and sufficiently to heighten my desire of making the farther discoveries which I had in my thoughts.

We pitched our little camp here, and sat down to our repast; for I found that though we were to go back to lodge, yet my patron had taken care we should be furnished sufficiently for dinner, and have a good house to eat it in, that is to say, a tent as before.

The place where we stood, though we had come down hill for a great way, yet seemed very high from the ordinary surface of the country, and gave us therefore an exceeding fine prospect of it, the country declining gradually for near ten miles; and we thought, as well as the distance of the place would allow us, we saw a great river, but, as I learned afterwards, it was rather a great lake than a river, which was supplied by the smaller rivers, or rivulets, from the mountains, which met there as in a great receptacle of waters, and out of this lake they all issued again in one river, of which I shall have occasion to give a farther account hereafter.

While we were at dinner, I ordered my midshipmen to take their observations of every distant object, and to look at everything with their glasses, which they did, and told me of this lake; but my patron could give no account of it, having never been, as he said before, one step farther that way than where we were.

However, my men showed me plainly that it was a great lake, and that there went a large river from it towards the east-south-east, and this was enough for me, for that way lay all the schemes I had laid.

I took this opportunity to ask my midshipmen, first, if they had taken such observations in their passage of the mountains as that they were sure they could find their way through to this place again without guides? And they assured me they could.

Then I put it to them whether they thought it might not be practicable to travel over that vast level country to the North Seas? and to make a sufficient discovery of the country, so as that hereafter

Englishmen coming to the coast on the side of those seas, might penetrate to these golden mountains, and reap the benefit of the treasure without going a prodigious length above Cape Horn and the Terra del Fuego, which was always attended with innumerable dangers, and without breaking through the kingdom of Chili and the Spaniards' settlements, which, perhaps, we might soon be at peace with, and so be shut out that way by our own consents?

One of my men began to speak of the difficulties of such an attempt, the want of provisions, and other dangers which we should be exposed to on the way; but the other, a bold, brisk fellow, told me he made no question but it might be easily done, and especially because all the rivers they should meet with would, of course, run along with us, so that we should be sure to have the tide with us, as he called it; and, at last, he added, that he would be content to be one of those men who should undertake it, provided he should be assured that the ships in the mean time would not go away, and pretend that they could not be found.

I told him, we would talk farther about it; that I had such a thought in my head, and a strong inclination to undertake it myself, but that I could not answer it to leave the ships, which depended so much upon my care of the voyage.

After some talk of the reasonableness of such an undertaking, and the methods of performing it, my second midshipman began to come into it, and to think it was practicable enough, and added, that though he used some cautions in his first hearing proposals, yet, if he undertook that enterprise, I should find that he would do as much of his duty in it as another man; and so he did at last, as will appear in its proper place.

We were, by this time, preparing to be satisfied with our journey, and my patron coming to me and asking if I was for returning, I told him I could not say how many days it would be before I should say I had enough of that prospect, but that I would return when he pleased, only I had one question to ask him, which was, whether the mountains were as full of gold on this side as they were on the side of Chili?

As to that, seignior, says he, the best way to be certain is to make a trial, that you may be sure we do not speak without proof; so he called his gentleman, and another servant that was with him, and desired me to call my two midshipmen, and, speaking something to his own servants first, in the language of the country, as I supposed, he turned to me, and said, Come, let us sit down and rest ourselves, while they go together, and see what they can do.

Accordingly, they went away, and, as my men told me afterwards, they searched in the small streams of water which they found running, and in some larger gulleys or channels, where they found little or no water running, but where, upon hasty rains, great shoots of water had been used to run, and where water stood still in the holes and falls, as I have described once before on the like occasion.

They had not been gone above an hour, when I plainly heard my two Englishmen halloo, which I could easily distinguish from the voices of any other nation, and immediately I ran out of the tent, Captain Merlotte followed, and then I saw one of my midshipmen running towards us, so we went to meet him, and, what with hallooing and running, he could hardly speak; but, recovering his breath, said, he came to desire me to come to them, if I would behold a sight which I never saw in my life.

I was eager enough to go, so I went with him, and left Captain Merlotte to go back to the tent to my patron, the Spaniard, and the Spanish doctor, who had not so much share in the curiosity; he did so, and they followed soon after.

When we came to the place, we saw such a wonder as indeed I never saw before, for there they were sitting down round a little puddle, or hole, as I might call it, of water, where, in the time of rain, the water running hastily from a piece of the rock, about two foot higher than the rest, had made a pit under it with the fall, like the tail of a mill, only much less.

Here they took up the sand or gravel with their hands, and every handful brought up with it such a quantity of gold as was surprising; for there they sat picking it out, just as the boys in London, who go with a broom and a hat, pick out old iron, nails, and pins from the channels, and it lay as thick.

I stood and looked at them awhile, and it must be confessed, it was a pleasant sight enough; but, reflecting immediately that there was no end of this, and that we were only upon the enquiry, Come away, said I, laughing to my men, and do not stand picking up of trash there all day; do you know how far we have to go to our lodgings?

I can make no guess what quantity might have been found here in places which had, for hundreds of years, washed gold from the hills, and, perhaps, never had a man come to pick any of it up before; but I was soon satisfied that here was enough, even to make all the world say they had enough; and so I called off my people, and came away.

It seems, the quantity of gold which is thus washed down is not small, since my men, inquiring afterwards among the Chilians, heard them talk of the great lake of water which I mentioned just now that we saw at a distance, which they call the Golden Lake, and where was, as they said, prodigious quantities of it; not that our men supposed any gold was there in mines, or in the ordinary soil, but that the waters from the hills, running with very rapid currents at certain times in the rainy seasons, and after the melting of the snows, had carried the gold so far as that lake; and, as it has been so, perhaps, from the days of the general deluge, no people ever applying themselves to gather the least grain of it up again, it might well be increased to such a quantity as might entitle that water to the name of the Golden Lake, and all the little streams and sluices of water that run into it deserved the name of Golden Rivers, as much as that of the Golden Lake.

But my present business was to know only if the gold was here, but not to trouble myself to pick it up; my views lay another way, and my end was fully answered, so I came back to my patron, and brought all my men with me.

You live in a golden country, seignior, says I; my men are stark mad to see so much gold, and nobody to take it.

Should the world know what treasure you have here, I would not answer for it that they should not flock hither in armies, and drive you all away. They need not do that, seignior, says he, for here is enough for them, and for us too.

We now packed up, and began our return; but it was not without regret that I turned my back upon this pleasant country, the most agreeable place of its kind that ever I was at in all my life, or ever shall be in again, a country rich, pleasant, fruitful, wholesome, and capable of everything for the life of man that the heart could entertain a wish for.

But my present work was to return; so we mounted our mules, and had, in the meantime, the pleasure of contemplating what we had seen, and applying ourselves to such farther measures as we had concerted among us. In about four hours we returned to our camp, as I called it, and, by the way, we found, to our no little pain, that though we had come down hill easily and insensibly to the opening for some miles, yet we had a hard pull uphill to go back again.

However, we reached to our tents in good time, and made our first encampment with pleasure enough, for we were very weary with the fatigue of a hard day's journey.

The next day we reached our good Chilian's mansion-house, or palace, for such it might be called, considering the place, and considering the entertainment; for now he had some time to provide for us, knowing we would come back again.

He met us with three mules, and two servants, about a mile before we came to the descent going down to his house, of which I took notice before, and this he did to guide us a way round to his house without going down those uneasy steps; so we came on our mules to his door, that is to say, on his mules, for he would have my patron, the Spaniard, to whom I observed he showed an extraordinary respect, and Captain Merlotte and myself, mount his fresh mules to carry us to his house.

When we came thither, I observed he wanted the assistance of my patron's servants for his cookery; for, though he had provided abundance of food, he owned he knew not how to prepare it to our liking, so they assisted him, and one of my midshipmen pretending to cook too, made them roast a piece of venison, and a piece of kid, or young goat, admirable well, and putting no garlick or onions into the sauce, but their own juices, with a little wine, it pleased the Spaniard so well, that my man passed for an extraordinary cook, and had the favour asked of him to dress some more after the same manner, when we came back to the Spaniard's house.

We had here several sorts of wildfowl, which the Chilian had shot while we were gone, but I knew none of them by any of the kinds we have in England, except some teal. However, they were very good.

The day was agreeable and pleasant, but the night dreadful, as before, being all fire and flame again, and though we understood both what it was, and where, yet I could not make it familiar to me, for my life. The Chilian persuaded us to stay all the next day, and did his endeavour to divert us as much as possible; my two midshipmen went out with him a-hunting, as he called it, that is, a-shooting; but, though he was a man of fifty years of age, he would have killed ten of them at his sport, running up the hills, and leaping from rock to rock like a boy of seventeen. At his gun he was so sure a marksman, that he seldom missed anything he shot at, whether running, flying, or sitting.

They brought home with them several fowls, two fawns, and a full-grown deer, and we had nothing but boiling, stewing, and broiling, all that evening. In the afternoon we walked out to view the hills, and to see the stupendous precipices which surrounded us. As for looking for gold, we saw the places where there was enough to be had, but that was become now so familiar to us, that we troubled not ourselves about it, as a business not worth our while; but the two midshipmen, I think, got about the quantity of five or six ounces apiece, while we were chatting or reposing in the Chilian's house.

Here it was that I entered into a confidence with my patron, the Spaniard, concerning my grand design. I told him, in the first place, that my view of the open country beyond these hills, and the particular account he had given me of it also, had raised a curiosity in me that I could scarce withstand; and that I had thereupon formed a design, which, if he would farther me with his assistance, I had a very great mind to put in practice, and that, though I was to hazard perishing in the attempt.

He told me very readily, nothing should be wanting on his part to give me any assistance he could, either by himself or any of his servants; but, smiling, and with abundance of good humour, Seignior, says he, I believe I guess at the design you speak of; you are fired now with a desire to traverse this great country to the Coasta Deserta and the North Seas; that is a very great undertaking, and you will be well advised before you undertake it.

True, Seignior, said I, you have guessed my design, and, were it not that I have two ships under my care, and some cargo of value on board, I would bring my whole ship's company on shore, and make the adventure, and, perhaps, we might be strong enough to defend ourselves against whatever might happen by the way.

As to that, seignior, says he, you would be in no danger that would require so many men; for you will find but few inhabitants anywhere, and those not in numbers sufficient to give you any trouble; fifty men would be as many as you would either want or desire, and, perhaps, as you would find provisions for; and, for fifty men, we might be able to carry provisions with us to keep them from distress. But, if you will accept of my advice, as well as assistance, seignior, says he, choose a faithful strong fellow out of your ship on whom you can depend, and give him fifty men with him, or thereabouts, and such instructions as you may find needful, as to the place on the coast where you would have them fix their stay, and let them take the first hazards of the adventure; and, as you are going round by sea, you will, if success follows, meet them on the shore, and if the account they give of their journey encourage you, you may come afterwards yourself up to these very mountains, and take a farther view; in which case, he added, with a solemn protestation, cost me what it will, I will come and meet you one hundred miles beyond the hills, with supplies of provisions and mules for your assistance.

This was such wholesome and friendly advice, and he offered it so sincerely, that though it was very little differing from my own design, yet I would not be seen so to lessen his prudence in the measures of his friendship in advising it, as to say that I had resolved to do so; but making all possible acknowledgment to him for his kind offers, I told him I would take his advice, and act just according to the measures he had prescribed; and, at the same time I assured him, that if I found a convenient port to settle and fortify in, I would not fail to come again from France (for we passed always as acting from France, whatever nation we were of) to relieve and supply them; and that, if ever I returned safe, I would not fail to correspond with him, by the passages of the mountains, and make a better acknowledgment for his kindness than I had been able to do yet.

He was going to break off the discourse upon the occasion of the Chilian's returning, who was just come in from his hunting, telling me, he would talk farther of it by the way; but I told him I could not quite dismiss the subject, because I must bespeak him to make some mention of it to the Chilian, that he might, on his account, be an assistant to our men, as we saw he was capable of being, in their passing by those difficult ways, and for their supply of provisions, &c. Trouble not yourself with that, seignior, said he, for when your men come, the care shall be mine; I will come myself as far as this wealthy Chilian's, and procure them all the assistance this place can afford them, and do anything that offers to forward them in the undertaking.

This was so generous, and so extraordinary, that I had nothing to say more, but to please myself with the apparent success of my attempt, and acknowledge the happiness of having an opportunity to oblige so generous, spirited, and grateful a person.

I would, however, have made some farther acknowledgment to our Chilian benefactor, but I had nothing left, except a couple of hats, and three pair of English stockings, one pair silk and the other two worsted, and those I gave him, and made him a great many acknowledgments for the favours he had shown us, and the next morning came away.

We made little stay anywhere else in our return; but, making much such stages back as we did forward, we came the fourteenth day to our patron's house, having made the passage through in something less than sixteen days, and the like back in fifteen days, including our stay at the Chilian's, one day.

The length of the way, according to the best of my calculations, I reckoned to be about one hundred and seventy-five English miles, taking it with all its windings and turnings, which were not a few, but which had this conveniency with them, that they gave a more easy and agreeable passage, and made the English proverb abundantly good, namely, that the farthest way about is the nearest way home.

The civilities I received after this from my generous Spaniard were agreeable to the rest of his usage of me; but we, that had so great a charge upon us at the sea-side, could not spare long time in those ceremonies, any more than I do now for relating them.

It is enough to mention, that he would not be excused, at parting, from going back with us quite to the ships, and when I would have excused it, he said, Nay, seignior, give me leave to go and fetch my hostages. In short, there was no resisting him, so we went all together, after staying two days more at his house, and came all safe to our ships, having been gone forty-six days from them.

We found the ship in very good condition, all safe on board, and well, except that the men seemed to have contracted something of the scurvy, which our Spanish doctor, however, soon recovered them from.

Here we found the two Spanish youths, our patron's hostages, very well also, and very well pleased with their entertainment; one of our lieutenants had been teaching them navigation, and something of the mathematics, and they made very good improvement in those studies, considering the time they had been there; and the Spaniard, their father, was so pleased with it, that not having gold enough to offer the lieutenant, as an acknowledgment for his teaching them, he gave him a very good ring from his finger, having a fine large emerald in it of some value, and made him a long Spanish compliment for having nothing of greater consequence to offer him.

We now made preparations for sailing, and our men, in my absence, had laid in a very considerable supply of provisions, particularly excellent pork, and tolerable good beef, with a great number of goats and hogs alive, as many as we could stow.

But I had now my principal undertaking to manage, I mean that of sending out my little army for discovery, and, having communicated my design to the supercargo, and the person whom I intrusted with him in the command of the ships, they unanimously approved of the scheme. My next business was to resolve upon whom to confer the command of the expedition; and this, by general consent, fell upon the lieutenant of the Madagascar ship, who had taught the young Spaniards navigation, and this the rather, because he was naturally a bold enterprising man, and also an excellent geographer; indeed, he was a general artist, and a man faithful and vigilant in whatever he undertook, nor was it a little consideration with me, that he was so agreeable to the Spaniard and his sons, of whose aid we knew he would stand in so much need.

When I had communicated to him the design, and he had both approved of the undertaking itself, and accepted the command, we constituted him captain, and the two midshipmen we made lieutenants for the expedition, promising each of them £500 if they performed it. As for the captain, we came to a good agreement with him for his reward; for I engaged to give him a thousand pounds in gold as soon as we met, if the journey was performed effectually.

We then laid open the design to the men, and left it to every one's choice to go, or not to go, as they pleased; but, instead of wanting men to go volunteers, we were fain to decide it by lot among some of them, they were all so eager to undertake it.

Then I gave them articles and conditions, which they who ventured should engage themselves to comply with, and particularly, that they should not mutiny, upon pain of being shot to death when we met, or upon the spot, if the captain thought it necessary; that they should not straggle from their company, nor be tempted by the view of picking up gold to stay behind, when the company beat to march; that all the gold they found in the way should be common, should be put together in a bulk every night, and be divided faithfully and equally at the end of the journey, allowing only five shares to each ship, to be divided as I should direct. Besides which, upon condition that every man behaved himself faithfully and quietly, and did his duty, I promised, that besides the gold he might get by the way, I would give to all one hundred pounds each at our meeting; and, if any man was sick, or maimed by the way, the rest were to engage not to forsake and leave him on any account whatsoever, death only excepted. And if any man died, except by any violence from the rest, his share of the gold which was gotten should be faithfully kept for his family, if he had any; but his reward of one hundred pounds, which was not due, because he did not live to demand it, should be divided among the rest; so that by this agreement, the undertaking was not so dear to me as I had expected, for the pay of the men amounted to no more than the sum following, viz.—

To the lieutenant, now made captain	£1000
To the midshipmen, now made lieutenants, each £500	£1000
To fifty men, each £100	£5000
To the surgeon £200, and his servant £100, over and above their £100 as being part of the fifty men	£300
	——
	£7300

Having pitched upon the men, I landed them, and made them encamp on shore; but, first of all, I made them every one make wills or letters of attorney, or other dispositions, of their effects to such persons as they thought fit, with an account under their hands, endorsed on the back of the said wills, &c., intimating what chests or cases or other things they had on board, and what was in them, and what pay was due to them; and those chests, &c., were sealed up before their faces with my seal, and writings signed by me, the contents unknown. Thus they were secure that all they had left in the ships, and all that was due to them, should be punctually and carefully kept and delivered as it was designed and directed by themselves, and this was greatly to their satisfaction.

As to the reward of one hundred pounds a man, and the articles about keeping together, obeying orders, gathering up gold, and the like, I did not read to them till they were all on shore, and till I was ready to leave them; because, if the rest of the men had heard it, I should have kept nobody with me to have sailed the ships.

There was as stout a company of bold, young brisk fellows of them, as ever went upon any expedition, fifty-three in number; among them a surgeon and his mate, very skilful and honest men both of them, a trumpeter and a drummer, three ship-carpenters, a cook, who was also a butcher by trade, and a barber, two shoemakers who had been soldiers among the pirates, a smith, and a tailor of the same, so that they wanted no mechanics, whatever might happen to them.

Give the fellows their due, they took but little baggage with them; but, however, what they had, I took care, with the assistance of my patron, the Spaniard, should be as much carried for them as possible.

I provided them three large tents made of a cotton stuff, which I bought in the country, and which we made up on board, which tents were large enough to cover them all, in case of rain or heat; but as for beds or bedding, they had only seven hammocks, in case any man was sick; for the rest, they were to shift as well as they could; the season was hot, and the climate good. Their way lay in the latitude of 40 to 50°, and they set out in the latter end of the month of October, which, on that side of the line, is the same as our April; so that the covering was more to keep them from the heat than the cold.

It was needful, in order to their defence, to furnish them with arms and ammunition; so I gave to every man a musket or fuzee, a pistol, and a sword, with cartouches and a good stock of ammunition, powder and shot, with three small barrels of fine powder for store, and lead in proportion; and these things were, indeed, the heaviest part of their baggage, excepting the carpenters' tools and the surgeon's box of medicines.

As for the carrying all these things, they might easily furnish themselves with mules or horses for carriage, while they had money to pay for them, and you may judge how that could be wanting, by what has been said of the country.

We gave them, however, a good large pack of European goods, to make agreeable presents where they received favours; such as black baize, pieces of say, serge, calamanco, drugget, hats and stockings; not forgetting another pack of hatchets, knives, scissors, beads, toys, and such things, to please the natives of the plain country, if they should meet with any.

They desired a few hand granadoes, and we gave them about a dozen; but, as they were heavy, it would have been very troublesome to have carried more.

The Spaniard stayed till all this was done, and till the men were ready to march, and then told us privately, that it would not be proper for him to march along with them, or to appear openly to countenance the enterprise; that my two lieutenants knew the way perfectly well; and that he would go before to his own house, and they should hear of him by the way.

All the mules and horses which he had lent us to bring us back he left with them to carry their baggage, and our new captain had bought six more privately in the country.

The last instructions I gave to our men were, that they should make the best of their way over the country beyond the mountains; that they should take the exact distances of places, and keep a journal of their march, set up crosses and marks at all proper stations; and that they should steer their course as near as they could between the latitude of 40°, where they would enter the country, and the latitude of 45° south, so that they would go an east-south-east course most of the way, and that wherever they made the shore they should seek for a creek or port where the ships might come to an anchor, and look out night and day for the ships; the signals also were agreed on, and they had two dozen of rockets to throw up if they discovered us at sea; they had all necessary instruments for observation also, and perspective glasses, pocket compasses, &c., and thus they set out, October 24th, 1715.

We stayed five days after they began their march, by agreement, that if any opposition should be offered them in the country, or any umbrage taken at their design, so that it could not be executed, we might have notice. But as the Spaniards in the country, who are the most supinely negligent people in the world, had not the least shadow of intelligence, and took them only to be French seamen belonging to the two French ships (such we past for) who had lain there so long, they knew nothing when they went away, much less whither; but, no question, they believed that they were all gone aboard again.

We stayed three days longer than we appointed, and hearing nothing amiss from them, we were satisfied that all was right with them; so we put to sea, standing off to the west, till we were out of sight of the shore, and then we stood away due south, with a fresh gale at north-west-by-west, and fair weather, though the wind chopped about soon after, and we had calms and hot weather that did us no good, but made our men sick and lazy.

The supposed journey of our travellers, their march, and the adventures they should meet with by the way, were, indeed, sufficient diversion, and employed us all with discourse, as well in the great cabin and roundhouse as afore the mast, and wagers were very rife among us, who should come first to the shore of Patagonia, for so we called it.

As for the place, neither they nor we could make any guess at what part of the country they should make the sea; but, as for us, we resolved to make the port St. Julian our first place to put in at, which is in the latitude of 50° 5' and that then, as wind and weather would permit, we would keep the coast as near as we could, till we came to Punta de St. Helena, where we would ride for some time, and, if possible, till we heard of them.

We had but a cross voyage to the mouth of the Straits of Magellan, having contrary winds, as I have said, and sometimes bad weather; so that it was the 13th of December when we made an observation, and found ourselves in the latitude of 52° 30', which is just the height of Cape Victoria, at the mouth of the passage.

Some of our officers were very much for passing the Straits, and not going about by Cape Horn; but the uncertainty of the winds in the passage, the danger of the currents, &c., made it by no means advisable, so we resolved to keep good sea-room.

The 25th of December, we found ourselves in the latitude of 62° 30', and being Christmas-day, I feasted the men, and drank the health of our travellers. Our course was south-east-by-south, the wind south-west; then we changed our course, and went east for eight days, and having changed our course, stood away, without observation, east-north-east, and in two days more, made the land, on the east of the Strait de la Mare, so that we were obliged to stand away east-south-east to take more sea-room, when the wind veering to the south-by-east, a fresh gale, we stood boldly away due north, and running large, soon found that we were entered into the North Sea on Twelfth Day; for joy of which, and to celebrate the day, I gave every mess a piece of English beef, and a piece of Chilian pork, and made a great bowl of punch afore the mast, as well as in the great cabin, which made our men very cheerful, and instead of a twelfth cake, I gave the cook order to make every mess a good plum-pudding, which pleased them all as well.

But while we were at our liquor and merry, the wind came about to the north-east and blew very hard, threatening us with a storm, and as the shore lay on our leeward quarter, we were not without apprehensions of being driven on some dangerous places, where we could have no shelter; I immediately therefore altered my course, and ran away east all night, to have as much sea-room as possible.

The next day the wind abated, and hauling away to the east, we stood northward again, and then north-west in three days more, and we made land, which appeared to be the head island of Port St. Julian, on the north side of the port, where we ran in, and about an hour before sunset came to an anchor in eleven fathom good holding ground, latitude 49° 18'.

We wanted fresh water, otherwise we would not have made any stay here, for we knew we were a little too far to the south; however, we were obliged to fill fresh water here for three days together, the watering-place being a good way up the river, and the swell of the sea running very high.

During this interval, Captain Merlotte and I went on shore with about thirty men, and marched up the country near twenty miles, getting up to the top of the hills, where we made fires, and at the farthest hill we encamped all night, and threw up five rockets, which was our signal; but we saw nothing to answer it, nor any sign either of English people or natives in all the country.

We saw a noble champaign country, the plains all smooth, and covered with grass like Salisbury Plain; very little wood to be seen anywhere, insomuch that we could not get any thing but grass to make a smoke with, which was another of our signals.

We shot some fowls here, and five or six hares; the hares are as large as an English fox, and burrow in the earth like a rabbit. The fowls we shot were duck and mallard, teal and widgeon, the same as in England in shape and size, only the colour generally grey, with white in the breast, and green heads; the flesh the same as ours, and very good.

We saw wild geese and wild swans, but shot none; we saw also guinacoes, or Peruvian sheep, as big as small mules, but could not get at them; for as soon as we stepped toward them, they would call to one another, to give notice of us, and then troop altogether and be gone.

This is an excellent country for feeding and breeding of sheep and horses, the grass being short, but very sweet and good on the plains, and very long and rich near the fresh rivers, and were it cultivated and stocked with cattle, would without doubt produce excellent kinds of all sorts of cattle; nor could it fail producing excellent corn, as well wheat as barley and oats; and as for peas, they grow wild all over the country, and nourish an infinite number of birds resembling pigeons, which fly in flights so great, that they seem in the air like clouds at a great distance.

As for the soil, that of the hills is gravel, and some stony; but that of the plains is a light black mould, and in some places a rich loam, and some marl, all of which are tokens of fruitfulness, such as indeed never fail.

The 14th of January (the weather being hot, and days long, for this was their July), we weighed and stood northerly along the shore, the coast running from Port St. Julian north-north-east, until we arrived at the famous islands called Penguin Islands; and here we came to an anchor again, in the same round bay which Sir John Narborough called Port Desire, it being the 17th of January.

Here we found a post or cross, erected by Sir John Narborough, with a plate of copper nailed to it, and an inscription, signifying that he had taken possession of that country in the name of Charles the Second.

Our men raised a shout for joy that they were in their own king's dominions, or as they said, in their own country; and indeed, excepting that it was not inhabited by Englishmen, and cultivated, planted, and enclosed after the English manner, I never saw a country so much like England.

Here we victualled our ships with a new kind of food, for we loaded ourselves with seals, of which here are an infinite number, and which we salted and ate, and our men liked them wonderfully for awhile, but they soon began to grow weary of them; also the penguins are a very wholesome diet, and very pleasant, especially when a little salted; and as for salt, we could have loaded our ships with it, being very good and white, made by the sun, and found in standing ponds of salt water, near the shore.

The penguins are so easily killed, and are found in such vast multitudes on that island (which for that reason is so called), that our men loaded the long-boat with them twice in one day, and we reckoned there were no less than seven thousand in the boat each time.

Here we travelled up into the country in search of our men, and made our signals, but had no answer to them, nor heard any intelligence of them. We saw some people here at a distance, scattering about; but they were but few, nor would they be brought by any means to converse with us, or come near us.

We spread ourselves over the country far and wide; and here we shot hares and wild-fowl again in abundance, the country being much the same as before, but something more bushy, and here and there a few trees, but they were a great way off. There is a large river which empties itself into this bay.

Finding no news here of our men, I ordered the Madagascar ship to weigh and stand farther north, keeping as near the shore as he might with safety, and causing his men to look out for the signals, which, if they discovered, they should give us notice by firing three guns.

They sailed the height of Cape Blanco, where the land falling back, makes a deep bay, and the sea receives into it a great river at several mouths, some of them twenty leagues from the other, all farther north. Here they stood into the bay until they made the land again; for at the first opening of the bay they could not see the bottom of it, the land lying very low.

The captain was doubtful what he should do upon the appearance of so large a bay, and was loath to stand farther in, lest the land, pushing out into the sea again afterwards, and a gale springing up from the seaward, they might be shut into a bay where they had no knowledge of the ground; and upon this caution, they resolved among themselves to come to an anchor for that evening, and to put farther out to sea the next morning.

Accordingly the next morning he weighed and stood off to sea; but the weather being very fine, and the little wind that blew being south-west-by-south, he ventured to stand in for the shore, where he found two or three small creeks, and one large river; and sending in his shallop to sound, and find out a good place to ride in, upon their making the signal to him that they had found such a place, he stood in, and came to an anchor in eleven fathom good ground, half a league from the shore, and well defended from the northerly and easterly winds, which were the winds we had any reason to fear.

Having thus brought his ship to an anchor, he sent his shallop along the shore to give me an account of it, and desire me to come up to him, which accordingly we did; and here we resolved to ride for some time, in hopes to hear from our little army.

We went on shore, some or other of us, every day, and especially when five of our men, going on shore on the north side of the river, had shot three Peruvian sheep and a black wild bull; for after that they ranged the country far and near to find more, but could never come within shot of them, except three bulls and a cow, which they killed after a long and tedious chase.

We lay here till the 16th of February, without any news of our travellers, as I called them. All the hopes we had was, that five of our men asking my leave to travel, swore to me they would go quite up to the Andes but they would find them; nay, they would go to the Spanish gentleman himself, if they did not hear of them; and obliged me to stay twenty days for them, and no longer. This I readily promised, and giving them everything they asked, and two Peruvian sheep to carry their ammunition, with two dozen of rockets for signals, a speaking trumpet, and a good perspective glass, away they went; and from them we had yet heard no news, so that was our present hope.

They travelled, as they afterwards gave an account, one hundred and twenty miles up the country, till they were at last forced to resolve to kill one of their guinacoes, or sheep, to satisfy their hunger, which was a great grief to them, for their luggage was heavy to carry; but, I say, they only resolved on it, for just as they were going to do it, one of them roused a deer with a fawn, and, by great good luck shot them both; for, having killed the doe, the fawn stood still by her till he had loaded his piece again, and shot that also.

This supplied them for four or five days plentifully, and the last day one of my men being by the bank of the river (for they kept as near the river as they could, in hopes to hear of them that way), saw something black come driving down the stream; he could not reach it, but calling one of his fellows, their curiosity was such, that the other, being a good swimmer, stripped and put off to it, and, when he came to it, he found it was a man's hat; this made them conclude their fellows were not far off, and that they were coming by water.

Upon this, they made to the first rising ground they could come at, and there they encamped, and at night fired some rockets, and after the third rocket was fired, they, to their great joy, saw two rockets rise up from the westward, and soon after that a third; and in two days more they all joyfully met.

We had been here, as I have said, impatiently expecting them a great while; but, at last, the man at the main-top, who was ordered to look out, called aloud to us below, that he saw a flash of fire; and immediately, the men looking to landward, they saw two rockets rise up in the air at a great distance, which we answered by firing three rockets again, and they returned by one rocket, to signify that they saw our men's signal.

This was a joyful exchange of distant language to both sides; but I was not there, for, being impatient, I had put out and sailed about ten leagues farther; but our ship fired three guns to give me notice, which, however, we heard not, and yet we knew they fired too; for, it being in the night, our men, who were very attentive with their eyes, as well as ears, saw plainly the three flashes of the guns, though they could not hear the report, the wind being contrary.

This was such certain intelligence to me, and I was so impatient to know how things went, that, having also a small gale of wind, I weighed immediately, and stood back again to our other ship; it was not, however, till the second day after we weighed that we came up to them, having little or no wind all the first day; the next day in the morning they spied us, and fired the three guns again, being the signal that they had got news of our friends.

Nothing could be more to my satisfaction than to hear that they had got news, and it was as much to their satisfaction as to ours to be sure, I mean our little army; for if any disaster had happened to us, they had been in a very odd condition; and though they might have found means to subsist, yet they would have been out of all hope of ever returning to their own country.

Upon the signal I stood into the bay, and came to an anchor at about a league to the northward of our other ship, and as far from the shore, and, as it were, in the mouth of the river, waiting for another signal from our men, by which, we might judge which side of the river to go ashore at, and might take some proper measures to come at them.

About five o'clock in the evening, our eyes being all up in the air, and towards the hills, for the appointed signals, beheld, to our great surprise, a canoe come rowing to us out of the mouth of the river. Immediately we went to work with our perspective glasses; one said it was one thing, and one said it was another, until I fetched a large telescope out of the cabin, and with that I could easily see they were my own men, and it was to our inexpressible satisfaction that they soon after came directly on board.

It might very well take up another volume to give a farther account of the particulars of their journey, or, rather, their journey and voyage.

How they got through the hills, and were entertained by the generous Spaniard, and afterwards by the wealthy Chilian; how the men, greedy for gold, were hardly brought away from the mountains; and how, once, they had much ado to persuade them not to rob the honest Chilian who had used them so well, till my lieutenant, then their captain, by a stratagem, seized on their weapons, and threatened to speak to the Spaniard to raise the Chilians in the mountains, and have all their throats cut; and yet even this did not suffice, till the two midshipmen, then their lieutenants, assured them that at the first opening of the hills, and in the rivers beyond, they would have plenty of gold; and one of the midshipmen told them, that if he did not see them have so much gold that they would not stoop to take up any more, they should have all his share to be divided among them, and should leave him behind in the first desolate place they could find.

How this appeased them till they came to the outer edge of the mountains, where I had been, and where my patron, the Spaniard, left them, having supplied them with sixteen mules to carry their baggage, and some guinacoes, or sheep of Peru, which would carry burdens, and afterwards be good to eat also.

Also, how here they mutinied again, and would not be drawn away, being insatiable in their thirst after gold, till about twenty, more reasonable than the rest, were content to move forward; and, after some time, the rest followed, though not till they were assured that the picking up of gold continued all along the river, which began at the bottom of the mountains, and that it was likely to continue a great way farther.

How they worked their way down these streams, with still an insatiable avarice and thirst after the gold, to the lake called the Golden Lake, and how here they were astonished at the quantity they found; how, after this, they had great difficulty to furnish themselves with provisions, and greater still in carrying it along with them until they found more.

I say, all these accounts might suffice to make another volume as large as this. How, at the farther end of the lake, they found that it evacuated itself into a large river, which, running away with a strong current to the south-south-east, and afterwards to the south-by-east, encouraged them to build canoes, in which they embarked, and which river brought them down to the very bay where we found them; but that they met with many difficulties, sank and staved their canoes several times, by which they lost some of their baggage, and, in one disaster, lost a great parcel of their gold, to their great surprise and mortification. How at one place, they split two of their canoes, where they could find no timber to build new ones, and the many hardships they were put to before they got other canoes. But I shall give a brief account of it all, and bring it into as narrow a compass as I can.

They set out, as I have said, with mules and horses to carry their baggage, and the Spaniard gave them a servant with them for a guide, who, carrying them by-ways, and unfrequented, so that they might give no alarm at the town of Villa Rica, or anywhere else, they came to the mouth of the entrance into the mountains, and there they pitched their tent.

N.B.—The lieutenant who kept their journal, giving an account of this, merrily, in his sea language, expresses it thus: "Being all come safe into the opening, that is, in the entrance of the mountains, and being there free from the observation of the country, we called it our first port, so we brought to, and came to an anchor."

Here the generous Spaniard, who at his own request was gone before, sent his gentleman and one of his sons to them, and sent them plenty of provisions, as also caused their mules to be changed for others that were fresh, and had not been fatigued with any of the other part of the journey.

These things being done, the Spaniard's gentleman caused them to decamp, and march two days farther into the mountains, and then they encamped again, where the Spaniard himself came incognito to them, and, with the utmost kindness and generosity, was their guide himself, and their purveyor also, though two or three times the fellows were so rude, so ungovernable and unbounded in their hunting after gold, that the Spaniard was almost frighted at them, and told the captain of it. Nor, indeed, was it altogether without cause, for the dogs were so ungrateful, that they robbed two of the houses of the Chilians, and took what gold they had, which was not much, indeed, but it hazarded so much the alarming the country, and raising all the mountaineers upon them, that the Spaniard was upon the point of flying from them, in spite of all their fire-arms and courage.

But the captain begged him to stay one night more, and promised to have the fellows punished, and satisfaction to be made; and so he brought all his men together and talked to them, and inquired who it was? but never was such a piece of work in the world. When the new captain came to talk of who did it, and of punishment, they cried, they all did it, and they did not value all the Spaniards or Indians in the country; they would have all the gold in the whole mountains, ay, that they would, and swore to it; and, if the Spaniard offered to speak a word to them, they would chop his head off, and put a stop to his farther jawing.

However, a little reasoning with them brought some of the men to their senses; and the captain, who was a man of sense and of a smooth tongue, managed so well, that he brought about twenty-two of the men, and the two lieutenants and surgeons, to declare for his opinion, and that they would act better for the future; and, with these, he stepped in between the other fellows, and separated about eighteen of them from their arms, for they had run scattering among the rocks to hunt for gold, and, when they were called to this parley, had not their weapons with them. By this stratagem, he seized eleven of the thieves, and made them prisoners; and then he told the rest, in so many words, that if they would not comply to keep order, and obey the rules they were at first sworn to, and had promised, he would force them to it, for he would deliver them, bound hand and foot, to the Spaniards, and they should do the poor Chilians justice upon them; for that, in short, he would not have the rest murdered for them; upon this, he ordered his men to draw up, to show them he would be as good as his word, when, after some consideration, they submitted.

But the Spaniard had taken a wiser course than this, or, perhaps, they had been all murdered; for he ran to the two Chilian houses which the rogues had plundered, and where, in short, there was a kind of tumult about it, and, with good words, promising to give them as much gold as they lost, and the price of some other things that were taken away, he appeased the people; and so our men were not ruined, as they would certainly have been if the mountaineers had taken the alarm.

After this, they grew a little more governable; but, in short, the sight of the gold, and the easy getting it (for they picked it up in abundance of places), I say, the sight of the gold made them stark mad. For now they were not, as they were before, trafficking for the owners and for the voyage; but as I had promised the gold they got should be their own, and that they were now working for themselves, there was no getting them to go on, but, in short, they would dwell here; and this was as fatal a humour as the other.

But to bring this part of the voyage to an end, after eight days they came to the hospitable wealthy Chilian's house, whom I mentioned before; and here, as the Spaniard had contrived it, they found all kind of needful stores for provisions laid up, as it were, on purpose; and, in a word, here they were not fed only, but feasted.

Here, again, the captain discovered a cursed conspiracy, which, had it taken effect, would, besides the baseness of the fact, have ended in their total destruction; in short, they had resolved to rob this Chilian, who was so kind to them; but, as I said, one of the lieutenants discovered and detected this villanous contrivance, and quashed it, so as never to let the Spaniard know of it.

But, I say, to end this part, they were one-and-twenty days in this traverse, for they could not go on so easy and so fast, now they were a little army, as we did, who were but six or seven; at length they came to the view of the open country, and, being all encamped at the edge of a descent, the generous Spaniard (and his three servants) took his leave, wishing them a good journey, and so went back, having, the day before, brought them some deer, five or six cows, and some sheep, for their subsisting at their entrance into, and travel through, the plain country.

And now they began to descend towards the plain, but they met with more difficulty here than they expected; for, as I observed that the way for some miles went with an ascent towards the farthest part of the hill; that continued ascent had, by degrees, brought them to a very great, and in some places, impassable descent; so that, however my guide found his way down, when I was through, it was not easy for them to do it, who were so many in number, and encumbered with mules and horses, and with their baggage, so that they knew not what to do; and, if they had not known that our ships were gone away, there had been some odds but, like the Israelites of old, they would have murmured against their leader, and have all gone back to Egypt. In a word, they were at their wits' end, and knew not what course to take for two or three days, trying and essaying to get down here and there, and then frightened with precipices and rocks, and climbing up to get back again. The whole of the matter was, that they had missed a narrow way, where they should have turned off to the south-east, the marks which our men had made before having not been so regular and exact just there, as in other parts of the way, or some other turning being so very like the same, that they took one for the other; and thus, going straight forward too far before they turned, they came to an opening indeed, and saw the plain country under them, as they had done before, but the descent was not so practicable.

After they had puzzled themselves here, as I said, two or three days, one of the lieutenants, and a man with him, seeing a hut or house of a Chilian at some distance, rode away towards it; but passing into a valley that lay between, he met with a river which he could by no means get over with the mules, so he came back again in despair. The captain then resolved to send back to the honest rich Chilian, who had entertained them so well, for a guide, or to desire him to give them such directions as they might not mistake.

But as the person sent back was one of those who had taken the journal which I mentioned, and was therefore greatly vexed at missing his way in such a manner, so he had his eyes in every corner, and pulled out his pocket-book at every turning, to see how the marks of the places agreed; and at last, the very next morning after he set out, he spied the turning where they should all have gone in, to have come to the place which they were at before; this being so remarkable a discovery, he came back again directly, without going on to the Chilian's house, which was two days' journey farther.

Our men were revived with this discovery, and all agreed to march back; so, having lost about six days in this false step, they got into the right way, and, in four more, came to the descent were I had been before.

Here the hill was still very high, and the passage down was steep and difficult enough; but still it was practicable, and our men could see the marks of cattle having passed there, as if they had gone in drifts or droves; also it was apparent, that, by some help and labour of hands, the way might be led winding and turning on the slope of the hill, so as to make it much easier to get down than it was now.

It cost them no small labour, however, to get down, chiefly because of the mules, which very often fell down with their loads; and our men said, they believed they could with much more ease have mounted up from the east side to the top than they came from the west side to the bottom.

They encamped one night on the declivity of the hill, but got up early, and were at the bottom and on the plain ground by noon. As soon as they came there they encamped and refreshed themselves, that is to say, went to dinner; but it being very hot there, the cool breezes of the mountains having now left them, they were more inclined to sleep than to eat; so the captain ordered the tent to be set up, and they made the whole day of it, calling a council in the morning to consider what course they should steer, and how they should go on.

Here they came to this resolution, that they should send two men a considerable way up the hill again, to take the strictest observation they could of the plain with the largest glasses they had, and to mark which way the nearest river or water was to be seen; and they should direct their course first to the water, and that, if the course of it lay south, or any way to the east of the south, they would follow on the bank of it, and, as soon as it was large enough to carry them, they would make them some canoes or shallops, or what they could do with the most ease, to carry them on by water; also, they directed them to observe if they could see any cattle feeding at a distance, or the like.

The messengers returned, and brought word that all the way to the east, and so on to south-east, they could discover nothing of water, but that they had seen a great lake, or lough of water, at a great distance, which looked like a sea, and lay from them to the northward of the east, about two points; adding, that they did not know but it might afterwards empty itself to the eastward, and it was their opinion to make the best of their way thither.

Accordingly, the next morning, the whole body decamped, and marched east-north-east, very cheerfully, but found the way much longer than they expected; for though from the mountains the country seemed to lie flat and plain, yet, when they came to measure it by their feet, they found a great many little hills; little, I say, compared to the great mountains, but great to them who were to travel over them in the heat, and with but very indifferent support as to provisions; so that, in a word, the captain very prudently ordered that they should travel only three hours in the morning and three in the evening, and encamp in the heat of the day, to refresh themselves as well as they could.

The best thing they met with in that part of the country was, that they had plenty of water, for though they were not yet come to any large, considerable river, yet every low piece of ground had a small rill of water in it; and the springs coming out from the rising grounds on the sides of the mountains being innumerable, made many such small brooks.

It cost them six days' travel, with two days' resting between, to advance to that river of water, which, from the height of the mountains, seemed to be but a little way off. They could not march, by their computation, above ten or twelve miles a day, and rest every third day too, for their luggage was heavy, and their mules but few; also some of their mules became tired and jaded by their long march, or fell lame, and were good for nothing.

Besides all this, the days which I call days of rest were really not so to them, for those intervals were employed to range about and hunt for food; and it was for want of that, more than for want of rest, that they halted every third day.

In this exercise they did, however, meet with such success, that they made shift to kill one sort of creature or another every day, sufficient to keep them from famishing; sometimes they met with some deer, other times with the guinacoes, or Peruvian sheep, and sometimes with fowls of several kinds, so that they did pretty well for food. At length, viz., the seventh day, they came to a river, which was at first small, but having received another small river or two from the northern part of the country, it began to seem large enough for their purpose; and, as it ran east-south-east, they concluded it would run into the lake, and that they might fleet down this river, if they could make anything to carry them.

But their first discouragement was, the country was all open, with very little wood, and no trees, or very few to be found large enough to make canoes, or boats of any sort; but the skill of their carpenters, of which they had four, soon conquered this difficulty; for, coming to a low swampy ground on the side of the river, they found a tree something like a beech, very firm good sort of wood, and yet soft enough to yield to their tools; and they went to work with this, and at first made them some rafts, which they thought might carry them along till the river was bigger.

While this was doing, which took up two or three days, the men straggled up and down; some with their guns to shoot fowls, some with contrivances to catch fish, some one thing, some another; when, on a sudden, one of their fishermen, not in the river, but in a little brook, which afterwards ran into the river, found a little bit of shining stuff among the sand or earth, in the bank, and cried, he had found a piece of gold. Now, it seems, all was not gold that glistened, for the lump had no gold in it, whatever it was; but the word being given out at first, it immediately set all our men a-rummaging the shores of every little rill of water they came at, to see if there was any gold; and they had not looked long till they found several little grains, very small and fine, not only in this brook, but in several others; so they spent their time more cheerfully, because they made some advantage.

All this while they saw no people, nor any signals of any; except once, on the other side of the river, at a great distance, they saw about thirty together, but whether men or women, or how many of each, they could not tell, nor would they come any nearer, only stood and gazed at our people at a distance.

They were now ready to quit their camp and embark, intending to lay all their baggage on the rafts, with three or four sick men, and so the rest to march by the river side, and as many as could, to ride upon the mules; when on a sudden, all their navigation was put to a stop, and their new vessels, such as they were, suffered a wreck.

The case was thus:—They had observed a great many black clouds to hang over the tops of the mountains, and some of them even below the tops, and they did believe it rained among the hills, but, in the plain where they lay, and all about them, it was fair, and the weather fine.

But, in the night, the carpenters and their assistants, who had set up a little tent near the river side, were alarmed with a great roaring noise, as they thought, in the river, though at a distance upwards; presently after, they found the water begin to come into their tent, when, running out, they found the river was swelling over its banks, and all the low grounds on both sides of them.

To their great satisfaction, it was just break of day, so that they could see enough to make their way from the water, and the land very happily rising a little to the south of the river, they immediately fled thither. Two of them had so much presence of mind with them, as to pick up their working-tools, at least some of them, and carry off, and the water rising gradually, the other two carpenters ventured back to save the rest, but they were put to some difficulty to get back again with them; in a word, the water rose to such a height that it carried away their tent, and everything that was in it, and which was worse, their rafts (for they had almost finished four large ones) were lifted off from the place where they were framed, which was a kind of a dry dock, and dashed all to pieces, and the timber, such as it was, all carried away. The smaller brooks also swelled in proportion to the large river; so that, in a word, our men lay as it were, surrounded with water, and began to be in a terrible consternation; for, though they lay in a hard dry piece of ground, too high for the land-flood to reach them, yet, had the rains continued in the mountains, they might have lain there till they had been obliged to eat one another, and so there had been an end of our new discovery.

But the weather cleared up among the hills the next day, which heartened them up again; and as the flood rose so soon, so the current being furiously rapid, the waters ran off again as easily as they came on, and in two days the water was all gone again. But our little float was shipwrecked, as I have said, and the carpenters finding how dangerous such great unwieldy rafts would be, resolved to set to it, and build one large float with sides to it, like a punt or ferry-boat. They worked so hard at this, ten of the men always working with them to help, that in five days they had her finished; the only thing they wanted was pitch and tar, to make her upper work keep out the water, and so they made a shift to fetch a juice out of some of the wood they had cut, by help of fire, that answered the end tolerably well.

But that which made this disappointment less afflicting was, that our men hunting about the small streams where this water had come down so furiously, found that there was more gold, and the more for the late flood. This made them run straggling up the streams, and, as the captain said, he thought once they would run quite back to the mountains again.

But this was his ignorance too; for after awhile, and the nearer they came to the rising of the hills the quantity abated; for where the streams were so furious, the water washed it all away, and carried it down with it, so that by the end of five days, the men found but little, and began to come back again.

But then they discovered that, though there was less in the higher part of the rivers, there was more farther down, and they found it so well worth while, that they went looking along for gold all the way towards the lake, and left their fellows and the boat to come after.

At last, when nothing else would do, hunger called them off, and so once more all the company were got together again; and now they began to load the float, indeed it might be called a luggage-boat; however, it answered very well, and was a great relief to our men; but when they came to load it, they found it would not carry near so much as they had to put in it. Besides that, they would be all obliged to march on foot by shore, which had this particular inconvenience in it, that whenever they came to any small river or brook which ran into the other, as was very often the case, they would be forced to march up a great way to get over it, or unload the great float to make a ferry-boat of it to waft them over.

Upon this they were resolved, that the first place they came at where timber was to be had for building, they would go to work again and make two or three more floats, not so big as the other, that so they might embark themselves, their baggage, and their provisions too, all together, and take the full benefit of the river, where it would afford them help; and not some sail on the water, and some go on foot upon the land, which would be very fatiguing.

Therefore, as soon as they found timber, as I have said, and a convenient place, they went all hands to work to build more floats or boats, and, while this was doing, all the spare men spent their time and pains in searching about for gold in the brooks and small streams, as well those they had been at before as others, and that after they had, as it were, plundered them at the first discovery; for, as they had found some gold after the hasty rain, they were loath to give it over, though they had been assured there was more to be found in the lake, where they were yet to come, than in the brooks.

All this while their making the floats went slowly on; for the men thought it a great hardship to keep chopping of blocks, as they called it, while their fellows were picking up gold, though they knew they were to have their share of what they found, as much as if they had been all the while with them; but it seems there is a kind of satisfaction in the work of picking up gold, besides the mere gain.

However, at length the gold failing, they began to think of their more immediate work, which was, going forward; and the carpenters having made three more floats, like flat-bottomed barges, which they brought to be able to carry their baggage and themselves too, if they thought fit, they began to embark and fall down the river; but they grew sick of their navigation in a very few days, for before they got to the lake, which was but three days' going, they ran several times on ground, and were obliged to lighten their floats to get them off again, then load again, and lighten again, and so off and on, till they were so tired of them that they would much rather have carried all their baggage, and have travelled by land; and, at last, they were forced to cast off two of them, and put all their baggage on board the other two, which, at best, though large, were but poor crazy things.

At length they came in sight of their beloved lake, and the next day they entered into the open part, or sea of it, which they found was very large, and in some places very deep.

Their floats, or by what other name they might be called, were by no means fit to carry them upon this inland sea; for if the water had been agitated by the least gust of wind, it would presently have washed over them, and have spoiled, if not sunk, their baggage; so they had no way to steer or guide them whenever they came into deep water, where they could not reach the ground with their poles.

This obliged them, as soon as they came into the open lake, to keep close under one shore, that is to say, to the right hand, where the land falling away to the south and the south-by-east, seemed to carry them still forward on their way; the other side widening to the north, made the lake seem there to be really a sea, for they could not look over it, unless they went on shore and got upon some rising ground.

Here, at first, they found the shore steep too, and a great depth of water close to land, which made them very uneasy; for, if the least gale of wind had disturbed the water, especially blowing from off the lake, they would have been shipwrecked close to the shore. However, after they had gone for two days along the side, by the help of towing and setting as well as they could, they came to a flatter shore and a fair strand, to their great joy and satisfaction.

But, if the shore proved to their satisfaction for its safety, it was much more so on another account; for they had not been long here before they found the sands or shore infinitely rich in gold, beyond all that they had seen, or thought of seeing before. They had no sooner made the discovery, than they resolved to possess themselves of a treasure that was to enrich them all for ever; accordingly, they went to work with such an avaricious spirit, that they seemed to be as if they were plundering an enemy's camp, and that there was an army at hand to drive them from the place; and, as it proved, they were in the right to do so; for, in this gust of their greedy appetite, they considered not where they were, and upon what tender and ticklish terms their navigation stood.

They had, indeed, drawn their two floats to the shore as well as they could, and with pieces of wood like piles, stuck in on every side, brought them to ride easy, but had not taken the least thought about change of weather, though they knew they had neither anchor or cable, nor so much as a rope large enough to fasten them with on the shore.

But they were taught more wit, to their cost, in two or three days; for, the very second night they felt a little unusual rising of the water, as they thought, though without any wind; and the next morning they found the water of the lake was swelled about two feet perpendicular, and that their floats, by that means, lay a great way farther from the shore than they did at first, and the water still increasing.

This made them imagine there was a tide in the lake, and that after a little time it would abate again, but they soon found their mistake; for after some time, they perceived the water, which was perfectly fine and clear before, grew by degrees of a paler colour, thick and whitish, till at last it was quite white and muddy, as is usual in land floods; and as it still continued rising, so they continued thrusting in their floats farther and farther towards the shore, till they had, in short, lost all the fine golden sands they were at work upon before, and found the lake overflowed the land so far beyond them, that, in short, they seemed to be in the middle of the lake, for they could scarce see to the end of the water, even on that very side where, but a few hours before, their floats were fast on the sands.

It may be easily judged that this put them into great consternation, and they might well conclude that they should be all drowned and lost; for they were now, as it were, in the middle of the sea upon two open floats or rafts, fenced nowhere from the least surge or swell of the water, except by a kind of waste board, about two feet high, built up on the sides, without any calking or pitching, or anything to keep out the water.

They had neither mast or sail, anchor or cable, head or stern, no bows to fence off the waves, or rudder to steer any course, or oars to give any motion to their floats, whose bottoms were flat like a punt, so that they were obliged to thrust them along with such poles as they had, some of which were about eight or ten feet long, which gained them a little way, though very slowly.

All the remedy they had in this case was, to set on with their poles towards the shore, and to observe, by their pocket compasses, which way it lay; and this they laboured hard at, lest they should be lost in the night, and not know which way to go.

Their carpenters, in the mean time, with some spare boards which they had, or rather made, raised their sides as well as they could, to keep off the wash of the sea, if any wind should rise so as to make the water rough; and thus they fenced against every danger as well as they could, though, all put together, they were but in a very sorry condition.

Now they had time to reflect upon their voracious fury, in ranging the shore to pick up gold, without considering where and in what condition they were, and without looking out on shore for a place of safety: nay, they might now have reflected on the madness of venturing out into a lake or inland sea of that vast extent, in such pitiful bottoms as they had under them. Their business, doubtless, had been to have stopped within the mouth of the river, and found a convenient place to land their goods and secure their lives; and when they had pitched their camp upon any safe high ground, where they might be sure they could neither be overflowed nor surrounded with water, they might have searched the shores of the lake as far as they thought fit; but thus to launch into an unknown water, and in such a condition, as to their vessels, as is described above, was most unaccountably rash and inconsiderate.

Never were a crew of fifty men, all able and experienced sailors, so embarked, nor drawn into such a snare; for they were surrounded with water for three or four miles in breadth on the nearest shore, and this all on a sudden, the country lying low and flat for such a breadth, all which appeared dry land and green, like the fields, the day before; and, without question, the men were sufficiently surprised.

Now they would have given all the gold they had got, which was very considerable too, to have been on shore on the wildest and most barren part of the country, and would have trusted to their own diligence to get food; but here, besides the imminent danger of drowning, they might also be in danger of starving; for had their floats grounded but upon any little hillock, they might have stuck there till they had starved and perished for hunger. Then they were in the utmost anxiety too for fear of wetting their powder, which, if it had happened, they could never have made serviceable again, and without it, they could not have killed anything for food, if they had got to the shore.

They had, in this exigence, some comforts, however, which might a little uphold their spirits; and without which, indeed, their condition must have been deplorable and desperate.

1. It was hot weather, so that as they had no shelter against the cold, if it had come, they had no cold to afflict them; but they rather wanted awnings to keep off the sun, than houses to keep off the cold.

2. The water of the lake was fresh and good; even when it looked white and thick, yet it was very sweet, wholesome, and good tasted; had it been salt water, and they thus in the middle of it, they must have perished with thirst.

3. They being now floating over the drowned lands only, the water was not very deep, so that they could reach ground, and set along their rafts with their poles, and this, to be sure, they failed not to do with the utmost diligence.

They had also the satisfaction to observe, though it was not without toiling in an inexpressible manner, that they gained upon the shore, and that there was a high land before them, which they were making for, though very slowly, and at a distance they hoped to overcome.

But soon after, they had another discouragement, namely, that they saw the day declining, and night coming on apace, and, in short, that it was impossible they could reach the high land, which they saw by daylight, nor did they know what to do or how to go on in the night.

At length two bold fellows offered themselves to strip and go off, either to wade or swim to the shore, which they had daylight to do, being, as they judged, about three miles, though they found it above four, and from thence to find means to make a fire or light to guide them to the shore in the dark.

This was, indeed, a desperate attempt, but the two fellows being good swimmers, and willing to venture, it was not impracticable. They had light linen drawers on, with pockets, and open at the knees, and their shirts; each of them took a little bottle with some gunpowder, close stopped, with other materials for kindling fire; weapons they had none, but each man a knife and a hatchet fastened round his waist in a little belt, and a light pole in his hands to help him when he waded, which it was expected they must do part of the way. They had no provisions with them, but a bottle with some good brandy in their pockets above mentioned.

When they went off, it was supposed the water to be about four feet to five feet deep, so they chose to swim rather than wade, and it was very seldom much deeper; they had often opportunity to stand on the firm ground to rest themselves.

In this posture they went on directly towards the land, and after they had, by swimming and wading together, advanced about a mile, they found the water grew shallower, which was a signal to them that they should reach the hard ground in a little time; so they walked cheerfully on in about three feet water, for near a mile more.

Their companions on board the rafts soon lost sight of them, for they being in white, and the water white too, and the light declining, they could not see them at a mile distance.

After this they found the ground falling lower, so that they had deeper water for half a mile more all the way; after which, they came to a flat ground again, for near two miles more, and at length to the dry land, to their great satisfaction, though it was then quite night.

They had been near an hour in the dark, that is to say, with only a dusky light, and began to be greatly at a loss, not being able to see the compass. They had made shift to get over the half mile of deeper water pretty well; for, though it was too deep for the two men to wade, as above, yet they could reach the bottom with their poles, and, at that time, they happened to feel a little breeze of wind fair in their way, which not only refreshed them, but gave them a kind of a jog on their way towards the shore.

At length, to their great joy, they saw a light; and it was the more to their joy, because they saw it just before them, or, as the seamen call it, right ahead; by which they had the satisfaction to know they had not varied their course in the dark. It seems their two men had landed upon a fair rising ground, where they found some low bushes and trees, and where they had good hard dry standing; and they soon found means to pick out a few withered dry sticks, with which they made a blaze for the present, having struck fire with the tools they were furnished with, as mentioned above.

By the light of this blaze, they gave the first notice to their comrades that they were landed; and they in return, as was agreed as before, fired two guns as a signal that they saw it, and were all safe.

By the light of this fire, the two men also gave themselves so much light as to find more dry wood; and, afterwards, their fire was so strong and good, that they made the green wood burn as well as the dry.

Their companions on the floats were now come into the shoal water, in which, as I said, these men waded, but, as their floats did not draw above a foot or eighteen inches water at most, they went on still; but, at length, being within about half a mile of the hillock where the two men were, they found the water so shallow that their floats would not swim. Upon this, more of the men went overboard with poles in their hands, sounding, as we call it, for a deeper water, and, with long paddling about, they found the ground fall off a little in one place, by which they got their floats about a quarter of a mile farther; but then the water was shallow again, not above a foot of water: so, in a word, they were fain to be content, and, running fast aground, they immediately began, though dark, and themselves very much fatigued, to unload their floats and carry all on shore on their backs.

The first thing they took care to land, was their ammunition, their gunpowder and arms, not forgetting the ammunition de bouche, as the French call it, I mean their victuals; and, with great joy, got to their comrades. Then they fetched their proper materials for their tent, and set it up, and having refreshed themselves, they went all to sleep, as they said, without so much as a sentinel placed for their guard; for, as they saw no inhabitants, so they feared no enemies; and, it may be supposed, they were weary enough to make them want rest, even in the extremest manner.

In the morning they had time enough to reflect upon the madness of such rash adventures. Their floats, indeed, remained as they had left them, and the water was ebbed away from them for more than two miles, that is to say, almost to the deep half mile mentioned above; but they heard a surprising noise and roaring of the water on the lake itself, the body of which was now above seven miles from them.

They could not imagine what this roaring should mean, for they felt no wind, nor could they perceive any clouds at a distance that looked as if they brought any squalls of wind with them, as they are often observed to do; but, when they came nearer the water, they found it had a kind of a swell, and that there was certainly some more violent motion at the farther distance; and, in a little while, looking behind them towards the shore where their comrades were, they found the water began to spread over the flat ground again; upon which, they hastened back, but having a good way to go, they were obliged to wade knee deep before they reached to the hillock where their tent stood.

They had not been many hours on shore before they found the wind began to rise, and the roaring, which before they heard at a distance, grew louder and nearer, till at length the floats were lifted up, and driven on shore by the wind, which increased to a storm, and the water swelled and grew rough; and, as they were upon the lee shore, the floats were soon broken in pieces, and went some one way and some another.

In the evening it overcast and grew cloudy, and, about midnight, they had their share of a violent rain, which yet, they could see was more violent towards the mountains of the Andes, and towards the course of the river which they came down in the floats.

The consequence of this was, that the third day, the waters of the lake swelled again to a frightful height; that is to say, it would have been frightful to them if they had been up in it, for they supposed it rose about two fathoms perpendicularly, and the wind continuing fresh, the water was all a white foam of froth; so that, had they been favoured with even a good large boat under them, she would scarce have lived there.

Their tent was a sufficient shelter from the rain, and, as they were on dry land, and too high to be reached by any inundation, they had no concern upon them about their safety, but took this for sufficient notice, not to come up the lake again in haste, unless they were better provided with boats to ride out a storm.

Our men began now to think they had taken their leave of the golden lake, and yet they knew not how to think of leaving it so soon. They were now fourteen or fifteen leagues from the shore where they had found so much gold, nor did they know the way to it by land; and as for going by water, that they were unprovided for several ways; besides, the waters kept up to a considerable height, and the winds blew fresh for six or eight days, without intermission.

All these obstructions joined together, put them upon considering of pursuing their march by land, in which, however, they resolved to coast the lake as near as they could to the eastward, till, if possible, they should find that the waters had some outlet, that is to say, that the lake emptied itself by some river towards the sea, as they concluded it certainly must.

They had not yet seen any inhabitants, or any sign of them, at least, not near them; they saw, or fancied they saw, some on the other side of the river, but, as none came within reach of them, it is doubtful whether they really saw them or not.

Before they decamped for a march, it was needful to get some provisions, if possible, and this made them the more desirous of finding out some conversible creatures, but it was in vain. They killed a wild cow and a deer, and this was all they could get for some time; and with this they set forward, taking their course east, and rather northerly, in order to come into the same latitude they set out in, at their first embarking on the river.

After they had marched thus for about three days, keeping the lake on the north side of them, and always in view, at length, on the third day, in the evening, coming to a little hill, which gave them the prospect of the country for some length north-east, they saw plainly a river issuing out of the lake, and running first east, then bending to the south; it was also easy to perceive that this river, was at that time, much broader than its usual course, for that they could see a great many trees, which probably grew on the banks of the river, standing as it were, in the middle of the water, the banks being overflowed both ways very considerably.

But, as they mounted the hill which they stood on, to greater height, they discovered farther north, at a distance of five or six miles, according to their account, a much larger river, which looked, compared to the first, rather like a sea than a river, which likewise issued out of the lake, and ran east-by-south towards the sea; which river they supposed to be in the same manner swelled with a land-water to a prodigious degree.

This prospect brought them to a more serious consultation as to the measures they should take to proceed on their journey; and as they could easily see there was little or no use to be made of the rivers for their travelling, while they were thus above the ordinary banks, so that they could not know the proper channels, and also that the currents were exceeding swift, so they resolved to stock themselves with provisions, if possible, and continue their journey by land.

To this purpose they first made it their business to catch some more guinacoes, or large sheep, which they knew would not only feed them, but also carry their luggage, which was still heavy and very troublesome to them, and yet absolutely necessary too. But all their endeavour was in vain, for though they saw several, and found that the country was pretty full of them, and some they killed, yet they could not take one alive by any means they could contrive.

Among other creatures they shot for food were a few wild cows and bulls, and especially on the north side of the river, where they found great plenty.

But the most surprising thing to them that they had yet met with, was still to come. They had descended from the hill where they at first discovered the smaller river, and where they had set up their tent, resolving to march on the lower grounds as near the river as they could, so as to be out of danger of the water, that they might find, if possible, some way over, to come at the great river, which they judged to be the stream most proper for their business.

Here they found a rich pleasant country, level and fruitful, not so low as to be exposed to the overflowing of the river, and not so high as to be dry and barren; several little brooks and streams of water rising on the side of the hill they came from, ran winding this way and that, as if to find out the river, and near the river were some woods of very large trees.

The men, not forgetting the main chance, fell to washing and searching the sand and gravel in these brooks for gold; but the harvest of gold seemed to be over, for here they found none.

They had also an occasion to discover, that till the land-waters were abated, there was no stirring for them, no not so much as to cross the first river; nor if they did, could they find in their hearts to venture, not knowing but the waters might still rise higher, and that the two rivers might swell into one, and so they should be swallowed up, or if not, they might be surrounded in some island, where they should perish for want of provisions; so they resolved to fetch their baggage from the hill as well as they could, and encamp in those pleasant plains, as near the river as they could, till the water should abate.

While they stayed here, they were so far from having hopes that the waters would abate, that it rained violently for almost three days and nights together; and one of those rainy mornings, looking out at their tent-door (for they could not stir abroad for the rain), they were surprised, when looking towards the river, which was just below them, they saw a prodigious number of black creatures in the water, and swimming towards the shore where they were.

They first imagined they were porpoises, or sea-hogs, but could not suggest anything of that kind at such a distance from the sea, when one of the men looking at them through the glass, cried out they were all black cattle, and that he could perceive their horns and heads; upon this, others looking with their glasses also, said the same; immediately every man ran to his gun, and, notwithstanding it rained hard, away they marched down to the river's side with all the speed they could make.

By that time they reached the river bank, their wonder increased, for they found it was a vast multitude of black cattle, who, finding the waters rise between the two rivers, and, by a natural sagacity, apprehensive of being swept away with the flood, had one and all took the waters, and were swimming over to this side for safety.

It may very well be imagined, the fellows, though they wanted a few such guests as these, yet were terrified with their multitude, and began to consider what course to take when the creatures should come to land, for there was a great number of them. Upon the whole, after a short consultation, for the creatures came on apace, they resolved to get into a low ground, where they perceived they directed their course, and in which there were a great many trees, and that they would all get up into the trees, and so lie ready to shoot among them as they landed.

Accordingly they did so, excepting five of them, who, by cutting down some large boughs of a tree, had got into a little thicket close to the water, and which they so fortified with the boughs of the trees, that they thought themselves secure within; and there they posted themselves, resolving to wait the coming of the cattle, and take their hazard.

When the creatures came to land, it was wonderful to observe how they lowed and roared, as it were to bid one another welcome on shore; and spreading themselves upon the neighbouring plain, immediately lay down, and rolling and stretching themselves, gave our people notice, that, in short, they had swam a great way and were very much tired.

Our fellows soon laid about them, and the five who had fixed themselves in the thicket had the fairest opportunity, for they killed eleven or twelve of them as soon as they set their foot on shore, and lamed as many.

And now they had a trial of skill, for as they killed as many as they knew what to do with, and had their choice of beef, if they killed a bull they let him lie, as having no use for him, but chose the cows, as what they thought was only fit for eating.

But, I say, now they had a trial of skill, namely, to see if they could maim some of the bulls so as not to kill them, and might bring them to carry their luggage. This was a kind of a fruitless attempt, as we afterwards told them, to make a baggage-horse of a wild bull.

However, they brought it so far to pass, that, having wounded several young bulls very much, after they had run roaring about with the hurt, they lay down and bled so, as that it was likely they would bleed to death, as several of them really did; but the surgeon observing two of them to be low enough that he might go to them, and do what he would with them, he soon stopped the bleeding, and in a word, healed the wounds. All the while they were under cure he caused grass and boughs of trees to be brought to them for food, and in four or five days the creatures were very well; then he caused them to be hampered with ropes, and tied together, so that they could neither fight with their heads, or run away with their heels; and having thus brought them to a place just by their tent, he caused them to be kept so hungry, and almost starved, that, when meat was carried them, they were so tame and thankful, that at last, they would eat out of his hand, and stretch out their heads for it, and when they were let a little looser, would follow him about for a handful of grass, like a dog for a bone.

When he had brought them thus to hand, he, by degrees, loaded them, and taught them to carry; and if they were unruly, as they were at first, he would load them with more than they could well carry, and make them stand under that load two or three hours, and then come himself and bring them meat, and take the load off; and thus in a few days they knew him so well, that they would let him do anything with them.

When our people came to decamp, they tied them both together, with such ropes as they had, and made them carry a very great weight. They tried the same experiment with two more, but they failed; one died, and the other proved untractable, sullen, and outrageous.

The men had now lain here twelve days, having plenty of provision, in which time, the weather proving fair, the land waters ran off, and the rivers came to their old channels, clear and calm. The men would gladly have gone back to the sands and flat shore of the lake, or to some other part, to look for gold; but that was impracticable now, so they marched on, and in about two days they found the first river seemed to turn so much to the south, that they thought it would carry them too far out of their way, for their orders were to keep about the latitude of 40 to 50° as is said before, so they resolved to get over the first river as soon as they could; they had not gone far, but they found the river so shallow, that they easily forded it, bulls and all, and, being safely landed, they travelled across the country to the great river, which they found also very low, though not like to be forded as the other was.

Now they thought they were in the way of their business, and here they resolved to see if a tree or two might be found, big enough to make a large canoe to carry them down this river, which, as it seemed large, so the current seemed to be less rapid and furious, the channel being deep and full.

They had not searched long but they found three trees that they thought large enough, and they immediately went to work with them, felled and shaped them, and, in four days' time they had three handsome canoes, one larger than the rest, and able to carry in all fifteen or sixteen men; but these were not enough, so they were forced to look out farther, for two trees more, and this took them up more time. However, in about a week, they launched them all; as for days, they had lost their account of time, so that, as they had sometimes no rule to distinguish one day from another, so at last they quite forgot the days, and knew not a Sunday from a working-day any longer.

While these canoes were making, the men, according to the old trade, fell to rummaging the shores of this river, as they had done the other, for gold, nor did they wholly lose their labour, for, in several places, they found some; and here it was that a certain number of them, taking one of the canoes that were first made, took a voyage of their own heads, not only without command, but against command; and, having made a little mast and sail to it, went up towards the lake, resolving to go quite into the lake to find another golden shore, or gold coast, as they called it.

To give a particular account of this wild undertaking, would be too long, nor would the rogues give much account of it themselves; only, in short, that they found a sand pretty rich in gold, worked upon it five days indefatigably, and got a sufficient quantity, had they brought it back, to have tempted the rest to have gone all away to the same place. But, at the end of five days, some were for returning and others for staying longer, till the majority prevailed to come back, representing to the rest, that their friends would be gone, and they should be left to starve in that wild country, and should never get home; so they all got into the canoe again, but quarrelled when they were in, and that to such an unreasonable height, that, in short, they fought, overset the boat, lost all their gold and their arms, except three muskets which were lashed under their thouts, or benches of the canoe, spoiled their ammunition and provisions, and drowned one of their company, so they came home to the rest mortified, wet, and almost famished.

This was a balk to them, and put a damp to their new projects; and yet six of the same men were so bold afterwards as to demand to be dismissed, and a canoe given them, and they would go back they said to the golden lake, where, they did not doubt, they should load the canoe with gold; and, if they found when they came back we were gone, they would find their way back through the mountains, and go to the rich Spaniard, who, they did not doubt, would get them license to go back to Europe with the galleons, and perhaps, they said, they might be in England before us.

But the captain quelled this mutiny, though there were four or five more came into it. By showing them the agreement they had made with me, their commander, the obligation they were under, and the madness of their other proposal, he prevailed with them to go forward with the rest, and pursue the voyage, which he now represented to be very easy, being as it were, all the way downhill, that is to say, with the stream, for they all knew the river they were in must go to the sea, and that in or near the latitude which they knew the ship had appointed to wait for them.

However, to soften them a little, and in some measure to please them, he promised, that if they met with any success in the search after gold in the river they were in, as he did not question but they should, he would consent to any reasonable stop that they should propose, not exceeding five days in a place, and the places to be not less than five leagues off from one another.

Upon these terms they consented, and all embarked and came away, though extremely mortified for the loss of one of their companions, who was a brave stout fellow, very well beloved by all the company, but there was no remedy; so they came on in five canoes, and with a good stock of provisions, such as it was, viz., good fresh beef cured in the sun, and fifteen Peruvian sheep alive; for, when they got into the country between the two rivers, they found it easy to catch those creatures, who before that would not come near them.

And now they came down the river apace, till they came to another golden shore, where, finding some quantity of gold, they claimed their captain's promise, and, accordingly, they went all on shore to work, and pretty good success they had, picking up from among the sands a considerable quantity of gold, and, having stayed four of the five days, they found that they had cleared the place, which was not of a long extent, and so they cheerfully came on.

They proceeded now for eleven days together very willingly, but then found the channel of the river divided itself, and one went away to the left, and the other to the right. They could not judge which was the best to take; but not questioning but that they would meet again soon, they took the southernmost channel, as being most direct in their latitude; and thus they coursed for three or four days more, when they were obliged to put into the mouth of a little river that fell into the other, and made a good harbour for their little fleet.

Here, I say, they were obliged to put in for want of provisions, for they had eaten up all their guinacoes, and their two tame bulls too, the last of which they soon repented, as will be shown presently.

After they had been a-hunting, and shot a couple of deer and a cow, with a kind of hare, as large as an English fox, they set forward again very merry, and the more, because they had another little piece of a gold coast, where, for two days, they had very good luck again; but judge how they were surprised, and in what a consternation they were, when, coming farther down the same river, they heard a terrible noise in the river, as of a mighty cataract, or waterfall, which increased as they came forward, till it grew so loud that they could not hear themselves speak, much less hear one another.

As they approached, it was the more frightful; so at length, lest they should be hurried into it before they were aware, they went all on shore, doing all by signs and dumb postures, for it was impossible to hear any sound but that of the cataract.

Though the noise was so great, it was near six miles to the place from whence it came, which, when they perceived, some of them went back to bring on the boats, and so brought them as near the place as they durst, and ran them on shore into a little hollow part of the bank, just large enough to hold them. When they had thus secured the boats, they went to view the waterfall; but how were they astonished, when they found that there were no less than five waterfalls, at the distance of about two miles from each other, some more, some less, and that the water fell from a prodigious height; so that it was impossible for any boat to launch down the cataract without being dashed in pieces.

The men now saw there was no remedy but that they must lose the benefit of their five canoes, which had been so comfortable to them, and by which they had come above four hundred miles in a little time, with safety and pleasure.

These cataracts made the river perfectly useless to them for above twenty miles, and it was impossible to drag their canoes that length over land; so, in short, they unloaded them, and, for their own satisfaction, they turned one, the biggest of them, adrift, and let it go to the first cataract, placing themselves so beyond that they might see it come down, which they did, and had the vexation of seeing it dashed all to pieces on the rocks below.

As there was no remedy, they plainly saw they must leave their boats behind them. And now, as I have said, they had time to repent killing their two tamed bulls, who would have done them good service; but it was too late to look back upon what was done and over so many days before. They had now no means left them, if they would go forward, but to take their baggage upon their shoulders and travel on foot. The only help they had was, that they had got five guinacoes left, which, though they were hungry, and would fain have eaten, yet, as they had carried at least five hundred weight of their luggage, they chose to fast and walk rather than feast and work; so they went on as well as they could till they got past these falls, which, though not above twenty miles, cost them five days' labour; at the end of which, they encamped again to refresh themselves, and consider of what was next to be done. They were thus long upon this short journey for many reasons.

1. Because they were obliged to employ the best part of two days in hunting for their food, in which time, five of them swimming over the river to shoot at some black cattle, extremely fatigued themselves in pursuing them, but did, however, shoot five cows and bulls; but then it was at such a distance, that it was more pains to drag the flesh along to the river's side than it was worth, only that they were indeed hunger-starved, and must have it.

2. They found still some little quantity of gold in the water, that is to say, below the falls, where the water, by falling with great force, had made a pit or hole of a vast depth, and had thrown up a shoal again, at perhaps a little distance, where they took up some gold whenever the water was low enough to come at it.

3. The weight of their baggage made them travel heavy, and seldom above five or six miles a day.

Being now come to the open river, they thought of building more floats; but they were discouraged from this consideration by not knowing but in a few days' march there might be more waterfalls, and then all their labour would be lost; so they took up their tent and began to travel again.

But here, as they kept the river close on board, as the seamen call it, they were at a full stop, by the coming in of another river from the south-west, which, when it joined the river they were along by, was above a quarter of a mile broad, and how to get over it they knew not.

They sent two men up the additional river some length, and they brought word that it was indeed narrower by much, but nowhere fordable, but deep and rapid.

At the same time they sent two more nimble fellows down the coast of the great river, to see if there were any more waterfalls, who brought them word that there were none for upwards of sixty miles.

While they lay here, at the point of the influx, expecting the return of their scouts, they used what diligence they could in getting provisions; and among the rest, they killed three cows and a bull on the other side of the largest river; but not knowing how to bring them over, they at last concluded to go, as many as could swim, which was the better half of them, and sit down by it, and roast and broil upon the spot as much as they could eat, and then bring with them, as much as they could for their companions.

For this purpose they got boughs of trees, and bound them together, then wrapped the meat in the hides, and laid it on the wood, and made a number of little contrivances to convey it, so that no part of the meat was lost. What they got on their own side of the river they made better shift with.

On the return of their scouts they found there was no remedy but to build some new vessels, of one kind or other, to take in their baggage and provision, which they made after the manner of their first floats; for they found no trees large enough to make canoes; when, therefore, they had made one great float, they resolved to make two small boats, like yawls or skiffs, with which they might tow their large float or barge; and as this they might do with small timbers, so they found means to line them within and without with the bulls' hides, and that so dexterously joined, and lapped and rolled one over another, that no water came through, or but very little.

With these two boats they ferried over the small rivers with ease, each boat carrying six men, besides two to row; and when they were over the small rivers, the two boats served to tow their great punt or barge close by the shore.

The greatest difficulty was for tow-lines to draw the boats by, and those they supplied by twisting a strong tough kind of flag or rush, which they found in the river, of which, with much application and labour, they made a kind of rope-yarn, and then twisting it again, made it very strong.

This was the voiture with which they conveyed themselves quite down to the sea, and one of these boats it was that we spied, as above, coming to us in the bay.

They had yet above four hundred and fifty miles to the sea, nor could they at any time tell or guess how far off it might be. They went on more or less every day, but it was but slowly, and not without great labour, both of rowing and towing. Their provisions also cost them much pains, for they were obliged first to hunt and kill it, and then bring it to the camp, which, however, was always close to the river's side.

After they had travelled thus some time, following the course of the river, they came to a place, where, on a sudden, they could see no farther bank of the river, but it looked all water, like the sea. This they could not account for; so, the next day, they rowed towards it with one of their little boats, when they were surprised to find that it was the northern branch of the river, which they had seen go off before they came at the waterfalls, which river being now increased with many other great waters, was now so great, that the mouth of it might be said to be four or five miles over, and rather received the river they were on, than ran into that; but, after this, it contracted itself again, though still it was to be supposed near a mile and a half over.

They were far from being pleased at this conjunction of the waters, because the great water being thus joined, they found the stream or current more violent, and the water, upon the least stirring of the wind, more turbulent than it was before, and as their great float drew but little water, and swam flat upon the surface, she was ready to founder upon every occasion. This obliged them almost every night to seek for some little cove or creek to run her into, as into a harbour, to preserve her; for, when the wind blew from shore, they had enough to do to keep her from driving off from the river, and, when there was but little wind, yet it made a rippling or chopping of the waves, that they had much difficulty to keep them from filling her.

All the country on the side of this river was a little higher ground than ordinary, which was its security from land-floods, and their security too; for sometimes the river was seen to rise, and that so much as to overflow a great extent of land on the other side. Hence, perhaps, the other side might be esteemed the most fruitful, and perhaps might be the better land, if it had but half the art and industry of an European nation to assist the natural fertility of the soil, by keeping the water in its bounds, banking and fencing the meadows from the inundations and freshes, which were frequently sent down from the Andes and from the country adjoining.

But, as it now was, those lower lands lay great part of the year under water; whether it was the better or worse for the soil, that no judgment can be made of, till some people come to settle there to whom it may be worth while to make experiments of that kind.

This part of the country they were now in resembled, as they hinted, the county of Dorsetshire and the downs about Salisbury, only not lying so high from the surface of the water, and the soil being a good fruitful dark mould, not a chalky solid rock, as in the country about Salisbury, and some other parts.

Here they found a greater quantity of deer than they had seen in all their journey, which they often had the good luck to kill for their supply of food, the creatures not being so shy and wild as they had found farther within the country.

It may be noted here, and it is very observable, that in all this journey I could not learn that they saw either wolf or fox, bear or lion, or, indeed, any other ravenous creature, which they had the least reason to be shy or afraid of, or which, indeed, were frightful to the deer; and this, perhaps, may be the reason why the number of the latter animals is so great, which, as I have said, is greater there than at other places.

After they had feasted themselves here for some days, they resolved to begin their new kind of navigation, and to see what they could make of it; but they went very heavily along, and every now and then, as I have said, the water was too rough for them, and they were fain to put into harbour, and sometimes lie there two or three days. However, they plyed their time as well as they could, and sometimes the current setting over to their side, and running strong by the shore, they would go at a great rate, insomuch that one time they said they went about thirty miles in a day, having, besides the current, a little gale of wind right astern.

They reckoned that they went near two hundred miles in this manner, for they made the best of it; and at the end of these two hundred miles, it was, by their reckoning, that our five men who travelled into the country so far, found them, when they saw the hat swimming down the stream; which hat, it seems, one of them let fall overboard in the night.

They had, I say, travelled thus far with great difficulty, the river being so large; but, as they observed it growing larger and larger the farther they went, so, they said, they did not doubt, but that, in a little more, they should come to the sea.

They also observed, that now, as they found the waters larger and the rivers wider, they killed more fowls than formerly, and, particularly, more of the duck-foot kind, though they could not perceive any sea-fowls, or such as they had been used to. They saw a great many wild swans, and some geese, as also duck, mallard, and teal; and these, I say, increased as they drew nearer the sea.

They could give very little account of the fish which the rivers produced, though they sometimes catched a few in the smaller river; but, as they had neither fishing-hook or nets, which was the only omission in my fitting them out, they had no opportunity to furnish themselves.

They had, likewise, no salt, neither was it possible to furnish them with any, so they cured their meat in the sun, and seasoned it with that excellent sauce called hunger.

The account they gave of discovering our five men was thus. They had been, for two days, pretty successful in their navigation, as I have described it, but were obliged to stop, and put in at the mouth of a little river, which made them a good harbour. The reason of their stay was, they had no victuals, so by consent they all went a-hunting, and, at night, having shot two guinacoes and a deer, they went to supper together in their great tent; and, having fed heartily on such good provisions, they began to be merry, and the captain and officers, having a little store left, though not much, they pulled out their bottles, and drank every one a dram to their good voyage, and to the merry meeting of their ships, and gave every man the same.

But their mirth was increased beyond expressing, when two of the men, who were without the tent door, cried out, it lightened. One said he saw the flash, he was sure, and the other said, he thought he saw it too; but, as it happened, their backs were towards the east, so that they did not see the occasion.

This lightning was certainly the first flash of one of our five men's rockets, or the breaking of it, and the stars that were at the end of it, up in the air.

When the captain heard the men say it lightened, he jumped from his seat, and called aloud to them to tell which way; but they foolishly replied, to the north-west, which was the way their faces were when they saw it; but the word was no sooner spoken but the two fellows fell a-hallooing and roaring, as if they were distracted, and said they saw a rocket rise up in the air to the eastward.

So nimble were the men at this word, that they were all out of the tent in a moment, and saw the last flash of the rocket with the stars, which, spreading themselves in the air, shone with the usual bright light that it is known those fireworks give.

This made them all set up a shout of joy, as if they imagined their fellows, who were yet many miles from them, should hear them; but the captain and officers, who knew what they were to do on this occasion, ran to their baggage, and took out their own rockets, and other materials, and prepared to answer the signal.

They were on a low ground, but, at less than a mile distant, the land went ascending up to a round crown or knoll, pretty high; away they ran thither, and set up a frame in an instant. But, as they were making these preparations, behold, to confirm their news, they saw a third rocket rise up in the air, in the same place as before.

It was near an hour from the first flash, as they called it, before they could get all things ready; but then they fired two rockets from the adjoining hill, soon after one another, and, after that, at about ten minutes' distance of time, a third, which was just as by agreement, and was perfectly understood, the rockets performing extremely well.

Upon this they saw another single rocket rise up, which was to let them know that their former was seen and understood.

This was, you will conclude, a very joyful night, and the next morning they went all hands to work at the boats, getting out of the creek early, and made the best of their way. However, with all they could do, they could not go above twelve miles that day, for the current setting over to the other shore, had left them, and in some places, they would rather have an eddy stream against them, and this discouraged them a little, but, depending that they were near their port, and that their friends were not far off, they were very cheerful. At night they looked out again for rockets, the sight of which failed not to rejoice their hearts again, and with this addition, that it appeared their friends were not above four or five miles off; they answered the rockets punctually, and proceeding early the next day, they met in the morning joyfully enough, as has been said.

We were overjoyed at meeting, as may be easily conceived; but, to see the pitiful boat, or periagua, they came on board in, a little surprised us; for, indeed, it was a wonder they should be able to make it swim under them, especially when they came out into the open sea.

As soon as we had the boat in reach, we hauled it up into the ship for a relic, and, taking two of the men with us, we manned out all our ship's boats to go and fetch the rest, for they were, as these men told us, about seventeen miles up the river still, and could not come any farther, their boats being not able to bring them along, and the river growing very broad and dangerous. The eldest of my midshipmen came in this first boat, but the captain and the other stayed with the men, who were very unruly, and frequently quarrelling and wrangling about their wealth, which, indeed, was very considerable; but they were above twice as far up the river as the men told us, having halted after the boat left them.

When our boats came to them, and took them in, I ordered they should be set on shore, and their tents put up there, till I had settled matters a little with them, having had an account how mutinous and fractious they had been; and I made them all stay there till I had fully adjusted everything with them about their treasure, which, indeed, was so much, that they scarce knew how to govern themselves under the thought of it.

Here I proposed conditions to them at first, that all the gold should be shared before they went on board, and that it should be put on board the ship, as goods for every man's single account; that I would give them bills of lading for it; and I offered to swear to them to deliver it into every man's possession, separately, at the first port we should come to an anchor at in England or France; and that, at that said port, they should every man have the £100 I had promised them, as above, for the undertaking this journey, delivered to them in gold dust, to that amount, and that they, alone, should have full liberty to go on shore with it, and go whither they would, no man whatever but themselves being allowed to set foot on shore in the same place, distress excepted. This they insisted on, because they had done some things, they said, which, if I would, I might bring some of them to the gallows. However, I promised to forgive them, and to inquire no more after it.

In a word, there had been a scuffle among them, in which one of their canoes was overset, as was said, and one of their number drowned, at the same time when they lost a great part of their gold; and some were thought to have done it maliciously too.

But, as I had no occasion to trouble them on that score, not having been upon the spot when it was done, so, having made this capitulation with them, I performed it punctually, and set them all on shore, with their wealth, in the river of Garonne, in France; their own gold, their $100's worth reward for their journey, their wages, and their share of pearl, and other advantages, made them very rich; for their cargo, when cast up on shore, amounted to about £400 a man. How they disposed of themselves, or their money, I never gave myself the trouble to inquire, and if I had, it is none of my business to give an account of it here.

We dismissed also near fourscore more of our men afterwards, in a little creek, which was at their own request; for most of them having been of the Madagascar men, and, by consequence, pirates, they were willing to be easy, and I was as willing to make them so, and therefore cleared with as many of them as desired it. But I return to our ship.

Having thus made a long capitulation with our travellers, I took them all on board, and had leisure enough to have a long narration from them of their voyage; and from which account, I take the liberty to recommend that part of America as the best and most advantageous part of the whole globe for an English colony, the climate, the soil, and, above all, the easy communication with the mountains of Chili, recommending it beyond any place that I ever saw or read of, as I shall farther make appear by itself.

We had nothing now to do, but to make the best of our way for England; and setting sail from the mouth of the river Camerones, so the Spaniards call it, the 18th of January, in which we had a more difficult and unpleasant voyage than in any other part of our way, chiefly because, being a rich ship, and not knowing how affairs stood in Europe, I kept to the northward as far as the banks of Newfoundland, steering thence to the coast of Galicia, where we touched as above; after which, we went through the Channel, and arrived safe in Dunkirk road the 12th of April; and from thence gave private notice of our good fortune to our merchants and owners; two of whom came over to us, and received at our hands such a treasure as gave them reason to be very well satisfied with their engagement. But, to my great grief, my particular friend, the merchant who put us upon this adventure, and who was the principal means of our making the discoveries that have been here mentioned and described, was dead before our return; which, if it had not happened, this new scheme of a trade round the world had, perhaps, not been made public till it had been put in practice by a set of merchants designed to be concerned in it from the New Austrian Netherlands.

Daniel Defoe – A Short Biography

Daniel Foe was born around 1660 in Fore Street in the parish of St. Giles Cripplegate in London.

The aristocratic-sounding 'De' was added to his name to create 'Defoe'. On occasion he was prone to claim descent from the family of De Beau Faux.

His father, James Foe, was a prosperous tallow chandler and a member of the Worshipful Company of Butchers and, with Defoe's mother, Annie, Presbyterian dissenters.

Defoe has been born into a time that was rich in dramatic history. In 1665, 70,000 were killed by the Great Plague of London. The following year the Great Fire of London destroyed much of mediaeval London. The Defoe house was one of the few to survive.

In 1667, a third calamity beset London when a Dutch fleet sailed up the Medway via the River Thames and attacked the town of Chatham, as well as destroying much of the British fleet.

By the time Defoe was aged ten accounts suggest his mother, Annie, had died.

Defoe's education began at James Fisher's boarding school in Pixham Lane in Dorking, Surrey. By 14 he was attending a dissenting academy at Newington Green in London run by Charles Morton, and he is then believed to have attended the Newington Green Unitarian Church. During this period, the English government persecuted those who chose to worship outside the Church of England.

Defoe entered the world of business as a general merchant, dealing at different times in hosiery, general woollen goods and wine. His ambitions were great and he was able to buy a country estate, a ship as well as civets, though he was rarely out of debt. (The civet produces an odorous secretion for the purpose of marking out their territory. Diluted, after some time, the odor of civet secretion, normally strong and repulsive, becomes pleasant with animalistic-musk nuance. The animals are kept in cages in order to be able to collect the secretions and thence perfume).

In 1684, Defoe married Mary Tuffley, the daughter of a London merchant, and received a dowry of £3,700 – a huge amount by the standards of the day. With his debts and political difficulties, the marriage may have been troubled, but it lasted 50 years.

In 1685, Defoe joined the ill-fated Monmouth Rebellion but gained a pardon, by which he escaped the Bloody Assizes of the notorious Judge George Jeffreys.

The Glorious Revolution brought Queen Mary and her husband William III to the crown in 1688, and Defoe became one of William's close allies and a secret agent. Some of the new Government policies led to conflict with France, thus damaging many of Defoe's trade relationships.

In 1692, Defoe was arrested for debts of £700 and his civets were taken away. His actual debts are thought to have been nearer £17,000. His laments were loud and he always sided with debtors, but there is evidence that his financial dealings were always above board.

With a wife and seven children to support it was essential that his release was quickly enabled. He achieved this and accounts then suggest he travelled to Europe and Scotland, perhaps to re-establish some business relationships and to trade wine.

By 1695, he was back in England, serving as a "commissioner of the glass duty", and responsible for collecting the tax on bottles. The following year, 1696, he ran a tile and brick factory in what is now Tilbury in Essex and the family lived in the parish of Chadwell St Mary.

Defoe's first notable publication was not one of his great fiction works but a series of proposals for social and economic improvements, a subject for which he had a keen eye and many ideas. An Essay upon Projects was published in 1697.

His most successful poem, The True-Born Englishman (1701), defended the king against the perceived xenophobia of his enemies, satirising the English claim to racial purity. That same year Defoe presented the Legion's Memorial to the Speaker of the House of Commons and later his employer, Robert Harley, flanked by a guard of sixteen gentlemen of quality. It demanded the release of the Kentish petitioners, who had asked Parliament to support the king in an imminent war against France.

In 1702 the death of William III once more created a political crisis. Queen Anne immediately began an attack against Non-conformists. Defoe was one of the first targets. His pamphleteering and political activities quickly resulted in his arrest. This seemed mainly predicated on his December 1702 pamphlet; The Shortest-Way with the Dissenters; Or, Proposals for the Establishment of the Church, which argued for their extermination. In it, he ruthlessly satirised both the High church Tories and those Dissenters who hypocritically practised so-called "occasional conformity". Although it was published anonymously, the Defoe's authorship was quickly unmasked and he was arrested and charged with seditious libel. In fact, Defoe's ironic writing had been misinterpreted, but, alas for him, his trial was to be at the Old bailey in front of the sadistic judge Salathiel Lovell.

Lovell sentenced him to a punitive fine of 200 marks, to public humiliation in a pillory at Charing Cross and an indeterminate length of imprisonment at the Queen's pleasure which would cease only on payment of the enormous fine.

This was an awful moment for Defoe. After his three days in the pillory, he was imprisoned at Newgate.

In despair, he wrote to William Paterson, the London Scot and founder of the Bank of England and who was in the confidence of Robert Harley, 1st Earl of Oxford and Earl Mortimer, a leading minister and spymaster in the English Government. Harley arranged Defoe's release, in 1703, in exchange for Defoe's co-operation as an intelligence agent for the Tories. In exchange for such co-operation with the rival political side, Harley paid some of Defoe's very large outstanding debts, which greatly improved his financial situation.

With his release from Newgate Defoe had, within a few days, witnessed the Great Storm of November 26th, 1703. It caused immense damage to an area from London to Bristol, uprooting millions of trees, and claiming the lives of over 8,000 people, mostly at sea. This became the subject of The Storm (1704), which included many eye-witness accounts and is regarded as one of the world's first examples of modern journalism.

In the same year, he set up his periodical A Review of the Affairs of France which supported the Harley Ministry, and chronicled the events of the War of the Spanish Succession (1702–1714). The Review initially ran weekly but was soon being printed three times a week. Defoe wrote most of the articles himself and although in effect the Review was a Government publication Defoe was enthusiastic and energetic as ever.

Harley was ousted from the ministry in 1708, but Defoe continued writing the Review to support a new master, Godolphin, then again to support Harley and his return in the Tory ministry of 1710–1714. The Tories fell from power with the death of Queen Anne, but Defoe continued his work, now for the Whig government, writing 'Tory' pamphlets that undermined the Tory point of view.

Not all of Defoe's pamphlet writing was political. One pamphlet was originally published anonymously, entitled 'A True Relation of the Apparition of One Mrs. Veal the Next Day after her Death to One Mrs. Bargrave at Canterbury the 8th of September, 1705.' it deals with the crossover between the spiritual and physical realms and describes Mrs. Bargrave's encounter with her old friend Mrs. Veal after she had died.

In 1709, Defoe authored a rather lengthy book entitled The History of the Union of Great Britain. The book attempts to explain the facts leading up to the Act of Union 1707, dating all the way back to December 6th, 1604 when King James was presented with a proposal for unification. (It should be remembered that since the death of Queen Elizabeth England and Scotland, although separate kingdoms, had a common monarch; known as James I of England and as James VI of Scotland. The act now brought the two countries into one; Great Britain.

Part of Defoe's duties as a Government spokesman and spy was the relaying of the Governments view to the public. He thought that his work on the Review would end the threat from the north and gain for the Treasury an "inexhaustible treasury of men", a valuable new market increasing the power of England, clearly the senior partner in the Union. In September 1706, Harley ordered Defoe to Edinburgh to do everything he could to secure loyalty to the Treaty of Union. Defoe was conscious of the risk he was taking. His reports were often vivid descriptions of violent demonstrations against the Union. "A Scots rabble is the worst of its kind", he reported.

Defoe was a Presbyterian who had suffered in England for his convictions, and as such he was accepted as an adviser to the General Assembly of the Church of Scotland and committees of the Parliament of Scotland with little problem.

Defoe received little in the way of reward or recognition from his pay-masters or the government. However, like any good writer, the experiences would be filed away for later use. The Scottish experience was helpful when he came to write his Tour Thro' the Whole Island of Great Britain, published in 1726.

Defoe continued to keep up a wide and varied output including in his apologia Appeal to Honour and Justice (1715), a defence of his part in Harley's Tory ministry (1710–14), The Family Instructor (1715), a conduct manual on religious duty; Minutes of the Negotiations of Monsr. Mesnager (1717), in which he impersonates Nicolas Mesnager, who negotiated the Treaty of Utrecht (1713); and A Continuation of the Letters Writ by a Turkish Spy (1718), a satire of European politics and religion, written by Defoe in the guise of a Muslim in Paris.

From this point Defoe would now enter a period of writing that would cement his place in the canon of English fiction. From 1719 to 1724, Defoe published the novels for which he is now world-famous including Robinson Crusoe in 1719 and Moll Flanders in 1724 amongst many others.

In the final decade of his life, he also wrote conduct manuals, including Religious Courtship (1722), The Complete English Tradesman (1726) and The New Family Instructor (1727).

Defoe seemed to have a natural knack of writing across a wide range of subjects and from a number of points of view. He published on the breakdown of the social order; The Great Law of Subordination Considered (1724) and Everybody's Business is Nobody's Business (1725), together with works on the supernatural; The Political History of the Devil (1726), A System of Magick (1727) and An Essay on the History and Reality of Apparitions (1727). His works on foreign travel and trade include A General History of Discoveries and Improvements (1727) and Atlas Maritimus and Commercialis (1728). Perhaps his greatest achievement is the magisterial A Tour Thro' the Whole Island of Great Britain (1724–27), which provided a panoramic survey of British trade on the eve of the Industrial Revolution.

Published in 1726, The Complete English Tradesman is a late example of Defoe's political and social work. He discusses the role of the tradesman in England in comparison to those abroad, arguing that the British system of trade is far superior. He also states that trade is the backbone of the British economy: "estate's a pond, but trade's a spring."

Defoe was obviously keenly aware of both political and economic structures. Trade, Defoe argues, is a much better vehicle for social and economic change than war. He states that through imperialism and trade expansion the British empire is able to "increase commerce at home" through job creation and increased consumption. This increased consumption, by laws of supply and demand, increases production which in turn raises wages for the poor therefore lifting part of British society further out of poverty.

Daniel Defoe died on April 24th, 1731. Some accounts say that it was whilst hiding from his creditors. Indeed, Defoe was known to enjoy walking on a Sunday when, legally, it was the only day of the week when he could not be legally pestered about his bills. The cause of his death was given as lethargy, but it is thought it was more probably a stroke.

He was interred in Bunhill Fields, London. A monument was erected to his memory there in 1870.

There are various suggestions as to the number of works in Defoe's literary output. Certainly, no less than 200 separate pieces but accounts suggest perhaps as many as 500 which seems, even for so prolific a writer as Defoe, rather too generous but perhaps is in keeping with the extravagance of his life.

Daniel Defoe – A Concise Bibliography

Defoe wrote an immense amount of works. Some were under pseudonyms or anonymously and others may merely have been attributed to him. The list below is by no means exhaustive but is certainly illustrative of both his range and scope.

Novels
Robinson Crusoe (1719)
The Farther Adventures of Robinson Crusoe (1719)
Serious Reflections During the Life and Surprising Adventures of Robinson Crusoe; With His Vision of the Angelic World (1720)
Captain Singleton (1720)
Memoirs of a Cavalier (1720)
A Journal of the Plague Year (1722)
Colonel Jack (1722)
Moll Flanders (1722)
Roxana: The Fortunate Mistress (1724)
Memoirs of a Cavalier: A Military Journal of the Wars in Germany, and the Wars in England.: From the Year 1632 to the Year 1648 (1724)
A New Voyage Round the World (1725)
Military Memoirs of Capt. George Carleton (1728)
A General History of the Pyrates, From their First Rise and Settlement in the Island of Providence, to the Present Time (1724)
The History of the Pyrates (1728)
Of Captain Misson and his Crew (1728)

Essays, Satires & Other Pieces
An Essay Upon Projects (1697)
The Shortest Way with the Dissenters (1702)
New Test of Church of England's Loyalty (1702)
Ode to the Athenian Society (1703)

Enquiry into Acgill's General Translation (1703)

The Storm– a description of the worst storm to hit Britain in recorded times, which includes eyewitness accounts. (1704)

The Great Law of Subordination Consider'd (1704)

Layman's Sermon on the Late Storm (1704)

Elegy on Author of 'True–Born Englishman,' (1704)

Hymn to Victory (1704)

An Essay on the Regulation of the Press (1704)

Giving Alms No Charity (1704)

The Consolidator or, Memoirs of Sundry Transactions from the World in the Moon (1705)

A True Relation of the Apparition of Mrs. Veal (1706)

Sermon on the Filling-up of Dr. Burgess's Meeting-house (1706)

History of the Union of Great Britain (1709)

Atalantis Major (1711)

A Short narrative of the Life and Actions of His Grace John, Duke of Marlborough (1711)

A Seasonable Warning and Caution Against the Insinuations of Papists and Jacobites in Favour of the Pretender (1712)

Short Enquiry into a Late Duel (1713)

A General History of Trade (1713)

An Answer to a Question That Nobody Thinks of, VIZ. But What if the Queen should die? (1713)

Reasons Against the Succession of the House of Hanover with an Enquiry How far the Abdication of King James, Supposing it to be Legal, Ought to Affect the Person of the Pretender (1713)

Wars of Charles III. (1715)

The Family Instructor (1715)

Hymn to the Mob (1715)

The Family Instructor (1715)

An Appeal to Honour and Justice, Though It Be of His Worst Enemies: Being A True Account of His Conduct in Public Affairs (1715)

A Friendly Epistle by Way of Reproof from one of the People Called Quakers, to T. B., a Dealer in Many Words (1715)

Memoirs of the Church of Scotland (1717)

Life and Death of Count Patkul (1717)

Memoirs of the Church of Scotland (1717)

Memoirs of Major Alexander Ramkins (1718)

Memoirs of Duke of Shrewsbury (1718)

Memoirs of Daniel Williams (1718)

A Vindication of the Press (1718)

Dickory Cronke: The Dumb Philosopher: or, Great Britain's Wonder (1719)

The King of Pirates (Capt. Avery) (1719)

Life of Baron de Goertz (1719)

Life and Adventures of Duncan Campbell (1720)

Mr. Campbell's Pacquet (1720)

The Supernatural Philosopher; or, The Mysteries of Magick (1720)

Due Preparations for the Plague (1722)

Life of Cartouche (1722)

Religious Courtship (1722)

History of Peter the Great (1723)

The Highland Rogue (Rob Roy) (1723)

Narrative of Murders at Calais (1724)
The History of The Remarkable Life of John Sheppard (1724)
A Narrative of All The Robberies, Escapes, &c. of John Sheppard (1724)
A Tour Thro' the Whole Island of Great Britain, Divided into Circuits or Journies (1724–1727)
The Great Law of Subordination; or, the Insolence and Insufferable Behaviour of Servants in England (1724)
Account of Jonathan Wild (1725)
Account of John Gow (1725)
Every-body's Business, Is No-body's Business (1725)
The Complete English Tradesman (1725; volume II, 1727)
The Friendly Demon (1726)
Mere Nature Delineated (Peter the Wild Boy) (1726)
Essay upon Literature and the Original of Letters (1726)
History of Discoveries (1726–7)
A System of Magic (1726)
The Protestant Monastery (1726)
The Political History of the Devil (1726)
An Essay Upon Literature (1726)
Mere Nature Delineated (1726)
Conjugal Lewdness (1727)
Treatise concerning Use and Abuse of Marriage (1727)
Secrets of Invisible World Discovered; or, History and Reality of Apparitions (1727)
Parochial Tyranny (1727)
A New Family Instructor (1728)
Augusta Triumphans: or, The Way to Make London the Most Flourishing City in the Universe (1728)
Plan of English Commerce (1728)
Second Thoughts are Best (on Street Robberies) (1728)
Street Robberies Considered (1728)
A Plan of the English Commerce (1728)
Humble Proposal to People of England for Increase of Trade, &c. (1729)
Preface to R. Dodsley's Poem 'Servitude' (1729)
Effectual Scheme for Preventing Street Robberies (1731)

Works in Verse
A New Discovery of an Old Intreague (1691)
Character of Dr. Samuel Annesley (1697)
The Pacificator (1700)
The True-Born Englishman: A Satyr (1701)
Reformation of Manners (1702)
The Mock Mourners (1702)
More Reformation (1703)
Hymn to the Pillory (1703)
The Dyet of Poland (1705)
Jure Divino. A Satyr in 12 books. (1706)
Caledonia (1706)
Translation of Du Fresnoy's "Compleat Art of Painting" (1720)

www.ingramcontent.com/pod-product-compliance
Lightning Source LLC
Chambersburg PA
CBHW051519170626
46811CB00002B/892